NEW YORK REVIEW BOOKS

CLASSICS

# PEASANTS

# AND OTHER STORIES

ANTON PAVLOVICH CHEKHOV (1860-1904), the son of a grocer and a former serf, worked as a physician and ran an open clinic for the poor, while also writing the plays and short stories that have established him as one of the greatest figures in Russian literature.

EDMUND WILSON (1895-1972) is widely regarded as the preeminent American man of letters of the twentieth century. Over his long career, he wrote for *Vanity Fair*, helped edit *The New Republic*, served as chief book critic for *The New Yorker*, and was a frequent contributor to *The New York Review of Books*. Wilson was the author of over twenty books, including *To the Finland Station*, *Patriotic Gore*, and a work of fiction, *Memoirs of Hecate County*.

# PEASANTS
# AND OTHER STORIES

Anton Chekhov

■

*Selected and with an Introduction by*

EDMUND WILSON

*Translated from the Russian by*

CONSTANCE GARNETT

NEW YORK REVIEW BOOKS

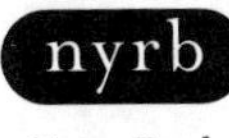

*New York*

THIS IS A NEW YORK REVIEW BOOK
PUBLISHED BY THE NEW YORK REVIEW OF BOOKS

PEASANTS AND OTHER STORIES



First published by Doubleday Anchor Books 1956

This edition published in 1999 in the United States of America by
The New York Review of Books
1755 Broadway
New York, NY 10019

3 5 7 9 10 8 6 4 2

Library of Congress Cataloging-in-Publication Data
Chekhov, Anton Pavlovich, 1860–1904.
[Short stories. English. Selections]
Peasants and other stories / Anton Chekhov; selected and with a preface by Edmund Wilson.
p. cm.
Originally published: Garden City, N.Y.: Doubleday Anchor Books, 1956.
Contents: A woman's kingdom — Three years — The murder — My life — Peasants — The new villa — In the ravine — The bishop — Betrothed.
ISBN 0-940322-14-5 (alk. paper)
1. Chekhov, Anton Pavlovich, 1860–1904 Translations into English.
2. Russia — Social life and customs Fiction. I. Wilson, Edmund, 1895–1972. II. Title.
PG3456.A15W53 1999
891.73'3—dc 21 99-14551

ISBN 0-940322-14-5

Printed in the United States of America on acid-free paper.
September 1999
www.nybooks.com

# CONTENTS


Introduction vii

A Woman's Kingdom 3

Three Years 53

The Murder 161

My Life 199

Peasants 311

The New Villa 363

In the Ravine 383

The Bishop 433

Betrothed 455

# INTRODUCTION

IT HAS ALWAYS been a serious obstacle to the understanding of Chekhov on the part of English-speaking readers that the volumes of translations of his stories made by Constance Garnett and others do not, as a rule, present his work in its chronological sequence. You get humorous sketches from his earliest phase, when he was writing for the comic papers, side by side with his most serious stories; and the various periods of this serious work are themselves all jumbled together: the terse ironical anecdote, which began by being funny and then turned pathetic; the more rounded-out drama of character and situation; the product of what Chekhov's English biographer, Mr. Ronald Hingley, calls his Tolstoyan period, when new moral preoccupations and a new psychological interest appear; and the more complex social study with which we are concerned in this volume. This garbling of Chekhov's development is one of the causes for the frequent complaints on the part of English-speaking critics that they cannot make out what he is driving at. What could one make of Mark Twain if one found *The Mysterious Stranger* followed immediately by *The Celebrated Jumping Frog of Calaveras County*, or of Joyce if a story from *Dubliners* were followed by a passage from *Finnegans Wake*.

In the later years of Chekhov's life—1894–1903—he was occupied mainly with a series of works, plays as well as stories, that were evidently intended to constitute a kind of analysis of Russian society, a miniature *Comédie Humaine*. The stories often run to greater length than is usual with his earlier pieces, and they differ from the longer of these, such as *The Steppe, The Duel*, and *Ward Number 6*, in that the latter deal with individuals, whereas the larger-scale stories of this latest period—though they sometimes, as in *The Bishop*, center about an individual—tend to be studies of milieux. The method here is like that of the full-scale plays, from *The Sea Gull* to *The Cherry Orchard*, which were written within these years, 1896–1904. In going through Chekhov in the Soviet edition, where his stories are printed in their proper sequence, one becomes aware that this final series begins with the story called *A Woman's Kingdom*. This follows immediately *The Black Monk*, a tale of the supernatural, rather suggestive of Hawthorne, which is also an inside presentation of a psychiatric case; but we find ourselves, with *A Woman's Kingdom*, definitely in a new domain. Up to now, we have had usually in Chekhov a certain vein of the grotesque or satiric, an exaggeration, comic or bitter, that is not always made quite plausible; but we are now in a provincial household of which the domestic incidents are soberly and solidly presented. The subject is a social phenomenon: the difficult readjustments of a new industrial middle class. And in each of the long stories that follows, you have a household or a local community which is intended to be significant of the life of some social group: the new factory owners in *A Woman's Kingdom*; the old Moscow merchant class in *Three Years*; in *The Murder*, the half-literate countrymen, fundamentalist and independent (*"raskolniki* or something of the sort"—*raskolniki* are dissident sectarians—Chekhov says in one of his letters); the Tolstoyan intelligentsia in *My Life*; the lowest stratum of the peasantry in *Peasants*; the new class of engineers in *The New Villa*; the kulaks, in *In the Ravine*, on their way to the commercial middle class; the professional churchmen in *The Bishop*; and in *Betrothed*, the old-fashioned provincial household and the revolt against it of the new generation. I have here brought these stories together, in the order in which they were written, omitting the more anecdotal ones with which they are interspersed.[1] That Chekhov was quite conscious that these interspersed pieces belonged to a different category from the more elaborate social studies would seem to be shown by his writing to his publisher (in a letter to A. S. Suvorin, June 21, 1897) that he did not want *An Artist's Story* brought out in the same volume with *Peasants*, on the ground that it had "nothing in common" with the more ambitious story. (Actually, *Peasants* and *My Life* were first published together in a volume by themselves.) It will be noticed that the life of the gentry is not treated at length in this series, but *The Sea Gull, Uncle Vanya* and *The Cherry Orchard* make up for this omission. It is probable that Chekhov preferred to deal with the land-owning class in the

1. Here is the complete chronology of the stories and plays of this period (I give all the titles in Constance Garnett's translation): 1894. *The Black Monk, A Woman's Kingdom, Rothschild's Fiddle, The Student, The Teacher of Literature, At the Manor, The Head Gardener's Story*; 1895. *Three Years, The Helpmate, Whitebrow, Anna on the Neck, The Murder, Ariadne*; 1896. *An Artist's Story, My Life, The Sea Gull*; 1897. *Peasants, Pechenyeg, At Home, The Schoolmistress, Uncle Vanya*; 1898. *The Man in the Case, Gooseberries, About Love, Ionich, A Doctor's Visit, The Darling*; 1899. *The New Villa, On Official Business, The Lady with the Dog, At Christmas Time*; 1900. *In the Ravine*; 1901. *The Three Sisters*; 1902. *The Bishop*; 1903. *Betrothed*; 1904. *The Cherry Orchard*. (If anyone should set out to read these consecutively in Constance Garnett's edition, he would be put to considerable inconvenience.)

theater, because they could be made more amusing as well as more attractive than his peasant and commercial and industrial groups. One does not find in any of his stories the same sort of atmosphere and tone that is characteristic of these three plays; and, conversely, one cannot imagine the incidents of *Peasants* or *In the Ravine* so effectively presented in a play.

If one reads these late stories, then, in conjunction with the late plays, one is presented with an anatomy of Russian society, as observed and estimated by Chekhov, at the end of the nineteenth century and just before the Revolution of 1905 (Chekhov died in 1904). This picture is anything but reassuring. The propertied classes are losing their grip but cannot merge in any healthy fashion with the rising serfs who are buying them up. The old merchant class are narrow and harsh, their world is almost a ghetto; when the young people try to escape from it by aping the intelligentsia or marrying into the gentry, they find that they do not pan out, that they cannot adapt themselves. The recently arrived bourgeoisie—factory owners and engineers—are uncomfortable because they find themselves cut off from the people from whom they have sprung. The hierarchy of the church is a routine affair, unilluminated by true religious feeling, and fanatical religion on a lower level does not rise beyond savagery and superstition. The well-to-do peasants who have been turning into shopkeepers and entrepreneurs now carry their cupidity to criminal lengths. The poor peasants are living in ignorance and filth: they crawl about their villages like badly kept beasts, and when they try their luck in the city—untrained at any trade that is practiced there—they are hardly better off. One is brought to the conclusion that Chekhov, whose family had been serfs till the Emancipation and who knew the life of the lower classes, is here contradicting deliberately the Tolstoyan idealization and the Turgenevian idylizing of the peasantry, as, in his stories about religion, he is confronting Dostoevsky's saints with something more degraded or prosaic. It is a picture, in general, of a feudal society attempting to modernize itself, but still in a state of transition that is considerably less than half-baked. One of the strongest impressions, in fact, conveyed by the whole of Chekhov's work is that, although the old order is petering out, there is not very much to build on for a sound democratic and up-to-date Russia. And yet there is just barely a note of hope. The architect's son of *My Life* does achieve a measure of satisfaction by abandoning his pretensions to gentility and settling down as a professional house-painter. In the last story Chekhov wrote, *Betrothed*—which counterbalances and to some extent offsets the first in this sequence, *A Woman's Kingdom*—he does allow his heroine to break away, at the cost of moral effort and some ruthlessness, from her stultifying provincial family, and to study for a career in St. Petersburg. A cousin, a *raté* intellectual, has egged her on to this. He has told her that the more people like her become trained and "dedicated," "the sooner the Kingdom of Heaven will descend upon the earth. In that time, little by little, there will not be left of your town one stone upon another. Everything will be changed, as if by magic. There will arise large and splendid houses, marvelous parks, extraordinary fountains, remarkable people." There is, of course, an element of parody, or irony, in this vision of the future on the part of one who has been so unsuccessful in the present, as there is in *The Three Sisters* in the case of a somewhat similar prophecy; yet Nadya does get to St. Petersburg as the sisters do not get to Moscow.

I hope that this volume may help to redeem Chekhov, one of the tersest, most lucid and most purposive of writers, from the Anglo-Saxon charges of vagueness; to give something of his true weight and point for readers who may have been bewildered by reading him in scrambled collections.

—Edmund Wilson

# PEASANTS AND OTHER STORIES

# A WOMAN'S KINGDOM

## 1. CHRISTMAS EVE

HERE WAS A thick roll of notes. It came from the bailiff at the forest villa; he wrote that he was sending fifteen hundred rubles, which he had been awarded as damages, having won an appeal. Anna Akimovna disliked and feared such words as "awarded damages" and "won the suit." She knew that it was impossible to do without the law, but for some reason, whenever Nazarich, the manager of the factory, or the bailiff of her villa in the country, both of whom frequently went to law, used to win lawsuits of some sort for her benefit, she always felt uneasy and, as it were, ashamed. On this occasion, too, she felt uneasy and awkward, and wanted to put that fifteen hundred rubles further away that it might be out of her sight.

She thought with vexation that other girls of her age—she was in her twenty-sixth year—were now busy looking after their households, were weary and would sleep sound, and would wake up tomorrow morning in holiday mood; many of them had long been married and had children. Only she, for some reason, was compelled to sit like an old woman over these letters, to make notes upon them, to write answers, then to do nothing the whole evening till midnight, but wait till she was sleepy; and tomorrow they would all day long be coming with Christmas greetings and asking for favors; and the day after tomorrow there would certainly be some scandal at the factory—someone would be beaten or would die of drinking too much vodka, and she would be fretted by pangs of conscience; and after the holidays Nazarich would turn off some twenty of the workpeople for absence from work, and all of the twenty would hang about at the front door, without their caps on, and she would be ashamed to go out to them, and they would be driven away like dogs. And all her acquaintances would say behind her back, and write to her in anonymous letters, that she was a millionaire and exploiter—that she was devouring other men's lives and sucking the blood of the workers.

Here there lay a heap of letters read through and laid aside already. They were all begging letters. They were from people who were hungry, drunken, dragged down by large families, sick, degraded, despised. . . . Anna Akimovna had already noted on each letter, three rubles to be paid to one, five to another; these letters would go the same day to the office, and next the distribution of assistance would take place, or, as the clerks used to say, the beasts would be fed.

They would distribute also in small sums four hundred and seventy rubles—the interest on a sum bequeathed by the late Akim Ivanovich for the relief of the poor and needy. There would be a hideous crush. From the gates to the doors of the office there would stretch a long file of strange people with brutal faces, in rags, numb with cold, hungry and already drunk, in husky voices calling down blessings upon Anna Akimovna, their benefactress, and her parents: those at the back would press upon those in front, and those in front would abuse them with bad language. The clerk would get tired of the noise, the swearing, and the singsong whining and blessing; would fly out and give someone a box on the ear, to the delight of all. And her own people, the factory hands, who received nothing at Christmas but their wages, and had already spent every farthing of it, would stand in the middle of the yard, looking on and laughing—some enviously, others ironically.

"Merchants, and still more their wives, are fonder of beggars than they are of their own workpeople," thought Anna Akimovna. "It's always so."

Her eye fell upon the roll of money. It would be nice to distribute that hateful, useless money among the workpeople tomorrow, but it did not do to give the workpeople anything for nothing, or they would demand it again next time. And what would be the good of fifteen hundred rubles when there were eighteen hundred workmen in the factory besides their wives and children? Or she might, perhaps, pick out one of the writers of those begging letters—some luckless man who had long ago lost all hope of anything better—and give him the fifteen hundred. The money would come upon the poor creature like a thunderclap, and perhaps for the first time in his life he would feel happy. This idea struck Anna Akimovna as original and amusing, and it fascinated her. She took one letter at random out of the pile and read it. Some petty official called Chalikov had long been out of a situation, was ill, and living in Gushchin's Buildings; his wife was in consumption, and he had five little girls. Anna Akimovna knew well the four-storied house, Gushchin's Buildings, in which Chalikov lived. Oh, it was a horrid, foul, unhealthy house!

"Well, I will give it to that Chalikov," she decided. "I won't send it; I had better take it myself to prevent unnecessary talk. Yes," she reflected as she put the fifteen hundred rubles in her pocket, "and I'll have to look at them, and perhaps I can do something for the little girls."

She felt lighthearted; she rang the bell and ordered the horses to be brought round.

When she got into the sledge it was past six o'clock in the evening. The windows in all the blocks of buildings were brightly lighted up, and that made the huge courtyard seem very dark: at the gates, and at the far end of the yard near the warehouses and the workpeople's barracks, electric lamps were gleaming.

Anna Akimovna disliked and feared those huge dark buildings, warehouses, and barracks where the workmen lived. She had only once been in the main building since her father's death. The high ceilings with iron girders; the multitude of huge, rapidly turning wheels, connecting straps and levers; the shrill hissing; the clank of steel; the rattle of the trolleys; the harsh puffing of steam; the faces—pale, crimson, or black with coal dust; the shirts soaked with sweat; the gleam of steel, of copper, and of fire; the smell of oil and coal; and the draught, at times very hot and at times very cold—gave her an impression of hell. It seemed to her as though the wheels, the levers, and the hot hissing cylinders were trying to tear themselves away from their fastenings to crush the men, while the men, not hearing one another, ran about with anxious faces and busied themselves about the machines, trying to stop their terrible movement. They showed Anna Akimovna something and respectfully explained it to her. She remembered how in the forge a piece of red-hot iron was pulled out of the furnace; and how an old man with a strap round his head, and another, a young man in a blue shirt with a chain on his breast, and an angry face, probably one of the foremen, struck the piece of iron with hammers; and how the golden sparks had been scattered in all directions; and how, a little afterwards, they had dragged out a huge piece of sheet iron with a clang. The old man had stood erect and smiled, while the young man had wiped his face with his sleeve and explained something to her.

And she remembered, too, how in another department an old man with one eye had been filing a piece of iron, and how the iron filings were scattered about; and how a red-haired man in black spectacles, with holes in his shirt, had been working at a lathe, making something out of a piece of steel: the lathe roared and hissed and squeaked, and Anna Akimovna felt sick at the sound, and it seemed as though they were boring into her ears. She looked, listened, did not understand, smiled graciously, and felt ashamed. To get hundreds of thousands of rubles from a business which one does not understand and cannot like—how strange it is!

And she had not once been in the workpeople's barracks. There, she was told, it was damp; there were bugs, debauchery, anarchy. It was an astonishing thing: a thousand rubles were spent annually on keeping the barracks in good order, yet, if she were to believe the anonymous letters, the condition of the workpeople was growing worse and worse every year.

"There was more order in my father's day," thought Anna Akimovna as she drove out of the yard, "because he had been a workman himself. I know nothing about it and only do silly things."

She felt depressed again, and was no longer glad that she had come, and the thought of the lucky man upon whom fifteen hundred rubles would drop from heaven no longer struck her as original and amusing. To go to some Chalikov or other, when at home a business worth a million was gradually going to pieces and being ruined, and the workpeople in the barracks were living worse than convicts, meant doing something silly and cheating her conscience. Along the highroad and across the fields near it, workpeople from the neighboring cotton and paper factories were walking towards the lights of the town. There was the sound of talk and laughter in the frosty air. Anna Akimovna looked at the women and young people, and she suddenly felt a longing for a plain rough life among a crowd. She recalled vividly that faraway time when she used to be called Anyutka, when she was a little girl and used to lie under the same quilt with her mother, while a washerwoman who lodged with them used to wash clothes in the next room; while through the thin walls there came from the neighboring flats the sounds of laughter, swearing, children's crying, the accordion, and the whir of carpenters' lathes and sewing machines; while her father, Akim Ivanovich, who was clever at almost every craft, would be soldering something near the stove, or drawing or planning, taking no notice whatever of the noise and stuffiness. And she longed to wash, to iron, to run to the shop and the tavern as she used to do every day when she lived with her mother. She ought to have been a workgirl and not the factory owner! Her big house with its chandeliers and pictures; her footman Mishenka, with his glossy mustache and swallow-tail coat; the devout and dignified Varvarushka, and smooth-tongued Agafyushka; and the young people of both sexes who came almost every day to ask her for money, and with whom she always for some reason felt guilty; and the clerks, the doctors, and the ladies who were charitable at her expense, who flattered her and secretly despised her for her humble origin—how wearisome and alien it all was to her!

Here were the railway crossing and the city gate; then came houses alternating with kitchen gardens; and at last the broad street where stood the renowned Gushchin's Buildings. The street, usually quiet, was now on Christmas Eve full of life and movement. The eating-houses and beer shops were noisy. If someone who did not belong to that quarter but lived in the center of the town had driven through the street now, he would have noticed nothing but dirty, drunken, and abusive people; but Anna Akimovna, who had lived in those parts all her life, was constantly recognizing in the crowd her own father or mother or uncle. Her father was a soft fluid character, a little fantastical, frivolous, and irresponsible. He did not care for money, respectability, or power; he used to say that a workingman had no time to keep the holy days and go to church; and if it had not been for his wife, he would probably never have gone to confession, taken the sacrament, or kept the fasts. While her uncle, Ivan Ivanovich, on the contrary, was like flint; in everything relating to religion, politics, and morality, he was harsh and relentless, and kept a strict watch, not only over himself, but also over all his servants and acquaintances. God forbid that one should go into his room without crossing oneself before the icon! The luxurious mansion in which Anna Akimovna now lived he had always kept locked up, and only opened it on great holidays for important visitors, while he lived himself in the office, in a little room covered with icons. He had leanings toward the Old Believers, and was continually entertaining priests and bishops of the old ritual, though he had been christened, and married, and had buried his wife in accordance with the Orthodox rites. He disliked Akim, his only brother and his heir, for his frivolity, which he called simpleness and folly, and for his indifference to religion. He treated him as an inferior, kept him in the position of a workman, paid him sixteen rubles a month. Akim addressed his brother with formal respect, and on the days of asking forgiveness, he and his wife and daughter bowed down to the ground before him. But three years before his death Ivan Ivanovich had drawn closer to his brother, forgave his shortcomings, and ordered him to get a governess for Anyutka.

There was a dark, deep, evil-smelling archway under Gushchin's Buildings; there was a sound of men coughing near the walls. Leaving the sledge in the street, Anna Akimovna went in at the gate and there inquired how to get to No. 46 to see a clerk called Chalikov. She was directed to the furthest door on the right in the third story. And in the courtyard and near the outer door, and even on the stairs, there was still the same loathsome smell as under the archway. In Anna Akimovna's childhood, when her father was a simple workman, she used to live in a building like that, and afterwards, when their circumstances were different, she had often visited them in the character of a Lady Bountiful. The narrow stone staircase with its steep dirty steps, with landings at every story; the greasy swinging lanterns; the stench; the troughs, pots, and rags on the landings near the doors—all this had been familiar to her long ago. . . . One door was open, and within could be seen Jewish tailors in caps, sewing. Anna Akimovna met people on the stairs, but it never entered her head that people might be rude to her. She was no more afraid of peasants or workpeople, drunk or sober, than of her acquaintances of the educated class.

There was no entry at No. 46; the door opened straight into the kitchen. As a rule, the dwellings of workmen and mechanics smell of varnish, tar, hides, smoke, according to the occupation of the tenant; the dwellings of persons of noble or official class who have come to poverty may be known by a peculiar rancid, sour smell. This disgusting smell enveloped Anna Akimovna on all sides, and as yet she was only on the threshold. A man in a black coat, no doubt Chalikov himself, was sitting in a corner at the table with his back to the door, and with him were five little girls. The eldest, a broad-faced thin girl with a comb in her hair, looked about fifteen, while the youngest, a chubby child with hair that stood up like a hedgehog, was not more than three. All the six were eating. Near the stove stood a very thin little woman with a yellow face, far gone in pregnancy. She was wearing a skirt and a white blouse, and had an oven fork in her hand.

"I did not expect you to be so disobedient, Liza," the man was saying reproachfully. "Fie, fie, for shame! Do you want Papa to whip you—eh?"

Seeing an unknown lady in the doorway, the thin woman started and put down the fork.

"Vassily Nikitich!" she cried, after a pause, in a hollow voice, as though she could not believe her eyes.

The man looked round and jumped up. He was a flat-chested, bony man with narrow shoulders and sunken temples. His eyes were small and hollow, with dark rings round them; he had a wide mouth and a long nose like a bird's beak—a little bit bent to the right. His beard was parted in the middle; his mustache was shaven, and this made him look more like a hired footman than a government clerk.

"Does Mr. Chalikov live here?" asked Anna Akimovna.

"Yes, madam," Chalikov answered severely, but immediately recognizing Anna Akimovna, he cried: "Anna Akimovna!" And all at once he gasped and clasped his hands as though in terrible alarm. "Benefactress!"

With a moan he ran to her, grunting inarticulately as though he were paralyzed—there was cabbage on his beard and he smelled of vodka—pressed his forehead to her muff, and seemed as though he were in a swoon.

"Your hand, your holy hand!" he brought out breathlessly. "It's a dream, a glorious dream! Children, awaken me!"

He turned towards the table and said in a sobbing voice, shaking his fists:

"Providence has heard us! Our savior, our angel, has come! We are saved! Children, down on your knees! On your knees!"

Madam Chalikov and the little girls, except the youngest one, began for some reason rapidly clearing the table.

"You wrote that your wife was very ill," said Anna Akimovna, and she felt ashamed and annoyed. "I am not going to give them the fifteen hundred," she thought.

"Here she is, my wife," said Chalikov in a thin feminine voice, as though his tears had gone to his head. "Here she is, unhappy creature! With one foot in the grave! But we do not complain, madam. Better death than such a life. Better die, unhappy woman!"

"Why is he playing these antics?" thought Anna Akimovna with annoyance. "One can see at once he is used to dealing with merchants."

"Speak to me like a human being," she said. "I don't care for farces."

"Yes, madam; five bereaved children round their mother's coffin with funeral candles—that's a farce? Eh?" said Chalikov bitterly, and turned away.

"Hold your tongue," whispered his wife, and she pulled at his sleeve. "The place has not been tidied up, madam," she said, addressing Anna Akimovna; "please excuse it . . . You know what it is where there are children. A crowded hearth, but harmony."

"I am not going to give them the fifteen hundred," Anna Akimovna thought again.

And to escape as soon as possible from these people and from the sour smell, she brought out her purse and made up her mind to leave them twenty-five rubles, not more; but she suddenly felt ashamed that she had come so far and disturbed people for so little.

"If you give me paper and ink, I will write at once to a doctor who is a friend of mine to come and see you," she said, flushing red. "He is a very good doctor. And I will leave you some money for medicine."

Madam Chalikov was hastening to wipe the table.

"It's messy here! What are you doing?" hissed Chalikov, looking at her wrathfully. "Take her to the lodger's room! I make bold to ask you, madam, to step into the lodger's room," he said, addressing Anna Akimovna. "It's clean there."

"Osip Ilyich told us not to go into his room!" said one of the little girls sternly.

But they had already led Anna Akimovna out of the kitchen, through a narrow passage room between two bedsteads: it was evident from the arrangement of the beds that in one two slept lengthwise, and in the other three slept across the bed. In the lodger's room, which came next, it really was clean. A neat-looking bed with a red woolen quilt, a pillow in a white pillow-case, even a slipper for the watch, a table covered with a hempen cloth and, on it, an inkstand of milky-looking glass, pens, paper, photographs in frames—everything as it ought to be; and another table for rough work, on which lay tidily arranged a watch-maker's tools and watches taken to pieces. On the walls hung hammers, pliers, awls, chisels, nippers, and so on, and there were three hanging clocks which were ticking; one was a big clock with thick weights, such as one sees in eating-houses.

As she sat down to write the letter, Anna Akimovna saw facing her on the table the photographs of her father and of herself. That surprised her.

"Who lives here with you?" she asked.

"Our lodger, madam, Pimenov. He works in your factory."

"Oh, I thought he must be a watchmaker."

"He repairs watches privately, in his leisure hours. He is an amateur."

After a brief silence during which nothing could be heard but the ticking of the clocks and the scratching of the pen on the paper, Chalikov heaved a sigh and said ironically, with indignation:

"It's a true saying: gentle birth and a grade in the service won't put a coat on your back. A cockade in your cap and a noble title, but nothing to eat. To my thinking, if anyone of humble class helps the poor he is much more of a gentleman than any Chalikov who has sunk into poverty and vice."

To flatter Anna Akimovna, he uttered a few more disparaging phrases about his gentle birth, and it was evident that he was humbling himself because he considered himself superior to her. Meanwhile she had finished her letter and had sealed it up. The letter would be thrown away and the money would not be spent on medicine—that she knew—but she put twenty-five rubles on the table all the same, and after a moment's thought added two more red notes. She saw the wasted, yellow hand of Madam Chalikov, like the claw of a hen, dart out and clutch the money tight.

"You have graciously given this for medicine," said Chalikov in a quivering voice, "but hold out a helping hand to me also . . . and the children!" he added with a sob. "My unhappy children! I am not afraid for myself; it is for my daughters I fear! It's the hydra of vice that I fear!"

Trying to open her purse, the catch of which had gone wrong, Anna Akimovna was confused and turned red. She felt ashamed that people should be standing before her, looking at her hands and waiting, and most likely at the bottom of their hearts laughing at her. At that instant someone came into the kitchen and stamped his feet, knocking the snow off.

"The lodger has come in," said Madam Chalikov.

Anna Akimovna grew even more confused. She did not want anyone from the factory to find her in this ridiculous position. As ill luck would have it, the lodger came in at the very moment when, having broken the catch at last, she was giving Chalikov some notes, and Chalikov, grunting as though he were paralyzed, was feeling about with his lips where he could kiss her. In the lodger she recognized the workman who had once clanked the sheet iron before her in the forge and had explained things to her. Evidently he had come in straight from the factory; his face looked dark and grimy, and on one cheek, near his nose, was a smudge of soot. His hands were perfectly black, and his unbelted shirt shone with oil and grease. He was a man of thirty, of medium height, with black hair and broad shoulders and a look of great physical strength. At the first glance Anna Akimovna perceived that he must be a foreman, who must be receiving at least thirty-five rubles a month, and a stern, loud-voiced man who struck the workmen in the face; all this was evident from his manner of standing, from the attitude he involuntarily assumed at once on seeing a lady in his room, and most of all from the fact that he did not wear top boots, that he had breast pockets and a pointed, picturesquely clipped beard. Her father, Akim Ivanovich, had been the brother of the factory owner, and yet he had been afraid of foremen like this lodger and had tried to win their favor.

"Excuse me for having come in here in your absence," said Anna Akimovna.

The workman looked at her in surprise, smiled in confusion, and did not speak.

"You must speak a little louder, madam . . ." said Chalikov softly. "When Mr. Pimenov comes home from the factory in the evenings he is a little hard of hearing."

But Anna Akimovna was by now relieved that there was nothing more for her to do here; she nodded to them and went rapidly out of the room. Pimenov went to see her out.

"Have you been long in our employment?" she asked in a loud voice, without turning to him.

"From nine years old. I entered the factory in your uncle's time."

"That's a long while! My uncle and my father knew all the workpeople, and I know hardly any of them. I had seen you before, but I did not know your name was Pimenov."

Anna Akimovna felt a desire to justify herself before him, to pretend that she had just given the money not seriously, but as a joke.

"Oh, this poverty," she sighed. "We give charity on holidays and working days, and still there is no sense in it. I believe it is useless to help such people as this Chalikov."

"Of course it is useless," he agreed. "However much you give him, he will drink it all away. And now the husband and wife will be snatching it from one another and fighting all night," he added with a laugh.

"Yes, one must admit that our philanthropy is useless,

boring, and absurd. But still, you must agree, one can't sit with one's hand in one's lap; one must do something. What's to be done with the Chalikovs, for instance?"

She turned to Pimenov and stopped, expecting an answer from him; he, too, stopped and slowly, without speaking, shrugged his shoulders. Obviously he knew what to do with the Chalikovs, but the treatment would have been so coarse and inhuman that he did not venture to put it into words. And the Chalikovs were to him so utterly uninteresting and worthless that a moment later he had forgotten them; looking into Anna Akimovna's eyes, he smiled with pleasure, and his face wore an expression as though he were dreaming about something very pleasant. Only, now standing close to him, Anna Akimovna saw from his face, and especially from his eyes, how exhausted and sleepy he was.

"Here, I ought to give him the fifteen hundred rubles!" she thought, but for some reason this idea seemed to her incongruous and insulting to Pimenov.

"I am sure you are aching all over after your work, and you come to the door with me," she said as they went down the stairs. "Go home."

But he did not catch her words. When they came out into the street, he ran on ahead, unfastened the cover of the sledge, and, helping Anna Akimovna in, said:

"I wish you a happy Christmas!"

## 2. CHRISTMAS MORNING

"They have left off ringing ever so long! It's dreadful; you won't be there before the service is over! Get up!"

"Two horses are racing, racing . . ." said Anna Akimovna, and she woke up; before her, candle in hand, stood her maid, red-haired Masha. "Well, what is it?"

"Service is over already," said Masha with despair. "I have called you three times! Sleep till evening for me, but you told me yourself to call you!"

Anna Akimovna raised herself on her elbow and glanced towards the window. It was still quite dark outside, and only the lower edge of the window frame was white with snow. She could hear a low, mellow chime of bells; it was not the parish church, but somewhere further away. The watch on the little table showed three minutes past six.

"Very well, Masha... In three minutes..." said Anna Akimovna in an imploring voice, and she snuggled under the bedclothes.

She imagined the snow at the front door, the sledge, the dark sky, the crowd in the church, and the smell of juniper, and she felt dread at the thought; but all the same, she made up her mind that she would get up at once and go to early service. And while she was warm in bed and struggling with sleep—which seems, as though to spite one, particularly sweet when one ought to get up—and while she had visions of an immense garden on a mountain and then Gushchin's Buildings, she was worried all the time by the thought that she ought to get up that very minute and go to church.

But when she got up it was quite light, and it turned out to be half-past nine. There had been a heavy fall of snow in the night; the trees were clothed in white, and the air was particularly light, transparent, and tender, so that when Anna Akimovna looked out of the window her first impulse was to draw a deep, deep breath. And when she had washed, a relic of faraway childish feelings—joy that today was Christmas—suddenly stirred within her; after that she felt lighthearted, free and pure in soul, as though her soul, too, had been washed or plunged in the white snow. Masha came in, dressed up and tightly laced, and wished her a happy Christmas; then she spent a long time combing her mistress's hair and helping her to dress. The fragrance and feeling of the new, gorgeous, splendid dress, its faint rustle, and the smell of fresh scent excited Anna Akimovna.

"Well, it's Christmas," she said gaily to Masha. "Now we will try our fortunes."

"Last year I was to marry an old man. It turned up three times the same."

"Well, God is merciful."

"Well, Anna Akimovna, what I think is, rather than neither one thing nor the other, I'd marry an old man," said Masha mournfully, and she heaved a sigh. "I am turned twenty; it's no joke."

Everyone in the house knew that red-haired Masha was in love with Mishenka, the footman, and this genuine, passionate, hopeless love had already lasted three years.

"Come, don't talk nonsense," Anna Akimovna consoled her. "I am going on for thirty, but I am still meaning to marry a young man."

While his mistress was dressing, Mishenka, in a new swallow-tail and polished boots, walked about the hall and drawing-room and waited for her to come out, to wish her a happy Christmas. He had a peculiar walk, stepping softly and delicately; looking at his feet, his hands, and the bend of his head, one might imagine that he was not simply walking, but learning to dance the first figure of a quadrille. In spite of his fine velvety mustache and handsome, rather flashy appearance, he was steady, prudent, and devout as an old man. He said his prayers, bowing down to the ground, and liked burning incense in his room. He respected people of wealth and rank and had a reverence for them; he despised poor people, and all who came to ask favors of any kind, with all the strength of his cleanly flunkey soul. Under his starched shirt he wore a flannel, winter and summer alike, being very careful of his health; his ears were plugged with cotton wool.

When Anna Akimovna crossed the hall with Masha, he bent his head downwards a little and said in his agreeable, honeyed voice:

"I have the honor to congratulate you, Anna Akimovna, on the most solemn feast of the birth of our Lord."

Anna Akimovna gave him five rubles, while poor Masha was numb with ecstasy. His holiday getup, his attitude, his voice, and what he said impressed her by their beauty and elegance; as she followed her mistress she could think of nothing, could see nothing; she could only smile, first blissfully and then bitterly. The upper story of the house was called the best or visitors' half, while the name of the business part—old people's or simply women's part—was given to the rooms on the lower story where Aunt Tatyana Ivanovna kept house. In the upper part the gentry and educated visitors were entertained; in the lower story, simpler folk and the aunt's personal friends. Handsome, plump, and healthy, still young and fresh, and feeling she had on a magnificent dress which seemed to her to diffuse a sort of radiance all about her, Anna Akimovna went down to the lower story. Here she was met with reproaches for forgetting God now that she was so highly educated, for sleeping too late for the service, and for not coming downstairs to break the fast, and they all clasped their hands and exclaimed with perfect sincerity that she was lovely, wonderful; and she believed it, laughed, kissed them, gave one a ruble, another three or five according to their position. She liked being downstairs. Wherever one looked there were shrines, icons, little lamps, portraits of ecclesiastical personages—the place smelled of monks; there was a rattle of knives in the kitchen, and already a smell of something savory, exceedingly appetizing, was pervading all the rooms. The yellow-painted floors shone, and from the doors narrow rugs with bright blue stripes ran like little paths to the icon corner, and the sunshine was simply pouring in at the windows.

In the dining-room some old women, strangers, were sitting; in Varvarushka's room, too, there were old women, and with them a deaf and dumb girl who seemed abashed about something and kept saying, "Bli, bli! . . ." Two skinny-looking little girls who had been brought out of the orphanage for Christmas came up to kiss Anna Akimovna's hand, and stood before her transfixed with admiration of her splendid dress; she noticed that one of the girls squinted, and in the midst of her lighthearted holiday mood she felt a sick pang at her heart at the thought that young men would despise the girl and that she would never marry. In the cook Agafya's room, five huge peasants in new shirts were sitting round the samovar; these were not workmen from the factory, but relations of the cook. Seeing Anna Akimovna, all the peasants jumped up from their seats and, from regard for decorum, ceased munching, though their mouths were full. The cook Stepan, in a white cap, with a knife in his hand, came into the room and gave her his greetings; porters in high felt boots came in, and they, too, offered their greetings. The water carrier peeped in with icicles on his beard, but did not venture to come in.

Anna Akimovna walked through the rooms, followed by her retinue—the aunt, Varvarushka, Nikandrovna, the sewing-maid Marfa Petrovna, and the downstairs Masha. Varvarushka—a tall, thin, slender woman, taller than anyone in the house, dressed all in black, smelling of cypress and coffee—crossed herself in each room before the icon, bowing down from the waist. And whenever one looked at her one was reminded that she had already prepared her shroud and that lottery tickets were hidden away by her in the same box.

"Anyutinka, be merciful at Christmas," she said, opening the door into the kitchen. "Forgive him, bless the man! Have done with it!"

The coachman Pantelei, who had been dismissed for drunkenness in November, was on his knees in the middle of the kitchen. He was a good-natured man, but he used to be unruly when he was drunk, and could not go to sleep, but persisted in wandering about the buildings and shouting in a threatening voice, "I know all about it!" Now from his beefy and bloated face and from his bloodshot eyes it could be seen that he had been drinking continually from November till Christmas.

"Forgive me, Anna Akimovna," he brought out in a hoarse voice, striking his forehead on the floor and showing his bull-like neck.

"It was Auntie dismissed you; ask her."

"What about Auntie?" said her aunt, walking into the kitchen, breathing heavily; she was very stout, and on her bosom one might have stood a tray of teacups and a samovar. "What about Auntie now? You are mistress here, give your own orders; though these rascals might be all dead for all I care. Come, get up, you hog!" she shouted at Pantelei, losing patience. "Get out of my sight! It's the last time I forgive you, but if you transgress again—don't ask for mercy!"

Then they went into the dining-room to coffee. But they had hardly sat down when the downstairs Masha rushed headlong in, saying with horror, "The singers!" And ran back again. They heard someone blowing his nose, a low bass cough, and footsteps that sounded like horses' iron-shod hoofs tramping about the entry near the hall. For half a minute all was hushed. . . . The singers burst out so suddenly and loudly that everyone started. While they were singing, the priest from the almshouses, with the deacon and the sexton, arrived. Putting on the stole, the priest slowly said that when they were ringing for matins it was snowing and not cold, but that the frost was sharper towards morning, God bless it! and now there must be twenty degrees of frost.

"Many people maintain, though, that winter is healthier than summer," said the deacon; then immediately assumed an austere expression and chanted after the priest, "Thy Birth, O Christ our Lord . . ."

Soon the priest from the workmen's hospital came with the deacon, then the Sisters from the hospital, children from the orphanage, and then singing could be heard almost uninterruptedly. They sang, had lunch, and went away.

About twenty men from the factory came to offer their Christmas greetings. They were only the foremen, mechanicians, and their assistants, the pattern makers, the accountant, and so on—all of good appearance, in new black coats. They were all first-rate men, as it were picked men; each one knew his value—that is, knew that if he lost his berth today, people would be glad to take him on at another factory. Evidently they liked Auntie, as they behaved freely in her presence and even smoked, and when they had all trooped in to have something to eat, the accountant put his arm round her immense waist. They were free and easy, perhaps, partly also because Varvarushka, who under the old masters had wielded great power and had kept watch over the morals of the clerks, had now no authority whatever in the house; and perhaps because many of them still remembered the time when Auntie Tatyana Ivanovna, whose brothers kept a strict hand over her, had been dressed like a simple peasant woman like Agafya, and when Anna Akimovna used to run about the yard near the factory buildings and every one used to call her Anyutya.

The foremen ate, talked, and kept looking with amazement at Anna Akimovna; how she had grown up and how handsome she had become! But this elegant girl, educated by governesses and teachers, was a stranger to them; they could not understand her, and they instinctively kept closer to Auntie, who called them by their names, continually pressed them to eat and drink, and, clicking glasses with them, had already drunk two wineglasses of rowanberry wine with them. Anna Akimovna was always afraid of their thinking her proud, an upstart, or a crow in peacock's feathers; and now while the foremen were crowding round the food, she did not leave the dining-room, but took part in the conversation. She asked Pimenov, her acquaintance of the previous day:

"Why have you so many clocks in your room?"

"I mend clocks," he answered. "I take the work up between times, on holidays, or when I can't sleep."

"So if my watch goes wrong I can bring it to you to be repaired?" Anna Akimovna asked, laughing.

"To be sure, I will do it with pleasure," said Pimenov, and there was an expression of tender devotion in his face, when, not herself knowing why, she unfastened her magnificent watch from its chain and handed it to him; he looked at it in silence and gave it back. "To be sure, I will do it with pleasure," he repeated. "I don't mend watches now. My eyes are weak, and the doctors have forbidden me to do fine work. But for you I can make an exception."

"Doctors talk nonsense," said the accountant. They all laughed. "Don't you believe them," he went on, flattered by the laughing; "last year a tooth flew out of a cylinder and hit old Kalmykov such a crack on the head that you could see his brains, and the doctor said he would die; but he is alive and working to this day, only he has taken to stammering since that mishap."

"Doctors do talk nonsense, they do, but not so much," sighed Auntie. "Pyotr Andreyich, poor dear, lost his sight. Just like you, he used to work day in day out at the factory near the hot furnace, and he went blind. The eyes don't like heat. But what are we talking about?" she said, rousing herself. "Come and have a drink. My best wishes for Christmas, my dears. I never drink with anyone else, but I drink with you, sinful woman as I am. Please God!"

Anna Akimovna fancied that after yesterday Pimenov despised her as a philanthropist but was fascinated by her as a woman. She looked at him and thought that he behaved very charmingly and was nicely dressed. It is true that the sleeves of his coat were not quite long enough, and the coat itself seemed short-waisted, and his trousers were not wide and fashionable, but his tie was tied carefully and with taste and was not as gaudy as the others'. And he seemed to be a good-natured man, for he ate submissively whatever Auntie put on his plate. She remembered how black he had been the day before, and how sleepy, and the thought of it for some reason touched her.

When the men were preparing to go, Anna Akimovna put out her hand to Pimenov. She wanted to ask him to come in sometimes to see her, without ceremony, but she did not know how to—her tongue would not obey her; and that they might not think she was attracted by Pimenov, she shook hands with his companions, too.

Then the boys from the school of which she was a patroness came. They all had their heads closely cropped and all wore gray blouses of the same pattern. The teacher—a tall, beardless young man with patches of red on his face—was visibly agitated as he formed the boys into rows; the boys sang in tune, but with harsh, disagreeable voices. The manager of the factory, Nazarich, a bald, sharp-eyed Old Believer, could never get on with the teachers, but the one who was now anxiously waving his hands he despised and hated, though he could not have said why. He behaved rudely and condescendingly to the young man, kept back his salary, meddled with the teaching, and had finally tried to dislodge him by appointing, a fortnight before Christmas, as porter to the school, a drunken peasant, a distant relation of his wife, who disobeyed the teacher and said rude things to him before the boys.

Anna Akimovna was aware of all this, but she could be of no help, for she was afraid of Nazarich herself. Now she wanted at least to be very nice to the schoolmaster, to tell him she was very much pleased with him; but when after the singing he began apologizing for something in great confusion, and Auntie began to address him familiarly as she drew him without ceremony to the table, she felt, for some reason, bored and awkward, and, giving orders that the children should be given sweets, went upstairs.

"In reality there is something cruel in these Christmas customs," she said a little while afterwards, as it were to herself, looking out of window at the boys, who were flocking from the house to the gates and, shivering with cold, putting their coats on as they ran. "At Christmas one wants to rest, to sit at home with one's own people, and the poor boys, the teacher, and the clerks and foremen are obliged for some reason to go through the frost, then to offer their greetings, show their respect, be put to confusion . . ."

Mishenka, who was standing at the door of the drawing-room and overheard this, said:

"It has not come from us, and it will not end with us. Of course, I am not an educated man, Anna Akimovna, but I do understand that the poor must always respect the rich. It is well said, 'God marks the rogue.' In prisons, night refuges, and pothouses you never see any but the poor, while decent people, you may notice, are always rich. It has been said of the rich, 'Deep calls to deep.'"

"You always express yourself so tediously and incomprehensibly," said Anna Akimovna, and she walked to the other end of the big drawing-room.

It was only just past eleven. The stillness of the big room, only broken by the singing that floated up from below, made her yawn. The bronzes, the albums, and the pictures on the walls, representing a ship at sea, cows in a meadow, and views of the Rhine, were so absolutely stale that her eyes simply glided over them without observing them. The holiday mood was already growing tedious. As before, Anna Akimovna felt that she was beautiful, good-natured, and wonderful, but now it seemed to her that that was of no use to anyone; it seemed to her that she did not know for whom and for what she had put on this expensive dress, too, and, as always happened on all holidays, she began to be fretted by loneliness and the persistent thought that her beauty, her health, and her wealth were a mere cheat, since she was not wanted, was of no use to anyone, and nobody loved her. She walked through all the rooms, humming and looking out of window; stopping in the drawing-room, she could not resist beginning to talk to Mishenka.

"I don't know what you think of yourself, Misha," she said, and heaved a sigh. "Really, God might punish you for it."

"What do you mean?"

"You know what I mean. Excuse my meddling in your affairs. But it seems you are spoiling your own life out of obstinacy. You'll admit that it is high time you got married, and she is an excellent and deserving girl. You will never find anyone better. She's a beauty, clever, gentle, and devoted. . . . And her appearance! . . . If she belonged to our circle or a higher one, people would be falling in love with her for her red hair alone. See how beautifully her hair goes with her complexion. Oh, goodness! You don't understand anything, and don't know what you want," Anna Akimovna said bitterly, and tears came into her eyes. "Poor girl, I am so sorry for her! I know you want a wife with money, but I have told you already I will give Masha a dowry."

Mishenka could not picture his future spouse in his imagination except as a tall, plump, substantial, pious woman, stepping like a peacock, and, for some reason, with a long shawl over her shoulders; while Masha was thin, slender, tightly laced, and walked with little steps, and, worst of all, she was too fascinating and at times extremely attractive to Mishenka, and that, in his opinion, was incongruous with matrimony and only in keeping with loose behavior. When Anna Akimovna had promised to give Masha a dowry, he had hesitated for a time; but once a poor student in a brown overcoat over his uniform, coming with a letter for Anna Akimovna, was fascinated by Masha and could not resist embracing her near the hat-stand, and she had uttered a faint shriek; Mishenka, standing on the stairs above, had seen this, and from that time had begun to cherish a feeling of disgust for Masha. A poor student! Who knows, if she had been embraced by a rich student or an officer the consequences might have been different.

"Why don't you wish it?" Anna Akimovna asked. "What more do you want?"

Mishenka was silent and looked at the armchair fixedly and raised his eyebrows.

"Do you love someone else?"

Silence. The red-haired Masha came in with letters and visiting cards on a tray. Guessing that they were talking about her, she blushed to tears.

"The postmen have come," she muttered. "And there is a clerk called Chalikov waiting below. He says you told him to come today for something."

"What insolence!" said Anna Akimovna, moved to anger. "I gave him no orders. Tell him to take himself off; say I am not at home!"

A ring was heard. It was the priests from her parish. They were always shown into the aristocratic part of the house—that is, upstairs. After the priests, Nazarich, the manager of the factory, came to pay his visit, and then the factory doctor; then Mishenka announced the inspector of the elementary schools. Visitors kept arriving.

When there was a moment free, Anna Akimovna sat down in a deep armchair in the drawing-room, and, shutting her eyes, thought that her loneliness was quite natural because she had not married and never would marry.... But that was not her fault. Fate itself had flung her out of the simple working-class surroundings, in which, if she could trust her memory, she had felt so snug and at home, into these immense rooms, where she could never think what to do with herself and could not understand why so many people kept passing before her eyes. What was happening now seemed to her trivial, useless, since it did not and could not give her happiness for one minute.

"If I could fall in love," she thought, stretching; the very thought of this sent a rush of warmth to her heart. "And if I could escape from the factory . . ." she mused, imagining how the weight of those factory buildings, barracks, and schools would roll off her conscience, roll off her mind. . . . Then she remembered her father and thought if he had lived longer he would certainly have married her to a workingman—to Pimenov, for instance. He would have told her to marry, and that would have been all about it. And it would have been a good thing; then the factory would have passed into capable hands.

She pictured his curly head, his bold profile, his delicate, ironical lips, and the strength, the tremendous strength, in his shoulders, in his arms, in his chest, and the tenderness with which he had looked at her watch that day.

"Well," she said, "it would have been all right. . . . I would have married him."

"Anna Akimovna," said Mishenka, coming noiselessly into the drawing-room.

"How you frightened me!" she said, trembling all over. "What do you want?"

"Anna Akimovna," he said, laying his hand on his heart and raising his eyebrows, "you are my mistress and my benefactress, and no one but you can tell me what I ought to do about marriage, for you are as good as a mother to me. . . . But kindly forbid them to laugh and jeer at me downstairs. They won't let me pass without it."

"How do they jeer at you?"

"They call me Mashenka's Mishenka."

"Pooh, what nonsense!" cried Anna Akimovna indignantly. "How stupid you all are! What a stupid you are, Misha! How sick I am of you! I can't bear the sight of you."

## 3. DINNER

Just as the year before, the last to pay her visits were Krylin, an actual civil councillor, and Lysevich, a well-known barrister. It was already dark when they arrived. Krylin, a man of sixty, with a wide mouth and with gray whiskers close to his ears, with a face like a lynx, was wearing a uniform with an Anna ribbon, and white trousers. He held Anna Akimovna's hand in both of his for a long while, looked intently in her face, moved his lips, and at last said, drawling upon one note:

"I used to respect your uncle . . . and your father, and enjoyed the privilege of their friendship. Now I feel it an agreeable duty, as you see, to present my Christmas wishes to their honored heiress . . . in spite of my infirmities and the distance I have to come. . . . And I am very glad to see you in good health."

The lawyer Lysevich, a tall, handsome, fair man, with a slight sprinkling of gray on his temples and beard, was distinguished by exceptionally elegant manners; he walked with a swaying step, bowed as it were reluctantly, and shrugged his shoulders as he talked, and all this with an indolent grace, like a spoiled horse fresh from the stable. He was well fed, extremely healthy, and very well off; on one occasion he had won forty thousand rubles, but concealed the fact from his friends. He was fond of good fare, especially cheese, truffles, and grated radish with hemp oil; while in Paris he had eaten, so he said, baked but unwashed guts. He spoke smoothly, fluently, without hesitation, and only occasionally, for the sake of effect, permitted himself to hesitate and snap his fingers as if picking up a word. He had long ceased to believe in anything he had to say in the law courts, or perhaps he did believe in it, but attached no kind of significance to it; it had all so long been familiar, stale, ordinary. . . . He believed in nothing but what was original and unusual. A copybook moral in an original form would move him to tears. Both his notebooks were filled with extraordinary expressions which he had read in various authors; and when he needed to look up any expression, he would search nervously in both books and usually failed to find it. Anna Akimovna's father had in a good-humored moment ostentatiously appointed him legal advisor in matters concerning the factory and had assigned him a salary of twelve thousand rubles. The legal business of the factory had been confined to two or three trivial actions for recovering debts, which Lysevich handed to his assistants.

Anna Akimovna knew that he had nothing to do at the factory, but she could not dismiss him—she had not the moral courage; and besides, she was used to him. He used to call himself her legal adviser, and his salary, which he invariably sent for on the first of the month punctually, he used to call "stern prose." Anna Akimovna knew that when, after her father's death, the timber of her forest was sold for railway sleepers, Lysevich had made more than fifteen thousand out of the transaction and had shared it with Nazarich. When first she found out they had cheated her she had wept bitterly, but afterwards she had grown used to it.

Wishing her a happy Christmas, and kissing both her hands, be looked her up and down and frowned.

"You mustn't," he said with genuine disappointment. "I have told you, my dear, you mustn't!"

"What do you mean, Viktor Nikolaich?"

"I have told you you mustn't get fat. All your family have an unfortunate tendency to grow fat. You mustn't," he repeated in an imploring voice, and kissed her hand. "You are so handsome! You are so splendid! Here, Your Excellency, let me introduce the one woman in the world whom I have ever seriously loved."

"There is nothing surprising in that. To know Anna Akimovna at your age and not to be in love with her, that would be impossible."

"I adore her," the lawyer continued with perfect sincerity, but with his usual indolent grace. "I love her, but not because I am a man and she is a woman. When I am with her I always feel as though she belongs to some third sex, and I to a fourth, and we float away together into the domain of the subtlest shades, and there we blend into the spectrum. Leconte de Lisle defines such relations better than anyone. He has a superb passage, a marvelous passage. . . ."

Lysevich rummaged in one notebook, then in the other, and, not finding the quotation, subsided. They began talking of the weather, of the opera, of the arrival, expected shortly, of Duse. Anna Akimovna remembered that the year before Lysevich and, she fancied, Krylin had dined with her, and now when they were getting ready to go away, she began with perfect sincerity pointing out to them in an imploring voice that, as they had no more visits to pay, they ought to remain to dinner with her. After some hesitation the visitors agreed.

In addition to the family dinner, consisting of cabbage soup, suckling pig, goose with apples, and so on, a so-called "French" or "chef's" dinner used to be prepared in the kitchen on great holidays, in case any visitor in the upper story wanted a meal. When they heard the clatter of crockery in the dining-room, Lysevich began to betray a noticeable excitement; he rubbed his hands, shrugged his shoulders, screwed up his eyes, and described with feeling what dinners her father and uncle used to give at one time, and a marvelous matelote of turbots the cook here could make: it was not a matelote, but a veritable revelation! He was already gloating over the dinner, already eating it in imagination and enjoying it. When Anna Akimovna took his arm and led him to the dining-room, he tossed off a glass of vodka and put a piece of salmon in his mouth; he positively purred with pleasure. He munched loudly, disgustingly, emitting sounds from his nose, while his eyes grew oily and rapacious.

The hors d'oeuvres were superb; among other things, there were fresh white mushrooms stewed in cream, and sauce provençale made of fried oysters and crayfish, strongly flavored with some bitter pickles. The dinner, consisting of elaborate holiday dishes, was excellent, and so were the wines. Mishenka waited at table with enthusiasm. When he laid some new dish on the table and lifted the shining cover, or poured out the wine, he did it with the solemnity of a professor of black magic, and, looking at his face and his movements suggesting the first figure of a quadrille, the lawyer thought several times, "What a fool!"

After the third course Lysevich said, turning to Anna Akimovna:

"The fin-de-siècle woman—I mean when she is young, and of course wealthy—must be independent, clever, elegant, intellectual, bold, and a little depraved. Depraved within limits, a little; for excess, you know, is wearisome. You ought not to vegetate, my dear; you ought not to live like everyone else, but to get the full savor of life, and a slight flavor of depravity is the sauce of life. Revel among flowers of intoxicating fragrance, breathe the perfume of musk, eat hashish, and best of all, love, love, love. . . . To begin with, in your place I would set up seven lovers—one for each day of the week; and one I would call Monday, one Tuesday, the third Wednesday, and so on, so that each might know his day."

This conversation troubled Anna Akimovna; she ate nothing and only drank a glass of wine.

"Let me speak at last," she said. "For myself personally, I can't conceive of love without family life. I am lonely, lonely as the moon in the sky, and a waning moon, too; and whatever you may say, I am convinced, I feel that this waning can only be restored by love in its ordinary sense. It seems to me that such love would define my duties, my work, make clear my conception of life. I want from love peace of soul, tranquillity; I want the very opposite of musk, and spiritualism, and fin de siècle . . . in short"—she grew embarrassed—"a husband and children."

"You want to be married? Well, you can do that, too," Lysevich assented. "You ought to have all experiences: marriage, jealousy, and the sweetness of the first infidelity, and even children. . . . But make haste and live—make haste, my dear: time is passing; it won't wait."

"Yes, I'll go and get married!" she said, looking angrily at his well-fed, satisfied face. "I will marry in the simplest, most ordinary way and be radiant with happiness. And, would you believe it, I will marry some plain workingman, some mechanic or draughtsman."

"There is no harm in that, either. The Duchess Josiane loved Gwynplaine, and that was permissible for her because she was a grand duchess. Everything is permissible for you, too, because you are an exceptional woman: if, my dear, you want to love a Negro or an Arab, don't scruple; send for a Negro. Don't deny yourself anything. You ought to be as bold as your desires; don't fall short of them."

"Can it be so hard to understand me?" Anna Akimovna asked with amazement, and her eyes were bright with tears. "Understand, I have an immense business on my hands—two thousand workmen, for whom I must answer before God. The men who work for me grow blind and deaf. I am afraid to go on like this; I am afraid! I am wretched, and you have the cruelty to talk to me of Negroes and . . . and you smile!" Anna Akimovna brought her fist down on the table. "To go on living the life I am living now, or to marry someone as idle and incompetent as myself, would be a crime. I can't go on living like this," she said hotly, "I cannot!"

"How handsome she is!" said Lysevich, fascinated by her. "My God, how handsome she is! But why are you angry, my dear? Perhaps I am wrong; but surely you don't imagine that if, for the sake of ideas for which I have the deepest respect, you renounce the joys of life and lead a dreary existence, your workmen will be any the better for it? Not a scrap! No, frivolity, frivolity!" he said decisively. "It's essential for you; it's your duty to be frivolous and depraved! Ponder that, my dear, ponder it."

Anna Akimovna was glad she had spoken out, and her spirits rose. She was pleased she had spoken so well, and that her ideas were so fine and just, and she was already convinced that if Pimenov, for instance, loved her, she would marry him with pleasure.

Mishenka began to pour out champagne.

"You make me angry, Viktor Nikolaich," she said, clinking glasses with the lawyer. "It seems to me you give advice and know nothing of life yourself. According to you, if a man be a mechanic or a draughtsman, he is bound to be a peasant and an ignoramus! But they are the cleverest people! Extraordinary people!"

"Your uncle and father . . . I knew them and respected them . . ." Krylin said, pausing for emphasis (he had been sitting upright as a post, and had been eating steadily the whole time), "were people of considerable intelligence and . . . of lofty spiritual qualities."

"Oh, to be sure, we know all about their qualities," the lawyer muttered, and asked permission to smoke.

When dinner was over Krylin was led away for a nap. Lysevich finished his cigar, and, staggering from repletion, followed Anna Akimovna into her study. Cozy corners with photographs and fans on the walls, and the inevitable pink or pale blue lanterns in the middle of the ceiling, he did not like, as the expression of an insipid and unoriginal character; besides, the memory of certain of his love affairs of which he was now ashamed was associated with such lanterns. Anna Akimovna's study with its bare walls and tasteless furniture pleased him exceedingly. It was snug and comfortable for him to sit on a Turkish divan and look at Anna Akimovna, who usually sat on the rug before the fire, clasping her knees and looking into the fire and thinking of something; and at such moments it seemed to him that her peasant Old Believer blood was stirring within her.

Every time after dinner when coffee and liqueurs were handed, he grew livelier and began telling her various bits of literary gossip. He spoke with eloquence and inspiration and was carried away by his own stories; and she listened to him and thought every time that for such enjoyment it was worth paying not only twelve thousand, but three times that sum, and forgave him everything she disliked in him. He sometimes told her the story of some tale or novel he had been reading, and then two or three hours passed unnoticed like a minute. Now he began rather dolefully in a failing voice with his eyes shut.

"It's ages, my dear, since I have read anything," he said when she asked him to tell her something. "Though I do sometimes read Jules Verne."

"I was expecting you to tell me something new."

"Hm! . . . new," Lysevich muttered sleepily, and he settled himself further back in the corner of the sofa. "None of the new literature, my dear, is any use for you or me. Of course, it is bound to be such as it is, and to refuse to recognize it is to refuse to recognize—would mean refusing to recognize the natural order of things, and I do recognize it, but . . ." Lysevich seemed to have fallen asleep. But a minute later his voice was heard again:

"All the new literature moans and howls like the autumn wind in the chimney. 'Ah, unhappy wretch! Ah, your life may be likened to a prison! Ah, how damp and dark it is in your prison! Ah, you will certainly come to ruin, and there is no chance of escape for you!' That's very fine, but I should prefer a literature that would tell us how to escape from prison. Of all contemporary writers, however, I prefer Maupassant." Lysevich opened his eyes. "A fine writer, a perfect writer!" Lysevich shifted in his seat. "A wonderful artist! A terrible, prodigious, supernatural artist!" Lysevich got up from the sofa and raised his right arm. "Maupassant!" he said rapturously. "My dear, read Maupassant! One page of his gives you more than all the riches of the earth! Every line is a new horizon. The softest, tenderest impulses of the soul alternate with violent tempestuous sensations; your soul, as though under the weight of forty thousand atmospheres, is transformed into the most insignificant little bit of some great thing of an undefined rosy hue which I fancy, if one could put it on one's tongue, would yield a pungent, voluptuous taste. What a fury of transitions, of motives, of melodies! You rest peacefully on the lilies and the roses, and suddenly a thought—a terrible, splendid, irresistible thought—swoops down upon you like a locomotive, and bathes you in hot steam and deafens you with its whistle. Read Maupassant, dear girl; I insist on it."

Lysevich waved his arms and paced from corner to corner in violent excitement.

"Yes, it is inconceivable," he pronounced, as though in despair; "his last thing overwhelmed me, intoxicated me! But I am afraid you will not care for it. To be carried away by it you must savor it, slowly suck the juice from each line, drink it in. . . . You must drink it in! . . ."

After a long introduction, containing many words such as demonic sensuality, a network of the most delicate nerves, simoom, crystal, and so on, he began at last telling the story of the novel. He did not tell the story so whimsically, but told it in minute detail, quoting from memory whole descriptions and conversations; the characters of the novel fascinated him, and to describe them he threw himself into attitudes, changed the expression of his face and voice like a real actor.

He laughed with delight at one moment in a deep bass, and at another, on a high shrill note, clasped his hands and clutched at his head with an expression which suggested that it was just going to burst. Anna Akimovna listened enthralled, though she had already read the novel, and it seemed to her ever so much finer and more subtle in the lawyer's version than in the book itself. He drew her attention to various subtleties and emphasized the felicitous expressions and the profound thoughts, but she saw in it, only life, life, life and herself, as though she had been a character in the novel. Her spirits rose, and she, too, laughing and clasping her hands, thought that she could not go on living such a life, that there was no need to have a wretched life when one might have a splendid one. She remembered her words and thoughts at dinner and was proud of them; and when Pimenov suddenly rose up in her imagination, she felt happy and longed for him to love her.

When he had finished the story, Lysevich sat down on the sofa, exhausted.

"How splendid you are! How handsome!" he began, a little while afterwards in a faint voice as if he were ill. "I am happy near you, dear girl, but why am I forty-two instead of thirty? Your tastes and mine do not coincide: you ought to be depraved, and I have long passed that phase, and want a love as delicate and immaterial as a ray of sunshine—that is, from the point of view of a woman of your age, I am of no earthly use."

In his own words, he loved Turgenev, the singer of virginal love and purity, of youth, and of the melancholy Russian landscape; but he loved virginal love, not from knowledge but from hearsay, as something abstract, existing outside real life. Now he assured himself that he loved Anna Akimovna platonically, ideally, though he did not know what those words meant. But he felt comfortable, snug, warm. Anna Akimovna seemed to him enchanting, original, and he imagined that the pleasant sensation that was aroused in him by these surroundings was the very thing that was called platonic love.

He laid his cheek on her hand and said in the tone commonly used in coaxing little children:

"My precious, why have you punished me?"

"How? When?"

"I have had no Christmas present from you."

Anna Akimovna had never heard before of their sending a Christmas box to the lawyer, and now she was at a loss how much to give him. But she must give him something, for he was expecting it, though he looked at her with eyes full of love.

"I suppose Nazarich forgot it," she said, "but it is not too late to set it right."

She suddenly remembered the fifteen hundred she had received the day before, which was now lying in the toilet drawer in her bedroom. And when she brought that ungrateful money and gave it to the lawyer, and he put it in his coat pocket with indolent grace, the whole incident passed off charmingly and naturally. The sudden reminder of a Christmas box and this fifteen hundred was not unbecoming in Lysevich.

"*Merci,*" he said, and kissed her finger.

Krylin came in with blissful, sleepy face, but without his decorations.

Lysevich and he stayed a little longer and drank a glass of tea each and began to get ready to go. Anna Akimovna was a little embarrassed.... She had utterly forgotten in what department Krylin served, and whether she had to give him money or not; and if she had to, whether to give it now or send it afterwards in an envelope.

"Where does he serve?" she whispered to Lysevich.

"Goodness knows," muttered Lysevich, yawning.

She reflected that if Krylin used to visit her father and her uncle and respected them, it was probably not for nothing: apparently he had been charitable at their expense, serving in some charitable institution. As she said good-bye she slipped three hundred rubles into his hand; he seemed taken aback and looked at her for a minute in silence with his pewtery eyes, but then seemed to understand and said:

"The receipt, honored Anna Akimovna, you can only receive on the New Year."

Lysevich had become utterly limp and heavy, and he staggered when Mishenka put on his overcoat.

As he went downstairs he looked like a man in the last stage of exhaustion, and it was evident that he would drop asleep as soon as he got into his sledge.

"Your Excellency," he said languidly to Krylin, stopping in the middle of the staircase, "has it ever happened to you to experience a feeling as though some unseen force were drawing you out longer and longer? You are drawn out and turn into the finest wire. Subjectively this finds expression in a curious voluptuous feeling which is impossible to compare with anything."

Anna Akimovna, standing at the top of the stairs, saw each of them give Mishenka a note.

"Good-bye! Come again!" she called to them, and ran into her bedroom.

She quickly threw off her dress, which she was weary of already, put on a dressing gown, and ran downstairs; and as she ran downstairs she laughed and thumped with her feet like a schoolboy; she had a great desire for mischief.

## 4. EVENING

Auntie, in a loose print blouse, Varvarushka, and two old women, were sitting in the dining-room having supper. A big piece of salt meat, a ham, and various savories were lying on the table before them, and clouds of steam were rising from the meat, which looked particularly fat and appetizing. Wine was not served on the lower story, but they made up for it with a great number of spirits and homemade liqueurs. Agafyushka, the fat, white-skinned, well-fed cook, was standing with her arms crossed in the doorway and talking to the old women, and the dishes were being handed by the downstairs Masha, a dark girl with a crimson ribbon in her hair. The old women had had enough to eat before the morning was over, and an hour before supper had had tea and buns, and so they were now eating with effort—as it were, from a sense of duty.

"Oh, my girl!" sighed Auntie, as Anna Akimovna ran into the dining-room and sat down beside her. "You've frightened me to death!"

Everyone in the house was pleased when Anna Akimovna was in good spirits and played pranks; this always reminded them that the old men were dead and that the old women had no authority in the house, and anyone could do as he liked without any fear of being sharply called to account for it. Only the two old women glanced askance at Anna Akimovna with amazement: she was humming, and it was a sin to sing at table.

"Our mistress, our beauty, our picture," Agafyushka began chanting with sugary sweetness. "Our precious jewel! The people, the people that have come today to look at our queen. Lord have mercy upon us! Generals and officers and gentlemen.... I kept looking out of window and counting and counting till I gave it up."

"I'd as soon they did not come at all," said Auntie; she

looked sadly at her niece and added: "They only waste the time for my poor orphan girl."

Anna Akimovna felt hungry, as she had eaten nothing since the morning. They poured her out some very bitter liqueur; she drank it off, and tasted the salt meat with mustard, and thought it extraordinarily nice. Then the downstairs Masha brought in the turkey, the pickled apples, and the gooseberries. And that pleased her, too. There was only one thing that was disagreeable: there was a draught of hot air from the tiled stove; it was stiflingly close and everyone's cheeks were burning. After supper the cloth was taken off and plates of peppermint biscuits, walnuts, and raisins were brought in.

"You sit down, too . . . no need to stand there!" said Auntie to the cook.

Agafyushka sighed and sat down to the table; Masha set a wineglass of liqueur before her, too, and Anna Akimovna began to feel as though Agafyushka's white neck were giving out heat like the stove. They were all talking of how difficult it was nowadays to get married, and saying that in old days, if men did not court beauty, they paid attention to money, but now there was no making out what they wanted; and while hunchbacks and cripples used to be left old maids, nowadays men would not have even the beautiful and wealthy. Auntie began to set this down to immorality and said that people had no fear of God, but she suddenly remembered that Ivan Ivanich, her brother, and Varvarushka—both people of holy life—had feared God, but all the same had had children on the sly, and had sent them to the Foundling Asylum. She pulled herself up and changed the conversation, telling them about a suitor she had once had, a factory hand, and how she had loved him, but her brothers had forced her to marry a widower, an icon painter, who, thank God, had died two years after. The downstairs Masha sat down to the table, too, and told them with a mysterious air that for the last week some unknown man with a black mustache, in a greatcoat with an astrakhan collar, had made his appearance every morning in the yard, had stared at the windows of the big house, and had gone on further—to the buildings; the man was all right, nice-looking. . . .

All this conversation made Anna Akimovna suddenly long to be married—long intensely, painfully; she felt as though she would give half her life and all her fortune only to know that upstairs there was a man who was closer to her than anyone in the world, that he loved her warmly and was missing her; and the thought of such closeness, ecstatic and inexpressible in words, troubled her soul. And the instinct of youth and health flattered her with lying assurances that the real poetry of life was not over but still to come, and she believed it, and, leaning back in her chair (her hair fell down as she did so), she began laughing, and, looking at her, the others laughed, too. And it was a long time before this causeless laughter died down in the dining-room.

She was informed that the Stinging Beetle had come. This was a pilgrim woman called Pasha or Spiridonovna—a thin little woman of fifty, in a black dress with a white kerchief, with keen eyes, sharp nose, and a sharp chin; she had sly, viperish eyes and she looked as though she could see right through everyone. Her lips were shaped like a heart. Her viperishness and hostility to everyone had earned her the nickname of the Stinging Beetle.

Going into the dining-room without looking at anyone, she made for the icons and chanted in a high voice "Thy Holy Birth," then she sang, "The Virgin today gives birth to the Son," then, "Christ is born," then she turned round and bent a piercing gaze upon all of them.

"A happy Christmas," she said, and she kissed Anna Akimovna on the shoulder. "It's all I could do, all I could do to get to you, my kind friends." She kissed Auntie on the shoulder. "I should have come to you this morning, but I went in to some good people to rest on the way. 'Stay, Spiridonovna, stay,' they said, and I did not notice that evening was coming on."

As she did not eat meat, they gave her salmon and caviar. She ate looking from under her eyelids at the company and drank three glasses of vodka. When she had finished she said a prayer and bowed down to Anna Akimovna's feet.

They began to play a game of "kings," as they had done the year before, and the year before that, and all the servants in both stories crowded in at the doors to watch the game. Anna Akimovna fancied she caught a glimpse once or twice of Mishenka, with a patronizing smile on his face, among the crowd of peasant men and women. The first to be king was Stinging Beetle, and Anna Akimovna as the soldier paid her tribute; and then Auntie was king and Anna Akimovna was peasant, which excited general delight, and Agafyushka was prince and was quite abashed with pleasure. Another game was got up at the other end of the table—played by the two Mashas, Varvarushka, and the sewing-maid Marfa Petrovna, who was waked on purpose to play "kings," and whose face looked cross and sleepy.

While they were playing they talked of men, and of how difficult it was to get a good husband nowadays, and which state was to be preferred—that of an old maid or a widow.

"You are a handsome, healthy, sturdy lass," said Stinging Beetle to Anna Akimovna. "But I can't make out for whose sake you are holding back."

"What's to be done if nobody will have me?"

"Or maybe you have taken a vow to remain a maid?" Stinging Beetle went on, as though she did not hear. "Well, that's a good deed. . . . Remain one," she repeated, looking intently and maliciously at her cards. "All right, my dear, remain one. . . . Yes . . . only maids, these saintly maids, are not all alike." She heaved a sigh and played the king. "Oh no, my girl, they are not all alike! Some really watch over themselves like nuns, and butter would not melt in their mouths; and if such a one does sin in an hour of weakness, she is worried to death, poor thing! so it would be a sin to condemn her. While others will go dressed in black and sew their shroud, and yet love rich old men on the sly. Yes, y-es, my canary birds, some hussies will bewitch an old man and rule over him, my doves, rule over him and turn his head; and when they've saved up money and lottery tickets enough, they will bewitch him to his death."

Varvarushka's only response to these hints was to heave a sigh and look towards the icons. There was an expression of Christian meekness on her countenance.

"I know a maid like that, my bitterest enemy," Stinging Beetle went on, looking round at everyone in triumph; "she is always sighing, too, and looking at the icons, the she-devil. When she used to rule in a certain old man's house, if one went to her she would give one a crust and bid one bow down to the icons while she would sing: 'In conception Thou dost abide a Virgin . . . !' On holidays she will give one a bite, and on working days she will reproach one for it. But nowadays I will make merry over her! I will make as merry as I please, my jewel."

Varvarushka glanced at the icons again and crossed herself.

"But no one will have me, Spiridonovna," said Anna Akimovna to change the conversation. "What's to be done?"

"It's your own fault. You keep waiting for highly educated gentlemen, but you ought to marry one of your own sort, a merchant."

"We don't want a merchant," said Auntie, all in a flutter. "Queen of Heaven, preserve us! A gentleman will spend your money, but then he will be kind to you, you poor little fool. But a merchant will be so strict that you won't feel at home in your own house. You'll be wanting to fondle him and he will be counting his money, and when you sit down to meals with him, he'll grudge you every mouthful, though it's your own, the lout! . . . Marry a gentleman."

They all talked at once, loudly interrupting one another, and Auntie tapped on the table with the nutcrackers and said, flushed and angry:

"We won't have a merchant; we won't have one! If you choose a merchant, I shall go to an almshouse."

"Sh . . . Sh! . . . Hush!" cried Stinging Beetle; when all were silent she screwed up one eye and said: "Do you know what, Annushka, my birdie . . . ? There is no need for you to get married really like everyone else. You're rich and free, you are your own mistress; but yet, my child, it doesn't seem the right thing for you to be an old maid. I'll find you, you know, some trumpery and simple-witted man. You'll marry him for appearances and then have your fling, bonny lass! You can hand him five thousand or ten maybe and pack him off where he came from, and you will be mistress in your own house—you can love whom you like and no one can say anything to you. And then you can love your highly educated gentleman. You'll have a jolly time!" Stinging Beetle snapped her fingers and gave a whistle.

"It's sinful," said Auntie.

"Oh, sinful," laughed Stinging Beetle. "She is educated, she understands. To cut someone's throat or bewitch an old man—that's a sin, that's true; but to love some charming young friend is not a sin at all. And what is there in it, really? There's no sin in it at all! The old pilgrim women have invented all that to make fools of simple folk. I, too, say everywhere it's a sin; I don't know myself why it's a sin." Stinging Beetle emptied her glass and cleared her throat. "Have your fling, bonny lass," this time evidently addressing herself. "For thirty years, wenches, I have thought of nothing but sins and been afraid, but now I see I have wasted my time, I've let it slip by like a ninny! Ah, I have been a fool, a fool!" She sighed. "A woman's time is short and every day is precious. You are handsome, Annushka, and very rich; but as soon as thirty-five or forty strikes for you your time is up. Don't listen to anyone, my girl; live, have your fling till you are forty, and then you will have time to pray forgiveness—there will be plenty of time to bow down and to sew your shroud. A candle to God and a poker to the devil! You can do both at once! Well, how is it to be? Will you make some little man happy?"

"I will," laughed Anna Akimovna. "I don't care now; I would marry a workingman."

"Well, that would do all right! Oh, what a fine fellow you would choose then!" Stinging Beetle screwed up her eyes and shook her head. "O—o—oh!"

"I tell her myself," said Auntie, "it's no good waiting for a gentleman, so she had better marry, not a gentleman, but someone humbler; anyway we should have a man in the house to look after things. And there are lots of good men. She might have someone out of the factory. They are all sober, steady men. . . ."

"I should think so," Stinging Beetle agreed. "They are capital fellows. If you like, Aunt, I will make a match for her with Vassily Lebedinsky."

"Oh, Vasya's legs are so long," said Auntie seriously. "He is so lanky. He has no looks."

There was laughter in the crowd by the door.

"Well, Pimenov? Would you like to marry Pimenov?" Stinging Beetle asked Anna Akimovna.

"Very good. Make a match for me with Pimenov."

"Really?"

"Yes, do!" Anna Akimovna said resolutely, and she struck her fist on the table. "On my honor, I will marry him."

"Really?"

Anna Akimovna suddenly felt ashamed that her cheeks were burning and that everyone was looking at her; she flung the cards together on the table and ran out of the room. As she ran up the stairs and, reaching the upper story, sat down to the piano in the drawing-room, a murmur of sound reached her from below like the roar of the sea; most likely they were talking of her and of Pimenov, and perhaps Stinging Beetle was taking advantage of her absence to insult Varvarushka and was putting no check on her language.

The lamp in the big room was the only light burning in the upper story, and it sent a glimmer through the door into the dark drawing-room. It was between nine and ten, not later. Anna Akimovna played a waltz, then another, then a third; she went on playing without stopping. She looked into the dark corner beyond the piano, smiled, and inwardly called to it, and the idea occurred to her that she might drive off to the town to see someone, Lysevich for instance, and tell him what was passing in her heart. She wanted to talk without ceasing, to laugh, to play the fool, but the dark corner was sullenly silent, and all round in all the rooms of the upper story it was still and desolate.

She was fond of sentimental songs, but she had a harsh, untrained voice, and so she only played the accompaniment and sang hardly audibly, just above her breath. She sang in a whisper one song after another, for the most part about love, separation, and frustrated hopes, and she imagined how she would hold out her hands to him and say with entreaty, with tears, "Pimenov, take this burden from me!" And then, just as though her sins had been forgiven, there would be joy and comfort in her soul, and perhaps a free, happy life would begin. In an anguish of anticipation she leaned over the keys, with a passionate longing for the change in her life to come at once without delay, and was terrified of the thought that her old life would go on for some time longer. Then she played again and sang hardly above her breath, and all was stillness about her. There was no noise coming from downstairs now, they must have gone to bed. It had struck ten some time before. A long, solitary, wearisome night was approaching.

Anna Akimovna walked through all the rooms, lay down for a while on the sofa, and read in her study the letters that had come that evening; there were twelve letters of Christmas greetings and three anonymous letters. In one of them some workman complained in a horrible, almost illegible handwriting that Lenten oil sold in the factory shop was rancid and smelled of paraffin; in another, someone respectfully informed her that over a purchase of iron Nazarich had lately taken a bribe of a thousand rubles from someone; in a third she was abused for her inhumanity.

The excitement of Christmas was passing off, and to keep it up Anna Akimovna sat down at the piano again and softly played one of the new waltzes, then she remembered how cleverly and creditably she had spoken at dinner today. She looked round at the dark windows, at the walls with the pictures, at the faint light that came from the big room, and all at once she began suddenly crying, and she felt vexed that she was so lonely, and that she had no one to talk to and consult. To cheer herself she tried to picture Pimenov in her imagination, but it was unsuccessful.

It struck twelve. Mishenka, no longer wearing his swallowtail but in his reefer jacket, came in, and, without speaking, lighted two candles; then he went out and returned a minute later with a cup of tea on a tray.

"What are you laughing at?" she asked, noticing a smile on his face.

"I was downstairs and heard the jokes you were making about Pimenov . . ." he said, and put his hand before his laughing mouth. "If he were sat down to dinner today with Viktor Nikolaevich and the general, he'd have died of fright." Mishenka's shoulders were shaking with laughter. "He doesn't know even how to hold his fork, I bet."

The footman's laughter and words, his reefer jacket and mustache, gave Anna Akimovna a feeling of uncleanness. She shut her eyes to avoid seeing him, and, against her own will, imagined Pimenov dining with Lysevich and Krylin, and his timid, unintellectual figure seemed to her pitiful and helpless, and she felt repelled by it. And only now, for the first time in the whole day, she realized clearly that all she had said and thought about Pimenov and marrying a workman was nonsense, folly, and willfulness. To convince herself of the opposite, to overcome her repulsion, she tried to recall what she had said at dinner, but now she could not see anything in it: shame at her own thoughts and actions, and the fear that she had said something improper during the day, and disgust at her own lack of spirit, overwhelmed her completely. She took up a candle and, as rapidly as if someone were pursuing her, ran downstairs, woke Spiridonovna, and began assuring her she had been joking. Then she went to her bedroom. Red-haired Masha, who was dozing in an armchair near the bed, jumped up and began shaking up the pillows. Her face was exhausted and sleepy, and her magnificent hair had fallen on one side.

"Chalikov came again this evening," she said, yawning, "but I did not dare to announce him; he was very drunk. He says he will come again tomorrow."

"What does he want with me?" said Anna Akimovna, and she flung her comb on the floor. "I won't see him, I won't."

She made up her mind she had no one left in life but this Chalikov, that he would never leave off persecuting her, and would remind her every day how uninteresting and absurd her life was. So all she was fit for was to help the poor. Oh, how stupid it was!

She lay down without undressing and sobbed with shame and depression: what seemed to her most vexatious and stupid of all was that her dreams that day about Pimenov had been right, lofty, honorable, but at the same time she felt that Lysevich and even Krylin were nearer to her than Pimenov and all the workpeople taken together. She thought that if the long day she had just spent could have been represented in a picture, all that had been bad and vulgar—as, for instance, the dinner, the lawyer's talk, the game of "kings"—would have been true, while her dreams and talk about Pimenov would have stood out from the whole as something false, as out of drawing; and she thought, too, that it was too late to dream of happiness, that everything was over for her, and it was impossible to go back to the life when she had slept under the same quilt with her mother, or to devise some new special sort of life.

Red-haired Masha was kneeling before the bed, gazing at her in mournful perplexity; then she, too, began crying, and laid her face against her mistress's arm, and without words it was clear why she was so wretched.

"We are fools!" said Anna Akimovna, laughing and crying. "We are fools! Oh, what fools we are!"

# THREE YEARS

## 1.

IT WAS DARK, and already lights had begun to gleam here and there in the houses, and a pale moon was rising behind the barracks at the end of the street. Laptev was sitting on a bench by the gate waiting for the end of the evening service at the Church of St. Peter and St. Paul. He was reckoning that Yulia Sergeyevna would pass by on her way from the service, and then he would speak to her, and perhaps spend the whole evening with her.

He had been sitting there for an hour and a half already, and all that time his imagination had been busy picturing his Moscow rooms, his Moscow friends, his man Pyotr, and his writing table. He gazed half wonderingly at the dark, motion-less trees, and it seemed strange to him that he was living now, not in his summer villa at Sokolniki, but in a provincial town in a house by which a great herd of cattle was driven every morning and evening, accompanied by terrible clouds of dust and the blowing of a horn. He thought of long conversations in which he had taken part quite lately in Moscow—conversations in which it had been maintained that one could live without love, that passionate love was an obsession, that finally there is no such love, but only a physical attraction between the sexes—and so on, in the same style; he remembered them and thought mournfully that if he were asked now what love was, he could not have found an answer.

The service was over, the people began to appear. Laptev strained his eyes gazing at the dark figures. The bishop had been driven by in his carriage, the bells had stopped ringing, and the red and green lights in the belfry were one after another extinguished—there had been an illumination, as it was dedication day—but the people were still coming out, lingering, talking, and standing under the windows. But at last Laptev heard a familiar voice, his heart began beating violently, and he was overcome with despair on seeing that Yulia Sergeyevna was not alone, but walking with two ladies.

"It's awful, awful!" he whispered, feeling jealous. "It's awful!"

At the corner of the lane, she stopped to say good-bye to the ladies, and while doing so glanced at Laptev.

"I was coming to see you," he said. "I'm coming for a chat with your father. Is he at home?"

"Most likely," she answered. "It's early for him to have gone to the club."

There were gardens all along the lane, and a row of lime trees growing by the fence cast a broad patch of shadow in the moonlight, so that the gate and the fences were completely plunged in darkness on one side, from which came the sounds of women whispering, smothered laughter, and someone playing softly on a balalaika. There was a fragrance of lime flowers and of hay. This fragrance and the murmur of the unseen whispers worked upon Laptev. He was all at once overwhelmed with a passionate longing to throw his arms round his companion, to shower kisses on her face, her hands, her shoulders, to burst into sobs, to fall at her feet and to tell her how long he had been waiting for her. A faint, scarcely perceptible scent of incense hung about her; and that scent reminded him of the time when he, too, believed in God and used to go to evening service, and when he used to dream so much of pure romantic love. And it seemed to him that, because this girl did not love him, all possibility of the happiness he had dreamed of then was lost to him forever.

She began speaking sympathetically of the illness of his sister, Nina Fyodorovna. Two months before his sister had undergone an operation for cancer, and now everyone was expecting a return of the disease.

"I went to see her this morning," said Yulia Sergeyevna, "and it seemed to me that during the last week she has, not exactly grown thin, but has, as it were, faded."

"Yes, yes," Laptev agreed. "There's no return of the symptoms, but every day I notice she grows weaker and weaker, and is wasting before my eyes. I don't understand what's the matter with her."

"Oh dear! And how strong she used to be, plump and rosy!" said Yulia Sergeyevna after a moment's silence. "Everyone here used to call her the Moscow lady. How she used to laugh! On holidays she used to dress up like a peasant girl, and it suited her so well."

Dr. Sergei Borisovich was at home; he was a stout, red-faced man, wearing a long coat that reached below his knees, and looking as though he had short legs. He was pacing up and down his study, with his hands in his pockets, and humming to himself in an undertone, "Ru-ru-ru-ru." His gray whiskers looked unkempt, and his hair was unbrushed, as though he had just got out of bed. And his study, with pillows on the sofa, with stacks of papers in the corners, and with a dirty invalid poodle lying under the table, produced the same impression of unkemptness and untidiness as himself.

"Monsieur Laptev wants to see you," his daughter said to him, going into his study.

"Ru-ru-ru-ru," he hummed louder than ever, and, turning into the drawing-room, gave his hand to Laptev, and asked: "What good news have you to tell me?"

It was dark in the drawing-room. Laptev, still standing with his hat in his hand, began apologizing for disturbing him; he asked what was to be done to make his sister sleep at night, and why she was growing so thin; and he was embarrassed by the thought that he had asked those very questions at his visit that morning.

"Tell me," he said, "wouldn't it be as well to send for some specialist on internal diseases from Moscow? What do you think of it?"

The doctor sighed, shrugged his shoulders, and made a vague gesture with his hands.

It was evident that he was offended. He was a very huffy man, prone to take offense, and always ready to suspect that people did not believe in him, that he was not recognized or properly respected, that his patients exploited him, and that his colleagues showed him ill will. He was always jeering at himself, saying that fools like him were only made for the public to ride roughshod over them.

Yulia Sergeyevna lighted the lamp. She was tired out with the service, and that was evident from her pale, exhausted face, and her weary step. She wanted to rest. She sat down on the sofa, put her hands on her lap, and sank into thought. Laptev knew that he was ugly, and now he felt as though he were conscious of his ugliness all over his body. He was short, thin, with ruddy cheeks, and his hair had grown so thin that his head felt cold. In his expression there was none of that refined simplicity which makes even rough, ugly faces attractive; in the society of women, he was awkward, overtalkative, affected. And now he almost despised himself for it. He must talk that Yulia Sergeyevna might not be bored in his company. But what about? About his sister's illness again?

And he began to talk about medicine, saying what is usually said. He approved of hygiene and said that he had long ago wanted to found a night refuge in Moscow—in fact, he had already calculated the cost of it. According to his plan the workmen who came in the evening to the night refuge were to receive a supper of hot cabbage soup with bread, a warm, dry bed with a rug, and a place for drying their clothes and their boots.

Yulia Sergeyevna was usually silent in his presence, and in a strange way, perhaps by the instinct of a lover, he divined her thoughts and intentions. And now, from the fact that after the evening service she had not gone to her room to change her dress and drink tea, he deduced that she was going to pay some visit elsewhere.

"But I'm in no hurry with the night refuge," he went on, speaking with vexation and irritability, and addressing the doctor, who looked at him, as it were, blankly and in perplexity, evidently unable to understand what induced him to raise the question of medicine and hygiene. "And most likely it will be a long time, too, before I make use of our estimate. I fear our night shelter will fall into the hands of our pious humbugs and philanthropic ladies, who always ruin any undertaking."

Yulia Sergeyevna got up and held out her hand to Laptev.

"Excuse me," she said, "it's time for me to go. Please give my love to your sister."

"Ru-ru-ru-ru," hummed the doctor. "Ru-ru-ru-ru."

Yulia Sergeyevna went out, and, after staying a little longer, Laptev said good-bye to the doctor and went home. When a man is dissatisfied and feels unhappy, how trivial seem to him the shapes of the lime trees, the shadows, the clouds, all the beauties of nature, so complacent, so indifferent! By now the moon was high up in the sky, and the clouds were scudding quickly below. "But how naive and provincial the moon is, how threadbare and paltry the clouds!" thought Laptev. He felt ashamed of the way he had talked just now about medicine and the night refuge. He felt with horror that next day he would not have will enough to resist trying to see her and talk to her again, and would again be convinced that he was nothing to her. And the day after—it would be the same. With what object? And how and when would it all end?

At home he went in to see his sister. Nina Fyodorovna still looked strong and gave the impression of being a well-built, vigorous woman, but her striking pallor made her look like a corpse, especially when, as now, she was lying on her back with her eyes closed; her elder daughter Sasha, a girl of ten years old, was sitting beside her reading aloud from her reading book.

"Alyosha has come," the invalid said softly to herself.

There had long been established between Sasha and her uncle a tacit compact, to take turns in sitting with the patient. On this occasion Sasha closed her reading book, and, without uttering a word, went softly out of the room. Laptev took an historical novel from the chest of drawers, and, looking for the right page, sat down and began reading it aloud.

Nina Fyodorovna was born in Moscow of a merchant family. She and her two brothers had spent their childhood and early youth, living at home in Pyatnitsky Street. Their childhood was long and wearisome; her father treated her sternly, and had even on two or three occasions flogged her, and her mother had had a long illness and died. The servants were coarse, dirty, and hypocritical; the house was frequented by priests and monks, also hypocritical; they ate and drank and coarsely flattered her father, whom they did not like. The boys had the good fortune to go to school, while Nina was left practically uneducated. All her life she wrote an illegible scrawl and had read nothing but historical novels. Seventeen years ago, when she was twenty-two, on a summer holiday at Khimki, she made the acquaintance of her present husband, a landowner called

Panaurov, had fallen in love with him, and married him secretly against her father's will. Panaurov, a handsome, rather impudent fellow, who whistled and lighted his cigarette from the holy lamp, struck the father as an absolutely worthless person. And when the son-in-law began in his letters demanding a dowry, the old man wrote to his daughter that he would send her furs, silver, and various articles that had been left at her mother's death, as well as thirty thousand rubles, but without his paternal blessing. Later he sent another twenty thousand. This money, as well as the dowry, was spent; the estate had been sold and Panaurov moved with his family to the town and got a job in a provincial government office. In the town he formed another tie and had a second family, and this was the subject of much talk, as his illicit family was not a secret.

Nina Fyodorovna adored her husband. And now, listening to the historical novel, she was thinking how much she had gone through in her life, how much she had suffered, and that if anyone were to describe her life it would make a very pathetic story. As the tumor was in her breast, she was persuaded that love and her domestic grief were the causes of her illness, and that jealousy and tears had brought her to her hopeless state.

At last Alexei Fyodorovich closed the book and said:

"That's the end, and thank God for it. Tomorrow we'll begin a new one."

Nina Fyodorovna laughed. She had always been given to laughter, but of late Laptev had begun to notice that at moments her mind seemed weakened by illness, and she would laugh at the smallest trifle, and even without any cause at all.

"Yulia came before dinner while you were out," she said. "So far as I can see, she hasn't much faith in her papa. 'Let Papa go on treating you,' she said, 'but write in secret to the holy elder to pray for you, too.' There is a holy man somewhere here. Yulia forgot her parasol here; you must take it to her tomorrow," she went on after a brief pause. "No, when the end comes, neither doctors nor holy men are any help."

"Nina, why can't you sleep at night?" Laptev asked, to change the subject.

"Oh well, I don't go to sleep—that's all. I lie and think."

"What do you think about, dear?"

"About the children, about you . . . about my life. I've gone through a great deal, Alyosha, you know. When one begins to remember and remember. . . . My God!" She laughed. "It's no joke to have borne five children as I have, to have buried three. . . . Sometimes I was expecting to be confined while my Grigory Nikolaich would be sitting at that very time with another woman. There would be no one to send for the doctor or the midwife. I would go into the passage or the kitchen for the servant, and there Jews, tradesmen, money-lenders would be waiting for him to come home. My head used to go round. . . . He did not love me, though he never said so openly. Now I've grown calmer—it doesn't weigh on my heart; but in old days, when I was younger, it hurt me—ach! how it hurt me, darling! Once—while we were still in the country—I found him in the garden with a lady, and I walked away. . . . I walked on aimlessly, and I don't know how, but I found myself in the church porch. I fell on my knees: 'Queen of Heaven!' I said. And it was night, the moon was shining. . . ."

She was exhausted, she began gasping for breath. Then, after resting a little, she took her brother's hand and went on in a weak, toneless voice:

"How kind you are, Alyosha! . . . And how clever! . . . What a good man you've grown up into!"

At midnight Laptev said good night to her, and as he went away he took with him the parasol that Yulia Sergeyevna had forgotten. In spite of the late hour, the servants, male and female, were drinking tea in the dining-room. How disorderly! The children were not in bed, but were there in the dining-room, too. They were all talking softly in undertones and had not noticed that the lamp was smoking and would soon go out. All these people, big and little, were disturbed by a whole succession of bad omens and were in an oppressed mood. The glass in the hall had been broken, the samovar had been buzzing every day, and, as though on purpose, was even buzzing now. They were describing how a mouse had jumped out of Nina Fyodorovna's boot when she was dressing. And the children were quite aware of the terrible significance of these omens. The elder girl, Sasha, a thin little brunette, was sitting motionless at the table, and her face looked scared and woebegone, while the younger, Lida, a chubby fair child of seven, stood beside her sister looking from under her brows at the light.

Laptev went downstairs to his own rooms in the lower story, where under the low ceilings it was always close and smelled of geraniums. In his sitting-room, Panaurov, Nina Fyodorovna's husband, was sitting reading the newspaper. Laptev nodded to him and sat down opposite. Both sat still and said nothing. They used to spend whole evenings like this without speaking, and neither of them was in the least put out by this silence.

The little girls came down from upstairs to say good night. Deliberately and in silence, Panaurov made the sign of the cross over them several times and gave them his hand to kiss. They dropped curtseys and then went up to Laptev, who had to make the sign of the cross and give them his hand to kiss also. This ceremony with the hand-kissing and curtseying was repeated every evening.

When the children had gone out Panaurov laid aside the newspaper and said:

"It's not very lively in our God-fearing town! I must confess, my dear fellow," he added with a sigh, "I'm very glad that at last you've found some distraction."

"What do you mean?" asked Laptev.

"I saw you coming out of Dr. Byelavin's just now. I expect you don't go there for the sake of the papa."

"Of course not," said Laptev, and he blushed.

"Well, of course not. And by the way, you wouldn't find such another old brute as that papa if you hunted by daylight with a candle. You can't imagine what a foul, stupid, clumsy beast he is! You cultured people in the capitals are still interested in the provinces only on the lyrical side, only from the paysage and *Poor Anton* point of view, but I can assure you, my boy, there's nothing logical about it; there's nothing but barbarism, meanness, and nastiness—that's all. Take the local devotees of science—the local intellectuals, so to speak. Can you imagine there are here in this town twenty-eight doctors? They've all made their fortunes, and they are living in houses of their own, and meanwhile the population is in just as helpless a condition as ever. Here Nina had to have an operation, quite an ordinary one really, yet we were obliged to get a surgeon from Moscow; not one doctor here would undertake it. It's beyond all conception. They know nothing, they understand nothing. They take no interest in anything. Ask them, for instance, what cancer is—what it is, what it comes from."

And Panaurov began to explain what cancer was. He was a specialist on all scientific subjects and explained from a scientific point of view everything that was discussed. But he explained it all in his own way. He had a theory of his own about the circulation of the blood, about chemistry, about astronomy. He talked slowly, softly, convincingly.

"It's beyond all conception," he pronounced in an imploring voice, screwing up his eyes, sighing languidly, and smiling as graciously as a king, and it was evident that he was very well satisfied with himself and never gave a thought to the fact that he was fifty.

"I am rather hungry," said Laptev. "I should like something savory."

"Well, that can easily be managed."

Not long afterwards Laptev and his brother-in-law were sitting upstairs in the dining-room having supper. Laptev had a glass of vodka and then began drinking wine. Panaurov drank nothing. He never drank and never gambled, yet in spite of that he had squandered all his own and his wife's property and had accumulated debts. To squander so much in such a short time, one must have, not passions, but a special talent. Panaurov liked dainty fare, liked a handsome dinner service, liked music after dinner, speeches, bowing footmen, to whom he would carelessly fling tips of ten, even twenty-five rubles. He always took part in all lotteries and subscriptions, sent bouquets to ladies of his acquaintance on their birthdays, bought cups, stands for glasses, studs, ties, walking sticks, scents, cigarette holders, pipes, lap dogs, parrots, Japanese bric-a-brac, antiques; he had silk nightshirts, and a bedstead made of ebony inlaid with mother-of-pearl. His dressing gown was a genuine Bokhara, and everything was to correspond; and on all this there went every day, as he himself expressed, "a deluge" of money.

At supper he kept sighing and shaking his head.

"Yes, everything on this earth has an end," he said softly, screwing up his dark eyes. "You will fall in love and suffer. You will fall out of love; you'll be deceived, for there is no woman who will not deceive; you will suffer, will be brought to despair, and will be faithless too. But the time will come when all this will be a memory, and when you will reason about it coldly and look upon it as utterly trivial. . . ."

Laptev, tired, a little drunk, looked at his handsome head, his clipped black beard, and seemed to understand why women so loved this pampered, conceited, and physically handsome creature.

After supper Panaurov did not stay in the house but went off to his other lodgings. Laptev went out to see him on his way. Panaurov was the only man in the town who wore a top hat, and his elegant, dandified figure, his top hat and tan gloves, beside the gray fences, the pitiful little houses, with their three windows and the thickets of nettles, always made a strange and mournful impression.

After saying good-bye to him, Laptev returned home without hurrying. The moon was shining brightly; one could distinguish every straw on the ground, and Laptev felt as though the moonlight were caressing his bare head, as though someone were passing a feather over his hair.

"I love!" he pronounced aloud, and he had a sudden longing to run to overtake Panaurov, to embrace him, to forgive him, to make him a present of a lot of money, and then to run off into the open country, into a wood, to run on and on without looking back.

At home he saw, lying on the chair, the parasol Yulia Sergeyevna had forgotten; he snatched it up and kissed it greedily. The parasol was a silk one, no longer new, tied round with old elastic. The handle was a cheap one, of white bone. Laptev opened it over him, and he felt as though there were the fragrance of happiness about him.

He settled himself more comfortably in his chair, and, still keeping hold of the parasol, began writing to Moscow to one of his friends:

> Dear precious Kostya,
>
> Here is news for you: I'm in love again! I say *again*, because six years ago I fell in love with a Moscow actress, though I didn't even succeed in making her acquaintance, and for the last year and a half I have been living with a certain person you know—a woman neither young nor good-looking. Ah, my dear boy, how unlucky

I am in love. I've never had any success with women, and if I say *again* it's simply because it's rather sad and mortifying to acknowledge even to myself that my youth has passed entirely without love, and that I'm in love in a real sense now for the first time in my life, at thirty-four. Let it stand that I love *again*.

If only you knew what a girl she is! She couldn't be called a beauty—she has a broad face, she is very thin, but what a wonderful expression of goodness she has when she smiles! When she speaks; her voice is as clear as a bell. She never carries on a conversation with me—I don't know her; but when I'm beside her I feel she's a striking, exceptional creature, full of intelligence and lofty aspirations. She is religious, and you cannot imagine how deeply this touches me and exalts her in my eyes. On that point I am ready to argue with you endlessly. You may be right, to your thinking; but, still, I love to see her praying in church. She is a provincial, but she was educated in Moscow. She loves our Moscow; she dresses in the Moscow style, and I love her for that—love her, love her. . . . I see you frowning and getting up to read me a long lecture on what love is, and what sort of woman one can love, and what sort one cannot, and so on, and so on. But, dear Kostya, before I was in love I, too, knew quite well what love was.

My sister thanks you for your message. She often recalls how she used to take Kostya Kochevoi to the preparatory class, and never speaks of you except as *poor Kostya*, as she still thinks of you as the little orphan boy she remembers. And so, poor orphan, I'm in love. While it's a secret, don't say anything to a "certain person." I think it will all come right of itself, or, as the footman says in Tolstoi, will "come round."

When he had finished his letter Laptev went to bed. He was so tired that he couldn't keep his eyes open, but for some reason he could not get to sleep; the noise in the street seemed to prevent him. The cattle were driven by to the blowing of a horn, and soon afterwards the bells began ringing for early mass. At one minute a cart drove by creaking; at the next, he heard the voice of some woman going to market. And the sparrows twittered the whole time.

## 2.

The next morning was a cheerful one; it was a holiday. At ten o'clock Nina Fyodorovna, wearing a brown dress and with her hair neatly arranged, was led into the drawing-room, supported on each side. There she walked about a little and stood by the open window, and her smile was broad and naive, and, looking at her, one recalled a local artist, a great drunkard, who wanted her to sit to him for a picture of the Russian carnival. And all of them—the children, the servants, her brother, Alexei Fyodorovich, and she herself—were suddenly convinced that she was certainly going to get well. With shrieks of laughter the children ran after their uncle, chasing him and catching him, and filling the house with noise.

People called to ask how she was, brought her holy bread, told her that in almost all the churches they were offering up prayers for her that day. She had been conspicuous for her benevolence in the town, and was liked. She was very ready with her charity, like her brother Alexei, who gave away his money freely, without considering whether it was necessary to give it or not. Nina Fyodorovna used to pay the school fees for poor children; used to give away tea, sugar, and jam to old women; used to provide trousseaux for poor brides; and if she picked up a newspaper, she always looked first of all to see if there were any appeals for charity or a paragraph about somebody's being in a destitute condition.

She was holding now in her hand a bundle of notes, by means of which various poor people, her protégés, had procured goods from a grocer's shop. They had been sent her the evening before by the shopkeeper with a request for the payment of the total—eighty-two rubles.

"My goodness, what a lot they've had! They've no conscience!" she said, deciphering with difficulty her ugly handwriting. "It's no joke! Eighty-two rubles! I declare I won't pay it."

"I'll pay it today," said Laptev.

"Why should you? Why should you?" cried Nina Fyodorovna in agitation. "It's quite enough for me to take two hundred and fifty every month from you and our brother. God bless you!" she added, speaking softly, so as not to be overheard by the servants.

"Well, but I spend two thousand five hundred a month," he said. "I tell you again, dear: you have just as much right to spend it as I or Fyodor. Do understand that, once for all. There are three of us, and of every three kopecks of our father's money, one belongs to you."

But Nina Fyodorovna did not understand, and her expression looked as though she were mentally solving some very difficult problem. And this lack of comprehension in pecuniary matters always made Laptev feel uneasy and troubled. He suspected that she had private debts in addition which worried her and of which she scrupled to tell him.

Then came the sound of footsteps and heavy breathing; it was the doctor coming up the stairs, disheveled and unkempt as usual.

"Ru-ru-ru," he was humming. "Ru-ru."

To avoid meeting him, Laptev went into the dining-room and then went downstairs to his own room. It was clear to him that to get on with the doctor and to drop in at his house without formalities was impossible; and to meet the "old brute," as Panaurov called him, was distasteful. That was why he so rarely saw Yulia. He reflected now that the father was not at home, that if he were to take Yulia Sergeyevna her parasol, he would be sure to find her at home alone, and his heart ached with joy. Haste, haste!

He took the parasol and, violently agitated, flew on the wings of love. It was hot in the street. In the big courtyard of the doctor's house, overgrown with coarse grass and nettles, some twenty urchins were playing ball. These were all the children of working-class families who tenanted the three disreputable-looking lodges, which the doctor was always meaning to have done up, though he put it off from year to year. The yard resounded with ringing, healthy voices. At some distance on one side, Yulia Sergeyevna was standing at her porch, her hands folded, watching the game.

"Good morning!" Laptev called to her.

She looked round. Usually he saw her indifferent, cold, or tired as she had been the evening before. Now her face looked full of life and frolic, like the faces of the boys who were playing ball.

"Look, they never play so merrily in Moscow," she said, going to meet him. "There are no such big yards there, though; they've no place to run there. Papa has only just gone to you," she added, looking round at the children.

"I know; but I've not come to see him, but to see you," said Laptev, admiring her youthfulness, which he had not noticed till then and seemed only that day to have discovered in her; it seemed to him as though he were seeing her slender white neck with the gold chain for the first time. "I've come to see you . . ." he repeated. "My sister has sent you your parasol; you forgot it yesterday."

She put out her hand to take the parasol, but he pressed it to his bosom and spoke passionately, without restraint, yielding again to the sweet ecstasy he had felt the night before, sitting under the parasol.

"I entreat you, give it me. I shall keep it in memory of you . . . of our acquaintance. It's so wonderful!"

"Take it," she said, and blushed; "but there's nothing wonderful about it."

He looked at her in ecstasy, in silence, not knowing what to say.

"Why am I keeping you here in the heat?" she said after a brief pause, laughing. "Let us go indoors."

"I am not disturbing you?"

They went into the hall. Yulia Sergeyevna ran upstairs, her white dress with blue flowers on it rustling as she went.

"I can't be disturbed," she answered, stopping on the landing. "I never do anything. Every day is a holiday for me, from morning till night."

"What you say is inconceivable to me," he said, going up to her. "I grew up in a world in which everyone without exception, men and women alike, worked hard every day."

"But if one has nothing to do?" she asked.

"One has to arrange one's life under such conditions that work is inevitable. There can be no clean and happy life without work."

Again he pressed the parasol to his bosom, and to his own surprise spoke softly, in a voice unlike his own:

"If you would consent to be my wife I would give everything—I would give everything. There's no price I would not pay, no sacrifice I would not make."

She started and looked at him with wonder and alarm.

"What are you saying!" she brought out, turning pale. "It's impossible, I assure you. Forgive me."

Then with the same rustle of her skirts she went up higher and vanished through the doorway.

Laptev grasped what this meant, and his mood was transformed, completely, abruptly, as though a light in his soul had suddenly been extinguished.

Filled with the shame of a man humiliated, of a man who is disdained, who is not liked, who is distasteful, perhaps disgusting, who is shunned, he walked out of the house.

"I would give everything," he thought, mimicking himself as he went home through the heat and recalled the details of his declaration. "I would give everything—like a regular tradesman. As though she wanted your *everything*!"

All he had just said seemed to him repulsively stupid. Why had he lied, saying that he had grown up in a world where everyone worked, without exception? Why had he talked to her in a lecturing tone about a clean and happy life? It was not clever, not interesting; it was false—false in the Moscow style. But by degrees there followed that mood of indifference into which criminals sink after a severe sentence. He began thinking that, thank God! everything was at an end and that the terrible uncertainty was over; that now there was no need to spend whole days in anticipation, in pining, in thinking always of the same thing. Now everything was clear; he must give up all hope of personal happiness, live without desires, without hopes, without dreams, or expectations, and to escape that dreary sadness which he was so sick of trying to soothe, he could busy himself with other people's affairs, other people's happiness, and old age would come in imperceptibly, and life would reach its end—and nothing more was wanted. He did not care, he wished for nothing, and could reason about it coolly, but there was a sort of heaviness in his face especially under his eyes, his forehead felt drawn tight like elastic—and tears were almost starting into his eyes. Feeling weak all over, he lay down on his bed, and in five minutes was sound asleep.

## 3.

The proposal Laptev had made so suddenly threw Yulia Sergeyevna into despair.

She knew Laptev very little, had made his acquaintance by chance; he was a rich man, a partner in the well-known Moscow firm of "Fyodor Laptev and Sons"; always serious, apparently clever, and anxious about his sister's illness. It had seemed to her that he took no notice of her whatever, and she did not care about him in the least—and then all of a sudden that declaration on the stairs, that pitiful, ecstatic face. . . .

The offer had overwhelmed her by its suddenness and by the fact that the word *wife* had been uttered, and by the necessity of rejecting it. She could not remember what she had said to Laptev, but she still felt traces of the sudden, unpleasant feeling with which she had rejected him. He did not attract her; he looked like a shopman; he was not interesting; she could not have answered him except with a refusal, and yet she felt uncomfortable, as though she had done wrong.

"My God! without waiting to get into the room, on the stairs," she said to herself in despair, addressing the icon which hung over her pillow; "and no courting beforehand, but so strangely, so oddly. . . ."

In her solitude her agitation grew more intense every hour, and it was beyond her strength to master this oppressive feeling alone. She needed someone to listen to her story and to tell her that she had done right. But she had no one to talk to. She had lost her mother long before; she thought her father a queer man and could not talk to him seriously. He worried her with his whims, his extreme readiness to take offense, and his meaningless gestures; and as soon as one began to talk to him, he promptly turned the conversation on himself. And in her prayer she was not perfectly open, because she did not know for certain what she ought to pray for.

The samovar was brought in. Yulia Sergeyevna, very pale and tired, looking dejected, came into the dining-room to make tea—it was one of her duties—and poured out a glass for her father. Sergei Borisovich, in his long coat that reached below his knees, with his red face and unkempt hair, walked up and down the room with his hands in his pockets, pacing, not from corner to corner, but backwards and forwards at random, like a wild beast in its cage. He would stand still by the table, sip his glass of tea with relish, and pace about again, lost in thought.

"Laptev made me an offer today," said Yulia Sergeyevna, and she flushed crimson.

The doctor looked at her and did not seem to understand.

"Laptev?" he queried. "Panaurov's brother-in-law?"

He was fond of his daughter; it was most likely that she would sooner or later be married and leave him, but he tried not to think about that. He was afraid of being alone, and, for some reason, fancied that if he were left alone in that great house, he would have an apoplectic stroke, but he did not like to speak of this directly.

"Well, I'm delighted to hear it," he said, shrugging his shoulders. "I congratulate you with all my heart. It offers you a splendid opportunity for leaving me, to your great satisfaction. And I quite understand your feelings. To live with an old father, an invalid, half crazy, must be very irksome at your age. I quite understand you. And the sooner I'm laid out and in the devil's clutches, the better everyone will be pleased. I congratulate you with all my heart."

"I refused him."

The doctor felt relieved, but he was unable to stop himself and went on:

"I wonder, I've long wondered, why I've not yet been put into a madhouse—why I'm still wearing this coat instead of a strait jacket? I still have faith in justice, in goodness. I am a fool, an idealist, and nowadays that's insanity, isn't it? And how do they repay me for my honesty? They almost throw stones at me and ride roughshod over me. And even my nearest kith and kin do nothing but try to get the better of me. It's high time the devil fetched an old fool like me. . . ."

"There's no talking to you like a rational being!" said Yulia.

She got up from the table impulsively and went to her room in great wrath, remembering how often her father had been unjust to her. But a little while afterwards she felt sorry for her father, too, and when he was going to the club she went downstairs with him and shut the door after him. It was a rough and stormy night; the door shook with the violence of the wind, and there were draughts in all directions in the passage, so that the candle was almost blown out. In her own domain upstairs Yulia Sergeyevna went the round of all the rooms, making the sign of the cross over every door and window; the wind howled, and it sounded as though someone were walking on the roof. Never had it been so dreary, never had she felt so lonely.

She asked herself whether she had done right in rejecting a man, simply because his appearance did not attract her. It was true he was a man she did not love, and to marry him would mean renouncing forever her dreams, her conceptions of happiness in married life, but would she ever meet the man of whom she dreamed, and would he love her? She was twenty-one already. There were no eligible young men in the town. She pictured all the men she knew—government clerks, schoolmasters, officers, and some of them were married already, and their domestic life was conspicuous for its dreariness and triviality; others were uninteresting, colorless, unintelligent, immoral. Laptev was, anyway, a Moscow man, had taken his degree at the university, spoke French. He lived in the capital, where there were lots of clever, noble, remarkable people; where there was noise and bustle, splendid theaters, musical evenings, first-rate dressmakers, confectioners. . . . In the Bible it was written that a wife must love her husband, and great importance was given to love in novels, but wasn't there exaggeration in it? Was it out of the question to enter upon married life without love? It was said, of course, that love soon passed away, and that nothing was left but habit, and that the object of married life was not to be found in love, nor in happiness, but in duties, such as the bringing up of one's children, the care of one's household, and so on. And perhaps what was meant in the Bible was love for one's husband as one's neighbor, respect for him, charity.

At night Yulia Sergeyevna read the evening prayers attentively, then knelt down, and, pressing her hands to her bosom, gazing at the flame of the lamp before the icon, said with feeling:

"Give me understanding, Holy Mother, our Defender! Give me understanding, O Lord!"

She had in the course of her life come across elderly maiden ladies, poor and of no consequence in the world, who bitterly repented and openly confessed their regret that they had refused suitors in the past. Would not the same thing happen to her? Had not she better go into a convent or become a Sister of Mercy?

She undressed and got into bed, crossing herself and crossing the air around her. Suddenly the bell rang sharply and plaintively in the corridor.

"Oh, my God!" she said, feeling a nervous irritation all over her at the sound. She lay still and kept thinking how poor this provincial life was in events, monotonous and yet not peaceful. One was constantly having to tremble, to feel apprehensive, angry, or guilty, and in the end one's nerves were so strained that one was afraid to peep out of the bedclothes.

A little while afterwards the bell rang just as sharply again. The servant must have been asleep and had not heard. Yulia Sergeyevna lighted a candle, and, feeling vexed with the servant, began with a shiver to dress, and when she went out into the corridor, the maid was already closing the door downstairs.

"I thought it was the master, but it's someone from a patient," she said.

Yulia Sergeyevna went back to her room. She took a pack of cards out of the chest of drawers and decided that if, after shuffling the cards well and cutting, the bottom card turned out to be a red one, it would mean *yes*—that is, she would accept Laptev's offer; and that if it was a black, it would mean *no*. The card turned out to be the ten of spades.

That relieved her mind—she fell asleep; but in the morning she was wavering again between *yes* and *no*, and she was dwelling on the thought that she could, if she chose, change her life. The thought harassed her, she felt exhausted and unwell; but yet, soon after eleven, she dressed and went to see Nina Fyodorovna. She wanted to see Laptev: perhaps now he would seem more attractive to her; perhaps she had been wrong about him hitherto. . . .

She found it hard to walk against the wind. She struggled along, holding her hat on with both hands, and could see nothing for the dust.

## 4.

Going into his sister's room, and seeing to his surprise Yulia Sergeyevna, Laptev had again the humiliating sensation of a man who feels himself an object of repulsion. He concluded that if after what had happened yesterday she could bring herself so easily to visit his sister and meet him, it must be because she was not concerned about him and regarded him as a complete nonentity. But when he greeted her, and with a pale face and dust under her eyes she looked at him mournfully and remorsefully, he saw that she, too, was miserable.

She did not feel well. She only stayed ten minutes and began saying good-bye. And as she went out she said to Laptev:

"Will you see me home, Alexei Fyodorovich?"

They walked along the street in silence, holding their hats, and he, walking a little behind, tried to screen her from the wind. In the lane it was more sheltered, and they walked side by side.

"Forgive me if I was not nice yesterday"; and her voice quavered as though she were going to cry. "I was so wretched! I did not sleep all night."

"I slept well all night," said Laptev, without looking at her; "but that doesn't mean that I was happy. My life is broken. I'm deeply unhappy, and after your refusal yesterday I go about like a man poisoned. The most difficult thing was said yesterday. Today I feel no embarrassment and can talk to you frankly. I love you more than my sister, more than my dead mother. . . . I can live without my sister, and without my mother, and I have lived without them, but life without you—is meaningless to me; I can't face it. . . ."

And now too, as usual, he guessed her intention. He realized that she wanted to go back to what had happened the day before, and with that object had asked him to accompany her, and now was taking him home with her. But what could she add to her refusal? What new idea had she in her head? From everything, from her glances, from her smile, and even from her tone, from the way she held her head and shoulders as she walked beside him, he saw that, as before, she did not love him, that he was a stranger to her. What more did she want to say?

Dr. Sergei Borisovich was at home.

"You are very welcome. I'm always glad to see you, Fyodor Alexeyich," he said, mixing up his Christian name and his father's. "Delighted, delighted!"

He had never been so polite before, and Laptev saw that he

knew of his offer; he did not like that either. He was sitting now in the drawing-room, and the room impressed him strangely, with its poor, common decorations, its wretched pictures, and though there were armchairs in it, and a huge lamp with a shade over it, it still looked like an uninhabited place, a huge barn, and it was obvious that no one could feel at home in such a room, except a man like the doctor. The next room, almost twice as large, was called the reception-room, and in it there were only rows of chairs, as though for a dancing class. And while Laptev was sitting in the drawing-room talking to the doctor about his sister, he began to be tortured by a suspicion. Had not Yulia Sergeyevna been to his sister Nina's, and then brought him here to tell him that she would accept him? Oh, how awful it was! But the most awful thing of all was that his soul was capable of such a suspicion. And he imagined how the father and the daughter had spent the evening—and perhaps the night—before in prolonged consultation, perhaps dispute, and at last had come to the conclusion that Yulia had acted thoughtlessly in refusing a rich man. The words that parents use in such cases kept ringing in his ears:

"It is true you don't love him, but think what good you could do!"

The doctor was going out to see patients. Laptev would have gone with him, but Yulia Sergeyevna said:

"I beg you to stay."

She was distressed and dispirited and told herself now that to refuse an honorable, good man who loved her simply because he was not attractive—especially when marrying him would make it possible for her to change her mode of life, her cheerless, monotonous, idle life in which youth was passing with no prospect of anything better in the future—to refuse him under such circumstances was madness, caprice, and folly, and that God might even punish her for it.

The father went out. When the sound of his steps had died

away, she suddenly stood up before Laptev and said resolutely, turning horribly white as she did so:

"I thought for a long time yesterday, Alexei Fyodorovich. . . . I accept your offer."

He bent down and kissed her hand. She kissed him awkwardly on the head with cold lips.

He felt that in this love scene the chief thing—her love—was lacking, and that there was a great deal that was not wanted; and he longed to cry out, to run away, to go back to Moscow at once. But she was close to him, and she seemed to him so lovely, and he was suddenly overcome by passion. He reflected that it was too late for deliberation now; he embraced her passionately, and muttered some words, calling her *thou*; he kissed her on the neck, and then on the cheek, on the head. . . .

She walked away to the window, dismayed by these demonstrations, and both of them were already regretting what they had said and both were asking themselves in confusion:

"Why has this happened?"

"If only you knew how miserable I am!" she said, wringing her hands.

"What is it?" he said, going up to her, wringing his hands too. "My dear, for God's sake, tell me—what is it? Only tell the truth, I entreat you—nothing but the truth!"

"Don't pay any attention to it," she said, and forced herself to smile. "I promise you I'll be a faithful, devoted wife. . . . Come this evening."

Sitting afterwards with his sister and reading aloud an historical novel, he recalled it all and felt wounded that his splendid, pure, rich feeling was met with such a shallow response. He was not loved, but his offer had been accepted—in all probability because he was rich: that is, what was thought most of in him was what he valued least of all in himself. It was quite possible that Yulia, who was so pure and believed in

God, had not once thought of his money; but she did not love him—did not love him, and evidently she had interested motives, vague, perhaps, and not fully thought out—still, it was so. The doctor's house with its common furniture was repulsive to him, and he looked upon the doctor himself as a wretched, greasy miser, a sort of operatic Gaspard from "Les Cloches de Corneville." The very name "Yulia" had a vulgar sound. He imagined how he and his Yulia would stand at their wedding, in reality complete strangers to one another, without a trace of feeling on her side, just as though their marriage had been made by a professional matchmaker; and the only consolation left him now, as commonplace as the marriage itself, was the reflection that he was not the first, and would not be the last; that thousands of people were married like that; and that with time, when Yulia came to know him better, she would perhaps grow fond of him.

"Romeo and Juliet!" he said, as he shut the novel, and he laughed. "I am Romeo, Nina. You may congratulate me. I made an offer to Yulia Byelavin today."

Nina Fyodorovna thought he was joking, but when she believed it, she began to cry; she was not pleased at the news.

"Well, I congratulate you," she said. "But why is it so sudden?"

"No, it's not sudden. It's been going on since March, only you don't notice anything. . . . I fell in love with her last March when I made her acquaintance here, in your rooms."

"I thought you would marry someone in our Moscow set," said Nina Fyodorovna after a pause. "Girls in our set are simpler. But what matters, Alyosha, is that you should be happy—that matters most. My Grigory Nikolaich did not love me, and there's no concealing it; you can see what our life is. Of course any woman may love you for your goodness and your brains, but, you see, Yulichka is a girl of good family from a high-class boarding school; goodness and brains are not enough for her.

She is young, and, you, Alyosha, are not so young, and are not good-looking."

To soften the last words, she stroked his head and said:

"You're not good-looking, but you're a dear."

She was so agitated that a faint flush came into her cheeks, and she began discussing eagerly whether it would be the proper thing for her to bless Alyosha with the icon at the wedding. She was, she reasoned, his elder sister, and took the place of his mother; and she kept trying to convince her dejected brother that the wedding must be celebrated in proper style, with pomp and gaiety, so that no one could find fault with it.

Then he began going to the Byelavins' as an accepted suitor, three or four times a day; and now he never had time to take Sasha's place and read aloud the historical novel. Yulia used to receive him in her two rooms, which were at a distance from the drawing-room and her father's study, and he liked them very much. The walls in them were dark; in the corner stood a case of icons; and there was a smell of good scent and of the oil in the holy lamp. Her rooms were at the furthest end of the house; her bedstead and dressing table were shut off by a screen. The doors of the bookcase were covered on the inside with a green curtain, and there were rugs on the floor, so that her footsteps were noiseless—and from this he concluded that she was of a reserved character, and that she liked a quiet, peaceful, secluded life. In her own home she was treated as though she were not quite grown up. She had no money of her own, and sometimes when they were out for walks together, she was overcome with confusion at not having a farthing. Her father allowed her very little for dress and books, hardly ten pounds a year. And, indeed, the doctor himself had not much money in spite of his good practice. He played cards every night at the club, and always lost. Moreover, he bought mortgaged houses through a building society, and let them. The tenants were irregular in paying the rent, but he was convinced that such speculations were profitable. He had mortgaged his own house in which he and his daughter were living, and with the money so raised had bought a piece of waste ground and had already begun to build on it a large two-storied house, meaning to mortgage it, too, as soon as it was finished.

Laptev now lived in a sort of cloud, feeling as though he were not himself, but his double, and did many things which he would never have brought himself to do before. He went three or four times to the club with the doctor, had supper with him, and offered him money for housebuilding. He even visited Panaurov at his other establishment. It somehow happened that Panaurov invited him to dinner, and, without thinking, Laptev accepted. He was received by a lady of five-and-thirty. She was tall and thin, with hair touched with gray, and black eyebrows, apparently not Russian. There were white patches of powder on her face. She gave him a honeyed smile and pressed his hand jerkily, so that the bracelets on her white hands tinkled. It seemed to Laptev that she smiled like that because she wanted to conceal from herself and from others that she was unhappy. He also saw two little girls, aged five and three, who had a marked likeness to Sasha. For dinner they had milk soup, cold veal, and chocolate. It was insipid and not good; but the table was splendid, with gold forks, bottles of Soyer, and cayenne pepper, an extraordinary bizarre cruet stand, and a gold pepper pot.

It was only as he was finishing the milk soup that Laptev realized how very inappropriate it was for him to be dining there. The lady was embarrassed, and kept smiling, showing her teeth. Panaurov expounded didactically what being in love was, and what it was due to.

"We have in it an example of the action of electricity," he said in French, addressing the lady. "Every man has in his skin microscopic glands which contain currents of electricity. If you meet with a person whose currents are parallel with your own, then you get love."

When Laptev went home and his sister asked him where he had been he felt awkward and made no answer.

He felt himself in a false position right up to the time of the wedding. His love grew more intense every day, and Yulia seemed to him a poetic and exalted creature; but, all the same, there was no mutual love, and the truth was that he was buying her and she was selling herself. Sometimes, thinking things over, he fell into despair and asked himself: should he run away? He did not sleep for nights together, and kept thinking how he should meet in Moscow the lady whom he had called in his letters "a certain person," and what attitude his father and his brother, difficult people, would take towards his marriage and towards Yulia. He was afraid that his father would say something rude to Yulia at their first meeting. And something strange had happened of late to his brother Fyodor. In his long letters he had taken to writing of the importance of health, of the effect of illness on the mental condition, of the meaning of religion, but not a word about Moscow or business. These letters irritated Laptev, and he thought his brother's character was changing for the worse.

The wedding was in September. The ceremony took place at the Church of St. Peter and St. Paul, after mass, and the same day the young couple set off for Moscow. When Laptev and his wife, in a black dress with a long train, already looking not a girl but a married woman, said good-bye to Nina Fyodorovna, the invalid's face worked, but there was no tear in her dry eyes. She said:

"If—which God forbid—I should die, take care of my little girls."

"Oh, I promise!" answered Yulia Sergeyevna, and her lips and eyelids began quivering too.

"I shall come to see you in October," said Laptev, much moved. "You must get better, my darling."

They traveled in a special compartment. Both felt depressed and uncomfortable. She sat in the corner without taking off her hat, and made a show of dozing, and he lay on the seat opposite, and he was disturbed by various thoughts—of his father, of "a certain person," whether Yulia would like her Moscow flat. And looking at his wife, who did not love him, he wondered dejectedly "why this had happened."

## 5.

The Laptevs had a wholesale business in Moscow, dealing in fancy goods: fringe, tape, trimmings, crochet cotton, buttons, and so on. The gross receipts reached two million a year; what the net profit was, no one knew but the old father. The sons and the clerks estimated the profits at approximately three hundred thousand, and said that it would have been a hundred thousand more if the old man had not "been too freehanded"—that is, had not allowed credit indiscriminately. In the last ten years alone the bad debts had mounted up to the sum of a million; and when the subject was referred to, the senior clerk would wink slyly and deliver himself of sentences the meaning of which was not clear to everyone:

"The psychological sequences of the age."

Their chief commercial operations were conducted in the town market in a building which was called the warehouse. The entrance to the warehouse was in the yard, where it was always dark, and smelled of matting and where the dray horses were always stamping their hoofs on the asphalt. A very humble-looking door, studded with iron, led from the yard into a room with walls discolored by damp and scrawled over with charcoal, lighted up by a narrow window covered by an iron grating. Then on the left was another room larger and cleaner with an iron stove and a couple of chairs, though it, too, had a prison window: this was the office, and from it a narrow stone staircase led up to the second story, where the principal room was. This was rather a large room, but, owing to the perpetual darkness, the low-pitched ceiling, the piles of boxes and bales, and the numbers of men that kept flitting to and fro in it, it made as unpleasant an impression on a newcomer as the others. In the offices on the top story the goods lay in bales, in bundles, and in cardboard boxes on the shelves; there was no order nor neatness in the arrangement of it, and if crimson threads, tassels, ends of fringe had not peeped out here and there from holes in the paper parcels, no one could have guessed what was being bought and sold here. And looking at these crumpled paper parcels and boxes, no one would have believed that a million was being made out of such trash, and that fifty men were employed every day in this warehouse, not counting the buyers.

When at midday, on the day after his arrival at Moscow, Laptev went into the warehouse, the workmen packing the goods were hammering so loudly that in the outer room and the office no one heard him come in. A postman he knew was coming down the stairs with a bundle of letters in his hand; he was wincing at the noise, and he did not notice Laptev either. The first person to meet him upstairs was his brother Fyodor Fyodorovich, who was so like him that they passed for twins. This resemblance always reminded Laptev of his own personal appearance, and now, seeing before him a short, red-faced man with rather thin hair, with narrow plebeian hips, looking so uninteresting and so unintellectual, he asked himself:

"Can I really look like that?"

"How glad I am to see you!" said Fyodor, kissing his brother and pressing his hand warmly. "I have been impatiently looking forward to seeing you every day, my dear fellow. When you wrote that you were getting married, I was tormented with curiosity, and I've missed you, too, Brother. Only fancy, it's six months since we saw each other. Well? How goes it? Nina's very bad? Awfully bad?"

"Awfully bad."

"It's in God's hands," sighed Fyodor. "Well, what of your wife? She's a beauty, no doubt? I love her already. Of course, she is my little sister now. We'll make much of her between us."

Laptev saw the broad, bent back—so familiar to him—of his father, Fyodor Stepanovich. The old man was sitting on a stool near the counter, talking to a customer.

"Father, God has sent us joy!" cried Fyodor. "Brother has come!"

Fyodor Stepanovich was a tall man of exceptionally powerful build; so that, in spite of his wrinkles and eighty years, he still looked a hale and vigorous man. He spoke in a deep, rich, sonorous voice, which resounded from his broad chest as from a barrel. He wore no beard, but a short-clipped military mustache, and smoked cigars. As he was always too hot, he used all the year round to wear a canvas coat at home and at the warehouse. He had lately had an operation for cataract. His sight was bad, and he did nothing in the business but talk to the customers and have tea and jam with them.

Laptev bent down and kissed his head and then his lips.

"It's a good long time since we saw you, honored sir," said the old man, "a good long time. Well, am I to congratulate you on entering the state of holy matrimony? Very well, then; I congratulate you."

And he put his lips out to be kissed. Laptev bent down and kissed him.

"Well, have you brought your young lady?" the old man asked, and, without waiting for an answer, he said, addressing the customer: "'Herewith I beg to inform you, Father, that I'm going to marry such and such a young lady.' Yes. But as for asking for his father's counsel or blessing, that's not in the rules nowadays. Now they go their own way. When I married I was over forty, but I went on my knees to my father and asked his advice. Nowadays we've none of that."

The old man was delighted to see his son but thought it unseemly to show his affection or make any display of his joy. His voice and his manner of saying "your young lady" brought back to Laptev the depression he had always felt in the warehouse. Here every trifling detail reminded him of the past, when he used to be flogged and put on Lenten fare; he knew that even now boys were thrashed and punched in the face till their noses bled, and that when those boys grew up they would beat others. And before he had been five minutes in the warehouse, he always felt as though he were being scolded or punched in the face.

Fyodor slapped the customer on the shoulder and said to his brother:

"Here, Alyosha, I must introduce our Tambov benefactor, Grigory Timofeich. He might serve as an example for the young men of the day; he's passed his fiftieth birthday, and he has tiny children."

The clerks laughed, and the customer, a lean old man with a pale face, laughed too.

"Nature above the normal capacity," observed the head clerk, who was standing at the counter close by. "It always comes out when it's there."

The head clerk—a tall man of fifty, in spectacles, with a dark beard, and a pencil behind his ear—usually expressed his ideas vaguely in roundabout hints, while his sly smile betrayed that he attached particular significance to his words. He liked to obscure his utterances with bookish words, which he understood in his own way, and many such words he used in a wrong sense. For instance, the word "except." When he had expressed some opinion positively and did not want to be contradicted, he would stretch out his hand and pronounce:

"Except!"

And what was most astonishing, the customers and the other clerks understood him perfectly. His name was Ivan Vassilich Pochatkin, and he came from Kashira. Now, congratulating Laptev, he expressed himself as follows:

"It's the reward of valor, for the female heart is a strong opponent."

Another important person in the warehouse was a clerk called Makeichev—a stout, solid, fair man with whiskers and a perfectly bald head. He went up to Laptev and congratulated him respectfully in a low voice:

"I have the honor, sir. . . . The Lord has heard your parent's prayer. Thank God."

Then the other clerks began coming up to congratulate him on his marriage. They were all fashionably dressed and looked like perfectly well-bred, educated men. Since between every two words they put in a "sir," their congratulations—something like "Best wishes, sir, for happiness, sir," uttered very rapidly in a low voice—sounded rather like the hiss of a whip in the air—"Shshsh-s s s s s!"

Laptev was soon bored and longing to go home, but it was awkward to go away. He was obliged to stay at least two hours at the warehouse to keep up appearances. He walked away from the counter and began asking Makeichev whether things had gone well while he was away, and whether anything new had turned up, and the clerk answered him respectfully, avoiding his eyes. A boy with a cropped head, wearing a gray blouse, handed Laptev a glass of tea without a saucer; not long afterwards another boy, passing by, stumbled over a box and almost fell down, and Makeichev's face looked suddenly spiteful and ferocious like a wild beast's, and he shouted at him:

"Keep on your feet!"

The clerks were pleased that their young master was married and had come back at last; they looked at him with curiosity and friendly feeling, and each one thought it his duty to say something agreeable when he passed him. But Laptev was convinced that it was not genuine, and that they were only flattering him because they were afraid of him. He never could forget how fifteen years before, a clerk, who was mentally deranged, had run out into the street with nothing on but his shirt and, shaking his fists at the windows, shouted that he had been ill-treated; and how, when the poor fellow had recovered, the clerks had jeered at him for long afterwards, reminding him how he had called his employers "planters" instead of "exploiters." Altogether the employees at Laptevs' had a very poor time of it, and this fact was a subject of conversation for the whole market. The worst of it was that the old man, Fyodor Stepanovich, maintained something of an Asiatic despotism in his attitude to them. Thus, no one knew what wages were paid to the old man's favorites, Pochatkin and Makeichev. They received no more than three thousand a year, together with bonuses, but he made out that he paid them seven. The bonuses were given to all the clerks every year, but privately, so that the man who got little was bound from vanity to say he had got more. Not one boy knew when he would be promoted to be a clerk; not one of the men knew whether his employer was satisfied with him or not. Nothing was directly forbidden, and so the clerks never knew what was allowed, and what was not. They were not forbidden to marry, but they did not marry for fear of displeasing their employer and losing their place. They were allowed to have friends and pay visits, but the gates were shut at nine o'clock, and every morning the old man scanned them all suspiciously and tried to detect any smell of vodka about them: "Now then, breathe," he would say.

Every clerk was obliged to go to early service, and to stand in church in such a position that the old man could see them all. The fasts were strictly observed. On great occasions, such as the birthday of their employer or of any member of his family, the clerks had to subscribe and present a cake from Fley's, or an album. The clerks lived three or four in a room in the lower story, and in the lodges of the house in Pyatnitsky Street, and at dinner ate from a common bowl, though there was a plate set before each of them. If one of the family came into the room while they were at dinner, they all stood up.

Laptev was conscious that only, perhaps, those among them who had been corrupted by the old man's training could seriously regard him as their benefactor; the others must have looked on him as an enemy and a "planter." Now, after six months' absence, he saw no change for the better; there was indeed something new which boded nothing good. His brother Fyodor, who had always been quiet, thoughtful, and extremely refined, was now running about the warehouse with a pencil behind his ear, making a show of being very busy and businesslike, slapping customers on the shoulder and shouting "Friends!" to the clerks. Apparently he had taken up a new role, and Alexei did not recognize him in the part.

The old man's voice boomed unceasingly. Having nothing to do, he was laying down the law to a customer, telling him how he should order his life and his business, always holding himself up as an example. That boastfulness, that aggressive tone of authority, Laptev had heard ten, fifteen, twenty years ago. The old man adored himself; from what he said it always appeared that he had made his wife and all her relations happy, that he had been munificent to his children, and a benefactor to his clerks and employees, and that everyone in the street and all his acquaintances remembered him in their prayers. Whatever he did was always right, and if things went wrong with people it was because they did not take his advice; without his advice nothing could succeed. In church he stood in the foremost place, and even made observations to the priests, if in his opinion they were not conducting the service properly, and believed that this was pleasing God because God loved him.

At two o'clock everyone in the warehouse was hard at work, except the old man, who still went on booming in his deep voice. To avoid standing idle, Laptev took some trimmings from a workgirl and let her go; then listened to a customer, a merchant from Vologda, and told a clerk to attend to him.

"T. V. A.!" resounded on all sides (prices were denoted by letters in the warehouse and goods by numbers). "R. I. T.!" As he went away, Laptev said good-bye to no one but Fyodor.

"I shall come to Pyatnitsky Street with my wife tomorrow," he said; "but I warn you, if Father says a single rude thing to her, I shall not stay there another minute."

"You're the same as ever," sighed Fyodor. "Marriage has not changed you. You must be patient with the old man. So till eleven o'clock, then. We shall expect you impatiently. Come directly after mass, then."

"I don't go to mass."

"That does not matter. The great thing is not to be later than eleven, so you may be in time to pray to God and to lunch with us. Give my greetings to my little sister and kiss her hand for me. I have a presentiment that I shall like her," Fyodor added with perfect sincerity. "I envy you, Brother!" he shouted after him as Alexei went downstairs.

"And why does he shrink into himself in that shy way as though he fancied he was naked?" thought Laptev, as he walked along Nikolsky Street, trying to understand the change that had come over his brother. "And his language is new, too: 'Brother, dear Brother, God has sent us joy; to pray to God'— just like Iudushka in Shchedrin."

## 6.

At eleven o'clock the next day, which was Sunday, he was driving with his wife along Pyatnitsky Street in a light, one-horse carriage. He was afraid of his father's doing something outrageous and was already ill at ease. After two nights in her husband's house Yulia Sergeyevna considered her marriage a mistake and a calamity, and if she had had to live with her husband in any other town but Moscow, it seemed to her that she could not have endured the horror of it. Moscow entertained her—she was delighted with the streets, the churches; and if it had been possible to drive about Moscow in those splendid sledges with expensive horses, to drive the whole day from morning till night, and with the swift motion to feel the cold autumn air blowing upon her, she would perhaps not have felt herself so unhappy.

Near a white, lately stuccoed two-storied house the coachman pulled up his horse and began to turn to the right. They were expected, and near the gate stood two policemen and the porter in a new full-skirted coat, high boots, and galoshes. The whole space, from the middle of the street to the gates and all over the yard from the porch, was strewn with fresh sand. The porter took off his hat, the policemen saluted. Near the entrance Fyodor met them with a very serious face.

"Very glad to make your acquaintance, little sister," he said, kissing Yulia's hand. "You're very welcome."

He led her upstairs on his arm, and then along a corridor through a crowd of men and women. The anteroom was crowded too and smelled of incense.

"I will introduce you to our father directly," whispered Fyodor in the midst of a solemn, deathly silence. "A venerable old man, paterfamilias."

In the big drawing-room, by a table prepared for service, Fyodor Stepanovich stood, evidently waiting for them, and with him the priest in a calotte, and a deacon. The old man shook hands with Yulia without saying a word. Everyone was silent. Yulia was overcome with confusion.

The priest and the deacon began putting on their vestments. A censer was brought in, giving off sparks and fumes of incense and charcoal. The candles were lighted. The clerks walked into the drawing-room on tiptoe and stood in two rows along the wall. There was perfect stillness, no one even coughed.

"The blessing of God," began the deacon.

The service was read with great solemnity; nothing was left out and two canticles were sung—to sweetest Jesus and the most Holy Mother of God. The singers sang very slowly, holding up the music before them. Laptev noticed how confused his wife was. While they were singing the canticles, and the singers in different keys brought out "Lord have mercy on us," he kept expecting in nervous suspense that the old man would make some remark such as, "You don't know how to cross yourself," and he felt vexed. Why this crowd, and why this ceremony with priests and choristers? It was too bourgeois. But when she, like the old man, put her head under the gospel and afterwards several times dropped upon her knees, he realized that she liked it all, and was reassured.

At the end of the service, during "Many, many years," the priest gave the old man and Alexei the cross to kiss, but when Yulia went up, he put his hand over the cross, and showed he wanted to speak. Signs were made to the singers to stop.

"The prophet Samuel," began the priest, "went to Bethlehem at the bidding of the Lord, and there the elders of the town with fear and trembling asked him: 'Comest thou peaceably?' And the prophet answered: 'Peaceably: I am come to sacrifice unto the Lord: sanctify yourselves and come with me to the sacrifice.' Even so, Yulia, servant of God, shall we ask of thee, Dost thou come bringing peace into this house?"

Yulia flushed with emotion. As he finished, the priest gave her the cross to kiss and said in quite a different tone of voice:

"Now Fyodor Fyodorovich must be married; it's high time."

The choir began singing once more, people began moving, and the room was noisy again. The old man, much touched, with his eyes full of tears, kissed Yulia three times, made the sign of the cross over her face, and said:

"This is your home. I'm an old man and need nothing."

The clerks congratulated her and said something, but the choir was singing so loud that nothing else could be heard. Then they had lunch and drank champagne. She sat beside the old father, and he talked to her, saying that families ought not to be parted but live together in one house; that separation and disunion led to permanent rupture.

"I've made money and the children only do the spending of it," he said. "Now, you live with me and save money. It's time for an old man like me to rest."

Yulia had all the time a vision of Fyodor flitting about so like her husband, but shyer and more restless; he fussed about her and often kissed her hand.

"We are plain people, little sister," he said, and patches of red came into his face as he spoke. "We live simply in Russian style, like Christians, little sister."

As they went home, Laptev felt greatly relieved that everything had gone off so well, and that nothing outrageous had happened as he had expected. He said to his wife:

"You're surprised that such a stalwart, broad-shouldered father should have such stunted, narrow-chested sons as Fyodor and me. Yes; but it's easy to explain! My father married my mother when he was forty-five, and she was only seventeen. She turned pale and trembled in his presence. Nina was born first—born of a comparatively healthy mother, and so she was finer and sturdier than we were. Fyodor and I were begotten and born after mother had been worn out by terror. I can remember my father correcting me—or, to speak plainly, beating me—before I was five years old. He used to thrash me with a birch, pull my ears, hit me on the head, and every morning when I woke up my first thought was whether he would beat me that day. Play and childish mischief were forbidden us. We had to go to morning service and to early mass. When we met priests or monks we had to kiss their hands; at home we had to sing hymns. Here you are religious and love all that, but I'm afraid of religion, and when I pass a church I remember my childhood and am overcome with horror. I was taken to the warehouse as soon as I was eight years old. I worked like a working boy, and it was bad for my health, for I used to be beaten there every day. Afterwards when I went to the high school, I used to go to school till dinnertime, and after dinner I had to sit in that warehouse till evening; and things went on like that till I was twenty-two, till I got to know Yartsev, and he persuaded me to leave my father's house. That Yartsev did a great deal for me. I tell you what," said Laptev, and he laughed with pleasure: "let us go and pay Yartsev a visit at once. He's a very fine fellow! How touched he will be!"

## 7.

On a Saturday in November Anton Rubinstein was conducting in a symphony concert. It was very hot and crowded. Laptev stood behind the columns, while his wife and Kostya Kochevoi were sitting in the third or fourth row some distance in front. At the very beginning of an interval a "certain person," Polina Nikolaevna Razsudin, quite unexpectedly passed by him. He had often since his marriage thought with trepidation of a possible meeting with her. When now she looked at him openly and directly, he realized that he had all this time shirked having things out with her, or writing her two or three friendly lines, as though he had been hiding from her; he felt ashamed and flushed crimson. She pressed his hand tightly and impulsively and asked:

"Have you seen Yartsev?"

And, without waiting for an answer, she went striding on impetuously as though someone were pushing her on from behind.

She was very thin and plain, with a long nose; her face always looked tired, and exhausted, and it seemed as though it were an effort to her to keep her eyes open and not to fall down. She had fine, dark eyes, and an intelligent, kind, sincere expression, but her movements were awkward and abrupt. It was hard to talk to her, because she could not talk or listen quietly. Loving her was not easy. Sometimes when she was alone with Laptev she would go on laughing for a long time, hiding her face in her hands, and would declare that love was not the chief thing in life for her, and would be as whimsical as a girl of seventeen; and before kissing her he would have to put out all the candles. She was thirty. She was married to a schoolmaster but had not lived with her husband for years. She earned her living by giving music lessons and playing in quartets.

During the Ninth Symphony she passed again as though by accident, but the crowd of men standing like a thick wall behind the columns prevented her going further, and she remained beside him. Laptev saw that she was wearing the same little velvet blouse she had worn at concerts last year and the year before. Her gloves were new, and her fan, too, was new, but it was a common one. She was fond of fine clothes, but she did not know how to dress and grudged spending money on it. She dressed so badly and untidily that when she was going to her lessons, striding hurriedly down the street, she might easily have been taken for a young monk.

The public applauded and shouted encore.

"You'll spend the evening with me," said Polina Nikolaevna, going up to Laptev and looking at him severely. "When this is over we'll go and have tea. Do you hear? I insist on it. You owe me a great deal and haven't the moral right to refuse me such a trifle."

"Very well; let us go," Laptev assented.

Endless calls followed the conclusion of the concert. The audience got up from their seats and went out very slowly, and Laptev could not go away without telling his wife. He had to stand at the door and wait.

"I'm dying for some tea," Polina Nikolaevna said plaintively. "My very soul is parched."

"You can get something to drink here," said Laptev. "Let's go to the buffet."

"Oh, I've no money to fling away on waiters. I'm not a shopkeeper."

He offered her his arm; she refused in a long, wearisome sentence which he had heard many times, to the effect that she did not class herself with the feebler fair sex and did not depend on the services of gentlemen.

As she talked to him she kept looking about at the audience and greeting acquaintances; they were her fellow students at the higher courses and at the conservatorium, and her pupils. She gripped their hands abruptly, as though she were tugging at them. But then she began twitching her shoulders and trembling as though she were in a fever, and at last said softly, looking at Laptev with horror:

"Who is it you've married? Where were your eyes, you mad fellow? What did you see in that stupid, insignificant girl? Why, I loved you for your mind, for your soul, but that china doll wants nothing but your money!"

"Let us drop that, Polina," he said in a voice of supplication. "All that you can say to me about my marriage I've said to myself many times already. . . . Don't cause me unnecessary pain."

Yulia Sergeyevna made her appearance, wearing a black dress with a big diamond brooch, which her father-in-law had sent her after the service. She was followed by her suite—Kochevoi, two doctors of their acquaintance, an officer, and a stout young man in student's uniform, called Kish.

"You go on with Kostya," Laptev said to his wife. "I'm coming later."

Yulia nodded and went on. Polina Nikolaevna gazed after her, quivering all over and twitching nervously, and in her eyes there was a look of repulsion, hatred, and pain.

Laptev was afraid to go home with her, foreseeing an unpleasant discussion, cutting words, and tears, and he suggested that they should go and have tea at a restaurant. But she said:

"No, no. I want to go home. Don't dare to talk to me of restaurants."

She did not like being in a restaurant because the atmosphere of restaurants seemed to her poisoned by tobacco smoke and the breath of men. Against all men she did not know she cherished a strange prejudice, regarding them all as immoral rakes, capable of attacking her at any moment. Besides, the music played at restaurants jarred on her nerves and gave her a headache.

Coming out of the Hall of Nobility, they took a sledge in Ostozhenka and drove to Savelovsky Lane, where she lodged. All the way Laptev thought about her. It was true that he owed her a great deal. He had made her acquaintance at the flat of his friend Yartsev, to whom she was giving lessons in harmony. Her love for him was deep and perfectly disinterested, and her relations with him did not alter her habits; she went on giving her lessons and wearing herself out with work as before. Through her he came to understand and love music, which he had scarcely cared for till then.

"Half my kingdom for a cup of tea!" she pronounced in a hollow voice, covering her mouth with her muff that she might not catch cold. "I've given five lessons, confound them! My pupils are as stupid as posts; I nearly died of exasperation. I don't know how long this slavery can go on. I'm worn out. As soon as I can scrape together three hundred rubles, I shall throw it all up and go to the Crimea, to lie on the beach and drink in ozone. How I love the sea—oh, how I love the sea!"

"You'll never go," said Laptev. "To begin with, you'll never save the money; and, besides, you'd grudge spending it. Forgive me, I repeat again: surely it's quite as humiliating to collect the money by farthings from idle people who have music lessons to while away their time, as to borrow it from your friends."

"I haven't any friends," she said irritably. "And please don't talk nonsense. The working class to which I belong has one privilege: the consciousness of being incorruptible—the right to refuse to be indebted to wretched little shopkeepers, and to treat them with scorn. No, indeed, you don't buy me! I'm not a Yulichka!"

Laptev did not attempt to pay the driver, knowing that it would call forth a perfect torrent of words, such as he had often heard before. She paid herself.

She had a little furnished room in the flat of a solitary lady who provided her meals. Her big Becker piano was for the time at Yartsev's in Great Nikitsky Street, and she went there every day to play on it. In her room there were armchairs in loose covers, a bed with a white summer quilt, and flowers belonging to the landlady; there were oleographs on the walls, and there was nothing that would have suggested that there was a woman, and a woman of university education, living in it. There was no toilet table; there were no books; there was not even a writing table. It was evident that she went to bed as soon as she got home and went out as soon as she got up in the morning.

The cook brought in the samovar. Polina Nikolaevna made tea, and, still shivering—the room was cold—began abusing the singers who had sung in the Ninth Symphony. She was so tired she could hardly keep her eyes open. She drank one glass of tea, then a second, and then a third.

"And so you are married," she said. "But don't be uneasy; I'm not going to pine away. I shall be able to tear you out of my heart. Only it's annoying and bitter to me that you are just as contemptible as everyone else; that what you want in a woman is not brains or intellect, but simply a body, good looks, and youth. . . . Youth!" she pronounced through her nose, as though mimicking someone, and she laughed. "Youth! You must have purity, *reinheit! reinheit!*" she laughed, throwing herself back in her chair. "*Reinheit!*"

When she left off laughing her eyes were wet with tears.

"You're happy, at any rate?" she asked.

"No."

"Does she love you?"

"No."

Laptev, agitated, and feeling miserable, stood up and began walking about the room.

"No," he repeated. "If you want to know, Polina, I'm very unhappy. There's no help for it; I've done the stupid thing, and there's no correcting it now. I must look at it philosophically. She married me without love, stupidly, perhaps with mercenary motives, but without understanding, and now she evidently sees her mistake and is miserable. I see it. At night we sleep together, but by day she is afraid to be left alone with me for five minutes and tries to find distraction, society. With me she feels ashamed and frightened."

"And yet she takes money from you?"

"That's stupid, Polina!" cried Laptev. "She takes money from me because it makes absolutely no difference to her whether she has it or not. She is an honest, pure girl. She married me simply because she wanted to get away from her father, that's all."

"And are you sure she would have married you if you had not been rich?" asked Polina.

"I'm not sure of anything," said Laptev dejectedly. "Not of anything. I don't understand anything. For God's sake, Polina, don't let us talk about it."

"Do you love her?"

"Desperately."

A silence followed. She drank a fourth glass, while he paced up and down, thinking that by now his wife was probably having supper at the doctors' club.

"But is it possible to love without knowing why?" asked Polina, shrugging her shoulders. "No; it's the promptings of animal passion! You are poisoned, intoxicated by that beautiful body, that *reinheit!* Go away from me; you are unclean! Go to her!"

She brandished her hand at him, then took up his hat and hurled it at him. He put on his fur coat without speaking and went out, but she ran after him into the passage, clutched his arm above the elbow, and broke into sobs.

"Hush, Polina! Don't!" he said, and could not unclasp her fingers. "Calm yourself, I entreat you."

She shut her eyes and turned pale, and her long nose became an unpleasant waxy color like a corpse's, and Laptev still could not unclasp her fingers. She had fainted. He lifted her up carefully, laid her on her bed, and sat by her for ten minutes till she came to herself. Her hands were cold, her pulse was weak and uneven.

"Go home," she said, opening her eyes. "Go away, or I shall begin howling again. I must take myself in hand."

When he came out, instead of going to the doctors' club where his friends were expecting him, he went home. All the way home he was asking himself reproachfully why he had not settled down to married life with that woman who loved him so much, and was in reality his wife and friend. She was the one human being who was devoted to him; and, besides, would it not have been a grateful and worthy task to give happiness, peace, and a home to that proud, clever, overworked creature? Was it for him, he asked himself, to lay claim to youth and beauty, to that happiness which could not be, and which, as though in punishment or mockery, had kept him for the last three months in a state of gloom and oppression. The honeymoon was long over, and he still, absurd to say, did not know what sort of person his wife was. To her school friends and her father she wrote long letters of five sheets and was never at a loss for something to say to them, but to him she never spoke except about the weather or to tell him that dinner was ready, or that it was suppertime. When at night she said her lengthy prayers and then kissed her crosses and icons, he thought, watching her with hatred, "Here she's praying. What's she praying about? What about?" In his thoughts he showered insults on himself and her, telling himself that when he got into bed and took her into his arms, he was taking what he had paid for; but it was horrible. If only it had been a healthy, reckless, sinful woman; but here he had youth, piety, meekness, the pure eyes of innocence. . . . While they were engaged her piety had touched him; now the conventional definiteness of her views and convictions seemed to him a barrier, behind which the real truth could not be seen. Already everything in his married life was agonizing. When his wife, sitting beside him in the theater, sighed or laughed spontaneously, it was bitter to him that she enjoyed herself alone and would not share her delight with him. And it was remarkable that she was friendly with all his friends, and they all knew what she was like already, while he knew nothing about her and only moped and was dumbly jealous.

When he got home Laptev put on his dressing gown and slippers and sat down in his study to read a novel. His wife was not at home. But within half an hour there was a ring at the hall door, and he heard the muffled footsteps of Pyotr running to open it. It was Yulia. She walked into the study in her fur coat, her cheeks rosy with the frost.

"There's a great fire in Pryesnya," she said breathlessly. "There's a tremendous glow. I'm going to see it with Konstantin Ivanovich."

"Well, do, dear!"

The sight of her health, her freshness, and the childish horror in her eyes, reassured Laptev. He read for another half hour and went to bed.

Next day Polina Nikolaevna sent to the warehouse two books she had borrowed from him, all his letters and his photographs; with them was a note consisting of one word—"*basta.*"

## 8.

Towards the end of October Nina Fyodorovna had had unmistakable symptoms of a relapse. There was a change in her face, and she grew rapidly thinner. In spite of acute pain she still imagined that she was getting better, and got up and dressed every morning as though she were well, and then lay on her bed, fully dressed, for the rest of the day. And towards the end she became very talkative. She would lie on her back and talk in a low voice, speaking with an effort and breathing painfully. She died suddenly under the following circumstances.

It was a clear moonlight evening. In the street people were tobogganing in the fresh snow, and their clamor floated in at the window. Nina Fyodorovna was lying on her back in bed, and Sasha, who had no one to take turns with her now, was sitting beside her half asleep.

"I don't remember his father's name," Nina Fyodorovna was saying softly, "but his name was Ivan Kochevoi—a poor clerk. He was a sad drunkard, the Kingdom of Heaven be his!

He used to come to us, and every month we used to give him a pound of sugar and two ounces of tea. And money, too, sometimes, of course. Yes. . . . And then, this is what happened. Our Kochevoi began drinking heavily and died, consumed by vodka. He left a little son, a boy of seven. Poor little orphan! . . . We took him and hid him in the clerk's quarters, and he lived there for a whole year, without father's knowing. And when father did see him, he only waved his hand and said nothing. When Kostya, the little orphan, was nine years old—by that time I was engaged to be married—I took him round to all the day schools. I went from one to the other, and no one would take him. And he cried. . . . 'What are you crying for, little silly?' I said. I took him to Razgulyai to the second school, where—God bless them for it!—they took him, and the boy began going every day on foot from Pyatnitsky Street to Razgulyai Street and back again. . . . Alyosha paid for him. . . . By God's grace the boy got on, was good at his lessons, and turned out well. . . . He's a lawyer now in Moscow, a friend of Alyosha's, and so good in science. Yes, we had compassion on a fellow creature and took him into our house, and now, I daresay, he remembers us in his prayers. . . . Yes. . . ."

Nina Fyodorovna spoke more and more slowly with long pauses, then after a brief silence she suddenly raised herself and sat up.

"There's something the matter with me . . . something seems wrong," she said. "Lord have mercy on me! Oh, I can't breathe!"

Sasha knew that her mother would soon die; seeing now how suddenly her face looked drawn, she guessed that it was the end, and she was frightened.

"Mother, you mustn't!" she began sobbing. "You mustn't."

"Run to the kitchen; let them go for Father. I am very ill indeed."

Sasha ran through all the rooms calling, but there were none of the servants in the house, and the only person she found was Lida asleep on a chest in the dining-room with her clothes on and without a pillow. Sasha ran into the yard just as she was, without her galoshes, and then into the street. On a bench at the gate her nurse was sitting watching the tobogganing. From beyond the river, where the tobogganing slope was, came the strains of a military band.

"Nurse, Mother's dying!" sobbed Sasha. "You must go for Father! . . ."

The nurse went upstairs, and, glancing at the sick woman, thrust a lighted wax candle into her hand. Sasha rushed about in terror and besought someone to go for her father, then she put on a coat and a kerchief, and ran into the street. From the servants she knew already that her father had another wife and two children with whom he lived in Bazarny Street. She ran out of the gate and turned to the left, crying, and frightened of unknown people. She soon began to sink into the snow and grew numb with cold.

She met an empty sledge, but she did not take it: perhaps, she thought, the man would drive her out of town, rob her, and throw her into the cemetery (the servants had talked of such a case at tea). She went on and on, sobbing and panting with exhaustion. When she got into Bazarny Street, she inquired where Monsieur Panaurov lived. An unknown woman spent a long time directing her, and, seeing that she did not understand, took her by the hand and led her to a house of one story that stood back from the street. The door stood open. Sasha ran through the entry, along the corridor, and found herself at last in a warm, lighted room where her father was sitting by the samovar with a lady and two children. But by now she was unable to utter a word and could only sob. Panaurov understood.

"Mother's worse?" he asked. "Tell me, child: is Mother worse?"

He was alarmed and sent for a sledge.

When they got home, Nina Fyodorovna was sitting propped

up with pillows, with a candle in her hand. Her face looked dark and her eyes were closed. Crowding in the doorway stood the nurse, the cook, the housemaid, a peasant called Prokofy, and a few persons of the humbler class, who were complete strangers. The nurse was giving them orders in a whisper, and they did not understand. Inside the room at the window stood Lida, with a pale and sleepy face, gazing severely at her mother.

Panaurov took the candle out of Nina Fyodorovna's hand, and, frowning contemptuously, flung it on the chest of drawers.

"This is awful!" he said, and his shoulders quivered. "Nina, you must lie down," he said affectionately. "Lie down, dear."

She looked at him but did not know him. . . . They laid her down on her back.

When the priest and the doctor, Sergei Borisovich, arrived, the servants crossed themselves devoutly and prayed for her.

"What a sad business!" said the doctor thoughtfully, coming out into the drawing-room. "Why, she was still young—not yet forty."

They heard the loud sobbing of the little girls. Panaurov, with a pale face and moist eyes, went up to the doctor and said in a faint, weak voice:

"Do me a favor, my dear fellow. Send a telegram to Moscow. I'm not equal to it."

The doctor fetched the ink and wrote the following telegram to his daughter:

> MADAM PANAUROV DIED AT EIGHT O'CLOCK THIS EVENING. TELL YOUR HUSBAND: A MORTGAGED HOUSE FOR SALE IN DVORYANSKY STREET, NINE THOUSAND CASH. AUCTION ON TWELFTH. ADVISE HIM NOT MISS OPPORTUNITY.

## 9.

Laptev lived in one of the turnings out of Little Dmitrovka. Besides the big house facing the street, he rented also a two-storied lodge in the yard at the back of his friend Kochevoi, a lawyer's assistant whom all the Laptevs called Kostya, because he had grown up under their eyes. Facing this lodge, stood another, also of two stories, inhabited by a French family consisting of a husband and wife and five daughters.

There was a frost of twenty degrees. The windows were frozen over. Waking up in the morning, Kostya, with an anxious face, took twenty drops of a medicine; then, taking two dumbbells out of the bookcase, he did gymnastic exercises. He was tall and thin, with big reddish mustaches; but what was most noticeable in his appearance was the length of his legs.

Pyotr, a middle-aged peasant in a reefer jacket and cotton breeches tucked into his high boots, brought in the samovar and made the tea.

"It's very nice weather now, Konstantin Ivanovich," he said.

"It is, but I tell you what, brother, it's a pity we can't get on, you and I, without such exclamations."

Pyotr sighed from politeness.

"What are the little girls doing?" asked Kochevoi.

"The priest has not come. Alexei Fyodorovich is giving them their lesson himself."

Kostya found a spot in the window that was not covered with frost and began looking through a field glass at the windows of the house where the French family lived.

"There's no seeing," he said.

Meanwhile Alexei Fyodorovich was giving Sasha and Lida a Scripture lesson below. For the last six weeks they had been living in Moscow and were installed with their governess in the lower story of the lodge. And three times a week a teacher from a school in the town, and a priest, came to give them lessons. Sasha was going through the New Testament and Lida was going through the Old. The time before Lida had been set the story up to Abraham to learn by heart.

"And so Adam and Eve had two sons," said Laptev. "Very good. But what were they called? Try to remember them!"

Lida, still with the same severe face, gazed dumbly at the table. She moved her lips, but without speaking; and the elder girl, Sasha, looked into her face, frowning.

"You know it very well, only you mustn't be nervous," said Laptev. "Come, what were Adam's sons called?"

"Abel and Canel," Lida whispered.

"Cain and Abel," Laptev corrected her.

A big tear rolled down Lida's cheek and dropped on the book. Sasha looked down and turned red, and she, too, was on the point of tears. Laptev felt a lump in his throat and was so sorry for them he could not speak. He got up from the table and lighted a cigarette. At that moment Kochevoi came down the stairs with a paper in his hand. The little girls stood up, and, without looking at him, made curtseys.

"For God's sake, Kostya, give them their lessons," said Laptev, turning to him. "I'm afraid I shall cry, too, and I have to go to the warehouse before dinner."

"All right."

Alexei Fyodorovich went away. Kostya, with a very serious face, sat down to the table and drew the Scripture history towards him.

"Well," he said, "where have you got to?"

"She knows about the Flood," said Sasha.

"The Flood? All right. Let's peg in at the Flood. Fire away about the Flood." Kostya skimmed through a brief description of the Flood in the book, and said: "I must remark that there really never was a flood such as is described here. And there was no such person as Noah. Some thousands of years before the birth of Christ, there was an extraordinary inundation of the earth, and that's not only mentioned in the Jewish Bible, but in the books of other ancient peoples: the Greeks, the Chaldeans, the Hindus. But whatever the inundation may have been, it couldn't have covered the whole earth. It may have flooded the plains, but the mountains must have remained. You can read this book of course, but don't put too much faith in it."

Tears trickled down Lida's face again. She turned away and suddenly burst into such loud sobs that Kostya started and jumped up from his seat in great confusion.

"I want to go home," she said, "to Papa and to Nurse."

Sasha cried too. Kostya went upstairs to his own room and spoke on the telephone to Yulia Sergeyevna.

"My dear soul," he said, "the little girls are crying again; there's no doing anything with them."

Yulia Sergeyevna ran across from the big house in her indoor dress, with only a knitted shawl over her shoulders, and chilled through by the frost, began comforting the children.

"Do believe me, do believe me," she said in an imploring voice, hugging first one and then the other. "Your papa's coming today; he has sent a telegram. You're grieving for Mother, and I grieve too. My heart's torn, but what can we do? We must bow to God's will!"

When they left off crying, she wrapped them up and took them out for a drive. They stopped near the Iverskoi chapel, put up candles at the shrine, and, kneeling down, prayed. On the way back they went in Filippov's and had cakes sprinkled with poppy seeds.

The Laptevs had dinner between two and three. Pyotr handed the dishes. This Pyotr waited on the family, and by day ran to the post, to the warehouse, to the law courts for Kostya; he spent his evenings making cigarettes, ran to open the door at night, and before five o'clock in the morning was up lighting the stoves, and no one knew where he slept. He was very fond of opening seltzer-water bottles and did it easily, without a bang and without spilling a drop.

"With God's blessing," said Kostya, drinking off a glass of vodka before the soup.

At first Yulia Sergeyevna did not like Kostya; his bass voice, his phrases such as "Landed him one on the beak," "filth," "produce the samovar," etc., his habit of clinking glasses and making sentimental speeches seemed to her trivial. But as she got to know him better, she began to feel very much at home with him. He was open with her; he liked talking to her in a low voice in the evening and even gave her novels of his own composition to read, though these had been kept a secret even from such friends as Laptev and Yartsev. She read these novels and praised them, so that she might not disappoint him, and he was delighted because he hoped sooner or later to become a distinguished author.

In his novels he described nothing but country-house life, though he had only seen the country on rare occasions when visiting friends at a summer villa and had only been in a real country house once in his life, when he had been to Volokolamsk on law business. He avoided any love interest as though he were ashamed of it; he put in frequent descriptions of nature, and in them was fond of using such expressions as, "the capricious lines of the mountains, the miraculous forms of the clouds, the harmony of mysterious rhythms. . . ." His novels had never been published, and this he attributed to the censorship.

He liked the duties of a lawyer, but yet he considered that his most important pursuit was not the law but these novels. He believed that he had a subtle, aesthetic temperament, and he always had leanings towards art. He neither sang nor played on any musical instrument, and was absolutely without an ear for music, but he attended all the symphony and philharmonic concerts, got up concerts for charitable objects, and made the acquaintance of singers. . . .

They used to talk at dinner.

"It's a strange thing," said Laptev, "my Fyodor took my breath away again! He said we must find out the date of the centenary of our firm, so as to try and get raised to noble rank; and he said it quite seriously. What can be the matter with him? I confess I begin to feel worried about him."

They talked of Fyodor, and of its being the fashion nowadays to adopt some pose or other. Fyodor, for instance, tried to appear like a plain merchant, though he had ceased to be one; and when the teacher came from the school, of which old Laptev was the patron, to ask Fyodor for his salary, the latter changed his voice and deportment, and behaved with the teacher as though he were someone in authority.

There was nothing to be done; after dinner they went into the study. They talked about the decadents, about "The Maid of Orléans," and Kostya delivered a regular monologue; he fancied that he was very successful in imitating Ermolova. Then they sat down and played whist. The little girls had not gone back to the lodge but were sitting together in one armchair, with pale and mournful faces, and were listening to every noise in the street, wondering whether it was their father coming. In the evening when it was dark and the candles were lighted, they felt deeply dejected. The talk over the whist, the footsteps of Pyotr, the crackling in the fireplace jarred on their nerves, and they did not like to look at the fire. In the evenings they did not want to cry, but they felt strange, and there was a load on their hearts. They could not understand how people could talk and laugh when their mother was dead.

"What did you see through the field glasses today?" Yulia Sergeyevna asked Kostya.

"Nothing today, but yesterday I saw the old Frenchman having his bath."

At seven o'clock Yulia and Kostya went to the Little Theater. Laptev was left with the little girls.

"It's time your father was here," he said, looking at his watch. "The train must be late."

The children sat in their armchair dumb and huddling together like animals when they are cold, while he walked about the room looking impatiently at his watch. It was quiet in the house. But just before nine o'clock someone rang the bell. Pyotr went to open the door.

Hearing a familiar voice, the children shrieked, burst into sobs, and ran into the hall. Panaurov was wearing a sumptuous coat of antelope skin, and his head and mustaches were white with hoarfrost. "In a minute, in a minute," he muttered, while Sasha and Lida, sobbing and laughing, kissed his cold hands, his hat, his antelope coat. With the languor of a handsome man spoiled by too much love, he fondled the children without haste, then went into the study and said, rubbing his hands:

"I've not come to stay long, my friends. I'm going to Petersburg tomorrow. They've promised to transfer me to another town."

He was staying at the Dresden Hotel.

## 10.

A friend who was often at the Laptevs' was Ivan Gavrilich Yartsev. He was a strong, healthy man with black hair and a clever, pleasant face. He was considered to be handsome, but of late he had begun to grow stout, and that rather spoiled his face and figure; another thing that spoiled him was that he wore his hair cut so close that the skin showed through.

At the university his tall figure and physical strength had won him the nickname of "the pounder" among the students. He had taken his degree with the Laptev brothers in the faculty of philology—then he went in for science and now had the degree of magister in chemistry. But he had never given a lecture or even been a demonstrator. He taught physics and natural history in the modern school, and in two girls' high schools. He was enthusiastic over his pupils, especially the girls, and used to maintain that a remarkable generation was growing up. At home he spent his time studying sociology and Russian history, as well as chemistry, and he sometimes published brief notes in the newspapers and magazines, signing them "Y." When he talked of some botanical or zoological subject, he spoke like an historian; when he was discussing some historical question, he approached it as a man of science.

Kish, nicknamed "the eternal student," was also like one of the family at the Laptevs'. He had been for three years studying medicine. Then he took up mathematics, and spent two years over each year's course. His father, a provincial druggist, used to send him forty rubles a month, to which his mother, without his father's knowledge, added another ten. And this sum was not only sufficient for his board and lodging, but even for such luxuries as an overcoat lined with Polish beaver, gloves, scent, and photographs (he often had photographs taken of himself and used to distribute them among his friends). He was neat and demure, slightly bald, with golden side whiskers, and he had the air of a man nearly always ready to oblige. He was always busy looking after other people's affairs. At one time he would be rushing about with a subscription list; at another time he would be freezing in the early morning at a ticket office to buy tickets for ladies of his acquaintance, or at somebody's request would be ordering a wreath or a bouquet. People simply said of him: "Kish will go, Kish will do it, Kish will buy it." He was usually unsuccessful in carrying out his commissions. Reproaches were showered upon him, people frequently forgot to pay him for the things he bought, but he simply sighed in hard cases and never protested. He was never particularly delighted nor disappointed; his stories were always long and boring; and his jokes invariably provoked laughter just because they were not funny. Thus, one day, for instance, intending to make a joke, he said to Pyotr: "Pyotr, you're not a sturgeon;" and this aroused a general laugh, and he, too, laughed for a long time, much pleased at having made such a successful jest. Whenever one of the professors was buried, he walked in front with the mutes.

Yartsev and Kish usually came in the evening to tea. If the Laptevs were not going to the theater or a concert, the evening tea lingered on till supper. One evening in February the following conversation took place:

"A work of art is only significant and valuable when there are some serious social problems contained in its central idea," said Kostya, looking wrathfully at Yartsev. "If there is in the work a protest against serfdom or the author takes up arms against the vulgarity of aristocratic society, the work is significant and valuable. The novels that are taken up with 'Ach!' and 'Ooh!' and 'she loved him, while he ceased to love her,' I tell you, are worthless, and damn them all, I say!"

"I agree with you, Konstantin Ivanovich," said Yulia Sergeyevna. "One describes a love scene; another, a betrayal; and the third, meeting again after separation. Are there no other subjects? Why, there are many people sick, unhappy, harassed by poverty, to whom reading all that must be distasteful."

It was disagreeable to Laptev to hear his wife, not yet twenty-two, speaking so seriously and coldly about love. He understood why this was so.

"If poetry does not solve questions that seem so important," said Yartsev, "you should turn to works on technical subjects, criminal law, or finance, read scientific pamphlets. What need is there to discuss in *Romeo and Juliet*, liberty of speech, or the disinfecting of prisons, instead of love, when you can find all that in special articles and textbooks?"

"That's pushing it to the extreme," Kostya interrupted.

"We are not talking of giants like Shakespeare or Goethe; we are talking of the hundreds of talented mediocre writers who would be infinitely more valuable if they would let love alone and would employ themselves in spreading knowledge and humane ideas among the masses."

Kish, lisping and speaking a little through his nose, began telling the story of a novel he had lately been reading. He spoke circumstantially and without haste. Three minutes passed, then five, then ten, and no one could make out what he was talking about, and his face grew more and more indifferent, and his eyes more and more blank.

"Kish, do be quick over it," Yulia Sergeyevna could not resist saying; "it's really agonizing!"

"Shut up, Kish!" Kostya shouted to him.

They all laughed, and Kish with them.

Fyodor came in. Flushing red in patches, he greeted them all in a nervous flurry and led his brother away into the study. Of late he had taken to avoiding the company of more than one person at once.

"Let the young people laugh, while we speak from the heart in here," he said, settling himself in a deep armchair at a distance from the lamp. "It's a long time, my dear brother, since we've seen each other. How long is it since you were at the warehouse? I think it must be a week."

"Yes, there's nothing for me to do there. And I must confess that the old man wearies me."

"Of course, they could get on at the warehouse without you and me, but one must have some occupation. 'In the sweat of thy brow thou shalt eat bread,' as it is written. God loves work."

Pyotr brought in a glass of tea on a tray. Fyodor drank it without sugar and asked for more. He drank a great deal of tea and could get through as many as ten glasses in the evening.

"I tell you what, Brother," he said, getting up and going

to his brother. "Laying aside philosophic subtleties, you must get elected on to the town council, and little by little we will get you on to the local Board, and then to be an alderman. And as time goes on—you are a clever man and well-educated—you will be noticed in Petersburg and asked to go there—active men on the provincial assemblies and town councils are all the fashion there now—and before you are fifty you'll be a privy councillor and have a ribbon across your shoulders."

Laptev made no answer; he knew that all this—being a privy councillor and having a ribbon over his shoulder—was what Fyodor desired for himself, and he did not know what to say.

The brothers sat still and said nothing. Fyodor opened his watch and for a long, long time gazed into it with strained attention, as though he wanted to detect the motion of the hand, and the expression of his face struck Laptev as strange.

They were summoned to supper. Laptev went into the dining-room, while Fyodor remained in the study. The argument was over and Yartsev was speaking in the tones of a professor giving a lecture:

"Owing to differences of climate, of energy, of tastes, of age, equality among men is physically impossible. But civilized man can make this inequality innocuous, as he has already done with bogs and bears. A learned man succeeded in making a cat, a mouse, a falcon, a sparrow all eat out of one plate; and education, one must hope, will do the same thing with men. Life continually progresses, civilization makes enormous advances before our eyes, and obviously a time will come when we shall think, for instance, the present condition of the factory population as absurd as we now do the state of serfdom, in which girls were exchanged for dogs."

"That won't be for a long while, a very long while," said Kostya, with a laugh, "not till Rothschild thinks his cellars full of gold absurd, and till then the workers may bend their backs and die of hunger. No; that's not it. We mustn't wait for it; we must struggle for it. Do you suppose because the cat eats out of the same saucer as the mouse—do you suppose that she is influenced by a sense of conscious intelligence? Not a bit of it! She's made to do it by force."

"Fyodor and I are rich; our father's a capitalist, a millionaire. You will have to struggle with us," said Laptev, rubbing his forehead with his hand. "Struggle with me is an idea I cannot grasp. I am rich, but what has money given me so far? What has this power given me? In what way am I happier than you? My childhood was slavery, and money did not save me from the birch. When Nina was ill and died, my money did not help her. If people don't care for me, I can't make them like me if I spend a hundred million."

"But you can do a great deal of good," said Kish.

"Good, indeed! You spoke to me yesterday of a mathematical man who is looking for a job. Believe me, I can do as little for him as you can. I can give money, but that's not what he wants. I asked a well-known musician to help a poor violinist, and this is what he answered: 'You apply to me just because you are not a musician yourself.' In the same way I say to you that you apply for help to me so confidently because you've never been in the position of a rich man."

"Why you bring in the comparison with a well-known musician I don't understand!" said Yulia Sergeyevna, and she flushed crimson. "What has the well-known musician to do with it!"

Her face was quivering with hatred, and she dropped her eyes to conceal the feeling. And not only her husband, but all the men sitting at the table, knew what the look in her face meant.

"What has the well-known musician got to do with it?" she said slowly. "Why, nothing's easier than helping someone poor."

Silence followed. Pyotr handed the woodcock, but they all refused it and ate nothing but salad. Laptev did not remember what he had said, but it was clear to him that it was not his words that were hateful, but the fact of his meddling in the conversation at all.

After supper he went into his study; intently, with a beating heart, expecting further humiliation, he listened to what was going on in the hall. An argument had sprung up there again. Then Yartsev sat down to the piano and played a sentimental song. He was a man of varied accomplishments; he could play and sing and even perform conjuring tricks.

"You may please yourselves, my friends, but I'm not going to stay at home," said Yulia. "We must go somewhere."

They decided to drive out of town, and sent Kish to the merchant's club to order a three-horse sledge. They did not ask Laptev to go with them because he did not usually join these expeditions, and because his brother was sitting with him; but he took it to mean that his society bored them, and that he was not wanted in their lighthearted youthful company. And his vexation, his bitter feeling, was so intense that he almost shed tears. He was positively glad that he was treated so ungraciously, that he was scorned, that he was a stupid, dull husband, a moneybag; and it seemed to him that he would have been even more glad if his wife were to deceive him that night with his best friend and were afterwards to acknowledge it, looking at him with hatred. . . . He was jealous on her account of their student friends, of actors, of singers, of Yartsev, even of casual acquaintances; and now he had a passionate longing for her really to be unfaithful to him. He longed to find her in another man's arms, and to be rid of this nightmare forever. Fyodor was drinking tea, gulping it noisily. But he, too, got up to go.

"Our old father must have got cataract again," he said, as he put on his fur coat. "His sight has become very poor."

Laptev put on his coat, too, and went out. After seeing his brother part of the way home, he took a sledge and drove to Yar's.

"And this is family happiness!" he said, jeering at himself. "This is love!"

His teeth were chattering, and he did not know if it were jealousy or something else. He walked about near the tables; listened to a comic singer in the hall. He had not a single phrase ready if he should meet his own party; and he felt sure beforehand that if he met his wife, he would only smile pitifully and not cleverly, and that everyone would understand what feeling had induced him to come here. He was bewildered by the electric light, the loud music, the smell of powder, and the fact that the ladies he met looked at him. He stood at the doors trying to see and to hear what was going on in the private rooms, and it seemed to him that he was somehow playing a mean, contemptible part on a level with the comic singers and those ladies. Then he went to Strelna, but he found none of his circle there, either; and only when on the way home he was again driving up to Yar's, a three-horse sledge noisily overtook him. The driver was drunk and shouting, and he could hear Yartsev laughing: "Ha, ha, ha!"

Laptev returned home between three and four. Yulia Sergeyevna was in bed. Noticing that she was not asleep, he went up to her and said sharply:

"I understand your repulsion, your hatred, but you might spare me before other people; you might conceal your feelings."

She got up and sat on the bed with her legs dangling. Her eyes looked big and black in the lamplight.

"I beg your pardon," she said.

He could not utter a single word from excitement and the trembling of his whole body; he stood facing her and was dumb. She trembled, too, and sat with the air of a criminal waiting for explanations.

"How I suffer!" he said at last, and he clutched his head. "I'm in hell, and I'm out of my mind."

"And do you suppose it's easy for me?" she asked, with a quiver in her voice. "God alone knows what I go through."

"You've been my wife for six months, but you haven't a spark of love for me in your heart. There's no hope, not one ray of light! Why did you marry me?" Laptev went on with despair. "Why? What demon thrust you into my arms? What did you hope for? What did you want?"

She looked at him with terror, as though she were afraid he would kill her.

"Did I attract you? Did you like me?" he went on, gasping for breath. "No. Then what? What? Tell me what?" he cried. "Oh, the cursed money! The cursed money!"

"I swear to God, no!" she cried, and she crossed herself. She seemed to shrink under the insult, and for the first time he heard her crying. "I swear to God, no!" she repeated. "I didn't think about your money; I didn't want it. I simply thought I should do wrong if I refused you. I was afraid of spoiling your life and mine. And now I am suffering for my mistake. I'm suffering unbearably!"

She sobbed bitterly, and he saw that she was hurt, and, not knowing what to say, dropped down on the carpet before her.

"That's enough; that's enough," he muttered. "I insulted you because I love you madly." He suddenly kissed her foot and passionately hugged it. "If only a spark of love," he muttered. "Come, lie to me; tell me a lie! Don't say it's a mistake! . . ."

But she went on crying, and he felt that she was only enduring his caresses as an inevitable consequence of her mistake. And the foot he had kissed she drew under her like a bird. He felt sorry for her.

She got into bed and covered her head over; he undressed and got into bed, too. In the morning they both felt confused and did not know what to talk about, and he even fancied she walked unsteadily on the foot he had kissed.

Before dinner Panaurov came to say good-bye. Yulia had an irresistible desire to go to her own home; it would be nice, she thought, to go away and have a rest from married life, from the embarrassment and the continual consciousness that she had done wrong. It was decided at dinner that she should set off with Panaurov and stay with her father for two or three weeks until she was tired of it.

## 11.

She traveled with Panaurov in a reserved compartment; he had on his head an astrakhan cap of peculiar shape.

"Yes, Petersburg did not satisfy me," he said, drawling, with a sigh. "They promise much, but nothing definite. Yes, my dear girl. I have been a justice of the peace, a member of the local Board, chairman of the Board of Magistrates, and finally councillor of the provincial administration. I think I have served my country and have earned the right to receive attention; but—would you believe it?—I can never succeed in wringing from the authorities a post in another town. . . ."

Panaurov closed his eyes and shook his head.

"They don't recognize me," he went on, as though dropping asleep. "Of course I'm not an administrator of genius, but, on the other hand, I'm a decent, honest man, and nowadays even that's something rare. I regret to say I have not been always quite straightforward with women, but in my relations with the Russian government I've always been a gentleman. But enough of that," he said, opening his eyes; "let us talk of you. What put it into your head to visit your papa so suddenly?"

"Well . . . I had a little misunderstanding with my husband," said Yulia, looking at his cap.

"Yes. What a queer fellow he is! All the Laptevs are queer.

Your husband's all right—he's nothing out of the way—but his brother Fyodor is a perfect fool."

Panaurov sighed and asked seriously:

"And have you a lover yet?"

Yulia looked at him in amazement and laughed.

"Goodness knows what you're talking about."

It was past ten o'clock when they got out at a big station and had supper. When the train went on again Panaurov took off his greatcoat and his cap and sat down beside Yulia.

"You are very charming, I must tell you," he began. "Excuse me for the eating-house comparison, but you remind me of fresh salted cucumber; it still smells of the hotbed, so to speak, and yet has a smack of the salt and a scent of fennel about it. As time goes on you will make a magnificent woman, a wonderful, exquisite woman. If this trip of ours had happened five years ago," he sighed, "I should have felt it my duty to join the ranks of your adorers, but now, alas, I'm a veteran on the retired list."

He smiled mournfully, but at the same time graciously, and put his arm round her waist.

"You must be mad!" she said; she flushed crimson and was so frightened that her hands and feet turned cold.

"Leave off, Grigory Nikolaevich!"

"What are you afraid of, dear?" he asked softly. "What is there dreadful about it? It's simply that you're not used to it."

If a woman protested he always interpreted it as a sign that he had made an impression on her and attracted her. Holding Yulia round the waist, he kissed her firmly on the cheek, then on the lips, in the full conviction that he was giving her intense gratification. Yulia recovered from her alarm and confusion and began laughing. He kissed her once more and said, as he put on his ridiculous cap:

"That is all that the old veteran can give you. A Turkish Pasha, a kindhearted old fellow, was presented by someone—or inherited, I fancy it was—a whole harem. When his beautiful young wives drew up in a row before him, he walked round them, kissed each one of them, and said: 'That is all that I am equal to giving you.' And that's just what I say, too."

All this struck her as stupid and extraordinary and amused her. She felt mischievous. Standing up on the seat and humming, she got a box of sweets from the shelf, and, throwing him a piece of chocolate, shouted:

"Catch!"

He caught it. With a loud laugh she threw him another sweet, then a third, and he kept catching them and putting them into his mouth, looking at her with imploring eyes; and it seemed to her that in his face, his features, his expression, there was a great deal that was feminine and childlike. And when, out of breath, she sat down on the seat and looked at him, laughing, he tapped her cheek with two fingers, and said as though he were vexed:

"Naughty girl!"

"Take it," she said, giving him the box. "I don't care for sweet things."

He ate up the sweets—every one of them—and locked the empty box in his trunk; he liked boxes with pictures on them.

"That's mischief enough, though," he said. "It's time for the veteran to go bye-bye."

He took out of his holdall a Bokhara dressing gown and a pillow, lay down, and covered himself with the dressing gown.

"Good night, darling!" he said softly, and sighed as though his whole body ached.

And soon a snore was heard. Without the slightest feeling of constraint, she, too, lay down and went to sleep.

When next morning she drove through her native town from the station homewards, the streets seemed to her empty and deserted. The snow looked gray, and the houses small, as though someone had squashed them. She was met by a funeral procession: the dead body was carried in an open coffin with banners.

"Meeting a funeral, they say, is lucky," she thought.

There were white bills pasted in the windows of the house where Nina Fyodorovna used to live.

With a sinking at her heart she drove into her own courtyard and rang at the door. It was opened by a servant she did not know—a plump, sleepy-looking girl wearing a warm wadded jacket. As she went upstairs Yulia remembered how Laptev had declared his love there, but now the staircase was unscrubbed, covered with footmarks. Upstairs in the cold passage patients were waiting in their outdoor coats. And for some reason her heart beat violently, and she was so excited she could scarcely walk.

The doctor, who had grown even stouter, was sitting with a brick-red face and disheveled hair, drinking tea. Seeing his daughter, he was greatly delighted, and even lachrymose. She thought that she was the only joy in this old man's life, and much moved, she embraced him warmly, and told him she would stay a long time—till Easter. After taking off her things in her own room, she went back to the dining-room to have tea with him. He was pacing up and down with his hands in his pockets, humming, "Ru-ru-ru"; this meant that he was dissatisfied with something.

"You have a gay time of it in Moscow," he said. "I am very glad for your sake. . . . I'm an old man and I need nothing. I shall soon give up the ghost and set you all free. And the wonder is that my hide is so tough, that I'm alive still! It's amazing!"

He said that he was a tough old ass that everyone rode on. They had thrust on him the care of Nina Fyodorovna, the worry of her children, and of her burial; and that coxcomb Panaurov would not trouble himself about it and had even borrowed a hundred rubles from him and had never paid it back.

"Take me to Moscow and put me in a madhouse," said the doctor. "I'm mad; I'm a simple child, as I still put faith in truth and justice."

Then he found fault with her husband for his shortsightedness in not buying houses that were being sold so cheaply. And now it seemed to Yulia that she was not the one joy in this old man's life. While he was seeing his patients, and afterwards going his rounds, she walked through all the rooms, not knowing what to do or what to think about. She had already grown strange to her own town and her own home. She felt no inclination to go into the streets or see her friends; and at the thought of her old friends and her life as a girl, she felt no sadness nor regret for the past.

In the evening she dressed a little more smartly and went to the evening service. But there were only poor people in the church, and her splendid fur coat and hat made no impression. And it seemed to her that there was some change in the church as well as in herself. In old days she had loved it when they read the prayers for the day at evening service, and the choir sang anthems such as "I Will Open My Lips." She liked moving slowly in the crowd to the priest who stood in the middle of the church, and then to feel the holy oil on her forehead; now she only waited for the service to be over. And now, going out of the church, she was only afraid that beggars would ask for alms; it was such a bore to have to stop and feel for her pockets; besides, she had no coppers in her pocket now—nothing but rubles.

She went to bed early and was a long time in going to sleep. She kept dreaming of portraits of some sort, and of the funeral procession she had met that morning. The open coffin with the dead body was carried into the yard and brought to a standstill at the door; then the coffin was swung backwards and forwards on a sheet, and dashed violently against the door. Yulia woke and jumped up in alarm. There really was a bang at the door, and the wire of the bell rustled against the wall, though no ring was to be heard.

The doctor coughed. Then she heard the servant go downstairs, and then come back.

"Madam!" she said, and knocked at the door. "Madam!"

"What is it?" said Yulia.

"A telegram for you!"

Yulia went out to her with a candle. Behind the servant stood the doctor, in his night clothes and greatcoat, and he, too, had a candle in his hand.

"Our bell is broken," he said, yawning sleepily. "It ought to have been mended long ago."

Yulia broke open the telegram and read:

WE DRINK TO YOUR HEALTH—YARTSEV, KOCHEVOI.

"Ah, what idiots!" she said, and burst out laughing; and her heart felt light and gay.

Going back into her room, she quietly washed and dressed, then she spent a long time in packing her things, until it was daylight, and at midday she set off for Moscow.

## 12.

In Holy Week the Laptevs went to an exhibition of pictures in the school of painting. The whole family went together in the Moscow fashion, the little girls, the governess, Kostya, and all.

Laptev knew the names of all the well-known painters and never missed an exhibition. He used sometimes to paint little landscape paintings when he was in the country in the summer, and he fancied he had a good deal of taste, and that if he had studied he might have made a good painter. When he was abroad he sometimes used to go to curio shops, examining the antiques with the air of a connoisseur and giving his opinion on them. When he bought any article he gave just what the shopkeeper liked to ask for it and his purchase remained afterwards in a box in the coach house till it disappeared altogether. Or going into a print shop, he would slowly and attentively examine the engravings and the bronzes, making various remarks on them, and would buy a common frame or a box of wretched prints. At home he had pictures always of large dimensions but of inferior quality; the best among them were badly hung. It had happened to him more than once to pay large sums for things which had afterwards turned out to be forgeries of the grossest kind. And it was remarkable that, though as a rule timid in the affairs of life, he was exceedingly bold and self-confident at a picture exhibition. Why?

Yulia Sergeyevna looked at the pictures as her husband did, through her open fist or an opera glass, and was surprised that the people in the pictures were like live people, and the trees like real trees. But she did not understand art, and it seemed to her that many pictures in the exhibition were alike, and she imagined that the whole object in painting was that the figures and objects should stand out as though they were real, when you looked at the picture through your open fist.

"That forest is Shiskin's," her husband explained to her. "He always paints the same thing. . . . But notice snow's never such a lilac color as that. . . . And that boy's left arm is shorter than his right."

When they were all tired and Laptev had gone to look for Kostya, that they might go home, Yulia stopped indifferently before a small landscape. In the foreground was a stream, over it a little wooden bridge; on the further side a path that disappeared in the dark grass; a field on the right; a copse; near it a campfire—no doubt of watchers by night; and in the distance there was a glow of the evening sunset.

Yulia imagined walking herself along the little bridge, and then along the little path further and further, while all round was stillness, the drowsy land rails calling and the fire flickering in the distance. And for some reason she suddenly began to feel that she had seen those very clouds that stretched across the red part of the sky, and that copse, and that field before, many times before. She felt lonely, and longed to walk on and on along the path; and there, in the glow of sunset, was the calm reflection of something unearthly, eternal.

"How finely that's painted!" she said, surprised that the picture had suddenly become intelligible to her.

"Look, Alyosha! Do you see how peaceful it is?"

She began trying to explain why she liked the landscape so much, but neither Kostya nor her husband understood her. She kept looking at the picture with a mournful smile, and the fact that the others saw nothing special in it troubled her. Then she began walking through the rooms and looking at the pictures again. She tried to understand them and no longer thought that a great many of them were alike. When, on returning home, for the first time she looked attentively at the big picture that hung over the piano in the drawing-room, she felt a dislike for it, and said:

"What an idea to have pictures like that!"

And after that the gilt cornices, the Venetian looking glasses with flowers on them, the pictures of the same sort as the one that hung over the piano, and also her husband's and Kostya's reflections upon art, aroused in her a feeling of dreariness and vexation, even of hatred.

Life went on its ordinary course from day to day with no promise of anything special. The theatrical season was over, the warm days had come. There was a long spell of glorious weather. One morning the Laptevs attended the district court to hear Kostya, who had been appointed by the court to defend someone. They were late in starting and reached the court after the examination of the witnesses had begun. A soldier in the reserve was accused of theft and housebreaking. There were a great number of witnesses, washerwomen; they all testified that the accused was often in the house of their employer—a woman who kept a laundry. At the Feast of the Exaltation of the Cross he came late in the evening and began asking for money; he wanted a pick-me-up, as he had been drinking, but no one gave him anything. Then he went away, but an hour afterwards he came back and brought with him some beer and a soft gingerbread cake for the little girl. They drank and sang songs almost till daybreak, and when in the morning they looked about, the lock of the door leading up into the attic was broken, and of the linen three men's shirts, a petticoat, and two sheets were missing. Kostya asked each witness sarcastically whether she had not drunk the beer the accused had brought. Evidently he was insinuating that the washerwomen had stolen the linen themselves. He delivered his speech without the slightest nervousness, looking angrily at the jury.

He explained what robbery with housebreaking meant, and the difference between that and simple theft. He spoke very circumstantially and convincingly, displaying an unusual talent for speaking at length and in a serious tone about what had been known to everyone long before. And it was difficult to make out exactly what he was aiming at. From his long speech the foreman of the jury could only have deduced "that it was housebreaking but not robbery, as the washerwomen had sold the linen for drink themselves; or, if there had been robbery, there had not been housebreaking." But obviously, he said just what was wanted, as his speech moved the jury and the audience and was very much liked. When they gave a verdict of acquittal, Yulia nodded to Kostya, and afterwards pressed his hand warmly.

In May the Laptevs moved to a country villa at Sokolniki. By that time Yulia was expecting a baby.

## 13.

More than a year had passed. Yulia and Yartsev were lying on the grass at Sokolniki not far from the embankment of the Yaroslav railway; a little distance away Kochevoi was lying with hands under his head, looking at the sky. All three had been for a walk and were waiting for the six o'clock train to pass to go home to tea.

"Mothers see something extraordinary in their children; that is ordained by nature," said Yulia. "A mother will stand for hours together by the baby's cot looking at its little ears and eyes and nose, and fascinated by them. If anyone else kisses her baby the poor thing imagines that it gives him immense pleasure. And a mother talks of nothing but her baby. I know that weakness in mothers, and I keep watch over myself, but my Olga really is exceptional. How she looks at me when I'm nursing her! How she laughs! She's only eight months old, but, upon my word, I've never seen such intelligent eyes in a child of three."

"Tell me, by the way," asked Yartsev: "which do you love most—your husband or your baby?"

Yulia shrugged her shoulders.

"I don't know," she said. "I never was so very fond of my husband, and Olga is in reality my first love. You know that I did not marry Alexei for love. In old days I was foolish and miserable and thought that I had ruined my life and his, and now I see that love is not necessary—that it is all nonsense."

"But if it is not love, what feeling is it that binds you to your husband? Why do you go on living with him?"

"I don't know. . . . I suppose it must be habit. I respect him, I miss him when he's away for long, but that's—not love. He is a clever, honest man, and that's enough to make me happy. He is very kind and goodhearted. . . ."

"Alyosha's intelligent, Alyosha's good," said Kostya, raising his head lazily; "but, my dear girl, to find out that he is intelligent, good, and interesting, you have to eat a hundred-weight of salt with him. . . . And what's the use of his goodness and intelligence? He can fork out money as much as you want, but when character is needed to resist insolence or aggressiveness, he is fainthearted and overcome with nervousness. People like your amiable Alyosha are splendid people, but they are no use at all for fighting. In fact, they are no use for anything."

At last the train came in sight. Coils of perfectly pink smoke from the funnels floated over the copse, and two windows in the last compartment flashed so brilliantly in the sun, that it hurt their eyes to look at it.

"Teatime!" said Yulia Sergeyevna, getting up.

She had grown somewhat stouter of late, and her movements were already a little matronly, a little indolent.

"It's bad to be without love though," said Yartsev, walking behind her. "We talk and read of nothing else but love, but we do very little loving ourselves, and that's really bad."

"All that's nonsense, Ivan Gavrilich," said Yulia. "That's not what gives happiness."

They had tea in the little garden, where mignonette, stocks, and tobacco plants were in flower, and spikes of early gladioli were just opening. Yartsev and Kochevoi could see from Yulia's face that she was passing through a happy period of inward peace and serenity, that she wanted nothing but what she had, and they, too, had a feeling of peace and comfort in their hearts. Whatever was said sounded apt and clever; the pines were lovely—the fragrance of them was exquisite as it had never been before; and the cream was very nice; and Sasha was a good, intelligent child.

After tea Yartsev sang songs, accompanying himself on the piano, while Yulia and Kochevoi sat listening in silence, though Yulia got up from time to time, and went softly indoors, to take a look at the baby and at Lida, who had been in bed for the last two days, feverish and eating nothing.

"My friend, my tender friend," sang Yartsev. "No, my friends, I'll be hanged if I understand why you are all so against love!" he said, flinging back his head. "If I weren't busy for fifteen hours of the twenty-four, I should certainly fall in love."

Supper was served on the veranda; it was warm and still, but Yulia wrapped herself in a shawl and complained of the damp. When it got dark, she seemed not quite herself; she kept shivering and begging her visitors to stay a little longer. She regaled them with wine and after supper ordered brandy to keep them from going. She didn't want to be left alone with the children and the servants.

"We summer visitors are getting up a performance for the children," she said. "We have got everything—a stage and actors; we are only at a loss for a play. Two dozen plays of different sorts have been sent us, but there isn't one that is suitable. Now, you are fond of the theater and are so good at history," she said, addressing Yartsev. "Write an historical play for us."

"Well, I might."

The men drank up all the brandy and prepared to go.

It was past ten, and for summer-villa people that was late.

"How dark it is! One can't see a bit," said Yulia, as she went with them to the gate. "I don't know how you'll find your way. But, isn't it cold?"

She wrapped herself up more closely and walked back to the porch.

"I suppose my Alexei's playing cards somewhere," she called to them. "Good night!"

After the lighted rooms nothing could be seen. Yartsev and Kostya groped their way like blind men to the railway embankment and crossed it.

"One can't see a thing," said Kostya in his bass voice,

standing still and gazing at the sky. "And the stars, the stars, they are like new threepenny bits. Gavrilich!"

"Ah?" Yartsev responded somewhere in the darkness.

"I say, one can't see a thing. Where are you?"

Yartsev went up to him whistling and took his arm.

"Hi, there, you summer visitors!" Kostya shouted at the top of his voice. "We've caught a socialist."

When he was exhilarated he was always very rowdy, shouting, wrangling with policemen and cabdrivers, singing, and laughing violently.

"Nature be damned," he shouted.

"Come, come," said Yartsev, trying to pacify him. "You mustn't. Please don't."

Soon the friends grew accustomed to the darkness and were able to distinguish the outlines of the tall pines and telegraph posts. From time to time the sound of whistles reached them from the station and the telegraph wires hummed plaintively. From the copse itself there came no sound, and there was a feeling of pride, strength, and mystery in its silence, and on the right it seemed that the tops of the pines were almost touching the sky. The friends found their path and walked along it. There it was quite dark, and it was only from the long strip of sky dotted with stars, and from the firmly trodden earth under their feet, that they could tell they were walking along a path. They walked along side by side in silence, and it seemed to both of them that people were coming to meet them. Their tipsy exhilaration passed off. The fancy came into Yartsev's mind that perhaps that copse was haunted by the spirits of the Muscovite Tsars, boyars, and patriarchs, and he was on the point of telling Kostya about it, but he checked himself.

When they reached the town gate there was a faint light of dawn in the sky. Still in silence, Yartsev and Kochevoi walked along the wooden pavement, by the cheap summer cottages, eating-houses, timber stacks. Under the arch of interlacing branches, the damp air was fragrant of lime trees, and then a broad, long street opened before them, and on it not a soul, not a light. . . . When they reached the Red Pond, it was daylight.

"Moscow—it's a town that will have to suffer a great deal more," said Yartsev, looking at the Alexyevsky Monastery.

"What put that into your head?"

"I don't know. I love Moscow."

Both Yartsev and Kostya had been born in Moscow, and adored the town, and felt for some reason antagonistic to every other town. Both were convinced that Moscow was a remarkable town, and Russia a remarkable country. In the Crimea, in the Caucasus, and abroad, they felt dull, uncomfortable, and ill at ease, and they thought their gray Moscow weather very pleasant and healthy. And when the rain lashed at the window-panes and it got dark early, and when the walls of the churches and houses looked a drab, dismal color, days when one doesn't know what to put on when one is going out—such days excited them agreeably.

At last near the station they took a cab.

"It really would be nice to write an historical play," said Yartsev, "but not about the Lyapunovs or the Godunovs, but of the times of Yaroslav or of Monomach. . . . I hate all historical plays except the monologue of Pimen. When you have to do with some historical authority or even read a textbook of Russian history, you feel that everyone in Russia is exceptionally talented, gifted, and interesting; but when I see an historical play at the theater, Russian life begins to seem stupid, morbid, and not original."

Near Dmitrovka the friends separated, and Yartsev went on to his lodging in Great Nikitsky Street. He sat half dozing, swaying from side to side, and pondering on the play. He suddenly imagined a terrible din, a clanging noise, and shouts in some unknown language that might have been Kalmuck, and a village wrapped in flames, and forests near covered with hoarfrost and soft pink in the glow of the fire, visible for miles around, and so clearly that every little fir tree could be distinguished, and savage men darting about the village on horseback and on foot, and as red as the glow in the sky.

"The Polovtsy," thought Yartsev.

One of them, a terrible old man with a bloodstained face all scorched from the fire, binds to his saddle a young girl with a White Russian face, and the girl looks sorrowful, understanding. . . . Yartsev flung back his head and woke up.

"My friend, my tender friend . . ." he hummed.

As he paid the cabman and went up his stairs, he could not shake off his dreaminess; he saw the flames catching the village, and the forest beginning to crackle and smoke. A huge, wild bear frantic with terror rushed through the village. . . . And the girl tied to the saddle was still looking.

When at last he went into his room it was broad daylight. Two candles were burning by some open music on the piano. On the sofa lay Polina Razsudin, wearing a black dress and a sash, with a newspaper in her hand, fast asleep. She must have been playing late, waiting for Yartsev to come home, and, tired of waiting, fell asleep.

"Hullo, she's worn out," he thought.

Carefully taking the newspaper out of her hands, he covered her with a rug. He put out the candles and went into his bedroom. As he got into bed, he still thought of his historical play, and the tune of "My friend, my tender friend" was still ringing in his head. . . .

Two days later Laptev looked in upon him for a moment to tell him that Lida was ill with diphtheria, and that Yulia Sergeyevna and her baby had caught it from her, and five days later came the news that Lida and Yulia were recovering, but the baby was dead, and that the Laptevs had left their villa at Sokolniki and had hastened back to Moscow.

## 14.

It had become distasteful to Laptev to be long at home. His wife was constantly away in the lodge declaring that she had to look after the little girls, but he knew that she did not go to the lodge to give them lessons but to cry in Kostya's room. The ninth day came, then the twentieth, and then the fortieth, and still he had to go to the cemetery to listen to the requiem, and then to wear himself out for a whole day and night thinking of nothing but that unhappy baby, and trying to comfort his wife with all sorts of commonplace expressions. He went rarely to the warehouse now and spent most of his time in charitable work, seizing upon every pretext requiring his attention, and he was glad when he had for some trivial reason to be out for the whole day. He had been intending of late to go abroad, to study night refuges, and that idea attracted him now.

It was an autumn day. Yulia had just gone to the lodge to cry, while Laptev lay on a sofa in the study thinking where he could go. Just at that moment Pyotr announced Polina Razsudin. Laptev was delighted; he leaped up and went to meet the unexpected visitor, who had been his closest friend, though he had almost begun to forget her. She had not changed in the least since that evening when he had seen her for the last time and was just the same as ever.

"Polina," he said, holding out both hands to her. "What ages! If you only knew how glad I am to see you! Do come in!"

Polina greeted him, jerked him by the hand, and, without taking off her coat and hat, went into the study and sat down.

"I've come to you for one minute," she said. "I haven't time to talk of any nonsense. Sit down and listen. Whether you are glad to see me or not is absolutely nothing to me, for I don't care a straw for the gracious attentions of you lords of creation. I've only come to you because I've been to five other places already today, and everywhere I was met with a refusal, and it's a matter that can't be put off. Listen," she went on, looking into his face. "Five students of my acquaintance, stupid, unintelligent people, but certainly poor, have neglected to pay their fees and are being excluded from the university. Your wealth makes it your duty to go straight to the university and pay for them."

"With pleasure, Polina."

"Here are their names," she said, giving him a list. "Go this minute; you'll have plenty of time to enjoy your domestic happiness afterwards."

At that moment a rustle was heard through the door that led into the drawing-room; probably the dog was scratching itself. Polina turned crimson and jumped up.

"Your Dulcinea's eavesdropping," she said. "That's horrid!"

Laptev was offended at this insult to Yulia.

"She's not here; she's in the lodge," he said. "And don't speak of her like that. Our child is dead, and she is in great distress."

"You can console her," Polina scoffed, sitting down again; "she'll have another dozen. You don't need much sense to bring children into the world."

Laptev remembered that he had heard this, or something very like it, many times in old days, and it brought back a whiff of the romance of the past, of solitary freedom, of his bachelor life, when he was young and thought he could do anything he chose, when he had neither love for his wife nor memory of his baby.

"Let us go together," he said, stretching.

When they reached the university Polina waited at the gate, while Laptev went into the office; he came back soon afterwards and handed Polina five receipts.

"Where are you going now?" he asked.

"To Yartsev's."

"I'll come with you."

"But you'll prevent him from writing."

"No, I assure you I won't," he said, and looked at her imploringly.

She had on a black hat trimmed with crepe, as though she were in mourning, and a short, shabby coat, the pockets of which stuck out. Her nose looked longer than it used to be, and her face looked bloodless in spite of the cold. Laptev liked walking with her, doing what she told him, and listening to her grumbling. He walked along thinking about her, what inward strength there must be in this woman, since, though she was so ugly, so angular, so restless, though she did not know how to dress, and always had untidy hair, and was always somehow out of harmony, she was yet so fascinating.

They went into Yartsev's flat by the back way through the kitchen, where they were met by the cook, a clean little old woman with gray curls; she was overcome with embarrassment, and with a honeyed smile which made her little face look like a pie, said:

"Please walk in."

Yartsev was not at home. Polina sat down to the piano, and, beginning upon a tedious, difficult exercise, told Laptev not to hinder her. And without distracting her attention by conversation, he sat on one side and began turning over the pages of a *The Messenger of Europe*. After practicing for two hours—it was the task she set herself every day—she ate something in the kitchen and went out to her lessons. Laptev read the continuation of a story, then sat for a long time without reading and without being bored, glad to think that he was too late for dinner at home.

"Ha, ha, ha!" came Yartsev's laugh, and he walked in with ruddy cheeks, looking strong and healthy, wearing a new coat with bright buttons. "Ha, ha, ha!"

The friends dined together. Then Laptev lay on the sofa while Yartsev sat near and lighted a cigar. It got dark.

"I must be getting old," said Laptev. "Ever since my sister Nina died, I've taken to constantly thinking of death."

They began talking of death, of the immortality of the soul, of how nice it would be to rise again and fly off somewhere to Mars, to be always idle and happy, and, above all, to think in a new special way, not as on earth.

"One doesn't want to die," said Yartsev softly. "No sort of philosophy can reconcile me to death, and I look on it simply as annihilation. One wants to live."

"You love life, Gavrilich?"

"Yes, I love it."

"Do you know, I can never understand myself about that. I'm always in a gloomy mood or else indifferent. I'm timid, without self-confidence; I have a cowardly conscience; I never can adapt myself to life, or become its master. Some people talk nonsense or cheat, and even so enjoy life, while I consciously do good, and feel nothing but uneasiness or complete indifference. I explain all that, Gavrilich, by my being a slave, the grandson of a serf. Before we plebeians fight our way into the true path, many of our sort will perish on the way."

"That's all quite right, my dear fellow," said Yartsev, and he sighed. "That only proves once again how rich and varied Russian life is. Ah, how rich it is! Do you know, I feel more convinced every day that we are on the eve of the greatest triumph, and I should like to live to take part in it. Whether you like to believe it or not, to my thinking a remarkable generation is growing up. It gives me great enjoyment to teach the children, especially the girls. They are wonderful children!"

Yartsev went to the piano and struck a chord.

"I'm a chemist, I think in chemical terms, and I shall die a chemist," he went on. "But I am greedy, and I am afraid of dying unsatisfied; and chemistry is not enough for me, and I seize upon Russian history, history of art, the science of teaching music. . . . Your wife asked me in the summer to write an historical play, and now I'm longing to write and write. I feel as though I could sit for three days and three nights without moving, writing all the time. I am worn out with ideas—my brain's crowded with them, and I feel as though there were a pulse throbbing in my head. I don't in the least want to become anything special, to create something great. I simply want to live, to dream, to hope, to be in the midst of everything. . . . Life is short, my dear fellow, and one must make the most of everything."

After this friendly talk, which was not over till midnight, Laptev took to coming to see Yartsev almost every day. He felt drawn to him. As a rule he came towards evening, lay down on the sofa, and waited patiently for Yartsev to come in, without feeling in the least bored. When Yartsev came back from his work, he had dinner and sat down to work; but Laptev would ask him a question, a conversation would spring up, and there was no more thought of work and at midnight the friends parted very well pleased with one another.

But this did not last long. Arriving one day at Yartsev's, Laptev found no one there but Polina, who was sitting at the piano practicing her exercises. She looked at him with a cold, almost hostile expression, and asked, without shaking hands:

"Tell me, please: how much longer is this going on?"

"This? What?" asked Laptev, not understanding.

"You come here every day and hinder Yartsev from working. Yartsev is not a tradesman; he is a scientific man, and every moment of his life is precious. You ought to understand and to have some little delicacy!"

"If you think that I hinder him," said Laptev, mildly, disconcerted, "I will give up my visits."

"Quite right, too. You had better go, or he may be home in a minute and find you here."

The tone in which this was said, and the indifference in Polina's eyes, completely disconcerted him. She had absolutely no sort of feeling for him now, except the desire that he should go as soon as possible—and what a contrast it was to her old love for him! He went out without shaking hands with her, and he fancied she would call out to him, bring him back, but he heard the scales again, and as he slowly went down the stairs he realized that he had become a stranger to her now.

Three days later Yartsev came to spend the evening with him.

"I have news," he said, laughing. "Polina Nikolaevna has moved into my rooms altogether." He was a little confused and went on in a low voice: "Well, we are not in love with each other, of course, but I suppose that . . . that doesn't matter. I am glad I can give her a refuge and peace and quiet, and make it possible for her not to work if she's ill. She fancies that her coming to live with me will make things more orderly, and that under her influence I shall become a great scientist. That's what she fancies. And let her fancy it. In the South they have a saying: 'Fancy makes the fool a rich man.' Ha, ha, ha!"

Laptev said nothing. Yartsev walked up and down the study, looking at the pictures he had seen so many times before, and said with a sigh:

"Yes, my dear fellow, I am three years older than you are, and it's too late for me to think of real love, and in reality a woman like Polina Nikolaevna is a godsend to me, and, of course, I shall get on capitally with her till we're both old people; but, goodness knows why, one still regrets something, one still longs for something, and I still feel as though I am lying in the Vale of Daghestan and dreaming of a ball. In short, man's never satisfied with what he has."

He went into the drawing-room and began singing as though nothing had happened, and Laptev sat in his study with his eyes shut and tried to understand why Polina had gone to live with Yartsev. And then he felt sad that there were no lasting, permanent attachments. And he felt vexed that Polina Nikolaevna had gone to live with Yartsev, and vexed with himself that his feeling for his wife was not what it had been.

## 15.

Laptev sat reading and swaying to and fro in a rocking chair; Yulia was in the study, and she, too, was reading. It seemed there was nothing to talk about; they had both been silent all day. From time to time he looked at her from over his book and thought: "Whether one marries from passionate love, or without love at all, doesn't it come to the same thing?" And the time when he used to be jealous, troubled, distressed, seemed to him far away. He had succeeded in going abroad, and now he was resting after the journey and looking forward to another visit in the spring to England, which he had very much liked.

And Yulia Sergeyevna had grown used to her sorrow and had left off going to the lodge to cry. That winter she had given up driving out shopping, had given up the theaters and concerts, and had stayed at home. She never cared for big rooms and always sat in her husband's study or in her own room, where she had shrines of icons that had come to her on her marriage, and where there hung on the wall the landscape that had pleased her so much at the exhibition. She spent hardly any money on herself and was almost as frugal now as she had been in her father's house.

The winter passed cheerlessly. Card playing was the rule everywhere in Moscow, and if any other recreation was attempted, such as singing, reading, drawing, the result was even more tedious. And since there were few talented people in Moscow, and the same singers and reciters performed at every entertainment, even the enjoyment of art gradually palled and became for many people a tiresome and monotonous social duty.

Moreover, the Laptevs never had a day without something vexatious happening. Old Laptev's eyesight was still failing; he no longer went to the warehouse, and the oculist told them that he would soon be blind. Fyodor had for some reason given up going to the warehouse and spent his time sitting at home writing something. Panaurov had got a post in another town, and had been promoted an actual civil councillor, and was now staying at the Dresden. He came to the Laptevs' almost every day to ask for money. Kish had finished his studies at last, and, while waiting for Laptev to find him a job, used to spend whole days at a time with them, telling them long, tedious stories. All this was irritating and exhausting and made daily life unpleasant.

Pyotr came into the study and announced an unknown lady. On the card he brought in was the name "Josephina Iosefovna Milan."

Yulia Sergeyevna got up languidly and went out limping slightly, as her foot had gone to sleep. In the doorway appeared a pale, thin lady with dark eyebrows, dressed altogether in black. She clasped her hands on her bosom and said supplicatingly:

"Monsieur Laptev, save my children!"

The jingle of her bracelets sounded familiar to him, and he knew the face with patches of powder on it; he recognized her as the lady with whom he had once so inappropriately dined before his marriage. It was Panaurov's second wife.

"Save my children," she repeated, and her face suddenly quivered and looked old and pitiful. "You alone can save us, and I have spent my last penny coming to Moscow to see you! My children are starving!"

She made a motion as though she were going to fall on her knees. Laptev was alarmed and clutched her by the arm.

"Sit down, sit down . . ." he muttered, making her sit down. "I beg you to be seated."

"We have no money to buy bread," she said. "Grigory Nikolaevich is going away to a new post, but he will not take the children and me with him, and the money which you so generously send us he spends only on himself. What are we to do? What? My poor, unhappy children!"

"Calm yourself, I beg. I will give orders that that money shall be made payable to you."

She began sobbing and then grew calmer, and he noticed that the tears had made little pathways through the powder on her cheeks, and that she was growing a mustache.

"You are infinitely generous, Monsieur Laptev. But be our guardian angel, our good fairy, persuade Grigory Nikolaevich not to abandon me, but to take me with him. You know I love him—I love him insanely; he's the comfort of my life."

Laptev gave her a hundred rubles, and promised to talk to Panaurov, and saw her out to the hall in trepidation the whole time, for fear she should break into sobs or fall on her knees.

After her, Kish made his appearance. Then Kostya came in with his photographic apparatus. Of late he had been attracted by photography and took photographs of every one in the house several times a day. This new pursuit caused him many disappointments, and he had actually grown thinner.

Before evening tea Fyodor arrived. Sitting in a corner in the study, he opened a book and stared for a long time at a page, obviously not reading. Then he spent a long time drinking tea; his face turned red. In his presence Laptev felt a load on his heart; even his silence was irksome to him.

"Russia may be congratulated on the appearance of a new author," said Fyodor. "Joking apart, though, Brother, I have turned out a little article—the first fruits of my pen, so to say—and I've brought it to show you. Read it, dear boy, and tell me your opinion—but sincerely."

He took a manuscript out of his pocket and gave it to his brother. The article was called *The Russian Soul*; it was written tediously, in the colorless style in which people with no talent, but full of secret vanity, usually write. The leading idea of it was that the intellectual man has the right to disbelieve in the supernatural, but it is his duty to conceal his lack of faith that he may not be a stumbling block and shake the faith of others. Without faith there is no idealism, and idealism is destined to save Europe and guide humanity into the true path.

"But you don't say what Europe has to be saved from," said Laptev.

"That's intelligible of itself."

"Nothing is intelligible," said Laptev, and he walked about the room in agitation. "It's not intelligible to me why you wrote it. But that's your business."

"I want to publish it in pamphlet form."

"That's your affair."

They were silent for a minute. Fyodor sighed and said:

"It's an immense regret to me, dear Brother, that we think differently. Oh, Alyosha, Alyosha, my darling brother! You and I are true Russians, true believers, men of broad nature; all of these German and Jewish crochets are not for us. You and I are not wretched upstarts, you know, but representatives of a distinguished merchant family."

"What do you mean by a distinguished family?" said Laptev, restraining his irritation. "A distinguished family! The landowners beat our grandfather and every low little government clerk punched him in the face. Our grandfather thrashed our father, and our father thrashed us. What has your distinguished family done for us? What sort of nerves, what sort of blood, have we inherited? For nearly three years you've been arguing like an ignorant deacon, and talking all sorts of nonsense, and now you've written—this slavish drivel here! While I, while I! Look at me. . . . No elasticity, no boldness, no strength of will; I tremble over every step I take as though I should be flogged for it. I am timid before nonentities, idiots, brutes, who are immeasurably my inferiors mentally and morally; I am afraid of porters, doorkeepers, policemen, gendarmes. I am afraid of everyone because I was born of a mother who was terrified, and because from a child I was beaten and frightened! . . . You and I will do well to have no children. Oh God, grant that this distinguished merchant family may die with us!"

Yulia Sergeyevna came into the study and sat down at the table.

"Are you arguing about something here?" she asked. "Am I interrupting?"

"No, little sister," answered Fyodor. "Our discussion was of principles. Here you are abusing the family," he added, turning to his brother. "That family has created a business worth a million, though. That stands for something, anyway!"

"A great distinction—a business worth a million! A man with no particular brains, without abilities, by chance becomes a trader, and then when he has grown rich he goes on trading from day to day, with no sort of system, with no aim, without having any particular greed for money. He trades mechanically, and money comes to him of itself, without his going to meet it. He sits all his life at his work, likes it only because he can domineer over his clerks and get the better of his customers. He's a churchwarden because he can domineer over the choristers and keep them under his thumb; he's the patron of a school because he likes to feel the teacher is his subordinate and enjoys lording it over him. The merchant does not love trading, he loves dominating, and your warehouse is not so much a commercial establishment as a torture chamber! And for a business like yours, you want clerks who have been deprived of individual character and personal life—and you make them such by forcing them in childhood to lick the dust for a crust of bread, and you've trained them from childhood to believe that you are their benefactors. No fear of your taking a university man into your warehouse!"

"University men are not suitable for our business."

"That's not true," cried Laptev. "It's a lie!"

"Excuse me, it seems to me you spit into the well from which you drink yourself," said Fyodor, and he got up. "Our business is hateful to you, yet you make use of the income from it."

"Aha! We've spoken our minds," said Laptev, and he laughed, looking angrily at his brother. "Yes, if I didn't belong to your distinguished family—if I had an ounce of will and courage, I should long ago have flung away that income and have gone to work for my living. But in your warehouse you've destroyed all character in me from a child! I'm your product."

Fyodor looked at the clock and began hurriedly saying good-bye. He kissed Yulia's hand and went out, but instead of going into the hall, walked into the drawing-room, then into the bedroom.

"I've forgotten how the rooms go," he said in extreme confusion. "It's a strange house. Isn't it a strange house!"

He seemed utterly overcome as he put on his coat, and there was a look of pain on his face. Laptev felt no more anger; he was frightened, and at the same time felt sorry for Fyodor, and the warm, true love for his brother, which seemed to have died down in his heart during those three years, awoke, and he felt an intense desire to express that love.

"Come to dinner with us tomorrow, Fyodor," he said, and stroked him on the shoulder. "Will you come?"

"Yes, yes; but give me some water."

Laptev ran himself to the dining-room to take the first thing he could get from the sideboard. This was a tall beer jug. He poured water into it and brought it to his brother. Fyodor began drinking, but bit a piece out of the jug; they heard a crunch, and then sobs. The water ran over his fur coat and his jacket, and Laptev, who had never seen men cry, stood in confusion and dismay, not knowing what to do. He looked on helplessly while Yulia and the servant took off Fyodor's coat and helped him back again into the room, and went with him, feeling guilty.

Yulia made Fyodor lie down on the sofa and knelt beside him.

"It's nothing," she said, trying to comfort him. "It's your nerves. . . ."

"I'm so miserable, my dear!" he said. "I am so unhappy, unhappy . . . but all the time I've been hiding it, I've been hiding it!"

He put his arm round her neck and whispered in her ear:

"Every night I see my sister Nina. She comes and sits in the chair near my bed. . . ."

When, an hour later, he put on his fur coat in the hall, he was smiling again and ashamed to face the servant. Laptev went with him to Pyatnitsky Street.

"Come and have dinner with us tomorrow," he said on the way, holding him by the arm, "and at Easter we'll go abroad together. You absolutely must have a change, or you'll be getting quite morbid."

When he got home Laptev found his wife in a state of great nervous agitation. The scene with Fyodor had upset her, and she could not recover her composure. She wasn't crying but kept tossing on the bed, clutching with cold fingers at the quilt, at the pillows, at her husband's hands. Her eyes looked big and frightened.

"Don't go away from me, don't go away," she said to her husband. "Tell me, Alyosha, why have I left off saying my prayers? What has become of my faith? Oh, why did you talk of religion before me? You've shaken my faith, you and your friends. I never pray now."

He put compresses on her forehead, chafed her hands, gave her tea to drink, while she huddled up to him in terror. . . .

Towards morning she was worn out and fell asleep, while Laptev sat beside her and held her hand. So that he could get no sleep. The whole day afterwards he felt shattered and dull, and wandered listlessly about the rooms without a thought in his head.

## 16.

The doctor said that Fyodor's mind was affected. Laptev did not know what to do in his father's house, while the dark warehouse in which neither his father nor Fyodor ever appeared now seemed to him like a sepulcher. When his wife told him that he absolutely must go every day to the warehouse and also to his father's, he either said nothing or began talking irritably of his childhood, saying that it was beyond his power to forgive his father for his past, that the warehouse and the house in Pyatnitsky Street were hateful to him, and so on.

One Sunday morning Yulia went herself to Pyatnitsky Street. She found old Fyodor Stepanovich in the same big drawing-room in which the service had been held on her first arrival. Wearing slippers, and without a cravat, he was sitting motionless in his armchair, blinking with his sightless eyes.

"It's I—your daughter-in-law," she said, going up to him. "I've come to see how you are."

He began breathing heavily with excitement.

Touched by his affliction and his loneliness, she kissed his hand; and he passed his hand over her face and head, and, having satisfied himself that it was she, made the sign of the cross over her.

"Thank you, thank you," he said. "You know I've lost my eyes and can see nothing. . . . I can dimly see the window and the fire, but people and things I cannot see at all. Yes, I'm going blind, and Fyodor has fallen ill, and without the master's eye things are in a bad way now. If there is any irregularity there's no one to look into it; and folks soon get spoiled. And why is it Fyodor has fallen ill? Did he catch cold? Here I have never ailed in my life and never taken medicine. I never saw anything of doctors."

And, as he always did, the old man began boasting. Meanwhile the servants hurriedly laid the table and brought in lunch and bottles of wine. Ten bottles were put on the table; one of them was in the shape of the Eiffel Tower. There was a whole dish of hot pies smelling of jam, rice, and fish.

"I beg my dear guest to have lunch," said the old man.

She took him by the arm, led him to the table, and poured him out a glass of vodka.

"I will come to you again tomorrow," she said, "and I'll bring your grandchildren, Sasha and Lida. They will be sorry for you and fondle you."

"There's no need. Don't bring them. They are illegitimate."

"Why are they illegitimate? Why, their father and mother were married."

"Without my permission. I do not bless them, and I don't want to know them. Let them be."

"You speak strangely, Fyodor Stepanovich," said Yulia, with a sigh.

"It is written in the Gospel: children must fear and honor their parents."

"Nothing of the sort. The Gospel tells us that we must forgive even our enemies."

"One can't forgive in our business. If you were to forgive everyone, you would come to ruin in three years."

"But to forgive, to say a kind, friendly word to anyone, even a sinner, is something far above business, far above wealth."

Yulia longed to soften the old man, to awaken a feeling of compassion in him, to move him to repentance; but he only listened condescendingly to all she said, as a grown-up person listens to a child.

"Fyodor Stepanovich," said Yulia resolutely, "you are an old man, and God soon will call you to Himself. He won't ask you how you managed your business, and whether you were successful in it, but whether you were gracious to people; or whether you were harsh to those who were weaker than you, such as your servants, your clerks."

"I was always the benefactor of those that served me; they ought to remember me in their prayers forever," said the old man, with conviction, but touched by Yulia's tone of sincerity, and anxious to give her pleasure, he said: "Very well; bring my grandchildren tomorrow. I will tell them to buy me some little presents for them."

The old man was slovenly in his dress, and there was cigar ash on his breast and on his knees; apparently no one cleaned his boots or brushed his clothes. The rice in the pies was half cooked, the tablecloth smelled of soap, the servants tramped noisily about the room. And the old man and the whole house had a neglected look, and Yulia, who felt this, was ashamed of herself and of her husband.

"I will be sure to come and see you tomorrow," she said.

She walked through the rooms and gave orders for the old man's bedroom to be set to rights, and the lamp to be lighted under the icons in it. Fyodor, sitting in his own room, was looking at an open book without reading it. Yulia talked to him and told the servants to tidy his room, too; then she went downstairs to the clerks. In the middle of the room where the clerks used to dine, there was an unpainted wooden post to support the ceiling and to prevent its coming down. The ceilings in the basement were low, the walls covered with cheap paper, and there was a smell of charcoal fumes and cooking. As it was a holiday, all the clerks were at home, sitting on their bedsteads waiting for dinner. When Yulia went in they jumped up and answered her questions timidly, looking up at her from under their brows like convicts.

"Good heavens! What a horrid room you have!" she said, throwing up her hands. "Aren't you crowded here?"

"Crowded, but not aggrieved," said Makeichev. "We are greatly indebted to you and will offer up our prayers for you to our Heavenly Father."

"The congruity of life with the conceit of the personality," said Pochatkin.

And noticing that Yulia did not understand Pochatkin, Makeichev hastened to explain:

"We are humble people and must live according to our position."

She inspected the boys' quarters, and then the kitchen, made acquaintance with the housekeeper, and was thoroughly dissatisfied.

When she got home she said to her husband:

"We ought to move into your father's house and settle there for good as soon as possible. And you will go every day to the warehouse."

Then they both sat side by side in the study without speaking. His heart was heavy, and he did not want to move into Pyatnitsky Street or to go into the warehouse; but he guessed what his wife was thinking and could not oppose her. He stroked her cheek and said:

"I feel as though our life is already over and that a gray half life is beginning for us. When I knew that my brother Fyodor was hopelessly ill, I shed tears; we spent our childhood and youth together, when I loved him with my whole soul. And now this catastrophe has come, and it seems, too, as though, losing him, I am finally cut away from my past. And when you said just now that we must move into the house in Pyatnitsky Street, to that prison, it began to seem to me that there was no future for me either."

He got up and walked to the window.

"However that may be, one has to give up all thoughts of happiness," he said, looking out into the street. "There is none. I never have had any, and I suppose it doesn't exist at all.

I was happy once in my life, though, when I sat at night under your parasol. Do you remember how you left your parasol at Nina's?" he asked, turning to his wife. "I was in love with you then, and I remember I spent all night sitting under your parasol and was perfectly blissful."

Near the bookcase in the study stood a mahogany chest with bronze fittings where Laptev kept various useless things, including the parasol. He took it out and handed it to his wife.

"Here it is."

Yulia looked for a minute at the parasol, recognized it, and smiled mournfully.

"I remember," she said. "When you proposed to me you held it in your hand." And seeing that he was preparing to go out, she said: "Please come back early if you can. I am dull without you."

And then she went into her own room and gazed for a long time at the parasol.

## 17.

In spite of the complexity of the business and the immense turnover, there were no bookkeepers in the warehouse, and it was impossible to make anything out of the books kept by the cashier in the office. Every day the warehouse was visited by agents, German and English, with whom the clerks talked politics and religion. A man of noble birth, ruined by drink, an ailing, pitiable creature, came to translate the foreign correspondence in the office; the clerks called him a midge and put salt in his tea. And altogether the whole concern struck Laptev as a very queer business.

He went to the warehouse every day and tried to establish a new order of things; he forbade them to thrash the boys and to jeer at the buyers, and was violently angry when the clerks gleefully dispatched to the provinces worthless shop-soiled goods as though they were new and fashionable. Now he was the chief person in the warehouse, but still, as before, he did not know how large his fortune was, whether his business was doing well, how much the senior clerks were paid, and so on. Pochatkin and Makeichev looked upon him as young and inexperienced, concealed a great deal from him, and whispered mysteriously every evening with his blind old father.

It somehow happened at the beginning of June that Laptev went into the Bubnovsky restaurant with Pochatkin to talk business with him over lunch. Pochatkin had been with the Laptevs a long while and had entered their service when he was eight years old. He seemed to belong to them—they trusted him fully; and when on leaving the warehouse he gathered up all the takings from the till and thrust them into his pocket, it never aroused the slightest suspicion. He was the headman in the business and in the house, and also in the church, where he performed the duties of churchwarden in place of his old master. He was nicknamed Malyuta Skuratov on account of his cruel treatment of the boys and clerks under him.

When they went into the restaurant he nodded to a waiter and said:

"Bring us, my lad, half a bodkin and twenty-four unsavories."

After a brief pause the waiter brought on a tray half a bottle of vodka and some plates of various kinds of savories.

"Look here, my good fellow," said Pochatkin. "Give us a plateful of the source of all slander and evil-speaking, with mashed potatoes."

The waiter did not understand; he was puzzled and would have said something, but Pochatkin looked at him sternly and said:

"Except."

The waiter thought intently, then went to consult with his colleagues, and in the end, guessing what was meant, brought a plateful of tongue. When they had drunk a couple of glasses and had had lunch, Laptev asked:

"Tell me, Ivan Vassilich, is it true that our business has been dropping off for the last year?"

"Not a bit of it."

"Tell me frankly and honestly what income we have been making and are making, and what our profits are. We can't go on in the dark. We had a balancing of the accounts at the warehouse lately, but, excuse me, I don't believe in it; you think fit to conceal something from me and only tell the truth to my father. You have been used to being diplomatic from your childhood, and now you can't get on without it. And what's the use of it? So I beg you to be open. What is our position?"

"It all depends upon the fluctuation of credit," Pochatkin answered after a moment's pause.

"What do you understand by the fluctuation of credit?"

Pochatkin began explaining, but Laptev could make nothing of it and sent for Makeichev. The latter promptly made his appearance, had some lunch after saying grace, and in his sedate, mellow baritone began saying first of all that the clerks were in duty bound to pray night and day for their benefactors.

"By all means, only allow me not to consider myself your benefactor," said Laptev.

"Every man ought to remember what he is, and to be conscious of his station. By the grace of God you are a father and benefactor to us, and we are your slaves."

"I am sick of all that!" said Laptev, getting angry. "Please be a benefactor to me now. Please explain the position of our business. Give up looking upon me as a boy, or tomorrow I shall close the business. My father is blind, my brother is in the asylum, my nieces are only children. I hate the business; I should be glad to go away, but there's no one to take my place, as you know. For goodness' sake, drop your diplomacy!"

They went to the warehouse to go into the accounts; then

they went on with them at home in the evening, the old father himself assisting. Initiating his son into his commercial secrets, the old man spoke as though he were engaged, not in trade, but in sorcery. It appeared that the profits of the business were increasing approximately ten percent per annum, and that the Laptevs' fortune, reckoning only money and paper securities, amounted to six million rubles.

When at one o'clock at night, after balancing the accounts, Laptev went out into the open air, he was still under the spell of those figures. It was a still, sultry, moonlight night. The white walls of the houses beyond the river, the heavy barred gates, the stillness and the black shadows combined to give the impression of a fortress, and nothing was wanting to complete the picture but a sentinel with a gun. Laptev went into the garden and sat down on a seat near the fence, which divided them from the neighbor's yard, where there was a garden, too. The bird cherry was in bloom. Laptev remembered that the tree had been just as gnarled and just as big when he was a child, and had not changed at all since then. Every corner of the garden and of the yard recalled the faraway past. And in his childhood, too, just as now, the whole yard bathed in moonlight could be seen through the sparse trees, the shadows had been mysterious and forbidding, a black dog had lain in the middle of the yard, and the clerks' windows had stood wide open. And all these were cheerless memories.

The other side of the fence, in the neighbor's yard, there was a sound of light steps.

"My sweet, my precious . . ." said a man's voice so near the fence that Laptev could hear the man's breathing.

Now they were kissing. Laptev was convinced that the millions and the business which was so distasteful to him were ruining his life and would make him a complete slave. He imagined how, little by little, he would grow accustomed to his position; would, little by little, enter into the part of the head of a great firm; would begin to grow dull and old, die in the end, as the average man usually does die, in a decrepit, soured old age, making everyone about him miserable and depressed. But what hindered him from giving up those millions and that business and leaving that yard and garden which had been hateful to him from his childhood?

The whispering and kisses the other side of the fence disturbed him. He moved into the middle of the yard, and, unbuttoning his shirt over his chest, looked at the moon, and it seemed to him that he would order the gate to be unlocked and would go out and never come back again. His heart ached sweetly with the foretaste of freedom; he laughed joyously and pictured how exquisite, poetical, and even holy, life might be. . . .

But he still stood and did not go away, and kept asking himself: "What keeps me here?" And he felt angry with himself and with the black dog, which still lay stretched on the stone yard, instead of running off to the open country, to the woods, where it would have been free and happy. It was clear that that dog and he were prevented from leaving the yard by the same thing; the habit of bondage, or servitude. . . .

At midday next morning he went to see his wife, and that he might not be dull, asked Yartsev to go with him. Yulia Sergeyevna was staying in a summer villa at Butovo, and he had not been to see her for five days. When they reached the station the friends got into a carriage, and all the way there Yartsev was singing and in raptures over the exquisite weather. The villa was in a great park not far from the station. At the beginning of an avenue, about twenty paces from the gates, Yulia Sergeyevna was sitting under a broad, spreading poplar, waiting for her guests. She had on a light, elegant dress of a pale cream color trimmed with lace, and in her hand she had the old familiar parasol. Yartsev greeted her and went on to the villa from which came the sound of Sasha's and Lida's voices, while Laptev sat down beside her to talk of business matters.

"Why is it you haven't been here for so long?" she said, keeping his hand in hers. "I have been sitting here for days watching for you to come. I miss you so when you are away!"

She stood up and passed her hand over his hair, and scanned his face, his shoulders, his hat, with interest.

"You know I love you," she said, and flushed crimson. "You are precious to me. Here you've come. I see you, and I'm so happy I can't tell you. Well, let us talk. Tell me something."

She had told him she loved him, and he could only feel as though he had been married to her for ten years, and that he was hungry for his lunch. She had put her arm round his neck, tickling his cheek with the silk of her dress; he cautiously removed her hand, stood up, and, without uttering a single word, walked to the villa. The little girls ran to meet him.

"How they have grown!" he thought. "And what changes in these three years. . . . But one may have to live another thirteen years, another thirty years. . . . What is there in store for us in the future? If we live, we shall see."

He embraced Sasha and Lida, who hung upon his neck, and he said:

"Grandpapa sends his love. . . . Uncle Fyodor is dying. Uncle Kostya has sent a letter from America and sends you his love in it. He's bored at the exhibition and will soon be back. And Uncle Alyosha is hungry."

Then he sat on the veranda and saw his wife walking slowly along the avenue towards the house. She was deep in thought; there was a mournful, charming expression in her face, and her eyes were bright with tears. She was not now the slender, fragile, pale-faced girl she used to be; she was a mature, beautiful, vigorous woman. And Laptev saw the enthusiasm with which Yartsev looked at her when he met her, and the way her new, lovely expression was reflected in his face, which looked mournful and ecstatic too. One would have thought that he was seeing her for the first time in his life. And while they were at lunch on the veranda, Yartsev smiled with a sort of joyous shyness and kept gazing at Yulia and at her beautiful neck. Laptev could not help watching them while he thought that he had perhaps another thirteen, another thirty years of life before him. . . . And what would he have to live through in that time? What is in store for us in the future?

And he thought:

"Let us live, and we shall see."

# THE MURDER

## 1.

THE EVENING SERVICE was being celebrated at Progonnaya Station. Before the great icon, painted in glaring colors on a background of gold, stood the crowd of railway servants with their wives and children, and also the timbermen and sawyers who worked close to the railway line. All stood in silence, fascinated by the glare of the lights and the howling of the snowstorm which was aimlessly disporting itself outside, regardless of the fact that it was the Eve of the Annunciation. The old priest from Vedenyapino conducted the service; the sacristan and Matvei Terekhov were singing.

Matvei's face was beaming with delight; he sang stretching out his neck as though he wanted to soar upwards. He sang tenor and chanted the "Praises" too in a tenor voice with honeyed sweetness and persuasiveness. When he sang "Archangel Voices," he waved his arms like a conductor, and, trying to second the sacristan's hollow bass with his tenor, achieved something extremely complex, and from his face it could be seen that he was experiencing great pleasure.

At last the service was over, and they all quietly dispersed, and it was dark and empty again, and there followed that hush which is only known in stations that stand solitary in the open country, or in the forest when the wind howls and nothing else is heard, and when all the emptiness around, all the dreariness of life slowly ebbing away is felt.

Matvei lived not far from the station at his cousin's tavern. But he did not want to go home. He sat down at the refreshment bar and began talking to the waiter in a low voice.

"We had our own choir in the tile factory. And I must tell you that though we were only workmen, our singing was first-rate, splendid. We were often invited to the town, and when the deputy bishop, Father Ivan, took the service at Trinity Church, the bishop's singers sang in the right choir and we in the left. Only they complained in the town that we kept the singing on too long: 'the factory choirs drag it out,' they used to say. It is true we began St. Andrei's prayers and the "Praises" between six and seven, and it was past eleven when we finished, so that it was sometimes after midnight when we got home to the factory. It was good," sighed Matvei. "Very good it was, indeed, Sergei Nikanorich! But here in my father's house it is anything but joyful. The nearest church is four miles away; with my weak health I can't get so far; there are no singers there. And there is no peace or quiet in our family; day in, day out, there is an uproar, scolding, uncleanliness; we all eat out of one bowl like peasants; and there are beetles in the cabbage soup. . . . God has not given me health, else I would have gone away long ago, Sergei Nikanorich."

Matvei Terekhov was a middle-aged man about forty-five, but he had a look of ill-health; his face was wrinkled and his lank, scanty beard was quite gray, and that made him seem many years older. He spoke in a weak voice, circumspectly, and held his chest when he coughed, while his eyes assumed the uneasy and anxious look one sees in very apprehensive people. He never said definitely what was wrong with him, but he was fond of describing at length how once at the factory he had lifted a heavy box and had ruptured himself, and how this had led to "the gripes" and had forced him to give up his work in the tile factory and come back to his native place; but he could not explain what he meant by "the gripes."

"I must own I am not fond of my cousin," he went on, pouring himself out some tea. "He is my elder; it is a sin to censure him, and I fear the Lord, but I cannot bear it in patience. He is a haughty, surly, abusive man; he is the torment of his relations and workmen, and constantly out of humor. Last Sunday I asked him in an amiable way, 'Brother, let us go to Pakhomovo for the Mass!' but he said, 'I am not going; the priest there is a gambler'; and he would not come here today because, he said, the priest from Vedenyapino smokes and drinks vodka. He doesn't like the clergy! He reads Mass himself and the Hours and the Vespers, while his sister acts as sacristan; he says, 'Let us pray unto the Lord'! and she, in a thin little voice like a turkey hen, 'Lord, have mercy upon us! . . .' It's a sin, that's what it is. Every day I say to him, 'Think what you are doing, brother! Repent, brother!' and he takes no notice."

Sergei Nikanorich, the waiter, poured out five glasses of tea and carried them on a tray to the waiting room. He had scarcely gone in when there was a shout:

"Is that the way to serve it, pig's face? You don't know how to wait!"

It was the voice of the stationmaster. There was a timid mutter, then again a harsh and angry shout:

"Get along!"

The waiter came back, greatly crestfallen.

"There was a time when I gave satisfaction to counts and princes," he said in a low voice; "but now I don't know how to serve tea. . . . He called me names before the priest and the ladies!"

The waiter, Sergei Nikanorich, had once had money of his own and had kept a buffet at a first-class station, which was a junction in the principal town of a province. There he had worn a swallow-tail coat and a gold chain. But things had gone ill with him; he had squandered all his own money over expensive fittings and service; he had been robbed by his staff, and, getting gradually into difficulties, had moved to another station less bustling. Here his wife had left him, taking with her all the silver, and he moved to a third station of a still lower class, where no hot dishes were served. Then to a fourth. Frequently changing his situation and sinking lower and lower, he had at last come to Progonnaya, and here he used to sell nothing but tea and cheap vodka, and for lunch hard-boiled eggs and dry sausages, which smelled of tar, and which he himself sarcastically said were only fit for the orchestra. He was bald all over the top of his head, and had prominent blue eyes and thick bushy whiskers, which he often combed out, looking into the little looking glass. Memories of the past haunted him continually; he could never get used to sausage "only fit for the orchestra," to the rudeness of the stationmaster, and to the peasants who used to haggle over the prices, and in his opinion it was as unseemly to haggle over prices in a refreshment room as in a chemist's shop. He was ashamed of his poverty and degradation, and that shame was now the leading interest of his life.

"Spring is late this year," said Matvei, listening. "It's a good job; I don't like spring. In spring it is very muddy, Sergei Nikanorich. In books they write: Spring, the birds sing, the sun is setting, but what is there pleasant in that? A bird is a bird, and nothing more. I am fond of good company, of listening to folks, of talking of religion or singing something agreeable in chorus; but as for nightingales and flowers—bless them, I say!"

He began again about the tile factory, about the choir, but Sergei Nikanorich could not get over his mortification and kept shrugging his shoulders and muttering. Matvei said good-bye and went home.

There was no frost, and the snow was already melting on the roofs, though it was still falling in big flakes; they were whirling rapidly round and round in the air and chasing one another in white clouds along the railway lines. And the oak forest on both sides of the line, in the dim light of the moon, which was hidden somewhere high up in the clouds, resounded with a prolonged sullen murmur. When a violent storm shakes the trees, how terrible they are! Matvei walked along the causeway beside the line, covering his face and his hands, while the wind beat on his back. All at once a little nag, plastered all over with snow, came into sight; a sledge scraped along the bare stones of the causeway, and a peasant, white all over, too, with his head muffled up, cracked his whip. Matvei looked round after him, but at once, as though it had been a vision, there was neither sledge nor peasant to be seen, and he hastened his steps, suddenly scared, though he did not know why.

Here was the crossing and the dark little house where the signalman lived. The barrier was raised, and by it perfect mountains had drifted and clouds of snow were whirling round like witches on broomsticks. At that point the line was crossed by an old highroad, which was still called "the track." On the right, not far from the crossing, by the roadside stood Terekhov's tavern, which had been a posting inn. Here there was always a light twinkling at night.

When Matvei reached home there was a strong smell of incense in all the rooms and even in the entry. His cousin, Yakov Ivanich, was still reading the evening service. In the prayer-room, where this was going on, in the corner opposite the door, there stood a shrine of old-fashioned ancestral icons in gilt settings, and both walls to right and to left were decorated with icons of ancient and modern fashion, in shrines and without them. On the table, which was draped to the floor, stood an icon of the Annunciation, and close by a cypress-wood cross and the censer; wax candles were burning. Beside the table was a reading desk. As he passed by the prayer-room, Matvei stopped and glanced in at the door. Yakov Ivanich was reading at the desk at that moment; his sister Aglaia, a tall lean old woman in a dark blue dress and white kerchief, was praying with him. Yakov Ivanich's daughter Dashutka, an ugly freckled girl of eighteen, was there, too, barefoot as usual, and wearing the dress in which she had at nightfall taken water to the cattle.

"Glory to Thee Who hast shown us the light!" Yakov Ivanich boomed out in a chant, bowing low.

Aglaia propped her chin on her hand and chanted in a thin, shrill, drawling voice. And upstairs, above the ceiling, there was the sound of vague voices which seemed menacing or ominous of evil. No one had lived on the story above since a fire there a long time ago. The windows were boarded up, and empty bottles lay about on the floor between the beams. Now the wind was banging and droning, and it seemed as though someone were running and stumbling over the beams.

Half of the lower story was used as a tavern, while Terekhov's family lived in the other half, so that when drunken visitors were noisy in the tavern every word they said could be heard in the rooms. Matvei lived in a room next to the kitchen, with a big stove, in which, in old days, when this had been a posting inn, bread had been baked every day. Dashutka, who had no room of her own, lived in the same room behind the stove. A cricket chirped there always at night and mice ran in and out.

Matvei lighted a candle and began reading a book which he had borrowed from the station policeman. While he was sitting over it the service ended, and they all went to bed. Dashutka lay down, too. She began snoring at once but soon woke up and said, yawning:

"You shouldn't burn a candle for nothing, Uncle Matvei."

"It's my candle," answered Matvei; "I bought it with my own money."

Dashutka turned over a little and fell asleep again. Matvei sat up a good time longer—he was not sleepy—and when he had finished the last page he took a pencil out of a box and wrote on the book:

"I, Matvei Terekhov, have read this book and think it the very best of all books I have read, for which I express my gratitude to the noncommissioned officer of the Police Department of Railways, Kuzma Nikolaev Zhukov, as the possessor of this priceless book."

He considered it an obligation of politeness to make such inscriptions in other people's books.

## 2.

On Annunciation Day, after the mail train had been seen off, Matvei was sitting in the refreshment bar, talking and drinking tea with lemon in it.

The waiter and Zhukov, the policeman, were listening to him.

"I was, I must tell you," Matvei was saying, "inclined to religion from my earliest childhood. I was only twelve years old when I used to read the epistle in church, and my parents were greatly delighted, and every summer I used to go on a pilgrimage with my dear mother. Sometimes other lads would be singing songs and catching crayfish, while I would be all the time with my mother. My elders commended me, and, indeed, I was pleased myself that I was of such good behavior. And when my mother sent me with her blessing to the factory, I used between working hours to sing tenor there in our choir, and nothing gave me greater pleasure. I needn't say, I drank no vodka, I smoked no tobacco, and lived in chastity; but we all know such a mode of life is displeasing to the enemy of mankind, and he, the unclean spirit, once tried to ruin me and began to darken my mind, just as now with my cousin. First of all, I took a vow to fast every Monday and not to eat meat any day, and as time went on all sorts of fancies came over me. For the first week of Lent down to Saturday the holy fathers have ordained a diet of dry food, but it is no sin for the weak or those who work hard even to drink tea, yet not a crumb passed into my mouth till the Sunday, and afterwards all through Lent I did not allow myself a drop of oil, and on Wednesdays and Fridays I did not touch a morsel at all. It was the same in the lesser fasts. Sometimes in St. Peter's fast our factory lads would have fish soup, while I would sit a little apart from them and suck a dry crust. Different people have different powers, of course, but I can say of myself I did not find fast days hard, and, indeed, the greater the zeal the easier it seems. You are only hungry on the first days of the fast, and then you get used to it; it goes on getting easier, and by the end of a week you don't mind it at all, and there is a numb feeling in your legs as though you were not on earth, but in the clouds. And, besides that, I laid all sorts of penances on myself; I used to get up in the night and pray, bowing down to the ground, used to drag heavy stones from place to place, used to go out barefoot in the snow, and I even wore chains, too. Only, as time went on, you know, I was confessing one day to the priest and suddenly this reflection occurred to me: why, this priest, I thought, is married; he eats meat and smokes tobacco—how can he confess me, and what power has he to absolve my sins if he is more sinful than I? I even scruple to eat Lenten oil, while he eats sturgeon, I dare say. I went to another priest, and he, as ill luck would have it, was a fat fleshy man, in a silk cassock; he rustled like a lady, and he smelled of tobacco, too. I went to fast and confess in the monastery, and my heart was not at ease even there; I kept fancying the monks were not living according to their rules. And after that I could not find a service to my mind: in one place they read the service too fast, in another they sang the wrong prayer, in a third the sacristan stammered. Sometimes, the Lord forgive me a sinner, I would stand in church and my heart would throb with anger. How could one pray, feeling like that? And I fancied that the people in the church did not cross themselves properly, did not listen properly; wherever I looked it seemed to me that they were all drunkards, that they broke the fast, smoked, lived loose lives and played cards. I was the only one who lived according to the commandments. The wily spirit did not slumber; it got worse as it went on. I gave up singing in the choir and I did not go to church at all; since my notion was that I was a righteous man and that the church did not suit me, owing to its imperfections—that is, indeed, like a fallen angel, I was puffed up in my pride beyond all belief. After this I began attempting to make a church for myself. I hired from a deaf woman a tiny little room, a long way out of town near the cemetery, and made a prayer-room like my cousin's, only I had big church candlesticks, too, and a real censer. In this prayer-room of mine I kept the rules of holy Mount Athos—that is, every day my matins began at midnight without fail, and on the eve of the chief of the twelve great holy days my midnight service lasted ten hours and sometimes even twelve. Monks are allowed by rule to sit during the singing of the Psalter and the reading of the Bible, but I wanted to be better than the monks, and so I used to stand all through. I used to read and sing slowly, with tears and sighing, lifting up my hands, and I used to go straight from prayer to work without sleeping; and, indeed, I was always praying at my work, too. Well, it got all over the town 'Matvei is a saint; Matvei heals the sick and the senseless.' I never had healed anyone, of course, but we all know wherever any heresy or false doctrine springs up there's no keeping the female sex away. They are just like flies on the honey. Old maids and females of all sorts came trailing to me, bowing down to my feet, kissing my hands and crying out I was a saint and all the rest of it, and one even saw a halo round my head. It was too crowded in the prayer-room. I took a bigger room, and then we had a regular tower of Babel. The devil got hold of me completely and screened the light from my eyes with his unclean hoofs. We all behaved as though we were frantic. I read, while the old maids and other females sang, and then after standing on their legs for twenty-four hours or longer without eating or drinking, suddenly a trembling would come over them as though they were in a fever; after that, one would begin screaming and then another—it was horrible! I, too, would shiver all over like a Jew in a frying pan, I don't know myself why, and our legs began to prance about. It's a strange thing, indeed: you don't want to, but you prance about and waggle your arms; and after that, screaming and shrieking, we all danced and ran after one another—ran till we dropped; and in that way, in wild frenzy, I fell into fornication."

The policeman laughed, but, noticing that no one else was laughing, became serious and said:

"That's Molokanism. I have heard they are all like that in the Caucasus."

"But I was not killed by a thunderbolt," Matvei went on, crossing himself before the icon and moving his lips. "My dead mother must have been praying for me in the other world. When everyone in the town looked upon me as a saint, and even ladies and gentlemen of good family used to come to me in secret for consolation, I happened to go in to our landlord, Osip Varlamich, to ask forgiveness—it was the Day of Forgiveness—and he fastened the door with the hook, and we were left alone face to face. And he began to reprove me, and I must tell you Osip Varlamich was a man of brains, though without education, and everyone respected and feared him, for he was a man of stern, God-fearing life and worked hard. He had been the mayor of the town, and a warden of the church for twenty years maybe, and had done a great deal of good; he had covered all the New Moscow Road with gravel, had painted the church, and had decorated the columns to look like malachite. Well, he fastened the door, and—'I have been wanting to get at you for a long time, you rascal . . .' he said. 'You think you are a saint,' he said. 'No, you are not a saint, but a backslider from God, a heretic, and an evildoer! . . .' And he went on and on. . . . I can't tell you how he said it, so eloquently and cleverly, as though it were all written down, and so touchingly. He talked for two hours. His words penetrated my soul; my eyes were opened. I listened, listened and—burst into sobs! 'Be an ordinary man,' he said; 'eat and drink, dress and pray like everyone else. All that is above the ordinary is of the devil. Your chains,' he said, 'are of the devil; your fasting is of the devil; your prayer-room is of the devil. It is all pride,' he said. Next day, on Monday in Holy Week, it pleased God I should fall ill. I ruptured myself and was taken to the hospital. I was terribly worried and wept bitterly and trembled. I thought there was a straight road before me from the hospital to hell, and I almost died. I was in misery on a bed of sickness for six months, and when I was discharged the first thing I did I confessed, and took the sacrament in the regular way and became a man again. Osip Varlamich saw me off home and exhorted me: 'Remember, Matvei, that anything above the ordinary is of the devil.' And now I eat and drink like everyone else and pray like everyone else. . . . If it happens now that the priest smells of tobacco or vodka I don't venture to blame him, because the priest, too, of course, is an ordinary man. But as soon as I am told that in the town or in the village a saint has set up who does not eat for weeks and makes rules of his own, I know whose work it is. So that is how I carried on in the past, gentlemen. Now, like Osip Varlamich, I am continually exhorting my cousins and reproaching them, but I am a voice crying in the wilderness. God has not vouchsafed me the gift."

Matvei's story evidently made no impression whatever. Sergei Nikanorich said nothing, but began clearing the refreshments off the counter, while the policeman began talking of how rich Matvei's cousin was.

"He must have thirty thousand at least," he said.

Zhukov, the policeman, a sturdy, well-fed, red-haired man with a full face (his cheeks quivered when he walked), usually sat lolling and crossing his legs when not in the presence of his superiors. As he talked he swayed to and fro and whistled carelessly, while his face had a self-satisfied, replete air, as though he had just had dinner. He was making money, and he always talked of it with the air of a connoisseur. He undertook jobs as an agent, and when anyone wanted to sell an estate, a horse, or a carriage, he applied to Zhukov.

"Yes, it will be thirty thousand, I dare say," Sergei Nikanorich assented. "Your grandfather had an immense fortune," he said, addressing Matvei. "Immense it was; all left to your father and your uncle. Your father died as a young man and your uncle got hold of it all, and afterwards, of course, Yakov Ivanich. While you were going on pilgrimages with your mamma and singing tenor in the factory, they didn't let the grass grow under their feet."

"Fifteen thousand comes to your share," said the policeman, swaying from side to side. "The tavern belongs to you in common, so the capital is in common. Yes. If I were in your place, I should have taken it into court long ago. I would have taken it into court for one thing, and while the case was going on I'd have knocked his face to a jelly."

Yakov Ivanich was disliked because when anyone believes differently from others it upsets even people who are indifferent to religion. The policeman disliked him also because he, too, sold horses and carriages.

"You don't care about going to law with your cousin because you have plenty of money of your own," said the waiter to Matvei, looking at him with envy. "It is all very well for anyone who has means, but here I shall die in this position, I suppose. . . ."

Matvei began declaring that he hadn't any money at all, but Sergei Nikanorich was not listening. Memories of the past and of the insults which he endured every day came showering upon him. His bald head began to perspire; he flushed and blinked.

"A cursed life!" he said with vexation, and he banged a sausage on the floor.

## 3.

The story ran that the tavern had been built in the time of Alexander I by a widow who had settled here with her son; her name was Avdotya Terekhov. The dark roofed-in courtyard and the gates always kept locked excited, especially on moonlight nights, a feeling of depression and unaccountable uneasiness in people who drove by with posting horses, as though sorcerers or robbers were living in it; and the driver always looked back after he had passed, and whipped up his horses. Travelers did not care to put up here, as the people of the house were always unfriendly and charged heavily. The yard was muddy even in summer; huge fat pigs used to lie there in the mud, and the horses in which the Terekhovs dealt wandered about untethered, and often it happened that they ran out of the yard and dashed along the road like mad creatures, terrifying the pilgrim women. At that time there was a great deal of traffic on the road: long trains of loaded wagons trailed by, and all sorts of adventures happened; such as, for instance, that thirty years ago when some wagoners got up a quarrel with a passing merchant and killed him, and a slanting cross is standing to this day half a mile from the tavern; posting chaises with bells and the heavy dormeuses of country gentlemen drove by; and herds of horned cattle passed, bellowing and stirring up clouds of dust.

When the railway came there was at first at this place only a platform, which was called simply a halt; ten years afterwards the present station, Progonnaya, was built. The traffic on the old posting road almost ceased, and only local landowners and peasants drove along it now, but the working people walked there in crowds in spring and autumn. The posting inn was transformed into a restaurant; the upper story was destroyed by fire, the roof had grown yellow with rust, the roof over the yard had fallen by degrees, but huge fat pigs, pink and revolting, still wallowed in the mud in the yard. As before, the horses sometimes ran away and, lashing their tails, dashed madly along the road. In the tavern they sold tea, hay, oats, and flour, as well as vodka and beer, to be drunk on the premises and also to be taken away; they sold spirituous liquors warily, for they had never taken out a license.

The Terekhovs had always been distinguished by their piety, so much so that they had even been given the nickname of the "Godlies." But perhaps because they lived apart like bears, avoided people, and thought out all their ideas for themselves, they were given to dreams and to doubts and to changes of faith, and almost each generation had a peculiar faith of its own. The grandmother Avdotya, who had built the inn, was an Old Believer; her son and both her grandsons (the fathers of Matvei and Yakov) went to the Orthodox church, entertained the clergy, and worshiped before the new icons as devoutly as they had done before the old. The son in old age refused to eat meat and imposed upon himself the rule of silence, considering all conversation as sin; it was the peculiarity of the grandsons that they interpreted the Scripture not simply, but sought in it a hidden meaning, declaring that every sacred word must contain a mystery.

Avdotya's great-grandson Matvei had struggled from early

childhood with all sorts of dreams and fancies and had been almost ruined by it; the other great-grandson, Yakov Ivanich, was orthodox, but after his wife's death he gave up going to church and prayed at home. Following his example, his sister Aglaia had turned, too; she did not go to church herself and did not let Dashutka go. Of Aglaia it was told that in her youth she used to attend the Flagellant meetings in Vedenyapino, and that she was still a Flagellant in secret, and that was why she wore a white kerchief.

Yakov Ivanich was ten years older than Matvei; he was a very handsome tall old man with a big gray beard almost to his waist, and bushy eyebrows which gave his face a stern, even ill-natured expression. He wore a long jerkin of good cloth or a black sheepskin coat, and altogether tried to be clean and neat in dress; he wore galoshes even in dry weather. He did not go to church, because, to his thinking, the services were not properly celebrated and because the priests drank wine at unlawful times and smoked tobacco. Every day he read and sang the service at home with Aglaia. At Vedenyapino they left out the "Praises" at early matins, and had no evening service even on great holidays, but he used to read through at home everything that was laid down for every day, without hurrying or leaving out a single line, and in his spare time read aloud the *Lives of the Saints*. And in everyday life he adhered strictly to the rules of the church; thus, if wine were allowed on some day in Lent, "for the sake of the vigil," then he never failed to drink wine, even if he were not inclined.

He read, sang, burned incense, and fasted, not for the sake of receiving blessings of some sort from God, but for the sake of good order. Man cannot live without religion, and religion ought to be expressed from year to year and from day to day in a certain order, so that every morning and every evening a man might turn to God with exactly those words and thoughts that were befitting that special day and hour. One must live and, therefore, also pray as is pleasing to God, and so every day one must read and sing what is pleasing to God—that is, what is laid down in the rule of the church. Thus the first chapter of St. John must be read only on Easter Day, and "It is most meet" must not be sung from Easter to Ascension, and so on. The consciousness of this order and its importance afforded Yakov Ivanich great gratification during his religious exercises. When he was forced to break this order by some necessity—to drive to town or to the bank, for instance—his conscience was uneasy and he felt miserable.

When his cousin Matvei had returned unexpectedly from the factory and settled in the tavern as though it were his home, he had from the very first day disturbed this settled order. He refused to pray with them, had meals and drank tea at wrong times, got up late, drank milk on Wednesdays and Fridays on the pretext of weak health; almost every day he went into the prayer-room while they were at prayers and cried: "Think what you are doing, brother! Repent, brother!" These words threw Yakov into a fury, while Aglaia could not refrain from beginning to scold. Or at night Matvei would steal into the prayer-room and say softly: "Cousin, your prayer is not pleasing to God. For it is written, First be reconciled with thy brother and then offer thy gift. You lend money at usury, you deal in vodka—repent!"

In Matvei's words Yakov saw nothing but the usual evasions of empty-headed and careless people who talk of loving your neighbor, of being reconciled with your brother, and so on, simply to avoid praying, fasting, and reading holy books, and who talk contemptuously of profit and interest simply because they don't like working. Of course, to be poor, save nothing, put by nothing was a great deal easier than being rich.

But yet he was troubled and could not pray as before. As soon as he went into the prayer-room and opened the book he began to be afraid his cousin would come in and hinder him;

and, in fact, Matvei did soon appear and cry in a trembling voice: "Think what you are doing, brother! Repent, brother!" Aglaia stormed and Yakov, too, flew into a passion and shouted: "Go out of my house!" while Matvei answered him: "The house belongs to both of us."

Yakov would begin singing and reading again, but he could not regain his calm, and unconsciously fell to dreaming over his book. Though he regarded his cousin's words as nonsense, yet for some reason it had of late haunted his memory that it is hard for a rich man to enter the kingdom of heaven, that the year before last he had made a very good bargain over buying a stolen horse, that one day when his wife was alive a drunkard had died of vodka in his tavern. . . .

He slept badly at nights now and woke easily, and he could hear that Matvei, too, was awake, and continually sighing and pining for his tile factory. And while Yakov turned over from one side to another at night he thought of the stolen horse and the drunken man, and what was said in the gospels about the camel.

It looked as though his dreaminess were coming over him again. And as ill luck would have it, although it was the end of March, every day it kept snowing, and the forest roared as though it were winter, and there was no believing that spring would ever come. The weather disposed one to depression, and to quarreling and to hatred, and in the night, when the wind droned over the ceiling, it seemed as though someone were living overhead in the empty story; little by little the broodings settled like a burden on his mind, his head burned, and he could not sleep.

## 4.

On the morning of the Monday before Good Friday, from his room Matvei heard Dashutka say to Aglaia:

"Uncle Matvei said the other day that there is no need to fast."

Matvei remembered the whole conversation he had had the evening before with Dashutka, and he felt hurt all at once.

"Girl, don't do wrong!" he said in a moaning voice, like a sick man. "You can't do without fasting; our Lord Himself fasted forty days. I only explained that fasting does a bad man no good."

"You should just listen to the factory hands; they can teach you goodness," Aglaia said sarcastically as she washed the floor (she usually washed the floors on working days and was always angry with everyone when she did it). "We know how they keep the fasts in the factory. You had better ask that uncle of yours—ask him about his 'Darling,' how he used to guzzle milk on fast days with her, the viper. He teaches others; he forgets about his viper. But ask him who was it he left his money with—who was it?"

Matvei had carefully concealed from everyone, as though it were a foul sore, that during that period of his life when old women and unmarried girls had danced and run about with him at their prayers he had formed a connection with a workingwoman and had had a child by her. When he went home he had given this woman all he had saved at the factory and had borrowed from his landlord for his journey, and now he had only a few rubles which he spent on tea and candles. The "Darling" had informed him later on that the child was dead and asked him in a letter what she should do with the money. This letter was brought from the station by the laborer. Aglaia intercepted it and read it and had reproached Matvei with his "Darling" every day since.

"Just fancy, nine hundred rubles," Alglaia went on. "You gave nine hundred rubles to a viper, no relation, a factory jade, blast you!" She had flown into a passion by now and was shouting shrilly: "Can't you speak? I could tear you to pieces, wretched creature! Nine hundred rubles as though it were a farthing. You might have left it to Dashutka—she is a relation, not a stranger—or else have sent it to Byelev for Marya's poor orphans. And your viper did not choke, may she be thrice accursed, the she-devil! May she never look upon the light of day!"

Yakov Ivanich called to her; it was time to begin the Hours. She washed, put on a white kerchief, and, by now quiet and meek, went into the prayer-room to the brother she loved. When she spoke to Matvei or served peasants in the tavern with tea she was a gaunt, keen-eyed, ill-humored old woman; in the prayer-room her face was serene and softened, she looked younger altogether, she curtseyed affectedly, and even pursed up her lips.

Yakov Ivanich began reading the service softly and dolefully, as he always did in Lent. After he had read a little he stopped to listen to the stillness that reigned through the house, and then went on reading again, with a feeling of gratification; he folded his hands in supplication, rolled his eyes, shook his head, sighed. But all at once there was the sound of voices. The policeman and Sergei Nikanorich had come to see Matvei. Yakov Ivanich was embarrassed at reading aloud and singing when there were strangers in the house, and now, hearing voices, he began reading in a whisper and slowly. In the prayer-room he could hear the waiter say:

"The Tatar at Shchepovo is selling his business for fifteen hundred. He'll take five hundred down and an I.O.U. for the rest. And so, Matvei Vassilich, be so kind as to lend me that five hundred rubles. I will pay you two percent a month."

"What money have I got?" cried Matvei, amazed. "I have no money!"

"Two percent a month will be a godsend to you," the policeman explained. "While lying by, your money is simply eaten by the moth, and that's all that you get from it."

Afterwards the visitors went out and a silence followed. But

Yakov Ivanich had hardly begun reading and singing again when a voice was heard outside the door:

"Brother, let me have a horse to drive to Vedenyapino."

It was Matvei. And Yakov was troubled again.

"Which can you go with?" he asked after a moment's thought. "The man has gone with the sorrel to take the pig, and I am going with the little stallion to Shuteykino as soon as I have finished."

"Brother, why is it you can dispose of the horses and not I?" Matvei asked with irritation.

"Because I am not taking them for pleasure, but for work."

"Our property is in common, so the horses are in common, too, and you ought to understand that, brother."

A silence followed. Yakov did not go on praying, but waited for Matvei to go away from the door.

"Brother," said Matvei, "I am a sick man. I don't want possessions—let them go; you have them, but give me a small share to keep me in my illness. Give it to me and I'll go away."

Yakov did not speak. He longed to be rid of Matvei, but he could not give him money, since all the money was in the business; besides, there had never been a case of the family dividing in the whole history of the Terekhovs. Division means ruin.

Yakov said nothing, but still waited for Matvei to go away, and kept looking at his sister, afraid that she would interfere and that there would be a storm of abuse again as there had been in the morning. When at last Matvei did go Yakov went on reading, but now he had no pleasure in it. There was a heaviness in his head and a darkness before his eyes from continually bowing down to the ground, and he was weary of the sound of his soft dejected voice. When such a depression of spirit came over him at night, he put it down to not being able to sleep; by day it frightened him, and he began to feel as though devils were sitting on his head and shoulders.

Finishing the service after a fashion, dissatisfied and ill-humored, he set off for Shuteykino. In the previous autumn a gang of navvies had dug a boundary ditch near Progonnaya and had run up a bill at the tavern for eighteen rubles, and now he had to find their foreman in Shuteykino and get the money from him. The road had been spoiled by the thaw and the snowstorm; it was of a dark color and full of holes, and in parts it had given way altogether. The snow had sunk away at the sides below the road, so that he had to drive, as it were, upon a narrow causeway, and it was very difficult to turn off it when he met anything. The sky had been overcast ever since the morning and a damp wind was blowing. . . .

A long train of sledges met him; peasant women were carting bricks. Yakov had to turn off the road. His horse sank into the snow up to its belly; the sledge lurched over to the right, and to avoid falling out he bent over to the left, and sat so all the time the sledges moved slowly by him. Through the wind he heard the creaking of the sledge poles and the breathing of the gaunt horses, and the women saying about him, "There's 'Godly' coming," while one, gazing with compassion at his horse, said quickly:

"It looks as though the snow will be lying till Yegory's Day! They are worn out with it!"

Yakov sat uncomfortably huddled up, screwing up his eyes on account of the wind, while horses and red bricks kept passing before him. And perhaps because he was uncomfortable and his side ached, he felt all at once annoyed, and the business he was going about seemed to him unimportant, and he reflected that he might send the laborer next day to Shuteykino. Again, as in the previous sleepless night, he thought of the saying about the camel, and then memories of all sorts crept into his mind: of the peasant who had sold him the stolen horse, of the drunken man, of the peasant women who had brought their samovars to him to pawn. Of course, every merchant tries to get as much as he can, but Yakov felt depressed that he was in trade; he longed to get somewhere far away from this routine, and he felt dreary at the thought that he would have to read the evening service that day. The wind blew straight into his face and soughed in his collar, and it seemed as though it were whispering to him all these thoughts, bringing them from the broad white plain. . . . Looking at that plain, familiar to him from childhood, Yakov remembered that he had had just this same trouble and these same thoughts in his young days when dreams and imaginings had come upon him and his faith had wavered.

He felt miserable at being alone in the open country; he turned back and drove slowly after the sledges, and the women laughed and said: "'Godly' has turned back."

At home nothing had been cooked and the samovar was not heated, owing to the fast, and this made the day seem very long. Yakov Ivanich had long ago taken the horse to the stable, dispatched the flour to the station, and twice taken up the Psalms to read, and yet the evening was still far off. Aglaia had already washed all the floors, and, having nothing to do, was tidying up her chest, the lid of which was pasted over on the inside with labels off bottles. Matvei, hungry and melancholy, sat reading, or went up to the Dutch stove and slowly scrutinized the tiles which reminded him of the factory. Dashutka was asleep; then, waking up, she went to take water to the cattle. When she was getting water from the well the cord broke and the pail fell in. The laborer began looking for a boat hook to get the pail out, and Dashutka, barefooted, with legs as red as a goose's, followed him about in the muddy snow, repeating: "It's too far!" She meant to say that the well was too deep for the hook to reach the bottom, but the laborer did not understand her, and evidently she bothered him, so that he suddenly turned round and abused her in unseemly language. Yakov Ivanich, coming out that moment into the yard, heard

Dashutka answer the laborer in a long rapid stream of choice abuse, which she could only have learned from drunken peasants in the tavern.

"What are you saying, shameless girl!" he cried to her, and he was positively aghast. "What language!"

And she looked at her father in perplexity, dully, not understanding why she should not use those words. He would have admonished her, but she struck him as so savage and benighted; and for the first time he realized that she had no religion. And all this life in the forest, in the snow, with drunken peasants, with coarse oaths, seemed to him as savage and benighted as this girl, and instead of giving her a lecture he only waved his hand and went back into the room.

At that moment the policeman and Sergei Nikanorich came in again to see Matvei. Yakov Ivanich thought that these people, too, had no religion, and that that did not trouble them in the least; and human life began to seem to him as strange, senseless, and unenlightened as a dog's. Bareheaded he walked about the yard, then he went out on to the road, clenching his fists. Snow was falling in big flakes at the time. His beard was blown about in the wind. He kept shaking his head, as though there were something weighing upon his head and shoulders, as though devils were sitting on them; and it seemed to him that it was not himself walking about, but some wild beast, a huge terrible beast, and that if he were to cry out, his voice would be a roar that would sound all over the forest and the plain, and would frighten everyone. . . .

## 5.

When he went back into the house the policeman was no longer there, but the waiter was sitting with Matvei, counting something on the reckoning beads. He was in the habit of coming often, almost every day, to the tavern; in old days he had come to see Yakov Ivanich, now he came to see Matvei. He was continually reckoning on the beads, while his face perspired and looked strained, or he would ask for money or, stroking his whiskers, would describe how he had once been in a first-class station and used to prepare champagne punch for officers, and at grand dinners served the sturgeon soup with his own hands. Nothing in this world interested him but refreshment bars, and he could only talk about things to eat, about wines and the paraphernalia of the dinner table. On one occasion, handing a cup of tea to a young woman who was nursing her baby and wishing to say something agreeable to her, he expressed himself in this way:

"The mother's breast is the baby's refreshment bar."

Reckoning with the beads in Matvei's room, he asked for money; said he could not go on living at Progonnaya, and several times repeated in a tone of voice that sounded as though he were just going to cry:

"Where am I to go? Where am I to go now? Tell me that, please."

Then Matvei went into the kitchen and began peeling some boiled potatoes which he had probably put away from the day before. It was quiet, and it seemed to Yakov Ivanich that the waiter was gone. It was past the time for evening service; he called Aglaia, and, thinking there was no one else in the house, sang out aloud without embarrassment. He sang and read, but was inwardly pronouncing other words, "Lord, forgive me! Lord, save me!" and, one after another, without ceasing, he made low bows to the ground as though he wanted to exhaust himself, and he kept shaking his head, so that Aglaia looked at him with wonder. He was afraid Matvei would come in, and was certain that he would come in, and felt an anger against him which he could overcome neither by prayer nor by continually bowing down to the ground.

Matvei opened the door very softly and went into the prayer-room.

"It's a sin, such a sin!" he said reproachfully, and heaved a sigh. "Repent! Think what you are doing, brother!"

Yakov Ivanich, clenching his fists and not looking at him for fear of striking him, went quickly out of the room. Feeling himself a huge terrible wild beast, just as he had done before on the road, he crossed the passage into the gray, dirty room, reeking with smoke and fog, in which the peasants usually drank tea, and there he spent a long time walking from one corner to the other, treading heavily, so that the crockery jingled on the shelves and the tables shook. It was clear to him now that he was himself dissatisfied with his religion and could not pray as he used to do. He must repent, he must think things over, reconsider, live and pray in some other way. But how pray? And perhaps all this was a temptation of the devil, and nothing of this was necessary? . . . How was it to be? What was he to do? Who could guide him? What helplessness! He stopped and, clutching at his head, began to think, but Matvei's being near him prevented him from reflecting calmly. And he went rapidly into the room.

Matvei was sitting in the kitchen before a bowl of potato, eating. Close by, near the stove, Aglaia and Dashutka were sitting facing one another, spinning yarn. Between the stove and the table at which Matvei was sitting was stretched an ironing board; on it stood a cold iron.

"Sister," Matvei asked, "let me have a little oil!"

"Who eats oil on a day like this?" asked Aglaia.

"I am not a monk, sister, but a layman. And in my weak health I may take not only oil but milk."

"Yes, at the factory you may have anything."

Aglaia took a bottle of Lenten oil from the shelf and banged it angrily down before Matvei with a malignant smile, evidently pleased that he was such a sinner.

"But I tell you, you can't eat oil!" shouted Yakov.

Aglaia and Dashutka started, but Matvei poured the oil into the bowl and went on eating as though he had not heard.

"I tell you, you can't eat oil!" Yakov shouted still more loudly; he turned red all over, snatched up the bowl, lifted it higher than his head, and dashed it with all his force to the ground, so that it flew into fragments. "Don't dare to speak!" he cried in a furious voice, though Matvei had not said a word. "Don't dare!" he repeated, and struck his fist on the table.

Matvei turned pale and got up.

"Brother!" he said, still munching, "brother, think what you are about!"

"Out of my house this minute!" shouted Yakov; he loathed Matvei's wrinkled face, and his voice, and the crumbs on his mustache, and the fact that he was munching. "Out, I tell you!"

"Brother, calm yourself! The pride of hell has confounded you!"

"Hold your tongue!" (Yakov stamped.) "Go away, you devil!"

"If you care to know," Matvei went on in a loud voice, as he, too, began to get angry, "you are a backslider from God and a heretic. The accursed spirits have hidden the true light from you; your prayer is not acceptable to God. Repent before it is too late! The deathbed of the sinner is terrible! Repent, brother!"

Yakov seized him by the shoulders and dragged him away from the table, while Matvei turned whiter than ever, and, frightened and bewildered, began muttering, "What is it? What's the matter?" and, struggling and making efforts to free himself from Yakov's hands, he accidentally caught hold of his shirt near the neck and tore the collar; and it seemed to Aglaia that he was trying to beat Yakov. She uttered a shriek, snatched up the bottle of Lenten oil and with all her force brought it down straight on the skull of the cousin she hated. Matvei reeled, and in one instant his face became calm and indifferent.

Yakov, breathing heavily, excited, and feeling pleasure at the gurgle the bottle had made, like a living thing, when it had struck the head, kept him from falling and several times (he remembered this very distinctly) motioned Aglaia towards the iron with his finger; and only when the blood began trickling through his hands and he heard Dashutka's loud wail, and when the ironing board fell with a crash and Matvei rolled heavily on it, Yakov left off feeling anger and understood what had happened.

"Let him rot, the factory buck!" Aglaia brought out with repulsion, still keeping the iron in her hand. The white bloodstained kerchief slipped on to her shoulders and her gray hair fell in disorder. "He's got what he deserved!"

Everything was terrible. Dashutka sat on the floor near the stove with the yarn in her hands, sobbing, and continually bowing down, uttering at each bow a gasping sound. But nothing was so terrible to Yakov as the potato in the blood, on which he was afraid of stepping, and there was something else terrible which weighed upon him like a bad dream and seemed the worst danger, though he could not take it in for the first minute. This was the waiter, Sergei Nikanorich, who was standing in the doorway with the reckoning beads in his hands, very pale, looking with horror at what was happening in the kitchen. Only when he turned and went quickly into the passage and from there outside, Yakov grasped who it was and followed him.

Wiping his hands on the snow as he went, he reflected. The idea flashed through his mind that their laborer had gone away long before and had asked leave to stay the night at home in the village; the day before they had killed a pig, and there were huge bloodstains in the snow and on the sledge, and even one side of the top of the well was spattered with blood, so that it could not have seemed suspicious even if the whole of Yakov's family had been stained with blood. To conceal the murder would be agonizing, but for the policeman, who would whistle and smile ironically, to come from the station, for the peasants to arrive and bind Yakov's and Aglaia's hands and take them solemnly to the district courthouse and from there to the town, while everyone on the way would point at them and say mirthfully, "They are taking the 'Godlies!'"—this seemed to Yakov more agonizing than anything, and he longed to lengthen out the time somehow, so as to endure this shame not now, but later, in the future.

"I can lend you a thousand rubles . . ." he said, overtaking Sergei Nikanorich. "If you tell anyone, it will do no good. . . . There's no bringing the man back, anyway;" and with difficulty keeping up with the waiter, who did not look round, but tried to walk away faster than ever, he went on: "I can give you fifteen hundred. . . ."

He stopped because he was out of breath, while Sergei Nikanorich walked on as quickly as ever, probably afraid that he would be killed, too. Only after passing the railway crossing and going half the way from the crossing to the station, he furtively looked round and walked more slowly. Lights, red and green, were already gleaming in the station and along the line; the wind had fallen, but flakes of snow were still coming down and the road had turned white again. But just at the station Sergei Nikanorich stopped, thought a minute, and turned resolutely back. It was growing dark.

"Oblige me with the fifteen hundred, Yakov Ivanich," he said, trembling all over. "I agree."

## 6.

Yakov Ivanich's money was in the bank of the town and was invested in second mortgages; he only kept a little at home, just what was wanted for necessary expenses. Going into the kitchen, he felt for the matchbox, and while the sulphur was burning with a blue light he had time to make out the figure of Matvei, which was still lying on the floor near the table, but now it was covered with a white sheet, and nothing could be seen but his boots. A cricket was chirruping. Aglaia and Dashutka were not in the room; they were both sitting behind the counter in the tearoom, spinning yarn in silence. Yakov Ivanich crossed to his own room with a little lamp in his hand, and pulled from under the bed a little box in which he kept his money. This time there were in it four hundred and twenty one-ruble notes and silver to the amount of thirty-five rubles; the notes had an unpleasant heavy smell. Putting the money together in his cap, Yakov Ivanich went out into the yard and then out of the gate. He walked looking from side to side, but there was no sign of the waiter.

"Hi!" cried Yakov.

A dark figure stepped out from the barrier at the railway crossing and came irresolutely towards him.

"Why do you keep walking about?" said Yakov with vexation, as he recognized the waiter. "Here you are; there is a little less than five hundred. . . . I've no more in the house."

"Very well . . . very grateful to you," muttered Sergei Nikanorich, taking the money greedily and stuffing it into his pockets. He was trembling all over, and that was perceptible in spite of the darkness. "Don't worry yourself, Yakov Ivanich. . . . What should I chatter for? I came and went away, that's all I've to do with it. As the saying is, I know nothing and I can tell nothing. . . ." And at once he added with a sigh: "Cursed life!"

For a minute they stood in silence, without looking at each other.

"So it all came from a trifle, goodness knows how . . ." said the waiter, trembling. "I was sitting counting to myself when all at once a noise. . . . I looked through the door, and just on account of Lenten oil you—Where is he now?"

"Lying there in the kitchen."

"You ought to take him away somewhere. . . . Why put it off?"

Yakov accompanied him to the station without a word, then went home again and harnessed the horse to take Matvei to Limarovo. He had decided to take him to the forest of Limarovo, and to leave him there on the road, and then he would tell everyone that Matvei had gone off to Vedenyapino and had not come back, and then everybody would think that he had been killed by someone on the road. He knew there was no deceiving anyone by this, but to move, to do something, to be active was not so agonizing as to sit still and wait. He called Dashutka, and with her carried Matvei out. Aglaia stayed behind to clean up the kitchen.

When Yakov and Dashutka turned back they were detained at the railway crossing by the barrier being let down. A long goods train was passing, dragged by two engines, breathing heavily, and flinging puffs of crimson fire out of their funnels.

The foremost engine uttered a piercing whistle at the crossing in sight of the station.

"It's whistling . . ." said Dashutka.

The train had passed at last, and the signalman lifted the barrier without haste.

"Is that you, Yakov Ivanich? I didn't know you, so you'll be rich."

And then when they had reached home they had to go to bed.

Aglaia and Dashutka made themselves a bed in the tea-room and lay down side by side, while Yakov stretched himself on the counter. They neither said their prayers nor lighted the icon lamp before lying down to sleep. All three lay awake till morning but did not utter a single word, and it seemed to them that all night someone was walking about in the empty story overhead.

Two days later a police inspector and the examining magistrate came from the town and made a search, first in Matvei's room and then in the whole tavern. They questioned Yakov first of all, and he testified that on the Monday Matvei had gone to Vedenyapino to confess, and that he must have been killed by the sawyers who were working on the line.

And when the examining magistrate had asked him how it had happened that Matvei was found on the road, while his cap had turned up at home—surely he had not gone to Vedenyapino without his cap?—and why they had not found a single drop of blood beside him in the snow on the road, though his head was smashed in and his face and chest were black with blood, Yakov was confused, lost his head, and answered:

"I cannot tell."

And just what Yakov had so feared happened: the policeman came, the district police officer smoked in the prayer-room, and Aglaia fell upon him with abuse and was rude to the police inspector; and afterwards when Yakov and Aglaia were led out of the yard, the peasants crowded at the gates and said, "They are taking the 'Godlies!'" and it seemed that they were all glad.

At the inquiry the policeman stated positively that Yakov and Aglaia had killed Matvei in order not to share with him, and that Matvei had money of his own, and that if it was not found at the search evidently Yakov and Aglaia had got hold of it. And Dashutka was questioned. She said that Uncle Matvei and Aunt Aglaia quarreled and almost fought every day over money, and that Uncle Matvei was rich, so much so that he had given someone—"his Darling"—nine hundred rubles.

Dashutka was left alone in the tavern. No one came now to drink tea or vodka, and she divided her time between cleaning up the rooms, drinking mead and eating rolls; but a few days later they questioned the signalman at the railway crossing, and he said that late on Monday evening he had seen Yakov and Dashutka driving from Limarovo. Dashutka, too, was arrested, taken to the town, and put in prison. It soon became known, from what Aglaia said, that Sergei Nikanorich had been present at the murder. A search was made in his room, and money was found in an unusual place, in his snow boots under the stove, and the money was all in small change, three hundred one-ruble notes. He swore he had made this money himself, and that he hadn't been in the tavern for a year, but witnesses testified that he was poor, and had been in great want of money of late, and that he used to go every day to the tavern to borrow from Matvei; and the policeman described how on the day of the murder he had himself gone twice to the tavern with the waiter to help him to borrow. It was recalled at this juncture that on Monday evening Sergei Nikanorich had not been there to meet the passenger train but had gone off somewhere. And he, too, was arrested and taken to the town.

The trial took place eleven months later.

Yakov Ivanich looked much older and much thinner and spoke in a low voice like a sick man. He felt weak, pitiful, lower in stature than anyone else, and it seemed as though his soul, too, like his body, had grown older and wasted, from the pangs of his conscience and from the dreams and imaginings which never left him all the while he was in prison. When it came out that he did not go to church the president of the court asked him:

"Are you a dissenter?"

"I can't tell," he answered.

He had no religion at all now; he knew nothing and understood nothing; and his old belief was hateful to him now, and seemed to him darkness and folly. Aglaia was not in the least subdued, and she still went on abusing the dead man, blaming him for all their misfortunes. Sergei Nikanorich had grown a beard instead of whiskers. At the trial he was red and perspiring, and was evidently ashamed of his gray prison coat and of sitting on the same bench with humble peasants. He defended himself awkwardly, and, trying to prove that he had not been to the tavern for a whole year, got into an altercation with every witness, and the spectators laughed at him. Dashutka had grown fat in prison. At the trial she did not understand the questions put to her, and only said that when they killed Uncle Matvei she was dreadfully frightened, but afterwards she did not mind.

All four were found guilty of murder with mercenary motives. Yakov Ivanich was sentenced to penal servitude for twenty years; Aglaia for thirteen and a half; Sergei Nikanorich to ten; Dashutka to six.

## 7.

Late one evening a foreign steamer stopped in the roads of Dué in Sakhalin and asked for coal. The captain was asked to wait till morning, but he did not want to wait over an hour, saying that if the weather changed for the worse in the night there would be a risk of his having to go off without coal. In the Gulf of Tartary the weather is liable to violent changes in the course of half an hour, and then the shores of Sakhalin are dangerous. And already it had turned fresh, and there was a considerable sea running.

A gang of convicts were sent to the mine from the Voevodsky Prison, the grimmest and most forbidding of all the prisons in Sakhalin. The coal had to be loaded upon barges, and then they had to be towed by a steam cutter alongside the steamer which was anchored more than a quarter of a mile from the coast, and then the unloading and reloading had to begin—an exhausting task when the barge kept rocking against the steamer and the men could scarcely keep on their legs for seasickness. The convicts, only just roused from their sleep, still drowsy, went along the shore, stumbling in the darkness and clanking their fetters. On the left, scarcely visible, was a tall, steep, extremely gloomy-looking cliff, while on the right there was a thick impenetrable mist, in which the sea moaned with a prolonged monotonous sound, "Ah! . . . ah! . . . ah! . . . ah! . . ." And it was only when the overseer was lighting his pipe, casting as he did so a passing ray of light on the escort with a gun and on the coarse faces of two or three of the nearest convicts, or when he went with his lantern close to the water, that the white crests of the foremost waves could be discerned.

One of this gang was Yakov Ivanich, nicknamed among the convicts the "Brush," on account of his long beard. No one had addressed him by his name or his father's name for a long time now; they called him simply Yashka.

He was here in disgrace, as, three months after coming to Siberia, feeling an intense irresistible longing for home, he had succumbed to temptation and run away; he had soon been caught, had been sentenced to penal servitude for life, and given forty lashes. Then he was punished by flogging twice again for losing his prison clothes, though on each occasion they were stolen from him. The longing for home had begun from the very time he had been brought to Odessa, and the convict train had stopped in the night at Progonnaya; and Yakov, pressing to the window, had tried to see his own home, and could see nothing in the darkness. He had no one with whom to talk of home. His sister Aglaia had been sent right across Siberia, and he did not know where she was now. Dashutka was in Sakhalin, but she had been sent to live with some ex-convict in a faraway settlement; there was no news of her except that once a settler who had come to the Voevodsky Prison told Yakov that Dashutka had three children. Sergei Nikanorich was serving as a footman at a government official's at Dué, but he could not reckon on ever seeing him, as Sergei was ashamed of being acquainted with convicts of the peasant class.

The gang reached the mine, and the men took their places on the quay. It was said there would not be any loading, as the weather kept getting worse and the steamer was meaning to set off. They could see three lights. One of them was moving: that was the steam cutter going to the steamer, and it seemed to be coming back to tell them whether the work was to be done or not. Shivering with the autumn cold and the damp sea mist, wrapping himself in his short torn coat, Yakov Ivanich looked intently without blinking in the direction in which lay his home. Ever since he had lived in prison together with men banished here from all ends of the earth—with Russians, Ukrainians, Tatars, Georgians, Chinese, Gypsies, Jews—and ever since he had listened to their talk and watched their sufferings, he had begun to turn again to God, and it seemed to him at last that he had learned the true faith for which all his family, from his grandmother Avdotya down, had so thirsted, which they had sought so long and which they had never found. He knew it all now and understood where God was, and how He was to be served, and the only thing he could not understand was why men's destinies were so diverse, why this simple faith, which other men receive from God for nothing and together with their lives, had cost him such a price that his arms and legs trembled like a drunken man's from all the horrors and agonies which as far as he could see would go on without a break to the day of his death. He looked with strained eyes into the darkness, and it seemed to him that through the thousand miles of that mist he could see home, could see his native province, his district, Progonnaya, could see the darkness, the savagery, the heartlessness, and the dull, sullen, animal indifference of the men he had left there. His eyes were dimmed with tears; but still he gazed into the distance where the pale lights of the steamer faintly gleamed, and his heart ached with yearning for home, and he longed to live, to go back home to tell them there of his new faith and to save from ruin if only one man, and to live without suffering if only for one day.

The cutter arrived, and the overseer announced in a loud voice that there would be no loading.

"Back!" he commanded. "Steady!"

They could hear the hoisting of the anchor chain on the steamer. A strong piercing wind was blowing by now; somewhere on the steep cliff overhead the trees were creaking. Most likely a storm was coming.

# MY LIFE

## THE STORY OF A PROVINCIAL

## 1.

THE SUPERINTENDENT SAID to me: "I only keep you out of regard for your worthy father; but for that you would have been sent flying long ago." I replied to him: "You flatter me too much, Your Excellency, in assuming that I am capable of flying." And then I heard him say: "Take that gentleman away; he gets upon my nerves."

Two days later I was dismissed. And in this way I have, during the years I have been regarded as grown-up, lost nine situations, to the great mortification of my father, the architect of our town. I have served in various departments, but all these nine jobs have been as alike as one drop of water is to another: I had to sit, write, listen to rude or stupid observations, and go on doing so till I was dismissed.

When I came in to my father he was sitting buried in a low armchair with his eyes closed. His dry, emaciated face, with a shade of dark blue where it was shaved (he looked like an old Catholic organist), expressed meekness and resignation. Without responding to my greeting or opening his eyes, he said:

"If my dear wife and your mother were living, your life would have been a source of continual distress to her. I see the Divine Providence in her premature death. I beg you, unhappy boy," he continued, opening his eyes, "tell me: what am I to do with you?"

In the past when I was younger my friends and relations had known what to do with me: some of them used to advise me to volunteer for the army, others to get a job in a pharmacy, and others in the telegraph department; now that I am over twenty-five, that gray hairs are beginning to show on my temples, and that I have been already in the army, and in a pharmacy, and in the telegraph department, it would seem that all earthly possibilities have been exhausted, and people have given up advising me, and merely sigh or shake their heads.

"What do you think about yourself?" my father went on. "By the time they are your age, young men have a secure social position, while look at you: you are a proletarian, a beggar, a burden on your father!"

And as usual he proceeded to declare that the young people of today were on the road to perdition through infidelity, materialism, and self-conceit, and that amateur theatricals ought to be prohibited, because they seduced young people from religion and their duties.

"Tomorrow we shall go together, and you shall apologize to the superintendent and promise him to work conscientiously," he said in conclusion. "You ought not to remain one single day with no regular position in society."

"I beg you to listen to me," I said sullenly, expecting nothing good from this conversation. "What you call a position in society is the privilege of capital and education. Those who have neither wealth nor education earn their daily bread by manual labor, and I see no grounds for my being an exception."

"When you begin talking about manual labor it is always stupid and vulgar!" said my father with irritation. "Understand, you dense fellow—understand, you addlepate, that besides coarse physical strength you have the divine spirit, a spark of the holy fire, which distinguishes you in the most striking way from the ass or the reptile, and brings you nearer to the Deity! This fire is the fruit of the efforts of the best of mankind during thousands of years. Your great-grandfather Poloznev, the general, fought at Borodino; your grandfather was a poet, an orator, and a Marshal of Nobility; your uncle is a schoolmaster; and lastly, I, your father, am an architect! All the Poloznevs have guarded the sacred fire for you to put it out!"

"One must be just," I said. "Millions of people put up with manual labor."

"And let them put up with it! They don't know how to do anything else! Anybody, even the most abject fool or criminal, is capable of manual labor; such labor is the distinguishing mark of the slave and the barbarian, while the holy fire is vouchsafed only to a few!"

To continue this conversation was unprofitable. My father worshiped himself, and nothing was convincing to him but what he said himself. Besides, I knew perfectly well that the disdain with which he talked of physical toil was founded not so much on reverence for the sacred fire as on a secret dread that I should become a workman and should set the whole town talking about me; what was worse, all my contemporaries had long ago taken their degrees and were getting on well, and the son of the manager of the State Bank was already a collegiate assessor, while I, my father's only son, was nothing! To continue the conversation was unprofitable and unpleasant, but I still sat on and feebly retorted, hoping that I might at last be understood. The whole question, of course, was clear and simple, and only concerned with the means of my earning my living; but the simplicity of it was not seen, and I was talked to in mawkishly rounded phrases of Borodino, of the sacred fire, of my uncle a forgotten poet, who had once written poor and artificial verses; I was rudely called an addlepate and a dense fellow. And how I longed to be understood! In spite of everything, I loved my father and my sister and it had been my habit from childhood to consult them—a habit so deeply rooted that I doubt whether I could ever have got rid of it; whether I were in the right or the wrong, I was in constant dread of wounding them, constantly afraid that my father's thin neck would turn crimson and that he would have a stroke.

"To sit in a stuffy room," I began, "to copy, to compete with a typewriter, is shameful and humiliating for a man of my age. What can the sacred fire have to do with it?"

"It's intellectual work, anyway," said my father. "But that's enough; let us cut short this conversation, and in any case I warn you: if you don't go back to your work again, but follow your contemptible propensities, then my daughter and I will banish you from our hearts. I shall strike you out of my will, I swear by the living God!"

With perfect sincerity to prove the purity of the motives by which I wanted to be guided in all my doings, I said:

"The question of inheritance does not seem very important to me. I shall renounce it all beforehand."

For some reason or other, quite to my surprise, these words were deeply resented by my father. He turned crimson.

"Don't dare to talk to me like that, stupid!" he shouted in a thin, shrill voice. "Wastrel!" and with a rapid, skillful, and habitual movement he slapped me twice in the face. "You are forgetting yourself."

When my father beat me as a child I had to stand up straight, with my hands held stiffly to my trouser seams, and look him straight in the face. And now when he hit me I was utterly overwhelmed, and, as though I were still a child, drew myself up and tried to look him in the face. My father was old and very thin, but his delicate muscles must have been as strong as leather, for his blows hurt a good deal.

I staggered back into the passage, and there he snatched up his umbrella, and with it hit me several times on the head and shoulders; at that moment my sister opened the drawing-room door to find out what the noise was, but at once turned away with a look of horror and pity without uttering a word in my defense.

My determination not to return to the government office, but to begin a new life of toil, was not to be shaken. All that was left for me to do was to fix upon the special employment, and there was no particular difficulty about that, as it seemed to me that I was very strong and fitted for the very heaviest labor. I was faced with a monotonous life of toil in the midst of hunger, coarseness, and stench, continually preoccupied with earning my daily bread. And—who knows?—as I returned from my work along Great Dvoryansky Street, I might very likely envy Dolzhikov, the engineer, who lived by intellectual work, but, at the moment, thinking over all my future hardships made me lighthearted. At times I had dreamed of spiritual activity, imagining myself a teacher, a doctor, or a writer, but these dreams remained dreams. The taste for intellectual pleasures—for the theater, for instance, and for reading—was a passion with me, but whether I had any ability for intellectual work I don't know. At school I had had an unconquerable aversion for Greek, so that I was only in the fourth class when they had to take me from school. For a long while I had coaches preparing me for the fifth class. Then I served in various government offices, spending the greater part of the day in complete idleness, and I was told that was intellectual work. My activity in the scholastic and official sphere had required neither mental application nor talent, nor special qualifications, nor creative impulse; it was mechanical. Such intellectual work I put on a lower level than physical toil; I despise it, and I don't think that for one moment it could serve as a justification for an idle, careless life, as it is indeed nothing but a sham, one of the forms of that same idleness. Real intellectual work I have in all probability never known.

Evening came on. We lived in Great Dvoryansky Street; it was the principal street in the town, and in the absence of decent public gardens our beau monde used to use it as a promenade in the evenings. This charming street did to some extent take the place of a public garden, as on each side of it there was a row of poplars which smelled sweet, particularly after rain, and acacias, tall bushes of lilac, wild cherries and apple trees hung over the fences and palings. The May twilight, the tender young greenery with its shifting shades, the scent of the lilac, the buzzing of the insects, the stillness, the warmth—how fresh and marvelous it all is, though spring is repeated every year! I stood at the garden gate and watched the passers-by. With most of them I had grown up and at one time played pranks; now they might have been disconcerted by my being near them, for I was poorly and unfashionably dressed, and they used to say of my very narrow trousers and huge, clumsy boots that they were like sticks of macaroni stuck in boats. Besides, I had a bad reputation in the town because I had no decent social position, and used often to play billiards in cheap taverns, and also, perhaps, because I had on two occasions been hauled up before an officer of the police, though I had done nothing whatever to account for this.

In the big house opposite someone was playing the piano at Dolzhikov's. It was beginning to get dark, and stars were twinkling in the sky. Here my father, in an old top hat with wide upturned brim, walked slowly by with my sister on his arm, bowing in response to greetings.

"Look up," he said to my sister, pointing to the sky with the same umbrella with which he had beaten me that afternoon. "Look up at the sky! Even the tiniest stars are all worlds! How insignificant is man in comparison with the universe!"

And he said this in a tone that suggested that it was particularly agreeable and flattering to him that he was so insignificant. How absolutely devoid of talent and imagination he was! Sad to say, he was the only architect in the town, and in the fifteen to twenty years that I could remember not one single decent house had been built in it. When anyone asked him to plan a house, he usually drew first the reception hall and drawing-room: just as in old days the boarding-school misses always started from the stove when they danced, so his artistic ideas could only begin and develop from the hall and drawing-room. To them he tacked on a dining-room, a nursery, a study, linking the rooms together with doors, and so they all inevitably turned into passages, and every one of them had two or even three unnecessary doors. His imagination must have been lacking in clearness, extremely muddled, curtailed. As though feeling that something was lacking, he invariably had recourse to all sorts of outbuildings, planting one beside another; and I can see now the narrow entries, the pokey little passages, the crooked staircases leading to half landings where one could not stand upright, and where, instead of a floor, there were three huge steps like the shelves of a bathhouse; and the kitchen was invariably in the basement with a brick floor and vaulted ceilings. The front of the house had a harsh, stubborn expression; the lines of it were stiff and timid; the roof was low-pitched and, as it were, squashed down; and the fat, well-fed-looking chimneys were invariably crowned by wire caps with squeaking black cowls. And for some reason all these houses, built by my father exactly like one another, vaguely reminded me of his top hat and the back of his head, stiff and stubborn-looking. In the course of years they have grown used in the town to the poverty of my father's imagination. It has taken root and become our local style.

This same style my father had brought into my sister's life also, beginning with christening her Kleopatra (just as he had named me Misail). When she was a little girl he scared her by references to the stars, to the sages of ancient times, to our ancestors, and discoursed at length on the nature of life and duty; and now, when she was twenty-six, he kept up the same habits, allowing her to walk arm in arm with no one but himself, and imagining for some reason that sooner or later a suitable young man would be sure to appear, and desire to enter into matrimony with her from respect for her father's personal qualities. She adored my father, feared him, and believed in his exceptional intelligence.

It was quite dark, and gradually the street grew empty. The music had ceased in the house opposite; the gate was thrown wide open, and a team with three horses trotted frolicking along our street with a soft tinkle of little bells. That was the engineer going for a drive with his daughter. It was bedtime.

I had my own room in the house, but I lived in a shed in the yard, under the same roof as a brick barn which had been built some time or other, probably to keep harness in; great hooks were driven into the wall. Now it was not wanted, and for the last thirty years my father had stowed away in it his newspapers, which for some reason he had bound in half-yearly volumes and allowed nobody to touch. Living here, I was less liable to be seen by my father and his visitors, and I fancied that if I did not live in a real room, and did not go into the house every day to dinner, my father's words that I was a burden upon him did not sound so offensive.

My sister was waiting for me. Unseen by my father, she had brought me some supper: not a very large slice of cold veal and a piece of bread. In our house such sayings as: "A penny saved is a penny gained," and "Take care of the pence and the pounds will take care of themselves," and so on, were frequently repeated, and my sister, weighed down by these vulgar maxims, did her utmost to cut down the expenses, and so we fared badly. Putting the plate on the table, she sat down on my bed and began to cry.

"Misail," she said, "what a way to treat us!"

She did not cover her face; her tears dropped on her bosom and hands, and there was a look of distress on her face. She fell back on the pillow, and abandoned herself to her tears, sobbing and quivering all over.

"You have left the service again . . ." she articulated. "Oh, how awful it is!"

"But do understand, Sister, do understand . . ." I said, and I was overcome with despair because she was crying.

As ill luck would have it, the kerosene in my little lamp was exhausted; it began to smoke and was on the point of going out, and the old hooks on the walls looked down sullenly, and their shadows flickered.

"Have mercy on us," said my sister, sitting up. "Father is in terrible distress and I am ill; I shall go out of my mind. What will become of you?" she said, sobbing and stretching out her arms to me. "I beg you, I implore you, for our dear mother's sake, I beg you to go back to the office!"

"I can't, Kleopatra!" I said, feeling that a little more and I should give way. "I cannot!"

"Why not?" my sister went on. "Why not? Well, if you can't get on with the head, look out for another post. Why shouldn't you get a situation on the railway, for instance? I have just been talking to Anyuta Blagovo; she declares they would take you on the railway line and even promised to try and get a post for you. For God's sake, Misail, think a little! Think a little, I implore you."

We talked a little longer and I gave way. I said that the thought of a job on the railway that was being constructed had never occurred to me, and that if she liked I was ready to try it.

She smiled joyfully through her tears and squeezed my hand, and then went on crying because she could not stop, while I went to the kitchen for some kerosene.

## 2.

Among the devoted supporters of amateur theatricals, concerts, and tableaux vivants for charitable objects the Azhogins, who lived in their own house in Great Dvoryansky Street, took a foremost place; they always provided the room and took upon themselves all the troublesome arrangements and the expenses. They were a family of wealthy landowners who had an estate of some nine thousand acres in the district and a capital house, but they did not care for the country and lived winter and summer alike in the town. The family consisted of the mother, a tall, spare, refined lady, with short hair, a short jacket, and a flat-looking skirt in the English fashion, and three daughters who, when they were spoken of, were called not by their names but simply: the eldest, the middle, and the youngest. They all had ugly sharp chins, and were shortsighted and round-shouldered. They were dressed like their mother, they lisped disagreeably, and yet, in spite of that, infallibly took part in every performance and were continually doing something with a charitable object—acting, reciting, singing. They were very serious and never smiled, and even in a musical comedy they played without the faintest trace of gaiety, with a businesslike air, as though they were engaged in bookkeeping.

I loved our theatricals, especially the numerous, noisy, and rather incoherent rehearsals, after which they always gave a supper. In the choice of the plays and the distribution of the parts I had no hand at all. The post assigned to me lay behind the scenes. I painted the scenes, copied out the parts, prompted, made up the actors' faces; and I was entrusted, too, with various stage effects such as thunder, the singing of nightingales, and so on. Since I had no proper social position and no decent clothes, at the rehearsals I held aloof from the rest in the shadows of the wings and maintained a shy silence.

I painted the scenes at the Azhogins' either in the barn or in the yard. I was assisted by Andrei Ivanov, a house painter, or, as he called himself, a contractor for all kinds of house decorations, a tall, very thin, pale man of fifty, with a hollow chest, with sunken temples, with blue rings round his eyes, rather terrible to look at in fact. He was afflicted with some internal malady, and every autumn and spring people said that he wouldn't recover, but after being laid up for a while he would get up and say afterwards with surprise: "I have escaped dying again."

In the town he was called Radish, and they declared that this was his real name. He was as fond of the theater as I was, and as soon as rumors reached him that a performance was being got up he threw aside all his work and went to the Azhogins' to paint scenes.

The day after my talk with my sister, I was working at the Azhogins' from morning till night. The rehearsal was fixed for seven o'clock in the evening, and an hour before it began all the amateurs were gathered together in the hall, and the eldest, the middle, and the youngest Azhogins were pacing about the stage, reading from manuscript books. Radish, in a long rusty-red overcoat and a scarf muffled round his neck, already stood leaning with his head against the wall, gazing with a devout expression at the stage. Madam Azhogin went up first to one and then to another guest, saying something agreeable to each. She had a way of gazing into one's face and speaking softly as though telling a secret.

"It must be difficult to paint scenery," she said softly, coming up to me. "I was just talking to Madam Mufke about superstitions when I saw you come in. My goodness, my whole life I have been waging war against superstitions! To convince the servants what nonsense all their terrors are, I always light three candles, and begin all my important undertakings on the thirteenth of the month."

Dolzhikov's daughter came in, a plump, fair beauty, dressed, as people said, in everything from Paris. She did not act, but a chair was set for her on the stage at the rehearsals, and the performances never began till she had appeared in the front row, dazzling and astounding everyone with her fine clothes. As a product of the capital she was allowed to make remarks during the rehearsals; and she did so with a sweet indulgent smile, and one could see that she looked upon our performance as a childish amusement. It was said she had studied singing at the Petersburg Conservatory, and even sang for a whole winter in a private opera. I thought her very charming, and I usually watched her through the rehearsals and performances without taking my eyes off her.

I had just picked up the manuscript book to begin prompting when my sister suddenly made her appearance. Without taking off her cloak or hat, she came up to me and said:

"Come along, I beg you."

I went with her. Anyuta Blagovo, also in her hat and wearing a dark veil, was standing behind the scenes at the door. She was the daughter of the assistant president of the court, who had held that office in our town almost ever since the establishment of the circuit court. Since she was tall and had a good figure, her assistance was considered indispensable for tableaux vivants, and when she represented a fairy or something like Glory her face burned with shame; but she took no part in dramatic performances, and came to the rehearsals only for a moment on some special errand and did not go into the hall. Now, too, it was evident that she had only looked in for a minute.

"My father was speaking about you," she said drily, blushing and not looking at me. "Dolzhikov has promised you a post on the railway line. Apply to him tomorrow; he will be at home."

I bowed and thanked her for the trouble she had taken.

"And you can give up this," she said, indicating the exercise book.

My sister and she went up to Madam Azhogin and for two minutes they were whispering with her looking towards me; they were consulting about something.

"Yes, indeed," said Madam Azhogin, softly coming up to me and looking intently into my face. "Yes, indeed, if this distracts you from serious pursuits"—she took the manuscript book from my hands—"you can hand it over to someone else; don't distress yourself, my friend, go home, and good luck to you."

I said good-bye to her and went away overcome with confusion. As I went down the stairs I saw my sister and Anyuta Blagovo going away; they were hastening along, talking eagerly about something, probably about my going into the railway service. My sister had never been at a rehearsal before, and now she was most likely conscience-stricken and afraid her father might find out that, without his permission, she had been to the Azhogins'!

I went to Dolzhikov's next day between twelve and one. The footman conducted me into a very beautiful room, which was the engineer's drawing-room, and, at the same time, his working study. Everything here was soft and elegant, and, for a man so unaccustomed to luxury as I was, it seemed strange. There were costly rugs, huge armchairs, bronzes, pictures, gold and plush frames; among the photographs scattered about the walls there were very beautiful women, clever, lovely faces, easy attitudes; from the drawing-room there was a door leading straight into the garden on to a veranda: one could see lilac trees; one could see a table laid for lunch, a number of bottles, a bouquet of roses; there was a fragrance of spring and expensive cigars, a fragrance of happiness—and everything seemed as though it would say: "Here is a man who has lived and labored and has attained at last the happiness possible on earth."

The engineer's daughter was sitting at the writing table, reading a newspaper.

"You have come to see my father?" she asked. "He is having a shower bath; he will be here directly. Please sit down and wait."

I sat down.

"I believe you live opposite?" she questioned me, after a brief silence.

"Yes."

"I am so bored that I watch you every day out of the window; you must excuse me," she went on, looking at the newspaper. "And I often see your sister; she always has such a look of kindness and concentration."

Dolzhikov came in. He was rubbing his neck with a towel.

"Papa, Monsieur Poloznev," said his daughter.

"Yes, yes, Blagovo was telling me." He turned briskly to me without giving me his hand. "But listen, what can I give you? What sort of posts have I got? You are a queer set of people!" he went on aloud in a tone as though he were giving me a lecture. "A score of you keep coming to me every day; you imagine I am the head of a department! I am constructing a railway line, my friends; I have employment for heavy labor: I need mechanics, smiths, navvies, carpenters, well sinkers, and none of you can do anything but sit and write! You are all clerks."

And he seemed to me to have the same air of happiness as his rugs and easy chairs. He was stout and healthy, ruddy-cheeked and broad-chested, in a print cotton shirt and full trousers like a toy china sledge driver. He had a curly, round beard—and not a single gray hair—a hooked nose, and clear, dark, guileless eyes.

"What can you do?" he went on. "There is nothing you can do! I am an engineer. I am a man of an assured position, but before they gave me a railway line I was for years in harness; I have been a practical mechanic. For two years I worked in

Belgium as an oiler. You can judge for yourself, my dear fellow; what kind of work can I offer you?"

"Of course that is so . . ." I muttered in extreme confusion, unable to face his clear, guileless eyes.

"Can you work the telegraph, anyway?" he asked, after a moment's thought.

"Yes, I have been a telegraph clerk."

"Hm! Well, we will see then. Meanwhile, go to Dubechnya. I have got a fellow there, but he is a wretched creature."

"And what will my duties consist of?" I asked.

"We shall see. Go there; meanwhile I will make arrangements. Only please don't get drunk, and don't worry me with requests of any sort, or I shall send you packing."

He turned away from me without even a nod.

I bowed to him and his daughter, who was reading a newspaper, and went away. My heart felt so heavy that when my sister began asking me how the engineer had received me, I could not utter a single word.

I got up early in the morning, at sunrise, to go to Dubechnya. There was not a soul in out Great Dvoryansky Street; everyone was asleep, and my footsteps rang out with a solitary, hollow sound. The poplars, covered with dew, filled the air with soft fragrance. I was sad and did not want to go away from the town. I was fond of my native town. It seemed to be so beautiful and so snug! I loved the fresh greenery, the still, sunny morning, the chiming of our bells; but the people with whom I lived in this town were boring, alien to me, sometimes even repulsive. I did not like them nor understand them.

I did not understand what these sixty-five thousand people lived for and by. I knew that Kimry lived by boots, that Tula made samovars and guns, that Odessa was a seaport, but what our town was, and what it did, I did not know. Great Dvoryansky Street and the two other smartest streets lived on the interest of capital, or on salaries received by officials from the public treasury; but what the other eight streets, which ran parallel for over two miles and vanished beyond the hills, lived upon was always an insoluble riddle to me. And the way those people lived one is ashamed to describe! No garden, no theater, no decent band; the public library and the club library were only visited by Jewish youths, so that the magazines and new books lay for months uncut; rich and well-educated people slept in close, stuffy bedrooms, on wooden bedsteads infested with bugs; their children were kept in revoltingly dirty rooms called nurseries, and the servants, even the old and respected ones, slept on the floor in the kitchen, covered with rags. On ordinary days the houses smelled of beetroot soup, and on fast days of sturgeon cooked in sunflower oil. The food was not good, and the drinking water was unwholesome. In the town council, at the governor's, at the head priest's, on all sides in private houses, people had been saying for years and years that our town had not a good and cheap water supply, and that it was necessary to obtain a loan of two hundred thousand from the Treasury for laying on water; very rich people, of whom three dozen could have been counted up in our town, and who at times lost whole estates at cards, drank the polluted water, too, and talked all their lives with great excitement of a loan for the water supply—and I did not understand that; it seemed to me it would have been simpler to take the two hundred thousand out of their own pockets and lay it out on that object.

I did not know one honest man in the town. My father took bribes and imagined that they were given him out of respect for his moral qualities; at the high school, in order to be moved up rapidly from class to class, the boys went to board with their teachers, who charged them exorbitant sums; the wife of the military commander took bribes from the recruits when they were called up before the board and even deigned to accept refreshments from them, and on one occasion could not get up from her knees in church because she was drunk; the doctors took bribes, too, when the recruits came up for examination, and the town doctor and the veterinary surgeon levied a regular tax on the butchers' shops and the restaurants; at the district school they did a trade in certificates, qualifying for partial exemption from military service; the higher clergy took bribes from the humbler priests and from the church elders; at the municipal, the artisans', and all the other boards every petitioner was pursued by a shout: "Don't forget your thanks!" and the petitioner would turn back to give sixpence or a shilling. And those who did not take bribes, such as the higher officials of the Department of Justice, were haughty, offered two fingers instead of shaking hands, were distinguished by the frigidity and narrowness of their judgments, spent a great deal of time over cards, drank to excess, married heiresses, and undoubtedly had a pernicious corrupting influence on those around them. It was only the girls who had still the fresh fragrance of moral purity; most of them had higher impulses, pure and honest hearts; but they had no understanding of life and believed that bribes were given out of respect for moral qualities, and after they were married grew old quickly, let themselves go completely, and sank hopelessly in the mire of vulgar, petty bourgeois existence.

## 3.

A railway line was being constructed in our neighborhood. On the eve of feast days the streets were thronged with ragged fellows whom the townspeople called "navvies," and of whom they were afraid. And more than once I had see one of these tatterdemalions, with a blood-stained countenance, being led to the police station, while a samovar or some linen, wet from the wash, was carried behind by way of material evidence. The navvies usually congregated about the taverns and the market place; they drank, ate, and used bad language, and pursued with shrill whistles every woman of light behavior who passed by. To entertain this hungry rabble our shopkeepers made cats and dogs drunk with vodka, or tied an old kerosene can to a dog's tail; a hue and cry was raised, and the dog dashed along the street, jingling the can, squealing with terror; it fancied some monster was close upon its heels; it would run far out of the town into the open country and there sink exhausted. There were in the town several dogs who went about trembling with their tails between their legs; and people said this diversion had been too much for them and had driven them mad.

A station was being built four miles from the town. It was said that the engineers asked for a bribe of fifty thousand rubles for bringing the line right up to the town, but the town council would only consent to give forty thousand; they could not come to an agreement over the difference, and now the townspeople regretted it, as they had to make a road to the station and that, it was reckoned, would cost more. The sleepers and rails had been laid throughout the whole length of the line, and trains ran up and down it, bringing building materials and laborers, and further progress was only delayed on account of the bridges which Dolzhikov was building, and some of the stations were not yet finished.

Dubechnya, as our first station was called, was a little under twelve miles from the town. I walked. The cornfields, bathed in the morning sunshine, were bright green. It was a flat, cheerful country, and in the distance there were the distinct outlines of the station, of ancient barrows, and faraway homesteads. . . . How nice it was out there in the open! And how I longed to be filled with the sense of freedom, if only for that one morning, that I might not think of what was being done in the town, not think of my needs, not feel hungry!

Nothing has so marred my existence as an acute feeling of hunger, which made images of buckwheat porridge, rissoles, and baked fish mingle strangely with my best thoughts. Here I was, standing alone in the open country, gazing upward at a lark which hovered in the air at the same spot, trilling as though in hysterics, and meanwhile I was thinking: "How nice it would be to eat a piece of bread and butter!" Or I would sit down by the roadside to rest, and shut my eyes to listen to the delicious sounds of May, and what haunted me was the smell of hot potatoes. Though I was tall and strongly built, I had as a rule little to eat, and so the predominant sensation throughout the day was hunger, and perhaps that was why I knew so well how it is that such multitudes of people toil merely for their daily bread and can talk of nothing but things to eat.

At Dubechnya they were plastering the inside of the station and building a wooden upper story to the pumping shed. It was hot; there was a smell of lime, and the workmen sauntered listlessly between the heaps of shavings and mortar rubble. The pointsman lay asleep near his sentry box, and the sun was blazing full on his face. There was not a single tree. The telegraph wire hummed faintly and hawks were perching on it here and there. I, wandering, too, among the heaps of rubbish, and not knowing what to do, recalled how the engineer, in answer to my question what my duties would consist in, had said: "We shall see when you are there"; but what could one see in that wilderness?

The plasterers spoke of the foreman, and of a certain Fyodot Vasilyev. I did not understand, and gradually I was overcome by depression—the physical depression in which one is conscious of one's arms and legs and huge body and does not know what to do with them or where to put them.

After I had been walking about for at least a couple of hours, I noticed that there were telegraph poles running off to the right from the station, and that they ended a mile or a mile and a half away at a white stone wall. The workmen told me the office was there, and at last I reflected that that was where I ought to go.

It was a very old manor house, deserted long ago. The wall round it, of porous white stone, was moldering and had fallen away in places, and the lodge, the blank wall of which looked out on the open country, had a rusty roof with patches of tin plate gleaming here and there on it. Within the gates could be seen a spacious courtyard overgrown with rough weeds, and an old manor house with sun blinds on the windows, and a high roof red with rust. Two lodges, exactly alike, stood one on each side of the house to right and to left: one had its windows nailed up with boards; near the other, of which the windows were open, there was washing on the line, and there were calves moving about. The last of the telegraph poles stood in the courtyard, and the wire from it ran to the window of that lodge whose blank wall looked out into the open country. The door stood open; I went in. By the telegraph apparatus a gentleman with a curly dark head, wearing a reefer coat made of sailcloth, was sitting at a table; he glanced at me morosely from under his brows but immediately smiled and said:

"Hullo, Better-than-nothing!"

It was Ivan Cheprakov, an old schoolfellow of mine, who had been expelled from the second class for smoking. We used at one time, during autumn, to catch goldfinches, finches, and linnets together, and to sell them in the market early in the morning, while our parents were still in their beds. We watched for flocks of migrating starlings and shot at them with small shot; then we picked up those that were wounded, and some of them died in our hands in terrible agonies (I remember to this day how they moaned in the cage at night); those that recovered we sold and swore with the utmost effrontery that they were all cocks. On one occasion at the market I had only one starling left, which I had offered to purchasers in vain, till at last I sold it for a farthing. "Anyway, it's better than nothing," I said to comfort myself, as I put the farthing in my pocket, and from that day the street urchins and the schoolboys called after me: "Better-than-nothing;" and to this day the street boys and the shopkeepers mock at me with the nickname, though no one remembers how it arose.

Cheprakov was not of robust constitution: he was narrow-chested, round-shouldered, and long-legged. He wore a silk cord for a tie, had no trace of a waistcoat, and his boots were worse than mine, with the heels trodden down on one side. He stared, hardly even blinking, with a strained expression, as though he were just going to catch something, and he was always in a fuss.

"You wait a minute," he would say fussily. "You listen. . . . Whatever was I talking about?"

We got into conversation. I learned that the estate on which I now was had until recently been the property of the Cheprakovs, and had only the autumn before passed into the possession of Dolzhikov, who considered it more profitable to put his money into land than to keep it in notes, and had already bought up three good-sized mortgaged estates in our neighborhood. At the sale Cheprakov's mother had reserved for herself the right to live for the next two years in one of the lodges at the side and had obtained a post for her son in the office.

"I should think he could buy!" Cheprakov said of the engineer. "See what he fleeces out of the contractors alone! He fleeces everyone!"

Then he took me to dinner, deciding fussily that I should live with him in the lodge and have my meals from his mother.

"She is a bit stingy," he said, "but she won't charge you much."

It was very cramped in the little rooms in which his mother lived; they were all, even the passage and the entry, piled up with furniture which had been brought from the big house after the sale; and the furniture was all old-fashioned mahogany.

Madam Cheprakov, a very stout middle-aged lady with slanting Chinese eyes, was sitting in a big armchair by the window, knitting a stocking. She received me ceremoniously.

"This is Poloznev, Mamma," Cheprakov introduced me. "He is going to serve here."

"Are you a nobleman?" she asked in a strange, disagreeable voice: it seemed to me to sound as though fat were bubbling in her throat.

"Yes," I answered.

"Sit down."

The dinner was a poor one. Nothing was served but pies filled with bitter curd, and milk soup. Elena Nikiforovna, who presided, kept blinking in a queer way, first with one eye and then with the other. She talked, she ate, but yet there was something deathly about her whole figure, and one almost fancied the faint smell of a corpse. There was only a glimmer of life in her, a glimmer of consciousness that she had been a lady who had once had her own serfs, that she was the widow of a general whom the servants had to address as "Your Excellency"; and when these feeble relics of life flickered up in her for an instant she would say to her son:

"Jean, you are not holding your knife properly!"

Or she would say to me, drawing a deep breath, with the mincing air of a hostess trying to entertain a visitor:

"You know we have sold our estate. Of course, it is a pity, we are used to the place, but Dolzhikov has promised to make Jean stationmaster of Dubechnya, so we shall not have to go away; we shall live here at the station, and that is just the same as being on our own property! The engineer is so nice! Don't you think he is very handsome?"

Until recently the Cheprakovs had lived in a wealthy style, but since the death of the general everything had been changed. Elena Nikiforovna had taken to quarreling with the neighbors, to going to law, and to not paying her bailiffs or her laborers; she was in constant terror of being robbed, and in some ten years Dubechnya had become unrecognizable.

Behind the great house was an old garden which had already run wild, and was overgrown with rough weeds and bushes. I walked up and down the veranda, which was still solid and beautiful; through the glass doors one could see a room with parqueted floor, probably the drawing-room; an old-fashioned piano and pictures in deep mahogany frames—there was nothing else. In the old flower beds all that remained were peonies and poppies, which lifted their white and bright red heads above the grass. Young maples and elms, already nibbled by the cows, grew beside the paths, drawn up and hindering each other's growth. The garden was thickly overgrown and seemed impassable, but this was only near the house where there stood poplars, fir trees, and old lime trees, all of the same age, relics of the former avenues. Further on, beyond them, the garden had been cleared for the sake of hay, and here it was not moist and stuffy, and there were no spiders' webs in one's mouth and eyes. A light breeze was blowing. The further one went the more open it was, and here in the open space were cherries, plums, and spreading apple trees, disfigured by props and by canker, and pear trees so tall that one could not believe they were pear trees. This part of the garden was let to some shopkeepers of the town, and it was protected from thieves and starlings by a feeble-minded peasant who lived in a shanty in it.

The garden, growing more and more open, till it became definitely a meadow, sloped down to the river, which was overgrown with green weeds and osiers. Near the milldam was the millpond, deep and full of fish; a little mill with a thatched roof was working away with a wrathful sound, and frogs croaked furiously. Circles passed from time to time over the smooth, mirrorlike water, and the water lilies trembled, stirred by the lively fish. On the further side of the river was the little village Dubechnya. The still, blue millpond was alluring with its promise of coolness and peace. And now all this—the millpond and the mill and the snug-looking banks—belonged to the engineer!

And so my new work began. I received and forwarded telegrams, wrote various reports, and made fair copies of the notes of requirements, the complaints, and the reports sent to the office by the illiterate foremen and workmen. But for the greater part of the day I did nothing but walk about the room waiting for telegrams, or made a boy sit in the lodge while I went for a walk in the garden, until the boy ran to tell me that there was a tapping at the operating machine. I had dinner at Madam Cheprakov's. Meat we had very rarely: our dishes were all made of milk, and Wednesdays and Fridays were fast days, and on those days we had pink plates which were called Lenten plates. Madam Cheprakov was continually blinking—it was her invariable habit, and I always felt ill at ease in her presence.

As there was not enough work in the lodge for one, Cheprakov did nothing, but simply dozed, or went with his gun to shoot ducks on the millpond. In the evenings he drank too much in the village or the station, and, before going to bed, stared in the looking glass and said: "Hullo, Ivan Cheprakov."

When he was drunk he was very pale and kept rubbing his hands and laughing with a sound like a neigh: "Hee-hee-hee!" By way of bravado he used to strip and run about the country naked. He used to eat flies and say they were rather sour.

## 4.

One day, after dinner, he ran breathless into the lodge and said: "Go along, your sister has come."

I went out, and there I found a hired brake from the town standing before the entrance of the great house. My sister had come in it with Anyuta Blagovo and a gentleman in a military tunic. Going up closer I recognized the latter: it was the brother of Anyuta Blagovo, the army doctor.

"We have come to you for a picnic," he said; "is that all right?"

My sister and Anyuta wanted to ask how I was getting on here, but both were silent and simply gazed at me. I was silent too. They saw that I did not like the place, and tears came into my sister's eyes, while Anyuta Blagovo turned crimson.

We went into the garden. The doctor walked ahead of us all and said enthusiastically:

"What air! Holy Mother, what air!"

In appearance he was still a student. And he walked and talked like a student, and the expression of his gray eyes was as keen, honest, and frank as a nice student's. Beside his tall and handsome sister he looked frail and thin; and his beard was thin too, and his voice, too, was a thin but rather agreeable tenor. He was serving in a regiment somewhere and had come home to his people for a holiday, and said he was going in the autumn to Petersburg for his examination as a doctor of medicine. He was already a family man, with a wife and three children; he had married very young, in his second year at the university, and now people in the town said he was unhappy in his family life and was not living with his wife.

"What time is it?" my sister asked uneasily. "We must get back in good time. Papa let me come to see my brother on condition I was back at six."

"Oh, bother your papa!" sighed the doctor.

I set the samovar. We put down a carpet before the veranda of the great house and had our tea there, and the doctor knelt down, drank out of his saucer, and declared that he now knew what bliss was. Then Cheprakov came with the key and opened the glass door, and we all went into the house. There it was half dark and mysterious, and smelled of mushrooms, and our footsteps had a hollow sound as though there were cellars under the floor. The doctor stopped and touched the keys of the piano, and it responded faintly with a husky, quivering, but melodious chord; he tried his voice and sang a song, frowning and tapping impatiently with his foot when some note was mute. My sister did not talk about going home but walked about the rooms and kept saying:

"How happy I am! How happy I am!"

There was a note of astonishment in her voice, as though it seemed to her incredible that she, too, could feel lighthearted. It was the first time in my life I had seen her so happy. She actually looked prettier. In profile she did not look nice; her nose and mouth seemed to stick out and had an expression as though she were pouting, but she had beautiful dark eyes, a pale, very delicate complexion, and a touching expression of goodness and melancholy, and when she talked she seemed charming and even beautiful. We both, she and I, took after our mother, were broad-shouldered, strongly built, and capable of endurance, but her pallor was a sign of ill-health; she often had a cough, and I sometimes caught in her face that look one sees in people who are seriously ill, but for some reason conceal the fact. There was something naive and childish in her gaiety now, as though the joy that had been suppressed and smothered in our childhood by harsh education had now suddenly awakened in her soul and found a free outlet.

But when evening came on and the horses were brought round, my sister sank into silence and looked thin and shrunken, and she got into the brake as though she were going to the scaffold.

When they had all gone, and the sound had died away . . . I remembered that Anyuta Blagovo had not said a word to me all day.

"She is a wonderful girl!" I thought. "Wonderful girl!"

St. Peter's fast came, and we had nothing but Lenten dishes

every day. I was weighed down by physical depression due to idleness and my unsettled position, and dissatisfied with myself. Listless and hungry, I lounged about the garden and only waited for a suitable mood to go away.

Towards evening one day, when Radish was sitting in the lodge, Dolzhikov, very sunburnt and gray with dust, walked in unexpectedly. He had been spending three days on his land, and had come now to Dubechnya by the steamer, and walked to us from the station. While waiting for the carriage, which was to come for him from the town, he walked round the grounds with his bailiff, giving orders in a loud voice, then sat for a whole hour in our lodge, writing letters. While he was there telegrams came for him, and he himself tapped off the answers. We three stood in silence at attention.

"What a muddle!" he said, glancing contemptuously at a record book. "In a fortnight I am transferring the office to the station, and I don't know what I am to do with you, my friends."

"I do my best, your honor," said Cheprakov.

"To be sure, I see how you do your best. The only thing you can do is to take your salary." The engineer went on, looking at me, "You keep relying on patronage to *faire la carrière* as quickly and as easily as possible. Well, I don't care for patronage. No one took any trouble on my behalf. Before they gave me a railway contract I went about as a mechanic and worked in Belgium as an oiler. And you, Pantelei, what are you doing here?" he asked, turning to Radish. "Drinking with them?"

He, for some reason, always called humble people Pantelei, and such as me and Cheprakov he despised, and called them drunkards, beasts, and rabble to their faces. Altogether he was cruel to humble subordinates and used to fine them and turn them off coldly without explanations.

At last the horses came for him. As he said good-bye he promised to turn us all off in a fortnight; he called his bailiff a blockhead; and then, lolling at ease in his carriage, drove back to the town.

"Andrei Ivanich," I said to Radish, "take me on as a workman."

"Oh, all right!"

And we set off together in the direction of the town. When the station and the big house with its buildings were left behind I asked: "Andrei Ivanich, why did you come to Dubechnya this evening?"

"In the first place my fellows are working on the line, and in the second place I came to pay the general's lady my interest. Last year I borrowed fifty rubles from her, and I pay her now a ruble a month interest."

The painter stopped and took me by the button.

"Misail Alexeyich, our angel," he went on. "The way I look at it is that if any man, gentle or simple, takes even the smallest interest, he is doing evil. There cannot be truth and justice in such a man."

Radish, lean, pale, dreadful-looking, shut his eyes, shook his head, and, in the tone of a philosopher, pronounced:

"Lice consume the grass, rust consumes the iron, and lying the soul. Lord, have mercy upon us sinners."

## 5.

Radish was not practical and was not at all good at forming an estimate; he took more work than he could get through, and when calculating he was agitated, lost his head, and so was almost always out of pocket over his jobs. He undertook painting, glazing, paper hanging, and even tiling roofs, and I can remember his running about for three days to find tilers for the sake of a paltry job. He was a first-rate workman; he sometimes earned as much as ten rubles a day; and if it had not been for the desire at all costs to be a master, and to be called a contractor, he would probably have had plenty of money.

He was paid by the job, but he paid me and the other workmen by the day, from one and twopence to two shillings a day. When it was fine and dry we did all kinds of outside work, chiefly painting roofs. When I was new to the work it made my feet burn as though I were walking on hot bricks, and when I put on felt boots they were hotter than ever. But this was only at first; later on I got used to it, and everything went swimmingly. I was living now among people to whom labor was obligatory, inevitable, and who worked like cart horses, often with no idea of the moral significance of labor, and, indeed, never using the word "labor" in conversation at all. Beside them I, too, felt like a cart horse, growing more and more imbued with the feeling of the obligatory and inevitable character of what I was doing, and this made my life easier, setting me free from all doubt and uncertainty.

At first everything interested me, everything was new, as though I had been born again. I could sleep on the ground and go about barefoot, and that was extremely pleasant; I could stand in a crowd of the common people and be no constraint to anyone, and when a cab horse fell down in the street I ran to help it up without being afraid of soiling my clothes. And the best of it all was, I was living on my own account and no burden to anyone!

Painting roofs, especially with our own oil and colors, was regarded as a particularly profitable job, and so this rough, dull work was not disdained, even by such good workmen as Radish. In short breeches, and wasted, purple-looking legs, he used to go about the roofs, looking like a stork, and I used to hear him, as he plied his brush, breathing heavily and saying: "Woe, woe to us sinners!"

He walked about the roofs as freely as though he were upon

the ground. In spite of his being ill and pale as a corpse, his agility was extraordinary: he used to paint the domes and cupolas of the churches without scaffolding, like a young man, with only the help of a ladder and a rope, and it was rather horrible when standing on a height far from the earth; he would draw himself up erect, and for some unknown reason pronounce:

"Lice consume grass, rust consumes iron, and lying the soul!"

Or, thinking about something, would answer his thoughts aloud:

"Anything may happen! Anything may happen!"

When I went home from my work, all the people who were sitting on benches by the gates, all the shopmen and boys and their employers, made sneering and spiteful remarks after me, and this upset me at first and seemed to be simply monstrous.

"Better-than-nothing!" I heard on all sides. "House painter! Yellow ocher!"

And none behaved so ungraciously to me as those who had only lately been humble people themselves and had earned their bread by hard manual labor. In the streets full of shops I was once passing an ironmonger's when water was thrown over me as though by accident, and on one occasion someone darted out with a stick at me, while a fishmonger, a gray-headed old man, barred my way and said, looking at me angrily:

"I am not sorry for you, you fool! It's your father I am sorry for."

And my acquaintances were for some reason overcome with embarrassment when they met me. Some of them looked upon me as a queer fish and a comic fool; others were sorry for me; others did not know what attitude to take up to me, and it was difficult to make them out. One day I met Anyuta Blagovo in a side street near Great Dvoryansky Street. I was going to work, and was carrying two long brushes and a pail of paint. Recognizing me, Anyuta flushed crimson.

"Please do not bow to me in the street," she said nervously, harshly, and in a shaking voice, without offering me her hand, and tears suddenly gleamed in her eyes. "If to your mind all this is necessary, so be it . . . so be it, but I beg you not to meet me!"

I no longer lived in Great Dvoryansky Street, but in the suburb with my old nurse Karpovna, a good-natured but gloomy old woman, who always foreboded some harm, was afraid of all dreams, and even in the bees and wasps that flew into her room saw omens of evil, and the fact that I had become a workman, to her thinking, boded nothing good.

"Your life is ruined," she would say, mournfully shaking her head, "ruined."

Her adopted son Prokofy, a huge, uncouth, redheaded fellow of thirty, with bristling mustaches, a butcher by trade, lived in the little house with her. When he met me in the passage he would make way for me in respectful silence, and if he was drunk he would salute me with all five fingers at once. He used to have supper in the evening, and through the partition wall of boards I could hear him clear his throat and sigh as he drank off glass after glass.

"Mamma," he would call in an undertone.

Well," Karpovna, who was passionately devoted to her adopted son, would respond: "What is it, Sonny?"

"I can show you a testimony of my affection, Mamma. All this earthly life I will cherish you in your declining years in this vale of tears, and when you die I will bury you at my expense; I have said it, and you can believe it."

I got up every morning before sunrise and went to bed early. We house painters ate a great deal and slept soundly; the only thing amiss was that my heart used to beat violently at night. I did not quarrel with my mates. Violent abuse, desperate oaths, and wishes such as, "Blast your eyes," or "Cholera take you," never ceased all day, but, nevertheless, we lived on very friendly terms. The other fellows suspected me of being some sort of religious sectary and made good-natured jokes at my expense, saying that even my own father had disowned me, and thereupon would add that they rarely went into the temple of God themselves, and that many of them had not been to confession for ten years. They justified this laxity on their part by saying that a painter among men was like a jackdaw among birds.

The men had a good opinion of me, and treated me with respect; it was evident that my not drinking, not smoking, but leading a quiet, steady life pleased them very much. It was only an unpleasant shock to them that I took no hand in stealing oil and did not go with them to ask for tips from people on whose property we were working. Stealing oil and paints from those who employed them was a house painter's custom and was not regarded as theft, and it was remarkable that even so upright a man as Radish would always carry away a little white lead and oil as he went home from work. And even the most respectable old fellows, who owned the houses in which they lived in the suburb, were not ashamed to ask for a tip, and it made me feel vexed and ashamed to see the men go in a body to congratulate some nonentity on the commencement or the completion of the job and thank him with degrading servility when they had received a few coppers.

With people on whose work they were engaged they behaved like wily courtiers, and almost every day I was reminded of Shakespeare's Polonius.

"I fancy it is going to rain," the man whose house was being painted would say, looking at the sky.

"It is, there is not a doubt it is," the painters would agree.

"I don't think it is a rain cloud, though. Perhaps it won't rain after all."

"No, it won't, your honor! I am sure it won't."

But their attitude to their patrons behind their backs was usually one of irony, and when they saw, for instance, a gentleman sitting in the veranda reading a newspaper, they would observe:

"He reads the paper, but I daresay he has nothing to eat."

I never went home to see my own people. When I came back from work I often found waiting for me little notes, brief and anxious, in which my sister wrote to me about my father; that he had been particularly preoccupied at dinner and had eaten nothing, or that he had been giddy and staggering, or that he had locked himself in his room and had not come out for a long time. Such items of news troubled me; I could not sleep, and at times even walked up and down Great Dvoryansky Street at night by our house, looking in at the dark windows and trying to guess whether everything was well at home. On Sundays my sister came to see me, but came in secret, as though it were not to see me but our nurse. And if she came in to see me she was very pale, with tear-stained eyes, and she began crying at once.

"Our father will never live through this," she would say. "If anything should happen to him—God grant it may not—your conscience will torment you all your life. It's awful, Misail; for our mother's sake I beseech you: reform your ways."

"My darling sister," I would say, "how can I reform my ways if I am convinced that I am acting in accordance with my conscience? Do understand!"

"I know you are acting on your conscience, but perhaps it could be done differently, somehow, so as not to wound anybody."

"Ah, holy Saints!" the old woman sighed through the door. "Your life is ruined! There will be trouble, my dears, there will be trouble!"

## 6.

One Sunday Dr. Blagovo turned up unexpectedly. He was wearing a military tunic over a silk shirt and high boots of patent leather.

"I have come to see you," he began, shaking my hand heartily like a student. "I am hearing about you every day, and I have been meaning to come and have a heart-to-heart talk, as they say. The boredom in the town is awful, there is not a living soul, no one to say a word to. It's hot, Holy Mother," he went on, taking off his tunic and sitting in his silk shirt. "My dear fellow, let me talk to you."

I was dull myself and had for a long time been craving for the society of someone not a house painter. I was genuinely glad to see him.

"I'll begin by saying," he said, sitting down on my bed, "that I sympathize with you from the bottom of my heart and deeply respect the life you are leading. They don't understand you here in the town, and, indeed, there is no one to understand, seeing that, as you know, they are all, with very few exceptions, regular Gogolesque pig faces here. But I saw what you were at once that time at the picnic. You are a noble soul, an honest, high-minded man! I respect you and feel it a great honor to shake hands with you!" he went on enthusiastically. "To have made such a complete and violent change of life as you have done, you must have passed through a complicated spiritual crisis, and to continue this manner of life now, and to keep up to the high standard of your convictions continually, must be a strain on your mind and heart from day to day. Now to begin our talk, tell me, don't you consider that if you had spent your strength of will, this strained activity, all these powers on something else, for instance, on gradually becoming a great scientist, or artist, your life would have been broader and deeper and would have been more productive?"

We talked, and when we got upon manual labor I expressed this idea: that what is wanted is that the strong should not enslave the weak, that the minority should not be a parasite on the majority, nor a vampire for ever sucking its vital sap; that is, all, without exception, strong and weak, rich and poor, should take part equally in the struggle for existence, each one on his own account, and that there was no better means for equalizing things in that way than manual labor, in the form of universal service, compulsory for all.

"Then do you think everyone without exception ought to engage in manual labor?" asked the doctor.

"Yes."

"And don't you think that if everyone, including the best men, the thinkers and great scientists, taking part in the struggle for existence, each on his own account, is going to waste his time breaking stones and painting roofs, may not that threaten a grave danger to progress?"

"Where is the danger?" I asked. "Why, progress is in deeds of love, in fulfilling the moral law; if you don't enslave anyone, if you don't oppress anyone, what further progress do you want?"

"But, excuse me," Blagovo suddenly fired up, rising to his feet. "But, excuse me! If a snail in its shell busies itself over perfecting its own personality and muddles about with the moral law, do you call that progress?"

"Why muddles?" I said, offended. "If you don't force your neighbor to feed and clothe you, to transport you from place to place, and defend you from your enemies, surely in the midst of a life entirely resting on slavery, that is progress, isn't it? To my mind it is the most important progress, and perhaps the only one possible and necessary for man."

"The limits of universal world progress are in infinity, and to talk of some 'possible' progress limited by our needs and temporary theories is, excuse my saying so, positively strange."

"If the limits of progress are in infinity as you say, it follows that its aims are not definite," I said. "To live without knowing definitely what you are living for!"

"So be it! But that 'not knowing' is not so dull as your 'knowing.' I am going up a ladder which is called progress, civilization, culture; I go on and up without knowing definitely where I am going, but really it is worth living for the sake of that delightful ladder; while you know what you are living for, you live for the sake of some people's not enslaving others, that the artist and the man who rubs his paints may dine equally well. But you know that's the petty, bourgeois, kitchen, gray side of life, and surely it is revolting to live for that alone? If some insects do enslave others, bother them, let them devour each other! We need not think about them. You know they will die and decay just the same, however zealously you rescue them from slavery. We must think of that great millennium which awaits humanity in the remote future."

Blagovo argued warmly with me, but at the same time one could see he was troubled by some irrelevant idea.

"I suppose your sister is not coming?" he said, looking at his watch. "She was at our house yesterday, and said she would be seeing you today. You keep saying slavery, slavery . . ." he went on. "But you know that is a special question, and all such questions are solved by humanity gradually."

We began talking of doing things gradually. I said that "the question of doing good or evil everyone settles for himself, without waiting till humanity settles it by the way of gradual development. Moreover, this gradual process has more than one aspect. Side by side with the gradual development of human ideas the gradual growth of ideas of another order is observed. Serfdom is no more, but the capitalist system is growing. And in the very heyday of emancipating ideas, just as in the days of Baty, the majority feeds, clothes, and defends the minority while remaining hungry, inadequately clad, and defenseless. Such an order of things can be made to fit in finely with any tendencies and currents of thought you like, because the art of enslaving is also gradually being cultivated. We no longer flog our servants in the stable, but we give to slavery refined forms, at least, we succeed in finding a justification for it in each particular case. Ideas are ideas with us, but if now, at the end of the nineteenth century, it were possible to lay the burden of the most unpleasant of our physiological functions upon the working class, we should certainly do so, and afterwards, of course, justify ourselves by saying that if the best people, the thinkers and great scientists, were to waste their precious time on these functions, progress might be menaced with great danger."

But at this point my sister arrived. Seeing the doctor, she was flustered and troubled, and began saying immediately that it was time for her to go home to her father.

"Kleopatra Alexyevna," said Blagovo earnestly, pressing both hands to his heart, "what will happen to your father if you spend half an hour or so with your brother and me?"

He was frank and knew how to communicate his liveliness to others. After a moment's thought, my sister laughed, and all at once became suddenly gay as she had been at the picnic. We went out into the country, and, lying in the grass, went on with our talk, and looked towards the town where all the windows facing west were like glittering gold because the sun was setting.

After that, whenever my sister was coming to see me Blagovo turned up too, and they always greeted each other as though their meeting in my room was accidental. My sister listened while the doctor and I argued, and at such times her expression was joyfully enthusiastic, full of tenderness and curiosity, and it seemed to me that a new world she had never dreamed of before, and which she was now striving to fathom, was gradually opening before her eyes. When the doctor was not there she was quiet and sad, and now if she sometimes shed tears as she sat on my bed it was for reasons of which she did not speak.

In August Radish ordered us to be ready to go to the railway line. Two days before we were "banished" from the town my father came to see me. He sat down and in a leisurely way, without looking at me, wiped his red face, then took out of his pocket our town *Messenger*, and deliberately, with emphasis on each word, read out the news that the son of the branch manager of the State Bank, a young man of my age, had been appointed head of a department in the Exchequer.

"And now look at you," he said, folding up the newspaper; "a beggar, in rags, good for nothing! Even working-class people and peasants obtain education in order to become men, while you, a Poloznev, with ancestors of rank and distinction, aspire to the gutter! But I have not come here to talk to you; I have washed my hands of you—" he added in a stifled voice, getting up. "I have come to find out where your sister is, you worthless fellow. She left home after dinner, and here it is nearly eight and she is not back. She has taken to going out frequently without telling me; she is less dutiful—and I see in it your evil and degrading influence. Where is she?"

In his hand he had the umbrella I knew so well, and I was already flustered and drew myself up like a schoolboy, expecting my father to begin hitting me with it, but he noticed my glance at the umbrella and most likely that restrained him.

"Live as you please!" he said. "I shall not give you my blessing!"

"Holy Saints!" my nurse muttered behind the door. "You poor, unlucky child! Ah, my heart bodes ill!"

I worked on the railway line. It rained without stopping all August; it was damp and cold; they had not carried the corn in the fields, and on big farms where the wheat had been cut by machines it lay not in sheaves but in heaps, and I remember how those luckless heaps of wheat turned blacker every day and the grain was sprouting in them. It was hard to work; the pouring rain spoiled everything we managed to do. We were not allowed to live or to sleep in the railway buildings, and we took refuge in the damp and filthy mud huts in which the navvies had lived during the summer, and I could not sleep at night for the cold and the wood lice crawling on my face and hands. And when we worked near the bridges the navvies used to come in the evenings in a gang, simply in order to beat the painters—it was a form of sport to them. They used to beat us, to steal our brushes. And to annoy us and rouse us to fight they used to spoil our work; they would, for instance, smear over the signal boxes with green paint. To complete our troubles, Radish took to paying us very irregularly. All the painting work on the line was given out to a contractor; he gave it out to another; and this subcontractor gave it to Radish after subtracting twenty percent for himself. The job was not a profitable one in itself, and the rain made it worse; time was wasted; we could not work while Radish was obliged to pay the fellows by the day. The hungry painters almost came to beating him, called him a cheat, a bloodsucker, a Judas, while he, poor fellow, sighed, lifted up his hand to heaven in despair, and was continually going to Madam Cheprakov for money.

## 7.

Autumn came on, rainy, dark, and muddy. The season of unemployment set in, and I used to sit at home out of work for three days at a stretch, or did various little jobs, not in the painting line. For instance, I wheeled earth, earning about fourpence a day by it. Dr. Blagovo had gone away to Petersburg. My sister had given up coming to see me. Radish was laid up at home ill, expecting death from day to day.

And my mood was autumnal too. Perhaps because, having

become a workman, I saw our town life only from the seamy side, it was my lot almost every day to make discoveries which reduced me almost to despair. Those of my fellow citizens, about whom I had no opinion before, or who had externally appeared perfectly decent, turned out now to be base, cruel people, capable of any dirty action. We common people were deceived, cheated, and kept waiting for hours together in the cold entry or the kitchen; we were insulted and treated with the utmost rudeness. In the autumn I papered the reading-room and two other rooms at the club; I was paid a penny three-farthings the piece, but had to sign a receipt at the rate of twopence halfpenny, and when I refused to do so, a gentleman of benevolent appearance in gold-rimmed spectacles, who must have been one of the club committee, said to me:

"If you say much more, you blackguard, I'll pound your face into a jelly!"

And when the flunkey whispered to him who I was, the son of Poloznev, the architect, he became embarrassed, turned crimson, but immediately recovered himself and said: "Devil take him."

In the shops they palmed off on us workmen putrid meat, musty flour, and tea that had been used and dried again; the police hustled us in church, the assistants and nurses in the hospital plundered us, and if we were too poor to give them a bribe they revenged themselves by bringing us food in dirty vessels. In the post office the pettiest official considered he had a right to treat us like animals, and to shout with coarse insolence: "You wait!" "Where are you shoving to?" Even the house dogs were unfriendly to us and fell upon us with peculiar viciousness. But the thing that struck me most of all in my new position was the complete lack of justice, what is defined by the peasants in the words: "They have forgotten God." Rarely did a day pass without swindling. We were swindled by the merchants who sold us oil, by the contractors and the workmen and the people who employed us. I need not say that there could never be a question of our rights, and we always had to ask for the money we earned as though it were a charity, and to stand waiting for it at the back door, cap in hand.

I was papering a room at the club next to the reading-room; in the evening, when I was just getting ready to go, the daughter of Dolzhikov, the engineer, walked into the room with a bundle of books under her arm.

I bowed to her.

"Oh, how do you do!" she said, recognizing me at once, and holding out her hand. "I'm very glad to see you."

She smiled and looked with curiosity and wonder at my smock, my pail of paste, the paper stretched on the floor; I was embarrassed, and she, too, felt awkward.

"You must excuse my looking at you like this," she said. "I have been told so much about you. Especially by Dr. Blagovo; he is simply in love with you. And I have made the acquaintance of your sister too; a sweet, dear girl, but I can never persuade her that there is nothing awful about your adopting the simple life. On the contrary, you have become the most interesting man in the town."

She looked again at the pail of paste and the wallpaper, and went on:

"I asked Dr. Blagovo to make me better acquainted with you, but apparently he forgot, or had not time. Anyway, we are acquainted all the same, and if you would come to see me quite simply I should be extremely indebted to you. I so long to have a talk. I am a simple person," she added, holding out her hand to me, "and I hope that you will feel no constraint with me. My father is not here, he is in Petersburg."

She went off into the reading-room, rustling her skirts, while I went home, and for a long time could not get to sleep.

That cheerless autumn some kind soul, evidently wishing to alleviate my existence, sent me from time to time tea and lemons, or biscuits, or roast game. Karpovna told me that they were always brought by a soldier, and from whom they came she did not know; and the soldier used to inquire whether I was well, and whether I dined every day, and whether I had warm clothing. When the frosts began I was presented in the same way in my absence with a soft knitted scarf brought by the soldier. There was a faint elusive smell of scent about it, and I guessed who my good fairy was. The scarf smelled of lilies of the valley, the favorite scent of Anyuta Blagovo.

Towards winter there was more work and it was more cheerful. Radish recovered, and we worked together in the cemetery church, where we were putting the groundwork on the icon stand before gilding. It was a clean, quiet job, and, as our fellows used to say, profitable. One could get through a lot of work in a day, and the time passed quickly, imperceptibly. There was no swearing, no laughter, no loud talk. The place itself compelled one to quietness and decent behavior, and disposed one to quiet, serious thoughts. Absorbed in our work we stood or sat motionless like statues; there was a deathly silence in keeping with the cemetery, so that if a tool fell, or a flame spluttered in the lamp, the noise of such sounds rang out abrupt and resonant and made us look round. After a long silence we would hear a buzzing like the swarming of bees: it was the requiem of a baby being chanted slowly in subdued voices in the porch; or an artist, painting a dove with stars round it on a cupola would begin softly whistling, and, recollecting himself with a start, would at once relapse into silence; or Radish, answering his thoughts, would say with a sigh: "Anything is possible! Anything is possible!" or a slow disconsolate bell would begin ringing over our heads, and the painters would observe that it must be for the funeral of some wealthy person. . . .

My days I spent in this stillness in the twilight of the church, and in the long evenings I played billiards or went to the theater in the gallery wearing the new trousers I had bought out of my own earnings. Concerts and performances had already begun at the Azhogins'; Radish used to paint the scenes alone now. He used to tell me the plot of the plays and describe the tableaux vivants which he witnessed. I listened to him with envy. I felt greatly drawn to the rehearsals, but I could not bring myself to go to the Azhogins'.

A week before Christmas Dr. Blagovo arrived. And again we argued and played billiards in the evenings. When he played he used to take off his coat and unbutton his shirt over his chest, and for some reason tried altogether to assume the air of a desperate rake. He did not drink much but made a great uproar about it, and had a special faculty for getting through twenty rubles in an evening at such a poor cheap tavern as the Volga.

My sister began coming to see me again; they both expressed surprise every time on seeing each other, but from her joyful, guilty face it was evident that these meetings were not accidental. One evening, when we were playing billiards, the doctor said to me:

"I say, why don't you go and see Miss Dolzhikov? You don't know Marya Viktorovna; she is a clever creature, a charmer, a simple, good-natured soul."

I described how her father had received me in the spring.

"Nonsense!" laughed the doctor, "the engineer's one thing and she's another. Really, my dear fellow, you mustn't be nasty to her; go and see her sometimes. For instance, let's go and see her tomorrow evening. What do you say?"

He persuaded me. The next evening I put on my new serge trousers, and in some agitation I set off to Mademoiselle Dolzhikov's. The footman did not seem so haughty and terrible, nor the furniture so gorgeous, as on that morning when I had come to ask a favor. Marya Viktorovna was expecting me, and she received me like an old acquaintance, shaking hands with me in a friendly way. She was wearing a gray cloth dress with full sleeves, and had her hair done in the style which we used to call "dogs' ears," when it came into fashion in the town a year before. The hair was combed down over the ears, and this made Marya Viktorovna's face look broader, and she seemed to me this time very much like her father, whose face was broad and red, with something in its expression like a sledge driver. She was handsome and elegant, but not youthful looking; she looked thirty, though in reality she was not more than twenty-five.

"Dear Doctor, how grateful I am to you," she said, making me sit down. "If it hadn't been for him you wouldn't have come to see me. I am bored to death! My father has gone away and left me alone, and I don't know what to do with myself in this town."

Then she began asking me where I was working now, how much I earned, where I lived.

"Do you spend on yourself nothing but what you earn?" she asked.

"No."

"Happy man!" she sighed. "All the evil in life, it seems to me, comes from idleness, boredom, and spiritual emptiness, and all this is inevitable when one is accustomed to living at other people's expense. Don't think I am showing off. I tell you truthfully: it is not interesting or pleasant to be rich. 'Make to yourselves friends of the mammon of unrighteousness' is said because there is not and cannot be a mammon that's righteous."

She looked round at the furniture with a grave, cold expression, as though she wanted to count it over, and went on:

"Comfort and luxury have a magical power; little by little they draw into their clutches even strong-willed people. At one time Father and I lived simply, not in a rich style, but now you see how! It is something monstrous," she said, shrugging her shoulders; "we spent up to twenty thousand a year! In the provinces!"

"One comes to look at comfort and luxury as the invariable privilege of capital and education," I said, "and it seems to me that the comforts of life may be combined with any sort of labor, even the hardest and dirtiest. Your father is rich, and yet he says himself that it has been his lot to be a mechanic and an oiler."

She smiled and shook her head doubtfully: "My father sometimes eats bread dipped in kvass," she said. "It's a fancy, a whim!"

At that moment there was a ring and she got up.

"The rich and well-educated ought to work like everyone else," she said, "and if there is comfort it ought to be equal for all. There ought not to be any privileges. But that's enough philosophizing. Tell me something amusing. Tell me about the painters. What are they like? Funny?"

The doctor came in; I began telling them about the painters, but, being unaccustomed to talking, I was constrained, and described them like an ethnologist, gravely and tediously. The doctor, too, told us some anecdotes of workingmen: he staggered about, shed tears, dropped on his knees, and, even, mimicking a drunkard, lay on the floor; it was as good as a play, and Marya Viktorovna laughed till she cried as she looked at him. Then he played on the piano and sang in his thin, pleasant tenor, while Marya Viktorovna stood by and picked out what he was to sing and corrected him when he made a mistake.

"I've heard that you sing, too?" I inquired.

"Sing, too!" cried the doctor in horror. "She sings exquisitely, a perfect artist, and you talk of her 'singing too'! What an idea!"

"I did study in earnest at one time," she said, answering my question, "but now I have given it up."

Sitting on a low stool she told us of her life in Petersburg and mimicked some celebrated singers, imitating their voices and manner of singing. She made a sketch of the doctor in her album, then of me; she did not draw well, but both the portraits were like us. She laughed and was full of mischief and charming grimaces, and this suited her better than talking about the mammon of unrighteousness, and it seemed to me that she had been talking just before about wealth and luxury, not in earnest, but in imitation of someone. She was a superb comic actress. I mentally compared her with our young ladies, and even the handsome, dignified Anyuta Blagovo could not stand comparison with her; the difference was immense, like the difference between a beautiful, cultivated rose and a wild briar.

We had supper together, the three of us. The doctor and Marya Viktorovna drank red wine, champagne, and coffee with brandy in it; they clinked glasses and drank to friendship, to enlightenment, to progress, to liberty, and they did not get drunk but only flushed, and were continually, for no reason, laughing till they cried. So as not to be tiresome I drank claret too.

"Talented, richly endowed natures," said Mademoiselle Dolzhikov, "know how to live, and go their own way; mediocre people, like myself for instance, know nothing and can do nothing of themselves; there is nothing left for them but to discern some deep social movement, and to float where they are carried by it."

"How can one discern what doesn't exist?" asked the doctor.

"We think so because we don't see it."

"Is that so? The social movements are the invention of the new literature. There are none among us."

An argument began.

"There are no deep social movements among us and never have been," the doctor declared loudly. "There is no end to what the new literature has invented! It has invented intellectual workers in the country, and you may search through all our villages and find at the most some lout in a reefer jacket or a black frockcoat who will make four mistakes in spelling a word of three letters. Cultured life has not yet begun among us. There's the same savagery, the same uniform boorishness, the same triviality, as five hundred years ago. Movements, currents there have been, but it has all been petty, paltry, bent upon vulgar and mercenary interests—and one cannot see anything important in them. If you think you have discerned a deep social movement, and, in following it, you devote yourself to tasks in the modern taste, such as the emancipation of insects from slavery or abstinence from beef rissoles, I congratulate you, madam. We must study, and study, and study, and we must wait a bit with our deep social movements; we are not mature enough for them yet; and to tell the truth, we don't know anything about them."

"You don't know anything about them, but I do," said Marya Viktorovna. "Goodness, how tiresome you are today!"

"Our duty is to study and to study, to try to accumulate as much knowledge as possible, for genuine social movements arise where there is knowledge; and the happiness of mankind in the future lies only in knowledge. I drink to science!"

"There is no doubt about one thing: one must organize one's life somehow differently," said Marya Viktorovna, after a moment's silence and thought. "Life, such as it has been hitherto, is not worth having. Don't let us talk about it."

As we came away from her the cathedral clock struck two.

"Did you like her?" asked the doctor; "she's nice, isn't she?"

On Christmas Day we dined with Marya Viktorovna, and all through the holidays we went to see her almost every day. There was never anyone there but ourselves, and she was right when she said that she had no friends in the town but the doctor and me. We spent our time for the most part in conversation; sometimes the doctor brought some book or magazine and read aloud to us. In reality he was the first well-educated man I had met in my life: I cannot judge whether he knew a great deal, but he always displayed his knowledge as though he wanted other people to share it. When he talked about anything relating to medicine he was not like any one of the doctors in our town, but made a fresh, peculiar impression upon me, and I fancied that if he liked he might have become a real man of science. And he was perhaps the only person who had a real influence upon me at that time. Seeing him, and reading the books he gave me, I began little by little to feel a thirst for the knowledge which would have given significance to my cheerless labor. It seemed strange to me, for instance, that I had not known till then that the whole world was made up of sixty elements, I had not known what oil was, what paints were, and that I could have got on without knowing these things. My acquaintance with the doctor elevated me morally too. I was continually arguing with him and, though I usually remained of my own opinion, yet, thanks to him, I began to perceive that everything was not clear to me, and I began trying to work out as far as I could definite convictions in myself that the dictates of conscience might be definite, and that there might be nothing vague in my mind. Yet, though he was the most cultivated and best man in the town, he was nevertheless far from perfection. In his manners, in his habit of turning every conversation into an argument, in his pleasant tenor, even in his friendliness, there was something coarse, like a divinity student, and when he took off his coat and sat in his silk shirt, or flung a tip to a waiter in the restaurant, I always fancied that culture might be all very well, but the Tatar was fermenting in him still.

At Epiphany he went back to Petersburg. He went off in the morning, and after dinner my sister came in. Without taking off her fur coat and her cap, she sat down in silence, very pale, and kept her eyes fixed on the same spot. She was chilled by the frost and one could see that she was upset by it.

"You must have caught cold," I said.

Her eyes filled with tears; she got up and went out to Karpovna without saying a word to me, as though I had hurt her feelings. And a little later I heard her saying, in a tone of bitter reproach:

"Nurse, what have I been living for till now? What? Tell me, haven't I wasted my youth? All the best years of my life to know nothing but keeping accounts, pouring out tea, counting the halfpence, entertaining visitors, and thinking there was nothing better in the world! Nurse, do understand, I have the cravings of a human being, and I want to live, and they have turned me into something like a housekeeper. It's horrible, horrible!"

She flung her keys towards the door, and they fell with a jingle into my room. They were the keys of the sideboard, of the kitchen cupboard, of the cellar, and of the tea caddy, the keys which my mother used to carry.

"Oh, merciful heavens!" cried the old woman in horror. "Holy Saints above!"

Before going home, my sister came into my room to pick up the keys, and said:

"You must forgive me. Something queer has happened to me lately."

## 8.

On returning home late one evening from Marya Viktorovna's, I found waiting in my room a young police inspector in a new uniform; he was sitting at my table, looking through my books.

"At last," he said, getting up and stretching himself. "This is the third time I have been to you. The governor commands you to present yourself before him at nine o'clock in the morning. Without fail."

He took from me a signed statement that I would act upon

His Excellency's command, and went away. This late visit of the police inspector and unexpected invitation to the governor's had an overwhelmingly oppressive effect upon me. From my earliest childhood I have felt terror stricken in the presence of gendarmes, policemen, and law-court officials, and now I was tormented by uneasiness, as though I were really guilty in some way. And I could not get to sleep. My nurse and Prokofy were also upset and could not sleep. My nurse had earache too; she moaned, and several times began crying with pain. Hearing that I was awake, Prokofy came into my room with a lamp and sat down at the table.

"You ought to have a drink of pepper cordial," he said, after a moment's thought. "If one does have a drink in this vale of tears it does no harm. And if Mamma were to pour a little pepper cordial in her ear it would do her a lot of good."

Between two and three he was going to the slaughterhouse for the meat. I knew I should not sleep till morning now, and to get through the time till nine o'clock I went with him. We walked with a lantern, while his shopboy Nikolka, aged thirteen, with blue patches on his cheeks from frostbites, a regular young brigand to judge by his expression, drove after us in the sledge, urging on the horse in a husky voice.

"I suppose they will punish you at the governor's," Prokofy said to me on the way. "There are rules of the trade for governors, and rules for the higher clergy, and rules for the officers, and rules for the doctors, and every class has its rules. But you haven't kept to your rules, and you can't be allowed."

The slaughterhouse was behind the cemetery, and till then I had only seen it in the distance. It consisted of three gloomy barns, surrounded by a gray fence, and when the wind blew from that quarter on hot days in summer, it brought a stifling stench from them. Now, going into the yard in the dark, I did not see the barns; I kept coming across horses and sledges, some empty, some loaded up with meat. Men were walking about with lanterns, swearing in a disgusting way. Prokofy and Nikolka swore just as revoltingly, and the air was in a continual uproar with swearing, coughing, and the neighing of horses.

There was a smell of dead bodies and of dung. It was thawing, the snow was changing into mud; and in the darkness it seemed to me that I was walking through pools of blood.

Having piled up the sledges full of meat, we set off to the butcher's shop in the market. It began to get light. Cooks with baskets and elderly ladies in mantles came along one after another. Prokofy, with a chopper in his hand, in a white apron spattered with blood, swore fearful oaths, crossed himself at the church, shouted aloud for the whole market to hear that he was giving away the meat at cost price and even at a loss to himself. He gave short weight and short change, the cooks saw that, but, deafened by his shouts, did not protest and only called him a hangman. Brandishing and bringing down his terrible chopper he threw himself into picturesque attitudes, and each time uttered the sound "Geck" with a ferocious expression, and I was afraid he really would chop off somebody's head or hand.

I spent all the morning in the butcher's shop, and when at last I went to the governor's, my overcoat smelled of meat and blood. My state of mind was as though I were being sent spear in hand to meet a bear. I remember the tall staircase with a striped carpet on it, and the young official, with shiny buttons, who mutely motioned me to the door with both hands, and ran to announce me. I went into a hall luxuriously but frigidly and tastelessly furnished, and the high, narrow mirrors in the spaces between the walls, and the bright yellow window curtains, struck the eye particularly unpleasantly. One could see that the governors were changed, but the furniture remained the same. Again the young official motioned me with both hands to the door, and I went up to a big green table at which a military general, with the Order of Vladimir on his breast, was standing.

"Monsieur Poloznev, I have asked you to come," he began, holding a letter in his hand, and opening his mouth like a round "o," "I have asked you to come here to inform you of this. Your highly respected father has appealed by letter and by word of mouth to the Marshal of Nobility begging him to summon you and to lay before you the inconsistency of your behavior with the rank of the nobility to which you have the honor to belong. His excellency Alexandr Pavlovich, justly supposing that your conduct might serve as a bad example, and considering that mere persuasion on his part would not be sufficient, but that official intervention in earnest was essential, presents me here in this letter with his views in regard to you, which I share."

He said this, quietly, respectfully, standing erect, as though I were his superior officer and looking at me with no trace of severity. His face looked worn and wizened and was all wrinkles; there were bags under his eyes, his hair was dyed, and it was impossible to tell from his appearance how old he was—forty or sixty.

"I trust," he went on, "that you appreciate the delicacy of our honored Alexandr Pavlovich, who has addressed himself to me not officially, but privately. I, too, have asked you to come here unofficially, and I am speaking to you, not as a governor, but from a sincere regard for your father. And so I beg you either to alter your line of conduct and return to duties in keeping with your rank, or, to avoid setting a bad example, remove to another district where you are not known, and where you can follow any occupation you please. In the other case, I shall be forced to take extreme measures."

He stood for half a minute in silence, looking at me with his mouth open.

"Are you a vegetarian?" he asked.

"No, Your Excellency, I eat meat."

He sat down and drew some papers towards him. I bowed and went out.

It was not worth while now to go to work before dinner. I went home to sleep, but could not sleep from an unpleasant, sickly feeling, induced by the slaughterhouse and my conversation with the governor; and when the evening came I went, gloomy and out of sorts, to Marya Viktorovna. I told her how I had been at the governor's, while she stared at me in perplexity as though she did not believe it, then suddenly began laughing gaily, loudly, irrepressibly, as only good-natured laughter-loving people can.

"If only one could tell that in Petersburg!" she brought out, almost falling over with laughter, and propping herself against the table. "If one could tell that in Petersburg!"

## 9.

Now we used to see each other often, sometimes twice a day. She used to come to the cemetery almost every day after dinner, and read the epitaphs on the crosses and tombstones while she waited for me. Sometimes she would come into the church, and, standing by me, would look on while I worked. The stillness, the naive work of the painters and gilders, Radish's sage reflections, and the fact that I did not differ externally from the other workmen, and worked just as they did in my waistcoat with no socks on, and that I was addressed familiarly by them—all this was new to her and touched her. One day a workman, who was painting a dove on the ceiling, called out to me in her presence:

"Misail, hand me up the white paint."

I took him the white paint, and afterwards, when I let myself down by the frail scaffolding, she looked at me, touched to tears and smiling.

"What a dear you are!" she said.

I remembered from my childhood how a green parrot, belonging to one of the rich men of the town, had escaped from its cage, and how for quite a month afterwards the beautiful bird had haunted the town, flying from garden to garden, homeless and solitary. Marya Viktorovna reminded me of that bird.

"There is positively nowhere for me to go now but the cemetery," she said to me with a laugh. "The town has become disgustingly dull. At the Azhogins' they are still reciting, singing, lisping. I have grown to detest them of late; your sister is an unsociable creature; Mademoiselle Blagovo hates me for some reason. I don't care for the theater. Tell me where am I to go?"

When I went to see her I smelled of paint and turpentine, and my hands were stained—and she liked that; she wanted me to come to her in my ordinary working clothes; but in her drawing-room those clothes made me feel awkward. I felt embarrassed, as though I were in uniform, so I always put on my new serge trousers when I went to her. And she did not like that.

"You must own you are not quite at home in your new character," she said to me one day. "Your workman's dress does not feel natural to you; you are awkward in it. Tell me, isn't that because you haven't a firm conviction and are not satisfied? The very kind of work you have chosen—your painting—surely it does not satisfy you, does it?" she asked, laughing. "I know paint makes things look nicer and last longer, but those things belong to rich people who live in towns, and after all they are luxuries. Besides, you have often said yourself that everybody ought to get his bread by the work of his own hands, yet you get money and not bread. Why shouldn't you keep to the literal sense of your words? You ought to be getting bread, that is, you ought to be plowing, sowing, reaping, threshing, or doing something which has a direct connection with agriculture, for instance, looking after cows, digging, building huts of logs. . . ."

She opened a pretty cupboard that stood near her writing table, and said:

"I am saying all this to you because I want to let you into my secret. *Voilà*! This is my agricultural library. Here I have fields, kitchen garden and orchard, and cattle yard and beehives. I read them greedily and have already learned all the theory to the tiniest detail. My dream, my darling wish, is to go to our Dubechnya as soon as March is here. It's marvelous there, exquisite, isn't it? The first year I shall have a look round and get into things, and the year after I shall begin to work properly myself, putting my back into it as they say. My father has promised to give me Dubechnya and I shall do exactly what I like with it."

Flushed, excited to tears, and laughing, she dreamed aloud how she would live at Dubechnya, and what an interesting life it would be! I envied her. March was near, the days were growing longer and longer, and on bright sunny days water dripped from the roofs at midday, and there was a fragrance of spring; I, too, longed for the country.

And when she said that she should move to Dubechnya, I realized vividly that I should remain in the town alone, and I felt that I envied her with her cupboard of books and her agriculture. I knew nothing of work on the land and did not like it, and I should have liked to have told her that work on the land was slavish toil, but I remembered that something similar had been said more than once by my father, and I held my tongue.

Lent began. Viktor Ivanich, whose existence I had begun to forget, arrived from Petersburg. He arrived unexpectedly, without even a telegram to say he was coming. When I went in, as usual in the evening, he was walking about the drawing-room, telling some story, with his face freshly washed and shaven, looking ten years younger: his daughter was kneeling on the floor, taking out of his trunks boxes, bottles, and books, and handing them to Pavel, the footman. I involuntarily drew back a step when I saw the engineer, but he held out both hands to me and said, smiling, showing his strong white teeth that looked like a sledge driver's:

"Here he is, here he is! Very glad to see you, Monsieur House-painter! Masha has told me all about it; she has been singing your praises. I quite understand and approve," he went on, taking my arm. "To be a good workman is ever so much more honest and more sensible than wasting government paper and wearing a cockade on your head. I myself worked in Belgium with these very hands and then spent two years as a mechanic. . . ."

He was wearing a short reefer jacket and indoor slippers; he walked like a man with the gout, rolling slightly from side to side and rubbing his hands. Humming something, he softly purred and hugged himself with satisfaction at being at home again at last, and able to have his beloved shower bath.

"There is no disputing," he said to me at supper, "there is no disputing; you are all nice and charming people, but for some reason, as soon as you take to manual labor, or go in for saving the peasants, in the long run it all comes to no more than being a dissenter. Aren't you a dissenter? Here you don't take vodka. What's the meaning of that if it is not being a dissenter?"

To satisfy him I drank some vodka and I drank some wine, too. We tasted the cheese, the sausage, the pâtés, the pickles, and the savories of all sorts that the engineer had brought with him, and the wine that had come in his absence from abroad. The wine was first-rate. For some reason the engineer got wine and cigars from abroad without paying duty; the caviar and the dried sturgeon someone sent him for nothing; he did not pay rent for his flat as the owner of the house provided the kerosene for the line; and altogether he and his daughter produced on me the impression that all the best in the world was at their service and provided for them for nothing.

I went on going to see them, but not with the same eagerness. The engineer made me feel constrained. I could not face his clear, guileless eyes, his reflections wearied and sickened me; I was sickened, too, by the memory that so lately I had been in the employ of this red-faced, well-fed man, and that he had been brutally rude to me. It is true that he put his arm round my waist, slapped me on the shoulder in a friendly way, approved my manner of life, but I felt that, as before, he despised my insignificance, and only put up with me to please his daughter, and I couldn't now laugh and talk as I liked, and I behaved unsociably and kept expecting that in another minute he would address me as Pantelei as he did his footman Pavel. How my pride as a provincial and a workingman was revolted. I, a proletarian, a house painter, went every day to rich people who were alien to me, and whom the whole town regarded as though they were foreigners, and every day I drank costly wines with them and ate unusual dainties—my conscience refused to be reconciled to it! On my way to the house I sullenly avoided meeting people, and looked at them from under my brows as though I really were a dissenter, and when I was going home from the engineer's I was ashamed of my well-fed condition.

Above all I was afraid of being carried away. Whether I was walking along the street, or working, or talking to the other fellows, I was all the time thinking of one thing only, of going in the evening to see Marya Viktorovna and was picturing her voice, her laugh, her movements. When I was getting ready to go to her, I always spent a long time before my nurse's warped looking glass as I fastened my tie; my serge trousers were detestable in my eyes, and I suffered torments, and at the same time despised myself for being so trivial. When she called to me out of the other room that she was not dressed and asked me to wait, I listened to her dressing; it agitated me, I felt as though the ground were giving way under my feet. And when I saw a woman's figure in the street, even at a distance, I invariably compared it. It seemed to me that all our girls and women were vulgar, that they were absurdly dressed and did not know how to hold themselves; and these comparisons aroused a feeling of pride in me: Marya Viktorovna was the best of them all! And I dreamed of her and myself at night.

One evening at supper with the engineer we ate a whole lobster. As I was going home afterwards I remembered that the engineer twice called me "My dear fellow" at supper, and I reflected that they treated me very kindly in that house, as they might an unfortunate big dog that had been kicked out by its owners, that they were amusing themselves with me, and that when they were tired of me they would turn me out like a dog. I felt ashamed and wounded, wounded to the point of tears as though I had been insulted, and, looking up at the sky, I took a vow to put an end to all this.

The next day I did not go to the Dolzhikovs'. Late in the evening, when it was quite dark and raining, I walked along Great Dvoryansky Street, looking up at the windows. Everyone was asleep at the Azhogins', and the only light was in one of the furthest windows. It was Madam Azhogin in her own room, sewing by the light of three candles, imagining that she was combating superstition. Our house was in darkness, but at the Dolzhikovs', on the contrary, the windows were lighted up, but one could distinguish nothing through the flowers and the curtains. I kept walking up and down the street; the cold March rain drenched me through. I heard my father come home from the club; he stood knocking at the gate. A minute later a light appeared at the window, and I saw my sister, who was hastening down with a lamp, while with the other hand she was twisting her thick hair together as she went. Then my father walked about the drawing-room, talking and rubbing his hands, while my sister sat in a low chair, thinking and not listening to what he said.

But then they went away; the light went out. . . . I glanced round at the engineer's, and there, too, all was darkness now. In the dark and the rain I felt hopelessly alone, abandoned to the whims of destiny; I felt that all my doings, my desires, and everything I had thought and said till then were trivial in comparison with my loneliness, in comparison with my present suffering, and the suffering that lay before me in the future. Alas, the thoughts and doings of living creatures are not nearly so significant as their sufferings! And without clearly realizing what I was doing, I pulled at the bell of the Dolzhikovs' gate, broke it, and ran along the street like some naughty boy, with a feeling of terror in my heart, expecting every moment that they would come out and recognize me. When I stopped at the end of the street to take breath I could hear nothing but the sound of the rain, and somewhere in the distance a watchman striking on a sheet of iron.

For a whole week I did not go to the Dolzhikovs'. My serge trousers were sold. There was nothing doing in the painting trade. I knew the pangs of hunger again and earned from twopence to fourpence a day where I could, by heavy and unpleasant work. Struggling up to my knees in the cold mud, straining my chest, I tried to stifle my memories, and, as it were, to punish myself for the cheeses and preserves with which I had been regaled at the engineer's. But all the same, as soon as I lay in bed, wet and hungry, my sinful imagination immediately began to paint exquisite, seductive pictures, and with amazement I acknowledged to myself that I was in love, passionately in love, and I fell into a sound, heavy sleep, feeling that hard labor only made my body stronger and younger.

One evening snow began falling most inappropriately, and the wind blew from the north as though winter had come back again. When I returned from work that evening I found Marya Viktorovna in my room. She was sitting in her fur coat and had both hands in her muff.

"Why don't you come to see me?" she asked, raising her clear, clever eyes, and I was utterly confused with delight and stood stiffly upright before her, as I used to stand facing my father when he was going to beat me; she looked into my face and I could see from her eyes that she understood why I was confused.

"Why don't you come to see me?" she repeated. "If you don't want to come, you see, I have come to you."

She got up and came close to me.

"Don't desert me," she said, and her eyes filled with tears. "I am alone, utterly alone."

She began crying and, hiding her face in her muff, articulated:

"Alone! My life is hard, very hard, and in all the world I have no one but you. Don't desert me!"

Looking for a handkerchief to wipe her tears she smiled; we were silent for some time, then I put my arms round her and kissed her, scratching my cheek till it bled with her hatpin as I did it.

And we began talking to each other as though we had been on the closest terms for ages and ages.

## 10.

Two days later she sent me to Dubechnya and I was unutterably delighted to go. As I walked towards the station and afterwards, as I was sitting in the train, I kept laughing from no apparent cause, and people looked at me as though I were drunk. Snow was falling, and there were still frosts in the mornings, but the roads were already dark-colored and rooks hovered over them, cawing.

At first I had intended to fit up an abode for us two, Masha and me, in the lodge at the side opposite Madam Cheprakov's lodge, but it appeared that the doves and the ducks had been living there for a long time, and it was impossible to clean it without destroying a great number of nests. There was nothing for it but to live in the comfortless rooms of the big house with the sun blinds. The peasants called the house the palace; there were more than twenty rooms in it, and the only furniture was a piano and a child's armchair lying in the attic. And if Masha had brought all her furniture from the town we should even then have been unable to get rid of the impression of immense emptiness and cold. I picked out three small rooms with windows looking into the garden, and worked from early morning till night, setting them to rights, putting in new panes, papering the walls, filling up the holes and chinks in the floors. It was easy, pleasant work. I was continually running to the river to see whether the ice were not going; I kept fancying that starlings were flying. And at night, thinking of Masha, I listened with an unutterably sweet feeling, with clutching delight, to the noise of the rats and the wind droning and knocking above the ceiling. It seemed as though some old house spirit were coughing in the attic.

The snow was deep; a great deal had fallen even at the end of March, but it melted quickly, as though by magic, and the spring floods passed in a tumultuous rush, so that by the beginning of April the starlings were already noisy, and yellow butterflies were flying in the garden. It was exquisite weather. Every day, towards evening, I used to walk to the town to meet Masha, and what a delight it was to walk with bare feet along the gradually drying, still soft road. Halfway I used to sit down and look towards the town, not venturing to go near it. The sight of it troubled me. I kept wondering how the people I knew would behave to me when they heard of my love. What would my father say? What troubled me particularly was the thought that my life was more complicated, and that I had completely lost all power to set it right, and that, like a balloon, it was bearing me away, God knows whither. I no longer considered the problem how to earn my daily bread, how to live, but thought about—I really don't know what.

Masha used to come in a carriage; I used to get in with her, and we drove to Dubechnya, feeling lighthearted and free. Or, after waiting till the sun had set, I would go back dissatisfied and dreary, wondering why Masha had not come; at the gate or in the garden I would be met by a sweet, unexpected apparition—it was she! It would turn out that she had come by rail and had walked from the station. What a festival it was! In a simple woolen dress with a kerchief on her head, with a modest sunshade, but laced in, slender, in expensive foreign boots—it was a talented actress playing the part of a little workgirl. We looked round our domain and decided which should be her room, and which mine, where we would have our avenue, our kitchen garden, our beehives.

We already had hens, ducks, and geese, which we loved because they were ours. We had, all ready for sowing, oats, clover, timothy grass, buckwheat, and vegetable seeds, and we always looked at all these stores and discussed at length the crop we might get; and everything Masha said to me seemed extraordinarily clever and fine. This was the happiest time of my life.

Soon after St. Thomas's week we were married at our parish church in the village of Kurilovka, two miles from Dubechnya. Masha wanted everything to be done quietly; at her wish our "best men" were peasant lads, the sacristan sang alone, and we came back from the church in a small, jolting chaise which she drove herself. Our only guest from the town was my sister Kleopatra, to whom Masha sent a note three days before the wedding. My sister came in a white dress and wore gloves. During the wedding she cried quietly from joy and tenderness. Her expression was motherly and infinitely kind. She was intoxicated with our happiness and smiled as though she were absorbing a sweet delirium; and, looking at her during our wedding, I realized that for her there was nothing in the world higher than love, earthly love, and that she was dreaming of it secretly, timidly, but continually and passionately. She embraced and kissed Masha, and, not knowing how to express her rapture, said to her of me: "He is good! He is very good!"

Before she went away she changed into her ordinary dress and drew me into the garden to talk to me alone.

"Father is very much hurt," she said, "that you have written nothing to him. You ought to have asked for his blessing. But in reality he is very much pleased. He says that this marriage will raise you in the eyes of all society and that under the influence of Marya Viktorovna you will begin to take a more serious view of life. We talk of nothing but you in the evenings now, and yesterday he actually used the expression: 'Our Misail.' That pleased me. It seems as though he had some plan in his mind, and I fancy he wants to set you an example of magnanimity and be the first to speak of reconciliation. It is very possible he may come here to see you in a day or two."

She hurriedly made the sign of the cross over me several times and said:

"Well, God be with you. Be happy. Anyuta Blagovo is a very clever girl; she says about your marriage that God is sending you a fresh ordeal. To be sure—married life does not bring only joy but suffering too. That's bound to be so."

Masha and I walked a couple of miles to see her on her way; we walked back slowly and in silence, as though we were resting. Masha held my hand, my heart felt light, and I had no inclination to talk about love; we had become closer and more akin now that we were married, and we felt that nothing now could separate us.

"Your sister is a nice creature," said Masha, "but it seems as though she had been tormented for years. Your father must be a terrible man."

I began telling her how my sister and I had been brought up, and what a senseless torture our childhood had really been. When she heard how my father had so lately beaten me, she shuddered and drew closer to me.

"Don't tell me any more," she said. "It's horrible!"

Now she never left me. We lived together in the three rooms in the big house, and in the evenings we bolted the door which led to the empty part of the house, as though someone were living there whom we did not know and were afraid of. I got up early, at dawn, and immediately set to work of some sort. I mended the carts, made paths in the garden, dug the flower beds, painted the roof of the house. When the time came to sow the oats I tried to plow the ground over again, to harrow and to sow, and I did it all conscientiously, keeping up with our laborer; I was worn out, the rain and the cold wind made my face and feet burn for hours afterwards. I dreamed of plowed land at night. But field labor did not attract me. I did not understand farming, and I did not care for it; it was perhaps because my forefathers had not been tillers of the soil, and the very blood that flowed in my veins was purely of the city. I loved nature tenderly; I loved the fields and meadows and kitchen gardens, but the peasant who turned up the soil with his plow and urged on his pitiful horse, wet and tattered, with his craning neck, was to me the expression of coarse, savage, ugly force, and every time I looked at the peasant's uncouth movements I involuntarily began thinking of the legendary life of the remote past, before men knew the use of fire. The fierce bull that ran with the peasants' herd, and the horses, when they dashed about the village, stamping their hoofs, moved me to fear, and everything rather big, strong, and angry, whether it was the ram with its horns, the gander, or the yard dog, seemed to me the expression of the same coarse, savage force. This mood was particularly strong in me in bad weather, when heavy clouds were hanging over the black plowed land. Above all, when I was plowing or sowing, and two or three people stood looking at how I was doing it, I had not the feeling that this work was inevitable and obligatory, and it seemed to me that I was amusing myself. I preferred doing something in the yard, and there was nothing I liked so much as painting the roof.

I used to walk through the garden and the meadow to our mill. It was let to a peasant of Kurilovka called Stepan, a handsome, dark fellow with a thick black beard, who looked very strong. He did not like the miller's work, and looked upon it as dreary and unprofitable, and only lived at the mill in order not to live at home. He was a leatherworker and was always surrounded by a pleasant smell of tar and leather. He was not fond of talking; he was listless and sluggish and was always sitting in the doorway or on the riverbank, humming "oo-loo-loo." His wife and mother-in-law, both white-faced, languid, and meek, used sometimes to come from Kurilovka to see him; they made low bows to him and addressed him formally, "Stepan Petrovich," while he went on sitting on the riverbank, softly humming "oo-loo-loo," without responding by word or movement to their bows. One hour and then a second would pass in silence. His mother-in-law and wife, after whispering together, would get up and gaze at him for some time, expecting him to look round; then they would make a low bow, and in sugary, chanting voices, say:

"Good-bye, Stepan Petrovich!"

And they would go away. After that Stepan, picking up the parcel they had left, containing cracknels or a shirt, would heave a sigh and say, winking in their direction:

"The female sex!"

The mill with two sets of millstones worked day and night.

I used to help Stepan; I liked the work, and when he went off I was glad to stay and take his place.

## 11.

After bright warm weather came a spell of wet; all May it rained and was cold. The sound of the mill wheels and of the rain disposed one to indolence and slumber. The floor trembled, there was a smell of flour, and that, too, induced drowsiness. My wife in a short fur-lined jacket, and in men's high galosh boots, would make her appearance twice a day, and she always said the same thing:

"And this is called summer! Worse than it was in October!"

We used to have tea and make the porridge together, or we would sit for hours at a stretch without speaking, waiting for the rain to stop. Once, when Stepan had gone off to the fair, Masha stayed all night at the mill. When we got up we could not tell what time it was, as the rain clouds covered the whole sky; but sleepy cocks were crowing at Dubechnya, and landrails were calling in the meadows; it was still very, very early. . . . My wife and I went down to the millpond and drew out the net which Stepan had thrown in overnight in our presence. A big pike was struggling in it, and a crayfish was twisting about, clawing upwards with its pincers.

"Let them go," said Masha. "Let them be happy too."

Because we got up so early and afterwards did nothing, that day seemed very long, the longest day in my life. Towards evening Stepan came back and I went home.

"Your father came today," said Masha.

"Where is he?" I asked.

"He has gone away. I would not see him."

Seeing that I remained standing and silent, that I was sorry for my father, she said:

"One must be consistent. I would not see him and sent word to him not to trouble to come and see us again."

A minute later I was out at the gate and walking to the town to explain things to my father. It was muddy, slippery, cold. For the first time since my marriage I felt suddenly sad, and in my brain, exhausted by that long, gray day, there was stirring the thought that perhaps I was not living as I ought. I was worn out; little by little I was overcome by despondency and indolence, I did not want to move or think, and after going on a little I gave it up with a wave of my hand and turned back.

The engineer in a leather overcoat with a hood was standing in the middle of the yard.

"Where's the furniture? There used to be lovely furniture in the Empire style: there used to be pictures, there used to be vases, while now you could play ball in it! I bought the place with the furniture. The devil take her!"

Moisei, a thin, pock-marked fellow of twenty-five, with insolent little eyes, who was in the service of the general's widow, stood near him crumpling up his cap in his hands; one of his cheeks was bigger than the other, as though he had lain too long on it.

"Your honor was graciously pleased to buy the place without the furniture," he brought out irresolutely; "I remember."

"Hold your tongue!" shouted the engineer; he turned crimson and shook with anger . . . and the echo in the garden loudly repeated his shout.

## 12.

When I was doing anything in the garden or the yard, Moisei would stand beside me, and, folding his arms behind his back, he would stand lazily and impudently staring at me with his little eyes. And this irritated me to such a degree that I threw up my work and went away.

From Stepan we heard that Moisei was Madam Cheprakov's lover. I noticed that when people came to her to borrow money they addressed themselves first to Moisei, and once I saw a peasant, black from head to foot—he must have been a coal heaver—bow down at Moisei's feet. Sometimes, after a little whispering, he gave out money himself, without consulting his mistress, from which I concluded that he did a little business on his own account.

He used to shoot in our garden under our windows, carried off victuals from our cellar, borrowed our horses without asking permission, and we were indignant and began to feel as though Dubechnya were not ours; and Masha would say, turning pale:

"Can we really have to go on living with these reptiles another year?"

Madam Cheprakov's son, Ivan, was serving as a guard on our railway line. He had grown much thinner and feebler during the winter, so that a single glass was enough to make him drunk, and he shivered out of the sunshine. He wore the guard's uniform with aversion and was ashamed of it, but considered his post a good one, as he could steal the candles and sell them. My new position excited in him a mixed feeling of wonder, envy, and a vague hope that something of the same sort might happen to him. He used to watch Masha with ecstatic eyes, ask me what I had for dinner now, and his lean and ugly face wore a sad and sweetish expression, and he moved his fingers as though he were feeling my happiness with them.

"Listen, Better-than-nothing," he said fussily, relighting his cigarette at every instant; there was always a little where he stood, for he wasted dozens of matches lighting one cigarette. "Listen, my life now is the nastiest possible. The worst of it is any subaltern can shout: 'Hi, there, guard!' I have overheard all sorts of things in the train, my boy, and do you know, I have learned that life's a beastly thing! My mother has been the ruin of me! A doctor in the train told me that if parents are immoral, their children are drunkards or criminals. Think of that!"

Once he came into the yard, staggering; his eyes gazed about blankly, his breathing was labored; he laughed and cried and babbled as though in a high fever, and the only words I could catch in his muddled talk were, "My mother! Where's my mother?" which he uttered with a wail like a child who has lost his mother in a crowd. I led him into our garden and laid him down under a tree, and Masha and I took turns to sit by him all that day and all night. He was very sick, and Masha looked with aversion at his pale, wet face, and said:

"Is it possible these reptiles will go on living another year in our yard? It's awful! It's awful!"

And how many mortifications the peasants caused us! How many bitter disappointments in those early days in the spring months, when we so longed to be happy. My wife built a school. I drew a plan of a school for sixty boys, and the Zemstvo Board approved of it but advised us to build the school at Kurilovka, the big village which was only two miles from us. Moreover, the school at Kurilovka in which children—from four villages, our Dubechnya being one of the number—were taught, was old and too small, and the floor was scarcely safe to walk upon. At the end of March, at Masha's wish, she was appointed guardian of the Kurilovka school, and at the beginning of April we three times summoned the village assembly and tried to persuade the peasants that their school was old and overcrowded, and that it was essential to build a new one. A member of the Zemstvo Board and the inspector of peasant schools came, and they, too, tried to persuade them. After each meeting the peasants surrounded us, begging for a bucket of vodka; we were hot in the crowd; we were soon exhausted and returned home dissatisfied and a little ill at ease. In the end the peasants set apart a plot of ground for the school and were obliged to bring all the building material from the town with their own horses. And the very first Sunday after the spring corn was sown carts set off from Kurilovka and Dubechnya to fetch bricks for the foundations. They set off as soon as it was light and came back late in the evening; the peasants were drunk and said they were worn out.

As ill luck would have it, the rain and the cold persisted all through May. The road was in an awful state: it was deep in mud. The carts usually drove into our yard when they came back from the town—and what a horrible ordeal it was. A pot-bellied horse would appear at the gate, setting its front legs wide apart; it would stumble forward before coming into the yard; a beam, nine yards long, wet and slimy-looking, crept in on a wagon. Beside it, muffled up against the rain, strode a peasant with the skirts of his coat tucked up in his belt, not looking where he was going, but stepping through the puddles. Another cart would appear with boards, then a third with a beam, a fourth . . . and the space before our house was gradually crowded up with horses, beams, and planks. Men and women, with their heads muffled and their skirts tucked up, would stare angrily at our windows, make an uproar, and clamor for the mistress to come out to them; coarse oaths were audible. Meanwhile Moisei stood at one side, and we fancied he was enjoying our discomfiture.

"We are not going to cart any more," the peasants would shout. "We are worn out! Let her go and get the stuff herself."

Masha, pale and flustered, expecting every minute that they would break into the house, would send them out a half pail of vodka; after that the noise would subside and the long beams, one after another, would crawl slowly out of the yard.

When I was setting off to see the building my wife was worried and said:

"The peasants are spiteful; I only hope they won't do you a mischief. Wait a minute, I'll come with you."

We drove to Kurilovka together, and there the carpenters asked us for a drink. The framework of the house was ready. It was time to lay the foundation, but the masons had not come; this caused delay, and the carpenters complained. And when at last the masons did come, it appeared that there was no sand; it had been somehow overlooked that it would be needed. Taking advantage of our helpless position, the peasants demanded thirty kopecks for each cartload, though the distance from the building to the river where they got the sand was less than a quarter of a mile, and more than five hundred cartloads were found to be necessary. There was no end to the misunderstandings, swearing, and importunity; my wife was indignant, and the foreman of the masons, Tit Petrov, an old man of seventy, took her by the arm, and said:

"You look here! You look here! You only bring me the sand; I set ten men on at once, and in two days it will be done! You look here!"

But they brought the sand and two days passed, and four, and a week, and instead of the promised foundation there was still a yawning hole.

"It's enough to drive one out of one's senses," said my wife, in distress. "What people! What people!"

In the midst of these disorderly doings the engineer arrived; he brought with him parcels of wine and savories, and after a prolonged meal lay down for a nap in the veranda and snored so loudly that the laborers shook their heads and said: "Well!"

Masha was not pleased at his coming; she did not trust him, though at the same time she asked his advice. When, after sleeping too long after dinner, he got up in a bad humor and said unpleasant things about our management of the place, or expressed regret that he had bought Dubechnya, which had already been a loss to him, poor Masha's face wore an expression of misery. She would complain to him, and he would yawn and say that the peasants ought to be flogged.

He called our marriage and our life a farce and said it was a caprice, a whim.

"She has done something of the sort before," he said about Masha. "She once fancied herself a great opera singer and left me; I was looking for her for two months, and, my dear soul, I spent a thousand rubles on telegrams alone."

He no longer called me a dissenter or Monsieur Painter, and did not as in the past express approval of my living like a workman, but said:

"You are a strange person! You are not a normal person! I won't venture to prophesy, but you will come to a bad end!"

And Masha slept badly at night and was always sitting at our bedroom window thinking. There was no laughter at supper now, no charming grimaces. I was wretched, and when it rained every drop that fell seemed to pierce my heart, like small shot, and I felt ready to fall on my knees before Masha and apologize for the weather. When the peasants made a noise in the yard I felt guilty also. For hours at a time I sat still in one place, thinking of nothing but what a splendid person Masha was, what a wonderful person. I loved her passionately, and I was fascinated by everything she did, everything she said. She had a bent for quiet, studious pursuits; she was fond of reading for hours together, of studying. Although her knowledge of farming was only from books she surprised us all by what she knew; and ever piece of advice she gave was of value; not one was ever thrown away; and, with all that, what nobility, what taste, what graciousness, that graciousness which is only found in well-educated people.

To this woman, with her sound, practical intelligence, the disorderly surroundings with petty cares and sordid anxieties in which we were living now were an agony: I saw that and could not sleep at night; my brain worked feverishly and I had a lump in my throat. I rushed about not knowing what to do.

I galloped to the town and brought Masha books, newspapers,

sweets, flowers; with Stepan I caught fish, wading for hours up to my neck in the cold water in the rain to catch eelpout to vary our fare; I demeaned myself to beg the peasants not to make a noise; I plied them with vodka, bought them off, made all sorts of promises. And how many other foolish things I did!

At last the rain ceased, the earth dried. One would get up at four o'clock in the morning; one would go out into the garden—where there was dew sparkling on the flowers, the twitter of birds, the hum of insects, not one cloud in the sky; and the garden, the meadows, and the river were so lovely, yet there were memories of the peasants, of their carts, of the engineer. Masha and I drove out together in the racing droshky to the fields to look at the oats. She used to drive, I sat behind; her shoulders were raised and the wind played with her hair.

"Keep to the right!" she shouted to those she met.

"You are like a sledge driver," I said to her one day.

"Maybe! Why, my grandfather, the engineer's father, was a sledge driver. Didn't you know that?" she asked, turning to me, and at once she mimicked the way sledge drivers shout and sing.

"And thank God for that," I thought as I listened to her. "Thank God."

And again memories of the peasants, of the carts, of the engineer . . .

## 13.

Dr. Blagovo arrived on his bicycle. My sister began coming often. Again there were conversations about manual labor, about progress, about a mysterious millennium awaiting mankind in the remote future. The doctor did not like our farm-work because it interfered with arguments, and said that plowing, reaping, grazing calves were unworthy of a free man, and all these coarse forms of the struggle for existence men would in time relegate to animals and machines, while they would devote themselves exclusively to scientific investigation. My sister kept begging them to let her go home earlier, and if she stayed on till late in the evening, or spent the night with us, there would be no end to the agitation.

"Good heavens, what a baby you are still!" said Masha reproachfully. "It is positively absurd."

"Yes, it is absurd," my sister agreed, "I know it's absurd; but what is to be done if I haven't the strength to get over it? I keep feeling as though I were doing wrong."

At haymaking I ached all over from the unaccustomed labor; in the evening, sitting on the veranda and talking with the others, I suddenly dropped asleep, and they laughed aloud at me. They waked me up and made me sit down to supper; I was overpowered with drowsiness and I saw the lights, the faces, and the plates as it were in a dream, heard the voices, but did not understand them. And getting up early in the morning, I took up the scythe at once, or went to the building and worked hard all day.

When I remained at home on holidays I noticed that my sister and Masha were concealing something from me and even seemed to be avoiding me. My wife was tender to me as before, but she had thoughts of her own apart, which she did not share with me. There was no doubt that her exasperation with the peasants was growing, the life was becoming more and more distasteful to her, and yet she did not complain to me. She talked to the doctor now more readily than she did to me, and I did not understand why it was so.

It was the custom in our province at haymaking and harvest time for the laborers to come to the manor house in the evening and be regaled with vodka; even young girls drank a glass. We did not keep up this practice; the mowers and the peasant women stood about in our yard till late in the evening expecting vodka and then departed abusing us. And all the time Masha frowned grimly and said nothing, or murmured to the doctor with exasperation: "Savages! Pechenyegs!"

In the country newcomers are met ungraciously, almost with hostility, as they are at school. And we were received in this way. At first we were looked upon as stupid, silly people, who had bought an estate simply because we did not know what to do with our money. We were laughed at. The peasants grazed their cattle in our wood and even in our garden; they drove away our cows and horses to the village and then demanded money for the damage done by them. They came in whole companies into our yard and loudly clamored that at the mowing we had cut some piece of land that did not belong to us; and as we did not yet know the boundaries of our estate very accurately, we took their word for it and paid damages. Afterwards it turned out that there had been no mistake at the mowing. They barked the lime trees in our wood. One of the Dubechnya peasants, a regular shark, who did a trade in vodka without a license, bribed our laborers and in collaboration with them cheated us in a most treacherous way. They took the new wheels off our carts and replaced them with old ones, stole our plowing harness and actually sold them to us, and so on. But what was most mortifying of all was what happened at the building; the peasant women stole by night boards, bricks, tiles, pieces of iron. The village elder with witnesses made a search in their huts; the village meeting fined them two rubles each, and afterwards this money was spent on drink by the whole commune.

When Masha heard about this, she would say to the doctor or my sister indignantly:

"What beasts! It's awful! awful!"

And I heard her more than once express regret that she had ever taken it into her head to build the school.

"You must understand," the doctor tried to persuade her,

"that if you build this school and do good in general, it's not for the sake of the peasants, but in the name of culture, in the name of the future; and the worse the peasants are the more reason for building the school. Understand that!"

But there was a lack of conviction in his voice, and it seemed to me that both he and Masha hated the peasants.

Masha often went to the mill, taking my sister with her, and they both said, laughing, that they went to have a look at Stepan, he was so handsome. Stepan, it appeared, was torpid and taciturn only with men; in feminine society his manners were free and easy, and he talked incessantly. One day, going down to the river to bathe, I accidentally overheard a conversation. Masha and Kleopatra, both in white dresses, were sitting on the bank in the spreading shade of a willow, and Stepan was standing by them with his hands behind his back, and was saying:

"Are peasants men? They are not men, but, asking your pardon, wild beasts, impostors. What life has a peasant? Nothing but eating and drinking; all he cares for is victuals to be cheaper and swilling liquor at the tavern like a fool; and there's no conversation, no manners, no formality, nothing but ignorance! He lives in filth, his wife lives in filth, and his children live in filth. What he stands up in, he lies down to sleep in; he picks the potatoes out of the soup with his fingers; he drinks kvass with a cockroach in it and doesn't bother to blow it away!"

"It's their poverty, of course," my sister put in.

"Poverty? There is want to be sure, there's different sorts of want, madam. If a man is in prison, or let us say blind or crippled, that really is trouble I wouldn't wish anyone, but if a man's free and has all his senses, if he has his eyes and his hands and his strength and God, what more does he want? It's cockering themselves, and it's ignorance, madam, it's not poverty. If you, let us suppose, good gentlefolk, by your education, wish out of kindness to help him, he will drink away your money in his low way; or, what's worse, he will open a drinkshop, and with your money start robbing the people. You say poverty, but does the rich peasant live better? He, too, asking your pardon, lives like a swine: coarse, loudmouthed, cudgel-headed, broader than he is long, fat, red-faced mug, I'd like to swing my fist and send him flying, the scoundrel. There's Larion, another rich one at Dubechnya, and I bet he strips the bark off your trees as much as any poor one; and he is a foul-mouthed fellow; his children are the same, and when he has had a drop too much he'll topple with his nose in a puddle and sleep there. They are all a worthless lot, madam. If you live in a village with them it is like hell. It has stuck in my teeth, that village has, and thank the Lord, the King of Heaven, I've plenty to eat and clothes to wear, I served out my time in the dragoons, I was village elder for three years, and now I am a free Cossack, I live where I like. I don't want to live in the village, and no one has the right to force me. They say—my wife. They say you are bound to live in your cottage with your wife. But why so? I am not her hired man."

"Tell me, Stepan, did you marry for love?" asked Masha.

"Love among us in the village!" answered Stepan, and he gave a laugh. "Properly speaking, madam, if you care to know, this is my second marriage. I am not a Kurilovka man, I am from Zalegoshcho, but afterwards I was taken into Kurilovka when I married. You see my father did not want to divide the land among us. There were five of us brothers. I took my leave and went to another village to live with my wife's family, but my first wife died when she was young."

"What did she die of?"

"Of foolishness. She used to cry and cry and cry for no reason, and so she pined away. She was always drinking some sort of herbs to make her better-looking, and I suppose she damaged her inside. And my second wife is a Kurilovka woman too, there is nothing in her. She's a village woman, a peasant woman, and nothing more. I was taken in when they plighted me to her. I thought she was young and fair-skinned, and that they lived in a clean way. Her mother was just like a Flagellant and she drank coffee, and the chief thing, to be sure, they were clean in their ways. So I married her, and next day we sat down to dinner; I bade my mother-in-law give me a spoon, and she gives me a spoon, and I see her wipe it out with her finger. So much for you, thought I; nice sort of cleanliness yours is. I lived a year with them and then I went away. I might have married a girl from the town," he went on after a pause. "They say a wife is a helpmate to her husband. What do I want with a helpmate? I help myself; I'd rather she talked to me, and not clack, clack, clack, but circumstantially, feelingly. What is life without good conversation?"

Stepan suddenly paused, and at once there was the sound of his dreary, monotonous "oo-loo-loo." This meant that he had seen me.

Masha used often to go to the mill and evidently found pleasure in her conversations with Stepan. Stepan abused the peasants with such sincerity and conviction, and she was attracted to him. Every time she came back from the mill the feeble-minded peasant, who looked after the garden, shouted at her:

"Wench Palashka! Hulla, wench Palashka!" and he would bark like a dog: "Ga! Ga!"

And she would stop and look at him attentively, as though in that idiot's barking she found an answer to her thoughts, and probably he attracted her in the same way as Stepan's abuse. At home some piece of news would await her, such, for instance, as that the geese from the village had ruined our cabbage in the garden, or that Larion had stolen the reins; and shrugging her shoulders, she would say with a laugh:

"What do you expect of these people?"

She was indignant, and there was rancor in her heart, and meanwhile I was growing used to the peasants, and I felt more and more drawn to them. For the most part they were nervous, irritable, downtrodden people; they were people whose imagination had been stifled, ignorant, with a poor, dingy outlook on life, whose thoughts were ever the same—of the gray earth, of gray days, of black bread, people who cheated, but like birds hiding nothing but their heads behind the tree—people who could not count. They would not come to mow for us for twenty rubles, but they came for half a pail of vodka, though for twenty rubles they could have bought four pails. There really was filth and drunkenness and foolishness and deceit, but with all that one yet felt that the life of the peasants rested on a firm, sound foundation. However uncouth a wild animal the peasant following the plow seemed, and however he might stupefy himself with vodka, still, looking at him more closely, one felt that there was in him what was needed, something very important, which was lacking in Masha and in the doctor, for instance, and that was that he believed the chief thing on earth was truth and justice, and that his salvation, and that of the whole people, was only to be found in truth and justice, and so more than anything in the world he loved just dealing. I told my wife she saw the spots on the glass, but not the glass itself; she said nothing in reply, or hummed like Stepan "oo-loo-loo." When this good-hearted and clever woman turned pale with indignation, and with a quiver in her voice spoke to the doctor of the drunkenness and dishonesty, it perplexed me, and I was struck by the shortness of her memory. How could she forget that her father the engineer drank too, and drank heavily, and that the money with which Dubechnya had been bought had been acquired by a whole series of shameless, impudent dishonesties? How could she forget it?

## 14.

My sister, too, was leading a life of her own which she carefully hid from me. She was often whispering with Masha.

When I went up to her she seemed to shrink into herself, and there was a guilty, imploring look in her eyes; evidently there was something going on in her heart of which she was afraid or ashamed. So as to avoid meeting me in the garden, or being left alone with me, she always kept close to Masha, and I rarely had an opportunity of talking to her except at dinner.

One evening I was walking quietly through the garden on my way back from the building. It was beginning to get dark. Without noticing me, or hearing my step, my sister was walking near a spreading old apple tree, absolutely noiselessly as though she were a phantom. She was dressed in black and was walking rapidly backwards and forwards on the same track, looking at the ground. An apple fell from the tree; she started at the sound, stood still and pressed her hands to her temples. At that moment I went up to her.

In a rush of tender affection which suddenly flooded my heart, with tears in my eyes, suddenly remembering my mother and our childhood, I put my arm round her shoulders and kissed her.

"What is the matter?" I asked her. "You are unhappy; I have seen it for a long time. Tell me what's wrong?"

"I am frightened," she said, trembling.

"What is it?" I insisted. "For God's sake, be open!"

"I will, I will be open; I will tell you the whole truth. To hide it from you is so hard, so agonizing. Misail, I love . . ." she went on in a whisper, "I love him . . . I love him. . . . I am happy, but why am I so frightened?"

There was the sound of footsteps; between the trees appeared Dr. Blagovo in his silk shirt with his high top boots. Evidently they had arranged to meet near the apple tree. Seeing him, she rushed impulsively towards him with a cry of pain as though he were being taken from her.

"Vladimir! Vladimir!"

She clung to him and looked greedily into his face, and only then I noticed how pale and thin she had become of late. It was particularly noticeable from her lace collar which I had known for so long, and which now hung more loosely than ever before about her thin, long neck. The doctor was disconcerted, but at once recovered himself, and, stroking her hair, said:

"There, there. . . . Why so nervous? You see, I'm here."

We were silent, looking with embarrassment at each other, then we walked on, the three of us together, and I heard the doctor say to me:

"Civilized life has not yet begun among us. Old men console themselves by making out that if there is nothing now, there was something in the forties or the sixties; that's the old: you and I are young; our brains have not yet been touched by *marasmus senilis*; we cannot comfort ourselves with such illusions. The beginning of Russia was in 862, but the beginning of civilized Russia has not come yet."

But I did not grasp the meaning of these reflections. It was somehow strange, I could not believe it, that my sister was in love, that she was walking with and holding the arm of a stranger and looking tenderly at him. My sister, this nervous, frightened, crushed, fettered creature, loved a man who was married and had children! I felt sorry for something, but what exactly I don't know; the presence of the doctor was for some reason distasteful to me now, and I could not imagine what would come of this love of theirs.

## 15.

Masha and I drove to Kurilovka to the dedication of the school.

"Autumn, autumn, autumn . . ." said Masha softly, looking away. "Summer is over. There are no birds and nothing is green but the willows."

Yes, summer was over. There were fine, warm days, but it was fresh in the morning, and the shepherds went out in their sheepskins already; and in our garden the dew did not dry off the asters all day long. There were plaintive sounds all the time, and one could not make out whether they came from the shutters creaking on their rusty hinges, or from the flying cranes—and one's heart felt light, and one was eager for life.

"The summer is over," said Masha. "Now you and I can balance our accounts. We have done a lot of work, a lot of thinking; we are the better for it—all honor and glory to us—we have succeeded in self-improvement; but have our successes had any perceptible influence on the life around us, have they brought any benefit to anyone whatever? No. Ignorance, physical uncleanliness, drunkenness, an appallingly high infant mortality, everything remains as it was, and no one is the better for your having plowed and sown, and my having wasted money and read books. Obviously we have been working only for ourselves and have had advanced ideas only for ourselves." Such reasonings perplexed me, and I did not know what to think.

"We have been sincere from beginning to end," said I, "and if anyone is sincere he is right."

"Who disputes it? We were right, but we haven't succeeded in properly accomplishing what we were right in. To begin with, our external methods themselves—aren't they mistaken? You want to be of use to men, but by the very fact of your buying an estate, from the very start you cut yourself off from any possibility of doing anything useful for them. Then if you work, dress, eat like a peasant, you sanctify, as it were, by your authority, their heavy, clumsy dress, their horrible huts, their stupid beards. . . . On the other hand, if we suppose that you work for long, long years, your whole life, that in the end some practical results are obtained, yet what are they, your results, what can they do against such elemental forces as wholesale ignorance, hunger, cold, degeneration? A drop in the ocean! Other methods of struggle are needed, strong, bold, rapid! If one really wants to be of use one must get out of the narrow circle of ordinary social work, and try to act direct upon the mass! What is wanted, first of all, is a loud, energetic propaganda. Why is it that art—music, for instance—is so living, so popular, and in reality so powerful? Because the musician or the singer affects thousands at once. Precious, precious art!" she went on, looking dreamily at the sky. "Art gives us wings and carries us far, far away! Anyone who is sick of filth, of petty, mercenary interests, anyone who is revolted, wounded, and indignant can find peace and satisfaction only in the beautiful."

When we drove into Kurilovka the weather was bright and joyous. Somewhere they were threshing; there was a smell of rye straw. A mountain ash was bright red behind the hurdle fences, and all the trees wherever one looked were ruddy or golden. They were ringing the bells, they were carrying the icons to the school, and we could hear them sing: "Holy Mother, our Defender," and how limpid the air was, and how high the doves were flying.

The service was being held in the classroom. Then the peasants of Kurilovka brought Masha the icon, and the peasants of Dubechnya offered her a big loaf and a gilt saltcellar. And Masha broke into sobs.

"If anything has been said that shouldn't have been or anything done not to your liking, forgive us," said an old man, and he bowed down to her and to me.

As we drove home, Masha kept looking round at the school; the green roof, which I had painted, and which was glistening in the sun, remained in sight for a long while. And I felt that the look Masha turned upon it now was one of farewell.

## 16.

In the evening she got ready to go to the town. Of late she had taken to going often to the town and staying the night there. In her absence I could not work, my hands felt weak and limp; our huge courtyard seemed a dreary, repulsive, empty hole. The garden was full of angry noises, and without her the house, the trees, the horses were no longer "ours."

I did not go out of the house, but went on sitting at her table beside her bookshelf with the books on land work, those old favorites no longer wanted and looking at me now so shamefacedly. For whole hours together, while it struck seven, eight, nine, while the autumn night, black as soot, came on outside, I kept examining her old glove, or the pen with which she always wrote, or her little scissors. I did nothing and realized clearly that all I had done before, plowing, mowing, chopping, had only been because she wished it. And if she had sent me to clean a deep well, where I had to stand up to my waist in deep water, I should have crawled into the well without considering whether it was necessary or not. And now when she was not near, Dubechnya, with its ruins, its untidiness, its banging shutters, with its thieves by day and by night, seemed to me a chaos in which any work would be useless. Besides, what had I to work for here, why anxiety and thought about the future, if I felt that the earth was giving way under my feet, that I had played my part in Dubechnya, and that the fate of the books on farming was awaiting me too? Oh, what misery it was at night, in hours of solitude, when I was listening every minute in alarm, as though I were expecting someone to shout that it was time for me to go away! I did not grieve for Dubechnya. I grieved for my love, which, too, was threatened with its autumn. What an immense happiness it is to love and be loved, and how awful to feel that one is slipping down from that high pinnacle!

Masha returned from the town towards the evening of the next day. She was displeased with something, but she concealed it, and only said, why was it all the window frames had been put in for the winter; it was enough to suffocate one. I took out two frames. We were not hungry, but we sat down to supper.

"Go and wash your hands," said my wife; "you smell of putty."

She had brought some new illustrated papers from the town, and we looked at them together after supper. There were supplements with fashion plates and patterns. Masha looked through them casually and was putting them aside to examine them properly later on, but one dress, with a flat skirt as full as a bell and large sleeves, interested her, and she looked at it for a minute gravely and attentively.

"That's not bad," she said.

"Yes, that dress would suit you beautifully," I said, "beautifully."

And looking with emotion at the dress, admiring that patch of gray simply because she liked it, I went on tenderly:

"A charming, exquisite dress! Splendid, glorious, Masha! My precious Masha!"

And tears dropped on the fashion plate.

"Splendid Masha . . ." I muttered; "sweet, precious Masha . . ."

She went to bed, while I sat another hour looking at the illustrations.

"It's a pity you took out the window frames," she said from the bedroom, "I am afraid it may be cold. Oh dear, what a draught there is!"

I read something out of the column of odds and ends, a receipt for making cheap ink, and an account of the biggest diamond in the world. I came again upon the fashion plate of the dress she liked, and I imagined her at a ball, with a fan, bare shoulders, brilliant, splendid, with a full understanding of painting, music, literature, and how small and how brief my part seemed!

Our meeting, our marriage, had been only one of the episodes of which there would be many more in the life of this vital, richly gifted woman. All the best in the world, as I have said already, was at her service, and she received it absolutely for nothing, and even ideas and the intellectual movement in vogue served simply for her recreation, giving variety to her life, and I was only the sledge driver who drove her from one entertainment to another. Now she did not need me. She would take flight, and I should be alone.

And as though in response to my thought, there came a despairing scream from the garden.

"He-e-elp!"

It was a shrill, womanish voice, and as though to mimic it the wind whistled in the chimney on the same shrill note. Half a minute passed, and again through the noise of the wind, but coming, it seemed, from the other end of the yard:

"He-e-elp!"

"Misail, do you hear?" my wife asked me softly. "Do you hear?"

She came out from the bedroom in her nightgown, with her hair down, and listened, looking at the dark window.

"Someone is being murdered," she said. "That is the last straw."

I took my gun and went out. It was very dark outside, the wind was high, and it was difficult to stand. I went to the gate and listened, the trees roared, the wind whistled, and, probably at the feeble-minded peasant's, a dog howled lazily. Outside the gates the darkness was absolute, not a light on the railway line. And near the lodge, which a year before had been the office, suddenly sounded a smothered scream:

"He-e-elp!"

"Who's there?" I called.

There were two people struggling. One was thrusting the other out, while the other was resisting, and both were breathing heavily.

"Leave go," said one, and I recognized Ivan Cheprakov; it was he who was shrieking in a shrill, womanish voice: "Let go, you damned brute, or I'll bite your hand off."

The other I recognized as Moisei. I separated them, and as I did so I could not resist hitting Moisei two blows in the face. He fell down, then got up again, and I hit him once more.

"He tried to kill me," he muttered. "He was trying to get at his mamma's chest. . . . I want to lock him up in the lodge for security."

Cheprakov was drunk and did not recognize me; he kept drawing deep breaths, as though he were just going to shout "help" again.

I left them and went back to the house; my wife was lying on her bed; she had dressed. I told her what had happened in the yard and did not conceal the fact that I had hit Moisei.

"It's terrible to live in the country," she said. "And what a long night it is. Oh dear, if only it were over!"

"He-e-elp!" we heard again, a little later.

"I'll go and stop them," I said.

"No, let them bite each other's throats," she said with an expression of disgust.

She was looking up at the ceiling, listening, while I sat beside her, not daring to speak to her, feeling as though I were to blame for their shouting "help" in the yard and for the night's seeming so long.

We were silent, and I waited impatiently for a gleam of light at the window, and Masha looked all the time as though she had awakened from a trance and now was marveling how she, so clever and well-educated, so elegant, had come into this pitiful, provincial, empty hole among crew of petty, insignificant people, and how she could have so far forgotten herself as ever to be attracted by one of these people, and for more than six months to have been his wife. It seemed to me that at that moment it did not matter to her whether it was I, or Moisei, or Cheprakov; everything for her was merged in that savage drunken "help"—I and our marriage, and our work together, and the mud and slush of autumn, and when she sighed or moved into a more comfortable position I read in her face: "Oh, that morning would come quickly!"

In the morning she went away. I spent another three days at Dubechnya expecting her, then I packed all our things in one room, locked it, and walked to the town. It was already evening when I rang at the engineer's, and the street lamps were burning in Great Dvoryansky Street. Pavel told me there was no one at home; Viktor Ivanich had gone to Petersburg, and Marya Viktorovna was probably at the rehearsal at the Azhogins'. I remember with what emotion I went on to the Azhogins', how my heart throbbed and fluttered as I mounted the stairs and stood waiting a long while on the landing at the top, not daring to enter that temple of the muses! In the big room there were lighted candles everywhere, on a little table, on the piano, and on the stage, everywhere in threes; and the first performance was fixed for the thirteenth, and now the first rehearsal was on a Monday, an unlucky day. All part of the war against superstition! All the devotees of the scenic art were gathered together; the eldest, the middle, and the youngest sisters were walking about the stage, reading their parts in exercise books. Apart from all the rest stood Radish, motionless, with the side of his head pressed to the wall as he gazed with adoration at the stage, waiting for the rehearsal to begin. Everything as it used to be.

I was making my way to my hostess; I had to pay my respects to her, but suddenly everyone said "Hush!" and waved me to step quietly. There was a silence. The lid of the piano was raised; a lady sat down at it, screwing up her shortsighted eyes at the music, and my Masha walked up to the piano, in a low-necked dress, looking beautiful, but with a special, new sort of beauty not in the least like the Masha who used to come and meet me in the spring at the mill. She sang: "Why do I love the radiant night?"

It was the first time during our whole acquaintance that I had heard her sing. She had a fine, mellow, powerful voice, and while she sang I felt as though I were eating a ripe, sweet, fragrant melon. She ended, the audience applauded, and she smiled, very much pleased, making play with her eyes, turning over the music, smoothing her skirts, like a bird that has at last broken out of its cage and preens its wings in freedom. Her hair was arranged over her ears, and she had an unpleasant, defiant expression in her face, as though she wanted to throw down a challenge to us all, or to shout to us as she did to her horses: "Hey, there, my beauties!"

And she must at that moment have been very much like her grandfather the sledge driver.

"You here too?" she said, giving me her hand. "Did you hear me sing? Well, what did you think of it?" and without waiting for my answer she went on: "It's a very good thing you are here. I am going tonight to Petersburg for a short time. You'll let me go, won't you?"

At midnight I went with her to the station. She embraced me affectionately, probably feeling grateful to me for not asking unnecessary questions, and she promised to write to me, and I held her hands a long time, and kissed them, hardly able to restrain my tears and not uttering a word.

And when she had gone I stood watching the retreating lights, caressing her in imagination and softly murmuring:

"My darling Masha, glorious Masha . . ."

I spent the night at Karpovna's, and next morning I was at work with Radish, re-covering the furniture of a rich merchant who was marrying his daughter to a doctor.

## 17.

My sister came after dinner on Sunday and had tea with me.

"I read a great deal now," she said, showing me the books which she had fetched from the public library on her way to me. "Thanks to your wife and to Vladimir, they have awakened me to self-realization. They have been my salvation; they have made me feel myself a human being. In old days I used to lie awake at night with worries of all sorts, thinking what a lot of sugar we had used in the week, or hoping the cucumbers would not be too salt. And now, too, I lie awake at night, but I have different thoughts. I am distressed that half my life has been passed in such a foolish, cowardly way. I despise my past; I am ashamed of it. And look upon our father now as my enemy. Oh, how grateful I am to your wife! And Vladimir! He is such a wonderful person! They have opened my eyes!"

"That's bad that you don't sleep at night," I said.

"Do you think I am ill? Not at all. Vladimir sounded me, and said I was perfectly well. But health is not what matters, it is not so important. . . . Tell me: am I right?"

She needed moral support, that was obvious. Masha had gone away. Dr. Blagovo was in Petersburg, and there was no one left in the town but me to tell her she was right. She looked intently into my face, trying to read my secret thoughts, and if I were absorbed or silent in her presence, she thought this was on her account and was grieved. I always had to be on my guard, and when she asked me whether she was right I hastened to assure her that she was right, and that I had a deep respect for her.

"Do you know they have given me a part at the Azhogins'?" she went on. "I want to act on the stage, I want to live—in fact, I mean to drain the full cup. I have no talent, none, and the part is only ten lines, but still this is immeasurably finer and loftier than pouring out tea five times a day, and looking to see if the cook has eaten too much. Above all, let my father see I am capable of protest."

After tea she lay down on my bed, and lay for a little while with her eyes closed, looking very pale.

"What weakness," she said, getting up. "Vladimir says all city-bred women and girls are anemic from doing nothing. What a clever man Vladimir is! He is right, absolutely right. We must work!"

Two days later she came to the Azhogins' with her manuscript for the rehearsal. She was wearing a black dress with a string of coral round her neck, and a brooch that in the distance was like a pastry puff, and in her ears earrings sparkling with brilliants. When I looked at her I felt uncomfortable. I was struck by her lack of taste. That she had very inappropriately put on earrings and brilliants, and that she was strangely dressed, was remarked by other people too; I saw smiles on people's faces, and heard someone say with a laugh: "Kleopatra of Egypt."

She was trying to assume society manners, to be unconstrained and at her ease, and so seemed artificial and strange. She had lost simplicity and sweetness.

"I told Father just now that I was going to the rehearsal," she began, coming up to me, "and he shouted that he would not give me his blessing, and actually almost struck me. Only fancy, I don't know my part," she said, looking at her manuscript. "I am sure to make a mess of it. So be it, the die is cast," she went on in intense excitement. "The die is cast. . . ."

It seemed to her that everyone was looking at her, and that all were amazed at the momentous step she had taken, that everyone was expecting something special of her, and it would have been impossible to convince her that no one was paying attention to people so petty and insignificant as she and I were.

She had nothing to do till the third act, and her part, that of a visitor, a provincial crony, consisted only in standing at the door as though listening, and then delivering a brief monologue. In the interval before her appearance, an hour and a half at least, while they were moving about on the stage reading their parts, drinking tea and arguing, she did not leave my side, and was all the time muttering her part and nervously crumpling up the manuscript. And, imagining that everyone was looking at her and waiting for her appearance, with a trembling hand she smoothed back her hair and said to me:

"I shall certainly make a mess of it. . . . What a load on my heart, if only you knew! I feel frightened, as though I were just going to be led to execution."

At last her turn came.

"Kleopatra Alexyevna, it's your cue!" said the stage manager.

She came forward into the middle of the stage with an expression of horror on her face, looking ugly and angular, and for half a minute stood as though in a trance, perfectly motionlness, and only her big earrings shook in her ears.

"The first time you can read it," said someone.

It was clear to me that she was trembling, and trembling so much that she could not speak, and could not unfold her manuscript, and that she was incapable of acting her part; and I was already on the point of going to her and saying something, when she suddenly dropped on her knees in the middle of the stage and broke into loud sobs.

All was commotion and hubbub. I alone stood still, leaning against the side scene, overwhelmed by what had happened, not understanding and not knowing what to do. I saw them lift her up and lead her away. I saw Anyuta Blagovo come up to me; I had not seen her in the room before, and she seemed to have sprung out of the earth. She was wearing her hat and veil, and, as always, had an air of having come only for a moment.

"I told her not to take a part," she said angrily, jerking out each word abruptly and turning crimson. "It's insanity! You ought to have prevented her!"

Madam Azhogin, in a short jacket with short sleeves, with cigarette ash on her breast, looking thin and flat, came rapidly towards me.

"My dear, this is terrible," she brought out, wringing her hands, and, as her habit was, looking intently into my face. "This is terrible! Your sister is in a condition. . . . She is with child. Take her away, I implore you. . . ."

She was breathless with agitation, while on one side stood her three daughters, exactly like her, thin and flat, huddling together in a scared way. They were alarmed, overwhelmed, as though a convict had been caught in their house. What a disgrace, how dreadful! And yet this estimable family had spent its life waging war on superstition; evidently they imagined that all the superstition and error of humanity was limited to the three candles, the thirteenth of the month, and to the unluckiness of Monday!

"I beg you . . . I beg," repeated Madam Azhogin, pursing up her lips in the shape of a heart on the syllable "you." "I beg you to take her home."

## 18.

A little later my sister and I were walking along the street. I covered her with the skirts of my coat; we hastened, choosing back streets where there were no street lamps, avoiding passers-by; it was as though we were running away. She was no longer crying, but looked at me with dry eyes. To Karpovna's, where I took her, it was only twenty minutes' walk, and, strange to say, in that short time we succeeded in thinking of our whole life; we talked over everything, considered our position, reflected. . . .

We decided we could not go on living in this town, and that when I had earned a little money we would move to some other place. In some houses everyone was asleep, in others they were playing cards; we hated these houses; we were afraid of them. We talked of the fanaticism, the coarseness of feeling, the insignificance of these respectable families, these amateurs of dramatic art whom we had so alarmed, and I kept asking in what way these stupid, cruel, lazy, and dishonest people were superior to the drunken and superstitious peasants of Kurilovka, or in what way they were better than animals, who in the same way are thrown into a panic when some incident disturbs the monotony of their life limited by their instincts. What would have happened to my sister now if she had been left to live at home?

What moral agonies would she have experienced, talking with my father, meeting every day with acquaintances? I imagined this to myself, and at once there came into my mind people, all people I knew, who had been slowly done to death by their nearest relations. I remembered the tortured dogs, driven mad, the live sparrows plucked naked by boys and flung into the water, and a long, long series of obscure lingering miseries which I had looked on continually from early childhood in that town; and I could not understand what these sixty-five thousand people lived for, what they read the gospel for, why they prayed, why they read books and magazines. What good had they gained from all that had been said and written hitherto if they were still possessed by the same spiritual darkness and hatred of liberty, as they were a hundred and three hundred years ago? A master carpenter spends his whole life building houses in the town, and always, to the day of his death, calls a "gallery" a "galdery." So these sixty-five thousand people have been reading and hearing of truth, of justice, of mercy, of freedom for generations, and yet from morning till night, till the day of their death, they are lying, and tormenting each other, and they fear liberty and hate it as a deadly foe.

"And so my fate is decided," said my sister, as we arrived

home. "After what has happened I cannot go back *there*. Heavens, how good that is! My heart feels lighter."

She went to bed at once. Tears were glittering on her eyelashes, but her expression was happy; she fell into a sound sweet sleep, and one could see that her heart was lighter and that she was resting. It was a long, long time since she had slept like that.

And so we began our life together. She was always singing and saying that her life was very happy, and the books I brought her from the public library I took back unread, as now she could not read; she wanted to do nothing but dream and talk of the future, mending my linen, or helping Karpovna near the stove; she was always singing, or talking of her Vladimir, of his cleverness, of his charming manners, of his kindness, of his extraordinary learning, and I assented to all she said, though by now I disliked her doctor. She wanted to work, to lead an independent life on her own account, and she used to say that she would become a schoolteacher or a doctor's assistant as soon as her health would permit her and would herself do the scrubbing and the washing. Already she was passionately devoted to her child; he was not yet born, but she knew already the color of his eyes, what his hands would be like, and how he would laugh. She was fond of talking about education, and as her Vladimir was the best man in the world, all her discussion of education could be summed up in the question how to make the boy as fascinating as his father. There was no end to her talk, and everything she said made her intensely joyful. Sometimes I was delighted, too, though I could not have said why.

I suppose her dreaminess infected me. I, too, gave up reading and did nothing but dream. In the evenings, in spite of my fatigue, I walked up and down the room, with my hands in my pockets, talking of Masha.

"What do you think?" I would ask of my sister. "When will

she come back? I think she'll come back at Christmas, not later; what has she to do there?"

"As she doesn't write to you, it's evident she will come back very soon."

"That's true," I assented, though I knew perfectly well that Masha would not return to our town.

I missed her fearfully, and could no longer deceive myself, and tried to get other people to deceive me. My sister was expecting her doctor, and I—Masha; and both of us talked incessantly, laughed, and did not notice that we were preventing Karpovna from sleeping. She lay on the stove and kept muttering:

"The samovar hummed this morning, it did hum! Oh, it bodes no good, my dears, it bodes no good!"

No one ever came to see us but the postman, who brought my sister letters from the doctor, and Prokofy, who sometimes came in to see us in the evening, and, after looking at my sister, without speaking went away, and when he was in the kitchen said:

"Every class ought to remember its rules, and anyone who is so proud that he won't understand that will find it a vale of tears."

He was very fond of the phrase "a vale of tears." One day—it was in Christmas week, when I was walking by the bazaar—he called me into the butcher's shop, and, not shaking hands with me, announced that he had to speak to me about something very important. His face was red from the frost and vodka; near him, behind the counter, stood Nikolka, with the expression of a brigand, holding a bloodstained knife in his hand.

"I desire to express my word to you," Prokofy began. "This incident cannot continue, because, as you understand yourself that for such a vale, people will say nothing good of you or of us. Mamma, through pity, cannot say something unpleasant to you, that your sister should move into another lodging on account of her condition, but I won't have it any more, because I can't approve of her behavior."

I understood him, and I went out of the shop. The same day my sister and I moved to Radish's. We had no money for a cab, and we walked on foot; I carried a parcel of our belongings on my back; my sister had nothing in her hands, but she gasped for breath and coughed and kept asking whether we should get there soon.

## 19.

At last a letter came from Masha.

"Dear, good M.A." (she wrote), "our kind, gentle 'angel,' as the old painter calls you, farewell; I am going with my father to America for the exhibition. In a few days I shall see the ocean—so far from Dubechnya, it's dreadful to think! It's far and unfathomable as the sky, and I long to be there in freedom. I am triumphant, I am mad, and you see how incoherent my letter is. Dear, good one, give me my freedom, make haste to break the thread, which still holds, binding you and me together. My meeting and knowing you was a ray from heaven that lighted up my existence; but my becoming your wife was a mistake, you understand that, and I am oppressed now by the consciousness of the mistake, and I beseech you, on my knees, my generous friend, quickly, quickly, before I start for the ocean, telegraph that you consent to correct our common mistake, to remove the solitary stone from my wings, and my father, who will undertake all the arrangements, promised me not to burden you too much with formalities. And so I am free to fly whither I will? Yes?

"Be happy, and God bless you; forgive me, a sinner.

"I am well, I am wasting money, doing all sorts of silly things, and I thank God every minute that such a bad woman as I has no children. I sing and have success, but it's not an infatuation; no, it's my haven, my cell to which I go for peace. King David had a ring with an inscription on it: 'All things pass.' When one is sad those words make one cheerful, and when one is cheerful it makes one sad. I have got myself a ring like that with Hebrew letters on it, and this talisman keeps me from infatuations. All things pass, life will pass, one wants nothing. Or at least one wants nothing but the sense of freedom, for when anyone is free, he wants nothing, nothing, nothing. Break the thread. A warm hug to you and your sister. Forgive and forget your M."

My sister used to lie down in one room, and Radish, who had been ill again and was now better, in another. Just at the moment when I received this letter my sister went softly into the painter's room, sat down beside him and began reading aloud. She read to him every day, Ostrovsky or Gogol, and he listened, staring at one point, not laughing, but shaking his head and muttering to himself from time to time:

"Anything may happen! Anything may happen!"

If anything ugly or unseemly were depicted in the play he would say as though vindictively, thrusting his finger into the book:

"There it is, lying! That's what it does, lying does."

The plays fascinated him, both from their subjects and their moral, and from their skillful, complex construction, and he marveled at "him," never calling the author by his name. How neatly *he* has put it all together.

This time my sister read softly only one page and could read no more: her voice would not last out. Radish took her hand and, moving his parched lips, said, hardly audibly, in a husky voice:

"The soul of a righteous man is white and smooth as chalk, but the soul of a sinful man is like pumice stone. The soul of a righteous man is like clear oil, but the soul of a sinful man is gas tar. We must labor, we must sorrow, we must suffer sickness," he went on, "and he who does not labor and sorrow will not gain the Kingdom of Heaven. Woe, woe to them that are well fed, woe to the mighty, woe to the rich, woe to the moneylenders! Not for them is the Kingdom of Heaven. Lice eat grass, rust eats iron . . ."

"And lying the soul," my sister added laughing.

I read the letter through once more. At that moment there walked into the kitchen a soldier who had been bringing us twice a week parcels of tea, French bread, and game, which smelled of scent, from some unknown giver. I had no work. I had had to sit at home idle for whole days together, and probably whoever sent us the French bread knew that we were in want.

I heard my sister talking to the soldier and laughing gaily. Then, lying down, she ate some French bread and said to me:

"When you wouldn't go into the service, but became a house painter, Anyuta Blagovo and I knew from the beginning that you were right, but we were frightened to say so aloud. Tell me what force is it that hinders us from saying what one thinks? Take Anyuta Blagovo now, for instance. She loves you, she adores you, she knows you are right, she loves me too, like a sister, and knows that I am right, and I daresay in her soul envies me, but some force prevents her from coming to see us, she shuns us, she is afraid."

My sister crossed her arms over her breast, and said passionately:

"How she loves you, if only you knew! She has confessed her love to no one but me, and then very secretly in the dark. She led me into a dark avenue in the garden and began whispering how precious you were to her. You will see, she'll never marry, because she loves you. Are you sorry for her?"

"Yes."

"It's she who has sent the bread. She is absurd really, what is the use of being so secret? I used to be absurd and foolish, but now I have got away from that and am afraid of nobody. I think and say aloud what I like and am happy. When I lived at home I hadn't a conception of happiness, and now I wouldn't change with a queen."

Dr. Blagovo arrived. He had taken his doctor's degree, and was now staying in our town with his father; he was taking a rest, and said that he would soon go back to Petersburg again. He wanted to study anti-toxins against typhus, and, I believe, cholera; he wanted to go abroad to perfect his training, and then to be appointed a professor. He had already left the army service, and wore a roomy serge reefer jacket, very full trousers, and magnificent neckties. My sister was in ecstasies over his scarf pin, his studs, and the red silk handkerchief which he wore, I suppose from foppishness, sticking out of the breast pocket of his jacket. One day, having nothing to do, she and I counted up all the suits we remembered him wearing, and came to the conclusion that he had at least ten. It was clear that he still loved my sister as before, but he never once even in jest spoke of taking her with him to Petersburg or abroad, and I could not picture to myself clearly what would become of her if she remained alive and what would become of her child. She did nothing but dream endlessly and never thought seriously of the future; she said he might go where he liked and might abandon her even, so long as he was happy himself; that what had been was enough for her.

As a rule he used to sound her very carefully on his arrival and used to insist on her taking milk and drops in his presence. It was the same on this occasion. He sounded her and made her drink a glass of milk, and there was a smell of creosote in our room afterwards.

"That's a good girl," he said, taking the glass from her. "You mustn't talk too much now; you've taken to chattering like a magpie of late. Please hold your tongue."

She laughed. Then he came into Radish's room where I was sitting and affectionately slapped me on the shoulder.

"Well, how goes it, old man?" he said, bending down to the invalid.

"Your honor," said Radish, moving his lips slowly, "your honor, I venture to submit. . . . We all walk in the fear of God, we all have to die. . . . Permit me to tell you the truth. . . . Your honor, the Kingdom of Heaven will not be for you!"

"There's no help for it," the doctor said jestingly; "there must be somebody in hell, you know."

And all at once something happened with my consciousness; as though I were in a dream, as though I were standing on a winter night in the slaughterhouse yard, and Prokofy beside me, smelling of pepper cordial; I made an effort to control myself, and rubbed my eyes, and at once it seemed to me that I was going along the road to the interview with the governor. Nothing of the sort had happened to me before, or has happened to me since, and these strange memories that were like dreams I ascribed to overexhaustion of my nerves. I lived through the scene at the slaughterhouse, and the interview with the governor, and at the same time was dimly aware that it was not real.

When I came to myself I saw that I was no longer in the house, but in the street, and was standing with the doctor near a lamppost.

"It's sad, it's sad," he was saying, and tears were trickling down his cheeks. "She is in good spirits, she's always laughing and hopeful, but her position's hopeless, dear boy. Your Radish hates me and is always trying to make me feel that I have treated her badly. He is right from his standpoint, but I have my point of view too; and I shall never regret all that has happened. One must love; we ought all to love—oughtn't we? There would be no life without love; anyone who fears and avoids love is not free."

Little by little he passed to other subjects, began talking of science, of his dissertation which had been liked in Petersburg.

He was carried away by his subject, and no longer thought of my sister, nor of his grief, nor of me. Life was of absorbing interest to him. She has America and her ring with the inscription on it, I thought, while this fellow has his doctor's degree and a professor's chair to look forward to, and only my sister and I are left with the old things.

When I said good-bye to him, I went up to the lamppost and read the letter once more. And I remembered, I remembered vividly how that spring morning she had come to me at the mill, lain down and covered herself with her jacket—she wanted to be like a simple peasant woman. And how, another time—it was in the morning also—we drew the net out of the water, and heavy drops of rain fell upon us from the riverside willows, and we laughed. . . .

It was dark in our house in Great Dvoryansky Street. I got over the fence and, as I used to do in the old days, went by the back way to the kitchen to borrow a lantern. There was no one in the kitchen. The samovar hissed near the stove, waiting for my father. "Who pours out my father's tea now?" I thought. Taking the lantern I went out to the shed, built myself up a bed of old newspapers and lay down. The hooks on the walls looked forbidding, as they used to of old, and their shadows flickered. It was cold. I felt that my sister would come in in a minute and bring me supper, but at once I remembered that she was ill and was lying at Radish's, and it seemed to me strange that I should have climbed over the fence and be lying here in this unheated shed. My mind was in a maze, and I saw all sorts of absurd things.

There was a ring. A ring familiar from childhood: first the wire rustled against the wall, then a short plaintive ring in the kitchen. It was my father come back from the club. I got up and went into the kitchen. Axinya, the cook, clasped her hands on seeing me and for some reason burst into tears.

"My own!" she said softly. "My precious! O Lord!"

And she began crumpling up her apron in her agitation. In the window there were standing jars of berries in vodka. I poured myself out a teacupful and greedily drank it off, for I was intensely thirsty. Axinya had quite recently scrubbed the table and benches, and there was that smell in the kitchen which is found in bright, snug kitchens kept by tidy cooks. And that smell and the chirp of the cricket used to lure us as children into the kitchen and put us in the mood for hearing fairy tales and playing at "kings."

"Where's Kleopatra?" Axinya asked softly, in a fluster, holding her breath; "and where is your cap, my dear? Your wife, you say, has gone to Petersburg?"

She had been our servant in our mother's time and used once to give Kleopatra and me our baths, and to her we were still children who had to be talked to for their good. For a quarter of an hour or so she laid before me all the reflections which she had with the sagacity of an old servant been accumulating in the stillness of that kitchen, all the time since we had seen each other. She said that the doctor could be forced to marry Kleopatra; he only needed to be thoroughly frightened; and that if an appeal were promptly written the bishop would annul the first marriage; that it would be a good thing for me to sell Dubechnya without my wife's knowledge and put the money in the bank in my own name; that if my sister and I were to bow down at my father's feet and ask him properly, he might perhaps forgive us; that we ought to have a service sung to the Queen of Heaven. . . .

"Come, go along, my dear, and speak to him," she said, when she heard my father's cough. "Go along, speak to him; bow down, your head won't drop off."

I went in. My father was sitting at the table sketching a plan of a summer villa, with Gothic windows, and with a fat turret like a fireman's watchtower—something peculiarly stiff and tasteless. Going into the study I stood still where I could see his drawing. I did not know why I had gone in to my father, but I remember that when I saw his lean face, his red neck, and his shadow on the wall, I wanted to throw myself on his neck, and as Axinya had told me, bow down at his feet; but the sight of the summer villa with the Gothic windows, and the fat turret, restrained me.

"Good evening," I said.

He glanced at me and at once dropped his eyes to his drawing.

"What do you want?" he asked, after waiting a little.

"I have come to tell you my sister's very ill. She can't live very long," I added in a hollow voice.

"Well," sighed my father, taking off his spectacles and laying them on the table. "What thou sowest that shalt thou reap. What thou sowest," he repeated, getting up from the table, "that shalt thou reap. I ask you to remember how you came to me two years ago, and on this very spot I begged you, I besought you to give up your errors; I reminded you of your duty, of your honor, of what you owed to your forefathers whose traditions we ought to preserve as sacred. Did you obey me? You scorned my counsels and obstinately persisted in clinging to your false ideals; worse still you drew your sister into the path of error with you and led her to lose her moral principles and sense of shame. Now you are both in a bad way. Well, as thou sowest, so shalt thou reap!"

As he said this he walked up and down the room. He probably imagined that I had come to him to confess my wrong doings, and he probably expected that I should begin begging him to forgive my sister and me. I was cold, I was shivering as though I were in a fever and spoke with difficulty in a husky voice.

"And I beg you, too, to remember," I said, "on this very spot I besought you to understand me, to reflect, to decide with me how and for what we should live, and in answer you began talking about our forefathers, about my grandfather who wrote poems. One tells you now that your only daughter is hopelessly ill, and you go on again about your forefathers, your traditions. . . . And such frivolity in your old age, when death is close at hand, and you haven't more than five or ten years left!"

"What have you come here for?" my father asked sternly, evidently offended at my reproaching him for his frivolity.

"I don't know. I love you, I am unutterably sorry that we are so far apart—so you see I have come. I love you still, but my sister has broken with you completely. She does not forgive you and will never forgive you now. Your very name arouses her aversion for the past, for life."

"And who is to blame for it?" cried my father. "It's your fault, you scoundrel!"

"Well, suppose it is my fault," I said. "I admit I have been to blame in many things, but why is it that this life of yours, which you think binding upon us, too—why is it so dreary, so barren? How is it that in not one of these houses you have been building for the last thirty years has there been anyone from whom I might have learned how to live, so as not to be to blame? There is not one honest man in the whole town! These houses of yours are nests of damnation, where mothers and daughters are made away with, where children are tortured. . . . My poor mother!" I went on in despair. "My poor sister! One has to stupefy oneself with vodka, with cards, with scandal; one must become a scoundrel, a hypocrite, or go on drawing plans for years and years, so as not to notice all the horrors that lie hidden in these houses. Our town has existed for hundreds of years, and all that time it has not produced one man of service to our country—not one. You have stifled in the germ everything in the least living and bright. It's a town of shopkeepers, publicans, countinghouse clerks, canting hypocrites; it's a useless, unnecessary town, which not one soul would regret if it suddenly sank through the earth."

"I don't want to listen to you, you scoundrel!" said my father, and he took up his ruler from the table. "You are drunk.

Don't dare come and see your father in such a state! I tell you for the last time, and you can repeat it to your depraved sister, that you'll get nothing from me, either of you. I have torn my disobedient children out of my heart, and if they suffer for their disobedience and obstinacy I do not pity them. You can go whence you came. It has pleased God to chastise me with you, but I will bear the trial with resignation, and, like Job, I will find consolation in my sufferings and in unremitting labor. You must not cross my threshold till you have mended your ways. I am a just man, all I tell you is for your benefit, and if you desire your own good you ought to remember all your life what I say and have said to you. . . ."

I waved my hand in despair and went away. I don't remember what happened afterwards, that night and next day.

I am told that I walked about the streets bareheaded, staggering, and singing aloud, while a crowd of boys ran after me, shouting:

"Better-than-nothing!"

## 20.

If I wanted to order a ring for myself, the inscription I should choose would be: "Nothing passes away." I believe that nothing passes away without leaving a trace, and that every step we take, however small, has significance for our present and our future existence.

What I have been through has not been for nothing. My great troubles, my patience, have touched people's hearts, and now they don't call me "Better-than-nothing," they don't laugh at me, and when I walk by the shops they don't throw water over me. They have grown used to my being a workman, and see nothing strange in my carrying a pail of paint and putting in windows, though I am of noble rank; on the contrary, people are glad to give me orders, and I am now considered a first-rate workman, and the best foreman after Radish, who, though he has regained his health, and though, as before, he paints the cupola on the belfry without scaffolding, has no longer the force to control the workmen; instead of him I now run about the town looking for work, I engage the workmen and pay them, borrow money at a high rate of interest, and now that I myself am a contractor, I understand how it is that one may have to waste three days racing about the town in search of tilers on account of some twopenny-halfpenny job. People are civil to me, they address me politely, and in the houses where I work they offer me tea and send to inquire whether I wouldn't like dinner. Children and young girls often come and look at me with curiosity and compassion.

One day I was working in the governor's garden, painting an arbor there to look like marble. The governor, walking in the garden, came up to the arbor and, having nothing to do, entered into conversation with me, and I reminded him how he had once summoned me to an interview with him. He looked into my face intently for a minute, then made his mouth like a round "O," flung up his hands, and said: "I don't remember!"

I have grown older, have become silent, stern, and austere; I rarely laugh, and I am told that I have grown like Radish, and that like him I bore the workmen by my useless exhortations.

Marya Viktorovna, my former wife, is living now abroad, while her father is constructing a railway somewhere in the eastern provinces, and is buying estates there. Dr. Blagovo is also abroad. Dubechnya has passed again into the possession of Madam Cheprakov, who has bought it after forcing the engineer to knock the price down twenty percent. Moisei goes about now in a bowler hat; he often drives into the town in a racing droshky on business of some sort and stops near the bank. They say he has already bought up a mortgaged estate and is constantly making inquiries at the bank about Dubechnya, which he means to buy too. Poor Ivan Cheprakov was for a long while out of work, staggering about the town and drinking. I tried to get him into our work, and for a time he painted roofs and put in windowpanes in our company, and even got to like it, and stole oil, asked for tips, and drank like a regular painter. But he soon got sick of the work and went back to Dubechnya, and afterwards the workmen confessed to me that he had tried to persuade them to join him one night and murder Moisei and rob Madam Cheprakov.

My father has greatly aged; he is very bent, and in the evenings walks up and down near his house. I never go to see him.

During an epidemic of cholera Prokofy doctored some of the shopkeepers with pepper cordial and pitch, and took money for doing so, and, as I learned from the newspapers, was flogged for abusing the doctors as he sat in his shop. His shopboy Nikolka died of cholera. Karpovna is still alive and, as always, she loves and fears her Prokofy. When she sees me, she always shakes her head mournfully, and says with a sigh: "Your life is ruined."

On working days I am busy from morning till night. On holidays, in fine weather, I take my tiny niece (my sister reckoned on a boy, but the child is a girl) and walk in a leisurely way to the cemetery. There I stand or sit down, and stay a long time gazing at the grave that is so dear to me, and tell the child that her mother lies here.

Sometimes, by the graveside, I find Anyuta Blagovo. We greet each other and stand in silence, or talk of Kleopatra, of her child, of how sad life is in this world; then, going out of the cemetery, we walk along in silence and she slackens her pace on purpose to walk beside me a little longer. The little girl, joyous and happy, pulls at her hand, laughing and screwing up her eyes in the bright sunlight, and we stand still and join in caressing the dear child.

When we reach the town, Anyuta Blagovo, agitated and flushing crimson, says good-bye to me and walks on alone, austere and respectable.... And no one who met her could, looking at her, imagine that she had just been walking beside me and even caressing the child.

# PEASANTS

## 1.

NIKOLAI CHIKLDYEYEV, A waiter in the Moscow hotel, Slavyansky Bazaar, was taken ill. His legs went numb and his gait was affected, so that on one occasion, as he was going along the corridor, he tumbled and fell down with a tray full of ham and peas. He had to leave his job. All his own savings and his wife's were spent on doctors and medicines; they had nothing left to live upon. He felt dull with no work to do, and he made up his mind he must go home to the village. It is better to be ill at home, and living there is cheaper; and it is a true saying that the walls of home are a help.

He reached Zhukovo towards evening. In his memories of childhood he had pictured his home as bright, snug, comfortable. Now, going into the hut, he was positively frightened; it was so dark, so crowded, so unclean. His wife Olga and his daughter Sasha, who had come with him, kept looking in bewilderment at the big untidy stove, which filled up almost half the hut and was black with soot and flies. What lots of flies! The stove was on one side, the beams lay slanting on the walls, and it looked as though the hut were just going to fall to pieces. In the corner, facing the door, under the holy images, bottle labels and newspaper cuttings were stuck on the walls instead of pictures. The poverty, the poverty! Of the grown-up people there were none at home; all were at work at the harvest. On the stove was sitting a white-headed girl of eight, unwashed and apathetic; she did not even glance at them as they came in. On the floor a white cat was rubbing itself against the oven fork.

"Puss, puss!" Sasha called to her. "Puss!"

"She can't hear," said the little girl; "she has gone deaf."

"How is that?"

"Oh, she was beaten."

Nikolai and Olga realized from the first glance what life was like here but said nothing to one another; in silence they put down their bundles and went out into the village street. Their hut was the third from the end and seemed the very poorest and oldest-looking; the second was not much better; but the last one had an iron roof, and curtains in the windows. That hut stood apart, not enclosed; it was a tavern. The huts were in a single row, and the whole of the little village—quiet and dreamy, with willows, elders, and mountain-ash trees peeping out from the yards—had an attractive look.

Beyond the peasant's homesteads there was a slope down to the river, so steep and precipitous that huge stones jutted out bare here and there through the clay. Down the slope, among the stones and holes dug by the potters, ran winding paths; bits of broken pottery, some brown, some red, lay piled up in heaps, and below there stretched a broad, level, bright green meadow, from which the hay had been already carried, and in which the peasants' cattle were wandering. The river, three-quarters of a mile from the village, ran twisting and turning, with beautiful leafy banks; beyond it was again a broad meadow, a herd of cattle, long strings of white geese; then, just as on the near side, a steep ascent uphill, and on the top of the hill a hamlet, and a church with five domes, and at a little distance the manor house.

"It's lovely here in your parts!" said Olga, crossing herself at the sight of the church. "What space, oh Lord!"

Just at that moment the bell began ringing for service (it was Saturday evening). Two little girls, down below, who were dragging up a pail of water, looked round at the church to listen to the bell.

"At this time they are serving the dinners at the Slavyansky Bazaar," said Nikolai dreamily.

Sitting on the edge of the slope, Nikolai and Olga watched the sun setting, watched the gold and crimson sky reflected in the river, in the church windows, and in the whole air—which was soft and still and unutterably pure as it never was in Moscow. And when the sun had set, the flocks and herds passed, bleating and lowing; geese flew across from the further side of the river, and all sank into silence; the soft light died away in the air, and the dusk of evening began quickly moving down upon them.

Meanwhile Nikolai's father and mother, two gaunt, bent, toothless old people, just of the same height, came back. The women—the sisters-in-law Marya and Fyokla—who had been working on the landowner's estate beyond the river, arrived home, too. Marya, the wife of Nikolai's brother Kiryak, had six children, and Fyokla, the wife of Nikolai's brother Denis—who had gone for a soldier—had two; and when Nikolai, going into the hut, saw all the family, all those bodies big and little moving about on the lockers, in the hanging cradles, and in all the corners, and when he saw the greed with which the old father and the women ate the black bread, dipping it in water, he realized he had made a mistake in coming here, sick, penniless, and with a family, too—a great mistake!

"And where is Kiryak?" he asked after they had exchanged greetings.

"He is in service at the merchant's," answered his father; "a keeper in the woods. He is not a bad peasant, but too fond of his glass."

"He is no great help!" said the old woman tearfully. "Our men are a grievous lot; they bring nothing into the house, but take plenty out. Kiryak drinks, and so does the old man; it is no use hiding a sin; he knows his way to the tavern. The Heavenly Mother is wroth."

In honor of the visitors they brought out the samovar. The tea smelled of fish; the sugar was gray and looked as though it had been nibbled; cockroaches ran to and fro over the bread and among the crockery. It was disgusting to drink, and the conversation was disgusting, too—about nothing but poverty and illnesses. But before they had time to empty their first cups there came a loud, prolonged, drunken shout from the yard:

"Ma-arya!"

"It looks as though Kiryak were coming," said the old man. "Speak of the devil."

All were hushed. And again, soon afterwards, the same shout, coarse and drawn out as though it came out of the earth:

"Ma-arya!"

Marya, the elder sister-in-law, turned pale and huddled against the stove, and it was strange to see the look of terror on the face of the strong, broad-shouldered, ugly woman. Her daughter, the child who had been sitting on the stove and looked so apathetic, suddenly broke into loud weeping.

"What are you howling for, you plague?" Fyokla, a handsome woman, also strong and broad-shouldered, shouted to her. "Her won't kill you, no fear!"

From his old father Nikolai learned that Marya was afraid to live in the forest with Kiryak, and that when he was drunk he always came for her, made a row, and beat her mercilessly.

"Ma-arya!" the shout sounded close to the door.

"Protect me, for Christ's sake, good people!" faltered Marya, breathing as though she had been plunged into very cold water. "Protect me, kind people. . . ."

All the children in the hut began crying, and, looking at them, Sasha, too, began to cry. They heard a drunken cough, and a tall, black-bearded peasant wearing a winter cap came into the hut, and was the more terrible because his face could not be seen in the dim light of the little lamp. It was Kiryak. Going up to his wife, he swung his arm and punched her in the face with his fist. Stunned by the blow, she did not utter a sound, but sat down, and her nose instantly began bleeding.

"What a disgrace! What a disgrace!" muttered the old man, clambering up on to the stove. "Before visitors, too! It's a sin!"

The old mother sat silent, bowed, lost in thought; Fyokla rocked the cradle.

Evidently conscious of inspiring fear, and pleased at doing so, Kiryak seized Marya by the arm, dragged her towards the door, and bellowed like an animal in order to seem still more terrible; but at that moment he suddenly caught sight of the visitors and stopped.

"Oh, they have come . . ." he said, letting his wife go; "my own brother and his family. . . ."

Staggering and opening wide his red, drunken eyes, he said his prayer before the image and went on:

"My brother and his family have come to the parental home . . . from Moscow, I suppose. The great capital Moscow, to be sure, the mother of cities. . . . Excuse me."

He sank down on the bench near the samovar and began drinking tea, sipping it loudly from the saucer in the midst of general silence. . . . He drank off a dozen cups, then reclined on the bench and began snoring.

They began going to bed. Nikolai, as an invalid, was put on

the stove with his old father; Sasha lay down on the floor, while Olga went with the other women into the barn.

"Aye, aye, dearie," she said, lying down on the hay beside Marya; "you won't mend your trouble with tears. Bear it in patience, that is all. It is written in the Scriptures: 'If anyone smite thee on the right cheek, offer him the left one also.' . . . Aye, aye, dearie."

Then in a low singsong murmur she told them about Moscow, about her own life, how she had been a servant in furnished lodgings.

"And in Moscow the houses are big, built of brick," she said; "and there are ever so many churches, forty times forty, dearie; and they are all gentry in the houses, so handsome and so proper!"

Marya told her that she had not only never been in Moscow, but had not even been in their own district town; she could not read or write and knew no prayers, not even "Our Father." Both she and Fyokla, the other sister-in-law, who was sitting a little way off listening, were extremely ignorant and could understand nothing. They both disliked their husbands; Marya was afraid of Kiryak, and whenever he stayed with her she was shaking with fear, and always got a headache from the fumes of vodka and tobacco with which he reeked. And in answer to the question whether she did not miss her husband, Fyokla answered with vexation:

"Miss him!"

They talked a little and sank into silence.

It was cool, and a cock crowed at the top of his voice near the barn, preventing them from sleeping. When the bluish morning light was already peeping through all the crevices, Fyokla got up stealthily and went out, and then they heard the sound of her bare feet running off somewhere.

## 2.

Olga went to church, and took Marya with her. As they went down the path towards the meadow both were in good spirits. Olga liked the wide view, and Marya felt that in her sister-in-law she had someone near and akin to her. The sun was rising. Low down over the meadow floated a drowsy hawk. The river looked gloomy; there was a haze hovering over it here and there, but on the further bank a streak of light already stretched across the hill. The church was gleaming, and in the manor garden the rooks were cawing furiously.

"The old man is all right," Marya told her, "but Granny is strict; she is continually nagging. Our own grain lasted till Carnival. We buy flour now at the tavern. She is angry about it; she says we eat too much."

"Aye, aye, dearie! Bear it in patience, that is all. It is written: 'Come unto me, all ye that labor and are heavy laden.'"

Olga spoke sedately, rhythmically, and she walked like a pilgrim woman, with a rapid, anxious step. Every day she read the gospel, read it aloud like a deacon; a great deal of it she did not understand, but the words of the gospel moved her to tears, and words like "forasmuch as" and "verily" she pronounced with a sweet flutter at her heart. She believed in God, in the Holy Mother, in the Saints; she believed one must not offend anyone in the world—not simple folks, nor Germans, nor gypsies, nor Jews—and woe even to those who have no compassion on the beasts. She believed this was written in the Holy Scriptures; and so, when she pronounced phrases from Holy Writ, even though she did not understand them, her face grew softened, compassionate, and radiant.

"What part do you come from?" Marya asked her.

"I am from Vladimir. Only I was taken to Moscow long ago, when I was eight years old."

They reached the river. On the further side a woman was standing at the water's edge, undressing.

"It's our Fyokla," said Marya, recognizing her. "She has been over the river to the manor yard. To the stewards. She is a shameless hussy and foulmouthed—fearfully!"

Fyokla, young and vigorous as a girl, with her black eyebrows and her loose hair, jumped off the bank and began splashing the water with her feet, and waves ran in all directions from her.

"Shameless—dreadfully!" repeated Marya.

The river was crossed by a rickety little bridge of logs, and exactly below it in the clear, limpid water was a shoal of broad-headed mullets. The dew was glistening on the green bushes that looked into the water. There was a feeling of warmth; it was comforting! What a lovely morning! And how lovely life would have been in this world, in all likelihood, if it were not for poverty, horrible, hopeless poverty, from which one can find no refuge! One had only to look round at the village to remember vividly all that had happened the day before, and the illusion of happiness which seemed to surround them vanished instantly.

They reached the church. Marya stood at the entrance and did not dare to go farther. She did not dare to sit down either. Though they only began ringing for mass between eight and nine, she remained standing the whole time.

While the gospel was being read the crowd suddenly parted to make way for the family from the great house. Two young girls in white frocks and wide-brimmed hats walked in; with them a chubby, rosy boy in a sailor suit. Their appearance touched Olga; she made up her mind from the first glance that they were refined, well-educated, handsome people. Marya looked at them from under her brows, sullenly, dejectedly, as though they were not human beings coming in, but monsters who might crush her if she did not make way for them.

And every time the deacon boomed out something in his bass voice she fancied she heard "Ma-arya!" and she shuddered.

## 3.

The arrival of the visitors was already known in the village, and directly after mass a number of people gathered together in the hut. The Leonychevs and Matvyeichevs and the Ilyichovs came to inquire about their relations who were in service in Moscow. All the lads of Zhukovo who could read and write were packed off to Moscow and hired out as butlers or waiters (while from the village on the other side of the river the boys all became bakers), and that had been the custom from the days of serfdom long ago when a certain Luka Ivanich, a peasant from Zhukovo, now a legendary figure, who had been a waiter in one of the Moscow clubs, would take none but his fellow villagers into his service, and found jobs for them in taverns and restaurants; and from that time the village of Zhukovo was always called among the inhabitants of the surrounding districts "Slaveytown." Nikolai had been taken to Moscow when he was eleven, and Ivan Makarich, one of the Matvyeichevs, at that time a headwaiter in the "Hermitage" garden, had put him into a situation. And now, addressing the Matvyeichevs, Nikolai said emphatically:

"Ivan Makarich was my benefactor, and I am bound to pray for him day and night, as it is owing to him I have become a good man."

"My good soul!" a tall old woman, the sister of Ivan Makarich, said tearfully, "and not a word have we heard about him, poor dear."

"In the winter he was in service at Omon's, and this season there was a rumor he was somewhere out of town, in gardens. . . . He has aged! In old days he would bring home as much as ten rubles a day in the summer time, but now things are very quiet everywhere. The old man frets."

The women looked at Nikolai's feet, shod in felt boots, and at his pale face, and said mournfully:

"You are not one to get on, Nikolai Osipich; you are not one to get on! No, indeed!"

And they all made much of Sasha. She was ten years old, but she was little and very thin, and might have been taken for no more than seven. Among the other little girls, with their sunburnt faces and roughly cropped hair, dressed in long faded smocks, she, with her white little face, with her big dark eyes, with a red ribbon in her hair, looked funny, as though she were some little wild creature that had been caught and brought into the hut.

"She can read, too," Olga said in her praise, looking tenderly at her daughter. "Read a little, child!" she said, taking the gospel from the corner. "You read, and the good Christian people will listen."

The testament was an old and heavy one in leather binding, with dog's-eared edges, and it exhaled a smell as though monks had come into the hut. Sasha raised her eyebrows and began in a loud rhythmic chant:

"'And the angel of the Lord . . . appeared unto Joseph, saying unto him: Rise up, and take the Babe and His mother.'"

"The Babe and His mother," Olga repeated, and flushed all over with emotion.

"'And flee into Egypt . . . and tarry there until such time as . . .'"

At the word "tarry" Olga could not refrain from tears. Looking at her, Marya began to whimper, and after her Ivan Makarich's sister. The old father cleared his throat and bustled about to find something to give his granddaughter, but, finding nothing, gave it up with a wave of his hand. And when the reading was over the neighbors dispersed to their homes, feeling touched and very much pleased with Olga and Sasha.

As it was a holiday, the family spent the whole day at home. The old woman, whom her husband, her daughters-in-law, her grandchildren all alike called Granny, tried to do everything herself; she heated the stove and set the samovar with her own hands, even waited at the midday meal, and then complained that she was worn out with work. And all the time she was uneasy for fear someone should eat a piece too much, or that her husband and daughters-in-law would sit idle. At one time she would hear the tavern-keeper's geese going at the back of the huts to her kitchen garden, and she would run out of the hut with a long stick and spend half an hour screaming shrilly by her cabbages, which were as gaunt and scraggy as herself; at another time she fancied that a crow had designs on her chickens, and she rushed to attack it with loud words of abuse. She was cross and grumbling from morning till night. And often she raised such an outcry that passers-by stopped in the street.

She was not affectionate towards the old man, reviling him as a lazybones and a plague. He was not a responsible, reliable peasant, and perhaps if she had not been continually nagging at him he would not have worked at all but would have simply sat on the stove and talked. He talked to his son at great length about certain enemies of his, complained of the insults he said he had to put up with every day from the neighbors, and it was tedious to listen to him.

"Yes," he would say, standing with his arms akimbo, "yes. . . . A week after the Exaltation of the Cross I sold my hay willingly at thirty kopecks a pood. . . . Well and good. . . . So you see I was taking the hay in the morning with a good will; I was interfering with no one. In an unlucky hour I see the village elder, Antip Syedelnikov, coming out of the tavern. 'Where are you taking it, you ruffian?' says he, and takes me by the ear."

Kiryak had a fearful headache after his drinking bout and was ashamed to face his brother.

"What vodka does! Ah, my God!" he muttered, shaking his aching head. "For Christ's sake, forgive me, Brother and Sister; I'm not happy myself."

As it was a holiday, they bought a herring at the tavern and made a soup of the herring's head. At midday they all sat down to drink tea and went on drinking it for a long time, till they were all perspiring; they looked positively swollen from the tea drinking, and, after it, began sipping the broth from the herring's head, all helping themselves out of one bowl. But the herring itself Granny had hidden.

In the evening a potter began firing pots on the ravine. In the meadow below the girls got up a choral dance and sang songs. They played the concertina. And on the other side of the river a kiln for baking pots was lighted, too, and the girls sang songs, and in the distance the singing sounded soft and musical. The peasants were noisy in and about the tavern. They were singing with drunken voices, each on his own account, and swearing at one another, so that Olga could only shudder and say:

"Oh, holy saints!"

She was amazed that the abuse was incessant, and those who were loudest and most persistent in this foul language were the old men who were so near their end. And the girls and children heard the swearing, and were not in the least disturbed by it, and it was evident that they were used to it from their cradles.

It was past midnight, the kilns on both sides of the river were put out, but in the meadow below and in the tavern the merrymaking still went on. The old father and Kiryak, both drunk, walking arm in arm and, jostling against each other's shoulders, went to the barn where Olga and Marya were lying.

"Let her alone," the old man persuaded him; "let her alone. . . . She is a harmless woman. It's a sin. . . ."

"Ma-arya!" shouted Kiryak.

"Let her be. . . . It's a sin. . . . She is not a bad woman."

Both stopped by the barn and went on.

"I lo-ove the flowers of the fi-ield," the old man began singing suddenly in a high, piercing tenor. "I lo-ove to gather them in the meadows!"

Then he spat, and with a filthy oath went into the hut.

## 4.

Granny put Sasha by her kitchen garden and told her to keep watch that the geese did not go in. It was a hot August day. The tavern-keeper's geese could make their way into the kitchen garden by the backs of the huts, but now they were busily engaged picking up oats by the tavern, peacefully conversing together, and only the gander craned his head high as though trying to see whether the old woman were coming with her stick. The other geese might come up from below, but they were now grazing far away the other side of the river, stretched out in a long white garland about the meadow. Sasha stood about a little, grew weary, and, seeing that the geese were not coming, went away to the ravine.

There she saw Marya's eldest daughter Motka, who was standing motionless on a big stone, staring at the church. Marya had given birth to thirteen children, but she only had six living, all girls, not one boy, and the eldest was eight. Motka in a long smock was standing barefooted in the full sunshine; the sun was blazing down right on her head, but she did not notice that and seemed as though turned to stone. Sasha stood beside her and said, iooking at the church:

"God lives in the church. Men have lamps and candles, but God has little green and red and blue lamps like little eyes. At night God walks about the church, and with Him the Holy

Mother of God St. Nikolai, thud, thud, thud! . . . And the watchman is terrified, terrified! Aye, aye, dearie," she added, imitating her mother. "And when the end of the world comes all the churches will be carried up to heaven."

"With the-ir be-ells?" Motka asked in her deep voice, drawling every syllable.

"With their bells. And when the end of the world comes the good will go to Paradise, but the angry will burn in fire eternal and unquenchable, dearie. To my mother as well as to Marya, God will say: 'You never offended anyone, and for that go to the right to Paradise'; but to Kiryak and Granny, He will say: 'You go to the left into the fire.' And anyone who has eaten meat in Lent will go into the fire, too."

She looked upwards at the sky, opening wide her eyes, and said:

"Look at the sky without winking, you will see angels."

Motka began looking at the sky, too, and a minute passed in silence.

"Do you see them?" asked Sasha.

"I don't," said Motka in her deep voice.

"But I do. Little angels are flying about the sky and flap, flap with their little wings as though they were gnats."

Motka thought for a little, with her eyes on the ground, and asked:

"Will Granny burn?"

"She will,dearie."

From the stone an even gentle slope ran down to the bottom, covered with soft green grass, which one longed to lie down on or to touch with one's hands. . . . Sasha lay down and rolled to the bottom. Motka with a grave, severe face, taking a deep breath, lay down, too, and rolled to the bottom, and in doing so tore her smock from the hem to the shoulder.

"What fun it is!" said Sasha, delighted.

They walked up to the top to roll down again, but at

that moment they heard a shrill, familiar voice. Oh, how awful it was! Granny, a toothless, bony, hunchbacked figure, with short gray hair, which was fluttering in the wind, was driving the geese out of the kitchen garden with a long stick, shouting:

"They have trampled all the cabbages, the damned brutes! I'd cut your throats, thrice accursed plagues! Bad luck to you!"

She saw the little girls, flung down the stick and picked up a switch, and, seizing Sasha by the neck with her fingers, thin and hard as the gnarled branches of a tree, began whipping her. Sasha cried with pain and terror, while the gander, waddling and stretching his neck, went up to the old woman and hissed at her, and when he went back to his flock all the geese greeted him approvingly with "Ga-ga-ga!" Then Granny proceeded to whip Motka, and in this Motka's smock was torn again. Feeling in despair, and crying loudly, Sasha went to the hut to complain. Motka followed her; she, too, was crying on a deeper note, without wiping her tears, and her face was as wet as though it had been dipped in water.

"Holy saints!" cried Olga, aghast, as the two came into the hut. "Queen of Heaven!"

Sasha began telling her story, while at the same time Granny walked in with a storm of shrill cries and abuse; then Fyokla flew into a rage, and there was an uproar in the hut.

"Never mind, never mind!" Olga, pale and upset, tried to comfort them, stroking Sasha's head. "She is your grandmother; it's a sin to be angry with her. Never mind, my child."

Nikolai, who was worn out already by the everlasting hubbub, hunger, stifling fumes, filth, who hated and despised the poverty, who was ashamed for his wife and daughter to see his father and mother, swung his legs off the stove and said in an irritable, tearful voice, addressing his mother:

"You must not beat her! You have no right to beat her!"

"You lie rotting on the stove, you wretched creature!"

Fyokla shouted at him spitefully. "The devil brought you all on us, eating us out of house and home."

Sasha and Motka and all the little girls in the hut huddled on the stove in the corner behind Nikolai's back, and from that refuge listened in silent terror, and the beating of their little hearts could be distinctly heard. Whenever there is someone in a family who has long been ill, and hopelessly ill, there come painful moments when all, timidly, secretly, at the bottom of their hearts long for his death; and only the children fear the death of someone near them and always feel horrified at the thought of it. And now the children, with bated breath, with a mournful look on their faces, gazed at Nikolai and thought that he was soon to die; and they wanted to cry and to say something friendly and compassionate to him.

He pressed close to Olga, as though seeking protection, and said to her softly in a quavering voice:

"Olga darling, I can't stay here longer. It's more than I can bear. For God's sake, for Christ's sake, write to your sister-in-law, Klavdia Abramovna. Let her sell and pawn everything she has; let her send us the money. We will go away from here. Oh Lord," he went on miserably, "to have one peep at Moscow! If I could see it in my dreams, the dear place!"

And when the evening came on, and it was dark in the hut, it was so dismal that it was hard to utter a word. Granny, very ill-tempered, soaked some crusts of rye bread in a cup, and was a long time, a whole hour, sucking at them. Marya, after milking the cow, brought in a pail of milk and set it on a bench; then Granny poured it from the pail into a jug just as slowly and deliberately, evidently pleased that it was now the Fast of the Assumption, so that no one would drink milk and it would be left untouched. And she only poured out a very little in a saucer for Fyokla's baby. When Marya and she carried the jug down to the cellar, Motka suddenly stirred, clambered down from the stove, and, going to the bench where stood the wooden cup full of crusts, sprinkled into it some milk from the saucer.

Granny, coming back into the hut, sat down to her soaked crusts again, while Sasha and Motka, sitting on the stove, gazed at her, and they were glad that she had broken her fast and now would go to hell. They were comforted and lay down to sleep, and Sasha as she dozed off to sleep imagined the Day of Judgment: a huge fire was burning, somewhat like a potter's kiln, and the Evil One, with horns like a cow's, and black all over, was driving Granny into the fire with a long stick, just as Granny herself had been driving the geese.

## 5.

On the day of the Feast of the Assumption, between ten and eleven in the evening, the girls and lads who were merrymaking in the meadow suddenly raised a clamor and outcry and ran in the direction of the village; and those who were above on the edge of the ravine could not for the first moment make out what was the matter.

"Fire! Fire!" they heard desperate shouts from below. "The village is on fire!"

Those who were sitting above looked round, and a terrible and extraordinary spectacle met their eyes. On the thatched roof of one of the end cottages stood a column of flame, seven feet high, which curled round and scattered sparks in all directions as though it were a fountain. And all at once the whole roof burst into bright flame, and the crackling of the fire was audible.

The light of the moon was dimmed, and the whole village was by now bathed in a red quivering glow: black shadows moved over the ground, there was a smell of burning, and those who ran up from below were all gasping and could not speak for trembling; they jostled against each other, fell down, and they could hardly see in the unaccustomed light and did not recognize each other. It was terrible. What seemed particularly dreadful was that doves were flying over the fire in the smoke; and in the tavern, where they did not yet know of the fire, they were still singing and playing the concertina as though there were nothing the matter.

"Uncle Semyon's on fire," shouted a loud, coarse voice.

Marya was fussing about round her hut, weeping and wringing her hands, while her teeth chattered, though the fire was a long way off at the other end of the village. Nikolai came out in high felt boots, the children ran out in their little smocks. Near the village constable's hut an iron sheet was struck. Boom, boom, boom! floated through the air, and this repeated, persistent sound sent a pang to the heart and turned one cold. The old women stood with the holy icons. Sheep, calves, cows were driven out of the back yards into the street; boxes, sheepskins, tubs were carried out. A black stallion, who was kept apart from the drove of horses because he kicked and injured them, on being set free ran once or twice up and down the village, neighing and pawing the ground; then suddenly stopped short near a cart and began kicking it with his hind legs.

They began ringing the bells in the church on the other side of the river.

Near the burning hut it was hot and so light that one could distinctly see every blade of grass. Semyon, a red-haired peasant with a long nose, wearing a reefer jacket and a cap pulled down right over his ears, sat on one of the boxes which they had succeeded in bringing out: his wife was lying on her face, moaning and unconscious. A little old man of eighty, with a big beard, who looked like a gnome—not one of the villagers, though obviously connected in some way with the fire—walked about bareheaded, with a white bundle in his arms. The glare was reflected on his bald head. The village elder, Antip Syedelnikov, as swarthy and black-haired as a gypsy, went up to the hut with an ax, and hacked out the windows one after another—no one knew why—then began chopping up the roof.

"Women, water!" he shouted. "Bring the engine! Look sharp!"

The peasants who had been drinking in the tavern just before dragged the engine up. They were all drunk; they kept stumbling and falling down, and all had a helpless expression and tears in their eyes.

"Wenches, water!" shouted the elder, who was drunk, too. "Look sharp, wenches!"

The women and the girls ran downhill to where there was a spring, and kept hauling pails and buckets of water up the hill, and, pouring it into the engine, ran down again. Olga and Marya and Sasha and Motka all brought water. The women and the boys pumped the water; the pipe hissed, and the elder, directing it now at the door, now at the windows, held back the stream with his finger, which made it hiss more sharply still.

"Bravo, Antip!" voices shouted approvingly. "Do your best."

Antip went inside the hut into the fire and shouted from within.

"Pump! Bestir yourselves, good Christian folk, in such a terrible mischance!"

The peasants stood round in a crowd, doing nothing but staring at the fire. No one knew what to do, no one had the sense to do anything, though there were stacks of wheat, hay, barns, and piles of faggots standing all round. Kiryak and old Osip, his father, both tipsy, were standing there, too. And as though to justify his doing nothing, old Osip said, addressing the woman who lay on the ground:

"What is there to trouble about, old girl! The hut is insured—why are you taking on?"

Semyon, addressing himself first to one person and then to another, kept describing how the fire had started.

"That old man, the one with the bundle, a house serf of General Zhukov's. . . . He was cook at our general's, God rest his soul! He came over this evening: 'Let me stay the night,' says he. . . . Well, we had a glass, to be sure. . . . The wife got the samovar—she was going to give the old fellow a cup of tea, and in an unlucky hour she set the samovar in the entrance. The sparks from the chimney must have blown straight up to the thatch; that's how it was. We were almost burnt ourselves. And the old fellow's cap has been burnt; what a shame!"

And the sheet of iron was struck indefatigably, and the bells kept ringing in the church the other side of the river. In the glow of the fire Olga, breathless, looking with horror at the red sheep and the pink doves flying in the smoke, kept running down the hill and up again. It seemed to her that the ringing went to her heart with a sharp stab, that the fire would never be over, that Sasha was lost. . . . And when the ceiling of the hut fell in with a crash, the thought that now the whole village would be burnt made her weak and faint, and she could not go on fetching water, but sat down on the ravine, setting the pail down near her; beside her and below her, the peasant women sat wailing as though at a funeral.

Then the stewards and watchmen from the estate the other side of the river arrived in two carts, bringing with them a fire engine. A very young student in an unbuttoned white tunic rode up on horseback. There was the thud of axes. They put a ladder to the burning framework of the house, and five men ran up it at once. Foremost of them all was the student, who was red in the face and shouting in a harsh hoarse voice, and in a tone as though putting out fires was a thing he was used to. They pulled the house to pieces, a beam at a time; they dragged away the corn, the hurdles, and the stacks that were near.

"Don't let them break it up!" cried stern voices in the crowd. "Don't let them."

Kiryak made his way up to the hut with a resolute air, as though he meant to prevent the newcomers from breaking up the hut, but one of the workmen turned him back with a blow in his neck. There was the sound of laughter, the workman dealt him another blow, Kiryak fell down, and crawled back into the crowd on his hands and knees.

Two handsome girls in hats, probably the student's sisters, came from the other side of the river. They stood a little way off, looking at the fire. The beams that had been dragged apart were no longer burning, but were smoking vigorously; the student, who was working the hose, turned the water, first on the beams, then on the peasants, then on the women who were bringing the water.

"George!" the girls called to him reproachfully in anxiety, "George!"

The fire was over. And only when they began to disperse they noticed that the day was breaking, that everyone was pale and rather dark in the face, as it always seems in the early morning when the last stars are going out. As they separated, the peasants laughed and made jokes about General Zhukov's cook and his cap which had been burnt; they already wanted to turn the fire into a joke and even seemed sorry that it had so soon been put out.

"How well you extinguished the fire, sir!" said Olga to the student. "You ought to come to us in Moscow: there we have a fire every day."

"Why, do you come from Moscow?" asked one of the young ladies.

"Yes, mademoiselle. My husband was a waiter at the Slavyansky Bazaar. And this is my daughter," she said, indicating Sasha, who was cold and huddling up to her. "She is a Moscow girl, too."

The two young ladies said something in French to the student, and he gave Sasha a twenty-kopeck piece.

Old Father Osip saw this, and there was a gleam of hope in his face.

"We must thank God, your honor, there was no wind," he said, addressing the student, "or else we should have been all burnt up together. Your honor, kind gentlefolks," he added in embarrassment in a lower tone, "the morning's chilly . . . something to warm one . . . half a bottle to your honor's health."

Nothing was given him, and, clearing his throat, he slouched home. Olga stood afterwards at the end of the street and watched the two carts crossing the river by the ford and the gentlefolks walking across the meadow; a carriage was waiting for them the other side of the river. Going into the hut, she described to her husband with enthusiasm:

"Such good people! And so beautiful! The young ladies were like cherubim."

"Plague take them!" Fyokla, sleepy, said spitefully.

## 6.

Marya thought herself unhappy and said that she would be very glad to die; Fyokla, on the other hand, found all this life to her taste: the poverty, the uncleanliness, and the incessant quarreling. She ate what was given her without discrimination; slept anywhere, on whatever came to hand. She would empty the slops just at the porch, would splash them out from the doorway, and then walk barefoot through the puddle. And from the very first day she took a dislike to Olga and Nikolai just because they did not like this life.

"We shall see what you'll find to eat here, you Moscow gentry!" she said malignantly. "We shall see!"

One morning, it was at the beginning of September, Fyokla,

vigorous, good-looking, and rosy from the cold, brought up two pails of water; Marya and Olga were sitting meanwhile at the table drinking tea.

"Tea and sugar," said Fyokla sarcastically. "The fine ladies!" she added, setting down the pails. "You have taken to the fashion of tea every day. You better look out that you don't burst with your tea drinking," she went on, looking with hatred at Olga. "That's how you have come by your fat mug, having a good time in Moscow, you lump of flesh!" She swung the yoke and hit Olga such a blow on the shoulder that the two sisters-in-law could only clasp their hands and say:

"Oh, holy saints!"

Then Fyokla went down to the river to wash the clothes, swearing all the time so loudly that she could be heard in the hut.

The day passed and was followed by the long autumn evening. They wound silk in the hut; everyone did it except Fyokla; she had gone over the river. They got the silk from a factory close by, and the whole family working together earned next to nothing, twenty kopecks a week.

"Things were better in the old days under the gentry," said the old father as he wound silk. "You worked and ate and slept, everything in its turn. At dinner you had cabbage soup and boiled grain, and at supper the same again. Cucumbers and cabbage in plenty: you could eat to your heart's content, as much as you wanted. And there was more strictness. Everyone minded what he was about."

The hut was lighted by a single little lamp, which burnt dimly and smoked. When someone screened the lamp and a big shadow fell across the window, the bright moonlight could be seen. Old Osip, speaking slowly, told them how they used to live before the emancipation; how in those very parts, where life was now so poor and so dreary, they used to hunt with harriers, grayhounds, retrievers, and when they went out as beaters the peasants were given vodka; how whole wagonloads of game used to be sent to Moscow for the young masters; how the bad were beaten with rods or sent away to the Tver estate, while the good were rewarded. And Granny told them something, too. She remembered everything, positively everything. She described her mistress, a kind, God-fearing woman, whose husband was a profligate and a rake, and all of whose daughters made unlucky marriages: one married a drunkard, another married a workman, the other eloped secretly (Granny herself, at that time a young girl, helped in the elopement), and they had all three as well as their mother died early from grief. And remembering all this, Granny positively began to shed tears.

All at once someone knocked at the door, and they all started.

"Uncle Osip, give me a night's lodging."

The little bald old man, General Zhukov's cook, the one whose cap had been burnt, walked in. He sat down and listened, then he, too, began telling stories of all sorts. Nikolai, sitting on the stove with his legs hanging down, listened and asked questions about the dishes that were prepared in the old days for the gentry. They talked of rissoles, cutlets, various soups and sauces, and the cook, who remembered everything very well, mentioned dishes that were no longer served. There was one, for instance—a dish made of bulls' eyes, which was called "waking up in the morning."

"And used you to do cutlets *au maréchal*?" asked Nikolai.

"No."

Nikolai shook his head reproachfully and said:

"Tut, tut! You were not much of a cook!"

The little girls, sitting and lying on the stove, stared down without blinking; it seemed as though there were a great many of them, like cherubim in the clouds. They liked the stories: they were breathless; they shuddered and turned pale with alternate rapture and terror, and they listened breathlessly, afraid to stir, to Granny, whose stories were the most interesting of all.

They lay down to sleep in silence; and the old people, troubled and excited by their reminiscences, thought how precious was youth, of which, whatever it might have been like, nothing was left in the memory but what was living, joyful, touching, and how terribly cold was death, which was not far off, better not think of it! The lamp died down. And the dusk, and the two little windows sharply defined by the moonlight, and the stillness and the creak of the cradle, reminded them for some reason that life was over, that nothing one could do would bring it back. . . . You doze off, you forget yourself, and suddenly someone touches your shoulder or breathes on your cheek—and sleep is gone; your body feels cramped, and thoughts of death keep creeping into your mind. You turn on the other side: death is forgotten, but old, dreary, sickening thoughts of poverty, of food, of how dear flour is getting, stray through the mind, and a little later again you remember that life is over and you cannot bring it back. . . .

"Oh Lord!" sighed the cook.

Someone gave a soft, soft tap at the window. It must be Fyokla come back. Olga got up, and, yawning and whispering a prayer, opened the door, then drew the bolt in the outer room, but no one came in; only from the street came a cold draught and a sudden brightness from the moonlight. The street, still and deserted, and the moon itself, floating across the sky, could be seen at the open door.

"Who is there?" called Olga.

"I," she heard the answer, "it is I."

Near the door, crouching against the wall, stood Fyokla, absolutely naked. She was shivering with cold, her teeth were chattering, and in the bright moonlight she looked very pale, strange, and beautiful. The shadows on her, and the bright moonlight on her skin, stood out vividly, and her dark eyebrows and firm, youthful bosom were defined with peculiar distinctness.

"The ruffians over there undressed me and turned me out like this," she said. "I've come home without my clothes... naked as my mother bore me. Bring me something to put on."

"But go inside!" Olga said softly, beginning to shiver, too.

"I don't want the old folks to see." Granny was, in fact, already stirring and muttering, and the old father asked: "Who is there?" Olga brought her own smock and skirt, dressed Fyokla, and then both went softly into the inner room, trying not to make a noise with the door.

"Is that you, you sleek one?" Granny grumbled angrily, guessing who it was. "Fie upon you, nightwalker!... Bad luck to you!"

"It's all right, it's all right," whispered Olga, wrapping Fyokla up; "it's all right, dearie."

All was stillness again. They always slept badly; everyone was kept awake by something worrying and persistent: the old man by the pain in his back, Granny by anxiety and anger, Marya by terror, the children by itch and hunger. Now, too, their sleep was troubled; they kept turning over from one side to the other, talking in their sleep, getting up for a drink.

Fyokla suddenly broke into a loud, coarse howl, but immediately checked herself, and only uttered sobs from time to time, growing softer and on a lower note, until she relapsed into silence. From time to time from the other side of the river there floated the sound of the beating of the hours; but the time seemed somehow strange—five was struck and then three.

"Oh Lord!" sighed the cook.

Looking at the windows, it was difficult to tell whether it was still moonlight or whether the dawn had begun. Marya got up and went out, and she could be heard milking the cows and saying, "Stea-dy!" Granny went out, too. It was still dark in the hut, but all the objects in it could be discerned.

Nikolai, who had not slept all night, got down from the stove. He took his dress coat out of a green box, put it on, and, going to the window, stroked the sleeves and took hold of the coattails—and smiled. Then he carefully took off the coat, put it away in his box, and lay down again.

Marya came in again and began lighting the stove. She was evidently hardly awake and seemed dropping asleep as she walked. Probably she had had some dream, or the stories of the night before came into her mind as, stretching luxuriously before the stove, she said:

"No, freedom is better."

## 7.

The master arrived—that was what they called the police inspector. When he would come and what he was coming for had been known for the last week. There were only forty households in Zhukovo, but more than two thousand rubles of arrears of rates and taxes had accumulated.

The police inspector stopped at the tavern. He drank there two glasses of tea, and then went on foot to the village elder's hut, near which a crowd of those who were in debt stood waiting. The elder, Antip Syedelnikov, was, in spite of his youth—he was only a little over thirty—strict and always on the side of the authorities, though he himself was poor and did not pay his taxes regularly. Evidently he enjoyed being elder and liked the sense of authority, which he could only display by strictness. In the village council the peasants were afraid of him and obeyed him. It would sometimes happen that he would pounce on a drunken man in the street or near the tavern, tie his hands behind him, and put him in the lockup. On one occasion he even put Granny in the lockup because she went to the village council instead of Osip, and began swearing, and he kept her there for a whole day and night. He had never lived in a town or read a book but somewhere or other had picked up various learned expressions and loved to make use of them in conversation, and he was respected for this though he was not always understood.

When Osip came into the village elder's hut with his tax book, the police inspector, a lean old man with a long gray beard, in a gray tunic, was sitting at a table in the passage, writing something. It was clean in the hut; all the walls were dotted with pictures cut out of the illustrated papers, and in the most conspicuous place near the icon there was a portrait of the Battenberg who was the Prince of Bulgaria. By the table stood Antip Syedelnikov with his arms folded.

"There is one hundred and nineteen rubles standing against him," he said when it came to Osip's turn. "Before Easter he paid a ruble, and he has not paid a kopeck since."

The police inspector raised his eyes to Osip and asked:

"Why is this, brother?"

"Show Divine mercy, your honor," Osip began, growing agitated. "Allow me to say last year the gentleman at Lutorydsky said to me, 'Osip,' he said, 'sell your hay . . . you sell it,' he said. Well, I had a hundred poods for sale; the women mowed it on the water meadow. Well, we struck a bargain all right, willingly. . . ."

He complained of the elder and kept turning round to the peasants as though inviting them to bear witness; his face flushed red and perspired, and his eyes grew sharp and angry.

"I don't know why you are saying all this," said the police inspector. "I am asking you . . . I am asking you why you don't pay your arrears. You don't pay, any of you, and am I to be responsible for you?"

"I can't do it."

"His words have no sequel, your honor," said the elder. "The Chikildyeyevs certainly are of a defective class, but if you will just ask the others, the root of it all is vodka, and they are a very bad lot. With no sort of understanding."

The police inspector wrote something down, and said to Osip quietly, in an even tone, as though he were asking him for water:

"Be off."

Soon he went away; and when he got into his cheap chaise and cleared his throat, it could be seen from the very expression of his long thin back that he was no longer thinking of Osip or of the village elder, nor of the Zhukovo arrears, but was thinking of his own affairs. Before he had gone three quarters of a mile Antip was already carrying off the samovar from the Chikildyeyevs' cottage, followed by Granny, screaming shrilly and straining her throat:

"I won't let you have it, I won't let you have it, damn you!"

He walked rapidly with long steps, and she pursued him, panting, almost falling over, a bent, ferocious figure; her kerchief slipped on to her shoulders, her gray hair with greenish lights on it was blown about in the wind. She suddenly stopped short, and like a genuine rebel, fell to beating her breast with her fists and shouting louder than ever in a singsong voice, as though she were sobbing:

"Good Christians and believers in God! Neighbors, they have ill-treated me! Kind friends, they have oppressed me! Oh, oh! dear people, take my part."

"Granny, Granny!" said the village elder sternly, "have some sense in your head!"

It was hopelessly dreary in the Chikildyeyevs' hut without the samovar; there was something humiliating in this loss, insulting, as though the honor of the hut had been outraged. Better if the elder had carried off the table, all the benches, all the pots—it would not have seemed so empty. Granny screamed,

Marya cried, and the little girls, looking at her, cried, too. The old father, feeling guilty, sat in the corner with bowed head and said nothing. And Nikolai, too, was silent. Granny loved him and was sorry for him, but now, forgetting her pity, she fell upon him with abuse, with reproaches, shaking her fist right in his face. She shouted that it was all his fault; why had he sent them so little when he boasted in his letters that he was getting fifty rubles a month at the Slavyansky Bazaar? Why had he come, and with his family, too? If he died, where was the money to come from for his funeral . . . ? And it was pitiful to look at Nikolai, Olga, and Sasha.

The old father cleared his throat, took his cap, and went off to the village elder. Antip was soldering something by the stove, puffing out his cheeks; there was a smell of burning. His children, emaciated and unwashed, no better than the Chikildyeyevs, were scrambling about the floor; his wife, an ugly, freckled woman with a prominent stomach, was winding silk. They were a poor, unlucky family, and Antip was the only one who looked vigorous and handsome. On a bench there were five samovars standing in a row. The old man said his prayer to Battenberg and said:

"Antip, show the Divine mercy. Give me back the samovar, for Christ's sake!"

"Bring three rubles, then you shall have it."

"I can't do it!"

Antip puffed out his cheeks, the fire roared and hissed, and the glow was reflected in the samovar. The old man crumpled up his cap and said after a moment's thought:

"You give it me back."

The swarthy elder looked quite black, and was like a magician; he turned round to Osip and said sternly and rapidly:

"It all depends on the rural captain. On the twenty-sixth instant you can state the grounds for your dissatisfaction before the administrative session, verbally or in writing."

Osip did not understand a word, but he was satisfied with that and went home.

Ten days later the police inspector came again, stayed an hour and went away. During those days the weather had changed to cold and windy; the river had been frozen for some time past, but still there was no snow, and people found it difficult to get about. On the eve of a holiday some of the neighbors came in to Osip's to sit and have a talk. They did not light the lamp, as it would have been a sin to work, but talked in the darkness. There were some items of news, all rather unpleasant. In two or three households hens had been taken for the arrears and had been sent to the district police station, and there they had died because no one had fed them; they had taken sheep, and while they were being driven away tied to one another, shifted into another cart at each village, one of them had died. And now they were discussing the question, who was to blame?

"The Zemstvo," said Osip. "Who else?"

"Of course it is the Zemstvo."

The Zemstvo was blamed for everything—for the arrears, and for the oppressions, and for the failure of the crops, though no one of them knew what was meant by the Zemstvo. And this dated from the time when well-to-do peasants who had factories, shops, and inns of their own were members of the Zemstvos, were dissatisfied with them, and took to swearing at the Zemstvos in their factories and inns.

They talked of God's not sending the snow; they had to bring in wood for fuel, and there was no driving nor walking in the frozen ruts. In old days fifteen to twenty years ago conversation was much more interesting in Zhukovo. In those days every old man looked as though he were treasuring some secret; as though he knew something and was expecting something. They used to talk about an edict in golden letters, about the division of lands, about new land, about treasures; they hinted at something. Now the people of Zhukovo had no mystery at all; their whole life was bare and open in the sight of all, and they could talk of nothing but poverty, food, there being no snow yet. . . .

There was a pause. Then they thought again of the hens, of the sheep, and began discussing whose fault it was.

"The Zemstvo," said Osip wearily. "Who else?"

## 8.

The parish church was nearly five miles away at Kosogorovo, and the peasants only attended it when they had to do so for baptisms, weddings, or funerals; they went to the services at the church across the river. On holidays in fine weather the girls dressed up in their best and went in a crowd together to church, and it was a cheering sight to see them in their red, yellow, and green dresses cross the meadow; in bad weather they all stayed at home. They went for the sacrament to the parish church. From each of those who did not manage in Lent to go to confession in readiness for the sacrament the parish priest, going the round of the huts with the cross at Easter, took fifteen kopecks.

The old father did not believe in God, for he hardly ever thought about Him; he recognized the supernatural, but considered it was entirely the women's concern, and when religion or miracles were discussed before him, or a question were put to him, he would say reluctantly, scratching himself:

"Who can tell!"

Granny believed, but her faith was somewhat hazy; everything was mixed up in her memory, and she could scarcely begin to think of sins, of death, of the salvation of the soul, before poverty and her daily cares took possession of her mind, and she instantly forgot what she was thinking about. She did not remember the prayers, and usually in the evenings, before lying down to sleep, she would stand before the icons and whisper:

"Holy Mother of Kazan, Holy Mother of Smolensk, Holy Mother of Troeruchitsy. . . ."

Marya and Fyokla crossed themselves, fasted, and took the sacrament every year, but understood nothing. The children were not taught their prayers, nothing was told them about God, and no moral principles were instilled into them; they were only forbidden to eat meat or milk in Lent. In the other families it was much the same: there were few who believed, few who understood. At the same time everyone loved the Holy Scripture, loved it with a tender, reverent love; but they had no Bible, there was no one to read it and explain it, and because Olga sometimes read them the gospel, they respected her, and they all addressed her and Sasha as though they were superior to themselves.

For church holidays and services Olga often went to neighboring villages, and to the district town, in which there were two monasteries and twenty-seven churches. She was dreamy, and when she was on these pilgrimages she quite forgot her family, and only when she got home again suddenly made the joyful discovery that she had a husband and daughter, and then would say, smiling and radiant:

"God has sent me blessings!"

What went on in the village worried her and seemed to her revolting. On Elijah's Day they drank, at the Assumption they drank, at the Ascension they drank. The Feast of the Intercession was the parish holiday for Zhukovo, and the peasants used to drink then for three days; they squandered on drink fifty rubles of money belonging to the mir, and then collected more for vodka from all the households. On the first day of the feast the Chikildyeyevs killed a sheep and ate of it in the morning, at dinnertime, and in the evening; they ate it ravenously, and the children got up at night to eat more. Kiryak was fearfully drunk for three whole days; he drank up everything, even his boots and cap, and beat Marya so terribly that they had to pour water over her. And then they were all ashamed and sick.

However, even in Zhukovo, in this "Slaveytown," there was once an outburst of genuine religious enthusiasm. It was in August, when throughout the district they carried from village to village the Holy Mother, the giver of life. It was still and overcast on the day when they expected *Her* at Zhukovo. The girls set off in the morning to meet the icon, in their bright holiday dresses, and brought Her towards the evening, in procession with the cross and with singing, while the bells pealed in the church across the river. An immense crowd of villagers and strangers flooded the street; there was noise, dust, a great crush. . . . And the old father and Granny and Kiryak—all stretched out their hands to the icon, looked eagerly at it, and said, weeping:

"Defender! Mother! Defender!"

All seemed suddenly to realize that there was not an empty void between earth and heaven, that the rich and the powerful had not taken possession of everything, that there was still a refuge from injury, from slavish bondage, from crushing, unendurable poverty, from the terrible vodka.

"Defender! Mother!" sobbed Marya. "Mother!"

But the thanksgiving service ended and the icon was carried away and everything went on as before; and again there was a sound of coarse drunken oaths from the tavern.

Only the well-to-do peasants were afraid of death; the richer they were the less they believed in God, and in the salvation of souls, and only through fear of the end of the world put up candles and had services said for them, to be on the safe side. The peasants who were rather poorer were not afraid of death. The old father and Granny were told to their faces that they had lived too long, that it was time they were dead, and they did not mind. They did not hinder Fyokla from saying in Nikolai's presence that when Nikolai died her husband Denis would get exemption—to return home from the army. And Marya, far from fearing death, regretted that it was so slow in coming and was glad when her children died.

Death they did not fear, but of every disease they had an exaggerated terror. The merest trifle was enough—a stomach upset, a slight chill, and Granny would be wrapped up on the stove, and would begin moaning loudly and incessantly:

"I am dy-ing!"

The old father hurried off for the priest, and Granny received the sacrament and extreme unction. They often talked of colds, of worms, of tumors which move in the stomach and coil round to the heart. Above all, they were afraid of catching cold, and so put on thick clothes even in the summer and warmed themselves at the stove. Granny was fond of being doctored and often went to the hospital, where she used to say she was not seventy, but fifty-eight; she supposed that if the doctor knew her real age he would not treat her, but would say it was time she died instead of taking medicine. She usually went to the hospital early in the morning, taking with her two or three of the little girls, and came back in the evening, hungry and ill-tempered—with drops for herself and ointments for the little girls. Once she took Nikolai, who swallowed drops for a fortnight afterwards and said he felt better.

Granny knew all the doctors and their assistants and the wise men for twenty miles round, and not one of them she liked. At the Intercession, when the priest made the round of the huts with the cross, the deacon told her that in the town near the prison lived an old man who had been a medical orderly in the army, and who made wonderful cures, and advised her to try him. Granny took his advice. When the first snow fell she drove to the town and fetched an old man with a big beard, a converted Jew, in a long gown, whose face was covered with blue veins. There were outsiders at work in the hut at the time: an old tailor, in terrible spectacles, was cutting a waistcoat out of some rags, and two young men were making felt boots out of wool; Kiryak, who had been dismissed from his place for drunkenness, and now lived at home, was sitting beside the tailor mending a bridle. And it was crowded, stifling, and noisome in the hut. The converted Jew examined Nikolai and said that it was necessary to try cupping.

He put on the cups, and the old tailor, Kiryak, and the little girls stood round and looked on, and it seemed to them that they saw the disease being drawn out of Nikolai; and Nikolai, too, watched how the cups suckling at his breast gradually filled with dark blood, and felt as though there really were something coming out of him, and smiled with pleasure.

"It's a good thing," said the tailor. "Please God, it will do you good."

The Jew put on twelve cups and then another twelve, drank some tea, and went away. Nikolai began shivering; his face looked drawn, and, as the women expressed it, shrank up like a fist; his fingers turned blue. He wrapped himself up in a quilt and in a sheepskin, but got colder and colder. Towards the evening he began to be in great distress; asked to be laid on the ground, asked the tailor not to smoke; then he subsided under the sheepskin and towards morning he died.

## 9.

Oh, what a grim, what a long winter!

Their own grain did not last beyond Christmas, and they had to buy flour. Kiryak was noisy in the evenings, inspiring terror in everyone, and in the mornings he suffered from headache and was ashamed; and he was a pitiful sight. In the stall the starved cows bellowed day and night—a heartrending sound to Granny and Marya. And as ill luck would have it, there was a sharp frost all the winter, the snow drifted in high heaps, and the winter dragged on. At Annunciation there was a regular blizzard, and there was a fall of snow at Easter.

But in spite of it all the winter did end. At the beginning of April there came warm days and frosty nights. Winter would not give way, but one warm day overpowered it at last, and the streams began to flow and the birds began to sing. The whole meadow and the bushes near the river were drowned in the spring floods, and all the space between Zhukovo and the further side was filled up with a vast sheet of water, from which wild ducks rose up in flocks here and there. The spring sunset, flaming among gorgeous clouds, gave every evening something new, extraordinary, incredible—just what one does not believe in afterwards, when one sees those very colors and those very clouds in a picture.

The cranes flew swiftly, swiftly, with mournful cries, as though they were calling to people to come with them. Standing on the edge of the ravine, Olga looked a long time at the flooded meadow, at the sunshine, at the bright church, which looked as though it had grown younger; and her tears flowed and her breath came in gasps from her passionate longing to go away, to go far away to the end of the world. It was already settled that she should go back to Moscow to be a servant, and that Kiryak should set off with her to get a job as a porter or something. Oh, to get away quickly!

As soon as it dried up and grew warm they got ready to set off. Olga and Sasha, with wallets on their backs and shoes of plaited bark on their feet, came out before daybreak: Marya came out, too, to see them on their way. Kiryak was not well and was kept at home for another week. For the last time Olga prayed at the church and thought of her husband, and though she did not shed tears, her face puckered up and looked ugly like an old woman's. During the winter she had grown thinner and plainer, and her hair had gone a little gray, and instead of the old look of sweetness and the pleasant smile on her face, she had the resigned, mournful expression left by the sorrows she had been through, and there was something blank and irresponsive in her eyes, as though she did not hear what was said. She was sorry to part from the village and the peasants. She remembered how they had carried out Nikolai, and how a requiem had been ordered for him at almost every hut, and all had shed tears in sympathy with her grief. In the course of the summer and the winter there had been hours and days when it seemed as though these people lived worse than the beasts, and to live with them was terrible; they were coarse, dishonest, filthy, and drunken; they did not live in harmony, but quarreled continually, because they distrusted and feared and did not respect one another. Who keeps the tavern and makes the people drunken? A peasant. Who wastes and spends on drink the funds of the commune, of the schools, of the church? A peasant. Who stole from his neighbors, set fire to their property, gave false witness at the court for a bottle of vodka? At the meetings of the Zemstvo and other local bodies, who was the first to fall foul of the peasants? A peasant. Yes, to live with them was terrible; but yet, they were human beings, they suffered and wept like human beings, and there was nothing in their lives for which one could not find excuse. Hard labor that made the whole body ache at night, the cruel winters, the scanty harvests, the overcrowding; and they had no help and none to whom they could look for help. Those of them who were a little stronger and better off could be no help, as they were themselves coarse, dishonest, drunken, and abused one another just as revoltingly; the paltriest little clerk or official treated the peasants as though they were tramps, and addressed even the village elders and church wardens as inferiors, and considered they had a right to do so. And, indeed, can any sort of help or good example be given by mercenary, greedy, depraved, and idle persons who only visit the village in order to insult, to despoil, and to terrorize? Olga remembered the pitiful, humiliated look of the old people when in the winter Kiryak had been taken to be flogged. . . . And now she felt sorry for all these people, painfully so, and as she walked on she kept looking back at the huts.

After walking two miles with them, Marya said good-bye, then kneeling, and falling forward with her face on the earth, she began wailing:

"Again I am left alone. Alas, for poor me! Poor, unhappy! . . ."

And she wailed like this for a long time, and for a long way Olga and Sasha could still see her on her knees, bowing down to someone at the side and clutching her head in her hands, while the rooks flew over her head.

The sun rose high; it began to get hot. Zhukovo was left far behind. Walking was pleasant. Olga and Sasha soon forgot both the village and Marya; they were gay and everything entertained them. Now they came upon an ancient barrow, now upon a row of telegraph posts running one after another into the distance and disappearing into the horizon, and the wires hummed mysteriously. Then they saw a homestead, all wreathed in green foliage; there came a scent from it of dampness, of hemp, and it seemed for some reason that happy people lived there. Then they came upon a horse's skeleton whitening in solitude in the open fields. And the larks trilled unceasingly, the corn crakes called to one another, and the land rail cried as though someone were really scraping at an old iron rail.

At midday Olga and Sasha reached a big village. There in the broad street they met the little old man who was General Zhukov's cook. He was hot, and his red, perspiring bald head shone in the sunshine. Olga and he did not recognize each other, then looked round at the same moment, recognized each other, and went their separate ways without saying a word. Stopping near the hut which looked newest and most prosperous, Olga bowed down before the open windows, and said in a loud, thin, chanting voice:

"Good Christian folk, give alms, for Christ's sake, that God's blessing may be upon you, and that your parents may be in the Kingdom of Heaven in peace eternal."

"Good Christian folk," Sasha began chanting, "give, for Christ's sake, that God's blessing, the Heavenly Kingdom . . ."

*Two further chapters of* Peasants *were found among Chekhov's papers and have been published in Volume 9 of the Soviet edition of his works. He had evidently, as the Soviet editors say, "planned to present, side by side with the rural peasant life, the life of the 'superfluous' peasant population under metropolitan conditions." That this was a part of his original intention and not an afterthought for a sequel is shown by the fact that his notes for it are found, in his notebooks, mixed in with his notes for the earlier parts of the story. Those entries that relate to the incidents which were to follow these two later chapters (from Volume 12 of the Soviet edition) have been made to follow them here.*

*It should also be mentioned that, in deference to the censor, a whole chapter from the story as written was omitted and has never been found. This contained, as Chekhov explains in a letter to F. D. Batyushkov of January 24, 1900, "a peasants' conversation about religion and the authorities."*

## 10.

Olga's sister-in-law, Klavdia Abramovna, lived in one of the little alleys near the Patriarch's Ponds,[1] in an ancient two-storied house. On the bottom floor was a laundry, and the

1. A small park in Moscow.

whole of the upper floor was rented by an elderly gentlewoman, a quiet retiring old maid, who in turn rented rooms to lodgers and supported herself in this way. Coming into the dark hallway, you found yourself facing two doors, one on the right and one on the left: behind the first of these, in a little room, lived Klavdia Abramovna and Sasha; behind the other lived a printer's make-up man. Beyond was a parlor, with a divan, armchairs, a lamp with a shade, and pictures on the walls —everything quite as it should be; but there was a smell there of steam and the washing of clothes that penetrated from the laundry below, and all day the sound of singing was heard. This parlor, which was used by all the lodgers, gave access to three apartments; in one of these the landlady lived, in another an aged lackey, Ivan Makarich Matvyeichev, a native of Zhukovo, the man who had once put Nikolai in the way of finding a job; on his door, which was white and was always kept closed, hung a big stable lock on a chain; on the other side of the third door lived a scrawny young woman, with sharp eyes and thick lips, who had three children that were always crying. On holidays a monastery priest came to see her. She usually went about all day wearing nothing but a skirt, without washing herself or doing her hair, but on the days when she was expecting her monastery priest, she would put on a silk dress and curl her hair.

In Klavdia Abramovna's room there was, as they say, not the space to turn around. There were a bed, a chest of drawers, a chair, and that was all—and yet it was somehow crowded. But the little room was tidily kept, and Klavdia Abramovna called it her boudoir. She was very much pleased with her furniture—especially with the things on the chest of drawers: a mirror, lip salve and powder, little bottles and little boxes, ceruse,[2] and every kind of luxury that she regarded as essential to her profession and on which she spent most of her earnings;

2. A cosmetic made of white lead.

and there were photographs in little frames that showed her in various guises. She had been taken with her husband, a postman, with whom she had lived only a year, after which she had left him, not feeling a vocation for family life. She had been photographed, as is common with women of that sort, with a bang on her forehead and frizzed like a sheep; in the uniform of a soldier, flourishing an unsheathed saber; and dressed as a page, astride a chair, so that her thighs, clad in tights, lay flat on the chair, like two fat boiled sausages. There were portraits of men, also—she was in the habit of calling them her visitors and did not always know their names; our friend Kiryak was even among them in his quality of family connection: he had had a full-length photograph taken of himself, wearing a pair of black trousers that he had somewhere or other acquired for a time.

Formerly Klavdia Abramovna had frequented costume balls and Filippov's[3] and spent whole evenings on the Tversky Boulevard; but with the years she had come gradually to stay at home, and now that she had reached forty-two, she rarely received visitors, and these were only a few left over from her earlier years, who came to her in memory of old times, and alas! had grown old themselves and visited her even more seldom, since they were dropping off every year. Among her new visitors there was only one who was very young, still beardless; he would come into the entrance hall, like a conspirator, noiselessly and sullenly, with the collar of his schoolboy coat pulled up around his ears in an attempt not to be seen from the parlor, and afterwards, when he went away, he would leave a ruble on the chest of drawers.

For whole days now Klavdia Abramovna would sit at home doing nothing; occasionally, however, when the weather was fine, she would walk along the Tverskaya or the Little Bronnaya, holding her head up proudly and feeling herself a lady of solid

3. A popular patisserie in Moscow.

position and dignity, and only when she dropped in at a druggist's, to inquire in a whisper about ointment to get rid of red hands or wrinkles, did she show any sense of shame. In the evening, not lighting the light, she would sit in her little room and wait for someone to come; and about eleven o'clock—this now occurred only infrequently, once or twice a week—somebody would be heard walking softly, groping up and down the stairs, and then rustling behind the door, in an effort to find the bell. The door would then open, a muttering would be heard, and the visitor with hesitation would come into the entrance hall—he would usually be bald and obese, old and unattractive—and Klavdia Abramovna would hasten to bring him into her little room. She adored a "respectable visitor." There was for her no higher or worthier being; to receive a respectable visitor, to conduct herself toward him with delicacy, to do him honor, to satisfy him, was her soul's need, her duty, her happiness, her pride; to refuse such a visitor, to treat him in an inhospitable manner was something of which she was quite incapable, even in the period of fasting in preparation for her Easter devotions.

When Olga had returned from the country, she had put Sasha to live with her sister-in-law, thinking that it would only be temporary and that the girl, while she was still so little, if she should see anything bad, would not understand it. But now Sasha was over thirteen, and really the time was approaching when she must look for some other place for her; yet Sasha and her aunt had by now become attached to one another, and it was difficult to separate them; nor was there anywhere for Sasha to go in view of the fact that Olga herself was taking shelter in the corridors of rooming houses and sleeping at night on chairs. The day was spent by Sasha with her mother, or on the street, or down below in the laundry; the nights she would spend at her aunt's, on the floor, between the chest of drawers and the bed, and in the case of a visitor's arriving, she would lie down in the entrance hall.

She liked to go in the evening to the place where Ivan Makarich worked, and to watch the dancing from the kitchen. There the music was always playing, it was bright and noisy; the cook and the kitchenmaids had about them a savory smell of food, and Grandpa Ivan Makarich would give her some tea or some ice and would pass to her some morsels from the saucers and plates he had brought back into the kitchen. Once in autumn, late in the evening, coming back from Ivan Makarich's, she had carried home, wrapped up in paper, a drumstick, a piece of sturgeon, and a piece of cake.... Her aunt was already in bed....

"Dear Auntie," said Sasha sadly, "I've brought you something to eat."

They lit the light. Klavdia Abramovna began to eat, sitting up in bed. And Sasha regarded her curlpapers, which made her aunt seem quite dreadful, and her old withered shoulders; she regarded her sadly and long as if she were looking at a sick woman; then suddenly the tears rolled down her cheeks.

"Dear Auntie," she brought out in a shaky voice. "Dear Auntie, the girls in the laundry were saying this morning that you'd be begging in the streets in your old age, and that you'd die in the hospital. That's not true, Auntie—it isn't true," Sasha went on, now sobbing. "I shan't leave you, I'll see that you're fed... and I shan't let you go to the hospital."

Klavdia Abramovna's chin began to quiver and tears glistened in her eyes, but she kept herself under control and only said, glancing sternly at Sasha: "It's not proper to listen to the washwomen."

## 11.

In the furnished rooms of the Lisbon, little by little the lodgers grew silent; there was a smell of burning in the air from the lamps that had been put out, and the long-legged upstairs waiter had stretched himself out on chairs. Olga took off her apron and her white-ribboned cap, put a kerchief over her head, and went off to see her family by the Patriarch's Ponds. Her work at the Lisbon kept her busy all day from morning till late at night; and she could only rarely get to see them, and then only at night; her work took up all her time, not leaving her a single free moment: she had not, since her return from the country, even once been to church.

She was hurrying now to show Sasha a letter she had had from Marya in the country. This letter contained nothing but messages of greeting and complaints about wants and woes, about the fact that the old people were still alive, contributing nothing and eating up bread; yet somehow in these crooked lines, in which each letter looked like a cripple, there was for Olga a peculiar hidden charm, and, along with the complaints and the greetings, she read also that just now in the country the clear and warm days had come, that it was quiet in the evenings and that the air was fragrant, that the hours were striking in the church beyond the river; she could see the country churchyard, where her husband lay: from the green graves tranquility breathed, you were envious of the dead—and so much space out there, such freedom! And yet, what a strange thing: when you were actually living in the country, you were eager to get to Moscow, but now, on the contrary, you longed for the country.

Olga awakened Sasha, and, nervously, in apprehension lest somebody might be disturbed by her whispering and the light, she read her the letter twice. After this, they descended together by the dark and stinking stairway and left the house. The windows were wide open, and they could see the women ironing; and two of them were standing behind the gate, smoking cigarettes. Quickly Olga and Sasha went out into the street and talked about how nice it would be to save up two rubles and send them to the country: one for Marya and the other to pay for a mass for the dead to be said over Nikolai's grave.

"Oh, I've just had the most awful scare!" Olga, clasping her hands, began to tell Sasha her tale. "We'd only just sat down to eat, darling, when suddenly, from goodness knows where, there was Kiryak just as drunk as drunk! 'Give me some money, Olga!' he says. And he shouts and stamps his feet—give him money and that's all there is to it. And where am I going to get money? They don't pay me any wages—I live on the alms the good gentlemen give me—that's all the money I've got. . . . He won't listen—'Give me money!' he says. The lodgers look out of their rooms, the landlord arrived on the scene—I thought I'd die of shame—what a scandal! I begged thirty kopecks from the students and gave them to him, and he went away. And all day I've been going around whispering, 'O Lord, soften his heart!' That's what I've been whispering all day. . . ."

It was quiet in the streets; from time to time the nocturnal cabs would pass, while from somewhere far away—it must have been in the amusement park—music was still heard playing and the muted burst of rockets.

She knew all the rooming houses in Moscow.

The old lackey from Omon's. His son a compositor.

The sixth day after Olga had left the rooming house and had not come back to sleep, her daughter became worried; in the evening she would feel depressed and weep, and that night she went out to get money.

Sitting on the boulevard at night, Sasha would think about God, about the soul, but the thirst for life overcame these thoughts.

K[lavdia] A[bramovna] wanted to take Sasha to a procuress, but Sasha did not want to go: "It won't do for anyone to see."

The make-up man was always on the wing, dropping fragmentary phrases; he will say: "We are all brothers," and go away without explaining.

"The rich have taken everything for themselves—even the churches, the sole refuge of the poor."

When Sasha would tell about the country, even the make-up man, sitting in his room, would listen.

Sasha worked in the laundry without grumbling: "We can't be happy, because we're simple people."

From Zhukovo many lackeys, thanks to the protection of Luke Ivanovich, an old man who had lived sometime a long while ago, a legendary character. From him this deterioration dated.

Sasha drank a great deal of tea: she would drink six glasses at a time.

Just as women of K[lavdia] A[bramovna]'s age want to see young girls get married, so she wanted to see young girls have a clientele of respectable visitors.

Having so many people about him at the printer's was wearing for the make-up man, so that at home he tried to be alone.

On the boulevard, noisy students were walking arm in arm; one of them felt Sasha's breasts.

Kiryak came at night and made a rumpus. The monastery priest was in his drawers. The make-up man gave him money. The janitor threw him downstairs so that he spun around like a top, and it was surprising he was still alive.

When Sasha was thirteen or fourteen, she considered herself more serious than her absent-minded mother, and she began to take care of Olga.

K[lavdia] A[bramovna] was not a believer, but the decencies, as she thought, demanded of her that she cross herself and make her Easter devotions, and if the simple people didn't believe, they'd all be killing one another in the street.

Nothing drugs one and makes one drunk like money; when there's a lot of it, the world seems better than it is.

Ivan Makarich in every kind of weather went about with an umbrella and galoshes.[4]

"The ladies and gentlemen are decent people; they talk about loving their neighbor, about freedom, about helping the poor, but just the same they're all owners of serfs, so that they can't get along without servants, whom they're humiliating every minute. They've been hiding something, they've been lying to the Holy Ghost."

The lackey talks to himself aloud. He begs Sasha to tell him about the country. He is seventy-six now, but says he is only sixty.

The lackey despises the merchants and their ladies.

---

4. This trait was later assigned to the classics teacher Belikov in the story called "The Man in the Case."

He likes to say clever things in conversation, and they respected him for this, though they did not always understand them.

Sasha's sensibilities were offended by the smell of washing, by the filth, by the stinking stairs; they were offended by life itself; but she was persuaded that, in her position, such a life as this was inescapable.

Sasha: death is still a long way off, and while you're alive, you need principles—and on that account she liked to listen to the phrases that the make-up man flung out.

They didn't teach the children to pray or to think about God, they didn't instill into them any principles: they just forbade them to eat meat in Lent.

Just as today we are astonished by the cruelties through which the Christian torturers distinguished themselves, so people will in time be astonished at the falsehood with which evil today is fought; for example, they talk about freedom while making general use of the services of slaves.

—Translated by Edmund Wilson

# THE NEW VILLA

## 1.

TWO MILES FROM the village of Obruchanovo a huge bridge was being built. From the village, which stood up high on the steep riverbank, its trellis-like skeleton could be seen, and in foggy weather and on still winter days, when its delicate iron girders and all the scaffolding around was covered with hoarfrost, it presented a picturesque and even fantastic spectacle. Kucherov, the engineer who was building the bridge, a stout, broad-shouldered, bearded man in a soft crumpled cap, drove through the village in his racing droshky or his open carriage. Now and then on holidays navvies working on the bridge would come to the village; they begged for alms, laughed at the women, and sometimes carried off something. But that was rare; as a rule the days passed quietly and peacefully as though no bridgebuilding were going on, and only in the evening, when campfires gleamed near the bridge, the wind faintly wafted the songs of the navvies. And by day there was sometimes the mournful clang of metal, don-don-don.

It happened that the engineer's wife came to see him. She

was pleased with the riverbanks and the gorgeous view over the green valley with trees, churches, flocks, and she began begging her husband to buy a small piece of ground and to build them a cottage on it. Her husband agreed. They bought sixty acres of land, and on the high bank in a field, where in earlier days the cows of Obruchanovo used to wander, they built a pretty house of two stories with a terrace and a veranda, with a tower and a flagstaff on which a flag fluttered on Sundays. They built it in about three months, and then all the winter they were planting big trees, and when spring came and everything began to be green there were already avenues to the new house—a gardener and two laborers in white aprons were digging near it—there was a little fountain, and a globe of looking glass flashed so brilliantly that it was painful to look at. The house had already been named the New Villa.

On a bright, warm morning at the end of May two horses were brought to Obruchanovo to the village blacksmith, Rodion Petrov. They came from the New Villa. The horses were sleek, graceful beasts, as white as snow, and strikingly alike.

"Perfect swans!" said Rodion, gazing at them with reverent admiration.

His wife Stepanida, his children, and grandchildren came out into the street to look at them. By degrees a crowd collected. The Lychkovs, father and son, both men with swollen faces and entirely beardless, came up bareheaded. Kozov, a tall, thin old man with a long, narrow beard, came up leaning on a stick with a crook handle: he kept winking with his crafty eyes and smiling ironically as though he knew something.

"It's only that they are white; what is there in them?" he said. "Put mine on oats, and they will be just as sleek. They ought to be in a plow and with a whip, too. . . ."

The coachman simply looked at him with disdain but did not utter a word. And afterwards, while they were blowing up the fire at the forge, the coachman talked while he smoked cigarettes. The peasants learned from him various details: his employers were wealthy people; his mistress, Elena Ivanovna, had till her marriage lived in Moscow in a poor way as a governess; she was kindhearted, compassionate, and fond of helping the poor. On the new estate, he told them, they were not going to plow or to sow, but simply to live for their pleasure, live only to breathe the fresh air. When he had finished and led the horses back a crowd of boys followed him, the dogs barked, and Kozov, looking after him, winked sarcastically.

"Landowners, too-oo!" he said. "They have built a house and set up horses, but I bet they are nobodies—landowners, too-oo."

Kozov for some reason took a dislike from the first to the new house, to the white horses, and to the handsome, well-fed coachman. Kozov was a solitary man, a widower; he had a dreary life (he was prevented from working by a disease which he sometimes called a rupture and sometimes worms); he was maintained by his son, who worked at a confectioner's in Kharkov and sent him money; and from early morning till evening he sauntered at leisure about the river or about the village; if he saw, for instance, a peasant carting a log, or fishing, he would say: "That log's dry wood—it is rotten," or, "They won't bite in weather like this." In times of drought he would declare that there would not be a drop of rain till the frost came; and when the rains came he would say that everything would rot in the fields, that everything was ruined. And as he said these things he would wink as though he knew something.

At the New Villa they burned Bengal lights and sent up fireworks in the evenings, and a sailing boat with red lanterns floated by Obruchanovo. One morning the engineer's wife, Elena Ivanovna, and her little daughter drove to the village in a carriage with yellow wheels and a pair of dark bay ponies; both mother and daughter were wearing broad-brimmed straw hats, bent down over their ears.

This was exactly at the time when they were carting manure, and the blacksmith Rodion, a tall, gaunt old man, bareheaded and barefooted, was standing near his dirty and repulsive-looking cart and, flustered, looked at the ponies, and it was evident by his face that he had never seen such little horses before.

"The Kucherov lady has come!" was whispered around. "Look, the Kucherov lady has come!"

Elena Ivanovna looked at the huts as though she were selecting one, and then stopped at the very poorest, at the windows of which there were so many children's heads—flaxen, red, and dark. Stepanida, Rodion's wife, a stout woman, came running out of the hut; her kerchief slipped off her gray head; she looked at the carriage facing the sun, and her face smiled and wrinkled up as though she were blind.

"This is for your children," said Elena Ivanovna, and she gave her three rubles.

Stepanida suddenly burst into tears and bowed down to the ground. Rodion, too, flopped to the ground, displaying his brownish bald head, and as he did so he almost caught his wife in the ribs with the fork. Elena Ivanovna was overcome with confusion and drove back.

## 2.

The Lychkovs, father and son, caught in their meadows two cart horses, a pony, and a broad-faced Aalhaus bull calf, and with the help of redheaded Volodka, son of the blacksmith Rodion, drove them to the village. They called the village elder, collected witnesses, and went to look at the damage.

"All right, let 'em!" said Kozov, winking, "le-et 'em! Let them get out of it if they can, the engineers! Do you think there is no such thing as law? All right! Send for the police inspector, draw up a statement! . . ."

"Draw up a statement," repeated Volodka.

"I don't want to let this pass!" shouted the younger Lychkov. He shouted louder and louder, and his beardless face seemed to be more and more swollen. "They've set up a nice fashion! Leave them free, and they will ruin all the meadows! You've no sort of right to ill-treat people! We are not serfs now!"

"We are not serfs now!" repeated Volodka.

"We got on all right without a bridge," said the elder Lychkov gloomily; "we did not ask for it. What do we want a bridge for? We don't want it!"

"Brothers, good Christians, we cannot leave it like this!"

"All right, let 'em!" said Kozov, winking. "Let them get out of it if they can! Landowners, indeed!"

They went back to the village, and as they walked the younger Lychkov beat himself on the breast with his fist and shouted all the way, and Volodka shouted, too, repeating his words. And meanwhile quite a crowd had gathered in the village round the thoroughbred bull calf and the horses. The bull calf was embarrassed and looked up from under his brows, but suddenly lowered his muzzle to the ground and took to his heels, kicking up his hind legs; Kozov was frightened and waved his stick at him, and they all burst out laughing. Then they locked up the beasts and waited.

In the evening the engineer sent five rubles for the damage, and the two horses, the pony, and the bull calf, without being fed or given water, returned home, their heads hanging with a guilty air as though they were convicted criminals.

On getting the five rubles the Lychkovs, father and son, the village elder, and Volodka, punted over the river in a boat and went to a hamlet on the other side where there was a tavern, and there had a long carousal. Their singing and the shouting of the younger Lychkov could be heard from the village. Their women were uneasy and did not sleep all night. Rodion did not sleep either.

"It's a bad business," he said, sighing and turning from side to side. "The gentleman will be angry, and then there will be trouble. . . . They have insulted the gentleman. . . . Oh, they've insulted him. It's a bad business. . . ."

It happened that the peasants, Rodion amongst them, went into their forest to divide the clearings for mowing, and as they were returning home they were met by the engineer. He was wearing a red cotton shirt and high boots; a setter dog with its long tongue hanging out, followed behind him.

"Good day, brothers," he said.

The peasants stopped and took off their hats.

"I have long wanted to have a talk with you, friends," he went on. "This is what it is. Ever since the early spring your cattle have been in my copse and garden every day. Everything is trampled down; the pigs have rooted up the meadow, are ruining everything in the kitchen garden, and all the undergrowth in the copse is destroyed. There is no getting on with your herdsmen; one asks them civilly, and they are rude. Damage is done on my estate every day and I do nothing—I don't fine you or make a complaint; meanwhile you impounded my horses and my bull calf and exacted five rubles. Was that right? Is that neighborly?" he went on, and his face was so soft and persuasive, and his expression was not forbidding. "Is that the way decent people behave? A week ago one of your people cut down two oak saplings in my copse. You have dug up the road to Eresnevo, and now I have to go two miles round. Why do you injure me at every step? What harm have I done you? For God's sake, tell me! My wife and I do our utmost to live with you in peace and harmony; we help the peasants as we can. My wife is a kind, warmhearted woman; she never refuses you help. That is her dream—to be of use to you and your children. You reward us with evil for our good. You are unjust, my friends. Think of that. I ask you earnestly to think it over. We treat you humanely; repay us in the same coin."

He turned and went away. The peasants stood a little longer, put on their caps and walked away. Rodion, who always understood everything that was said to him in some peculiar way of his own, heaved a sigh and said:

"We must pay. 'Repay in coin, my friends,' he said."

They walked to the village in silence. On reaching home, Rodion said his prayer, took off his boots, and sat down on the bench beside his wife. Stepanida and he always sat side by side when they were at home and always walked side by side in the street; they ate and they drank and they slept always together, and the older they grew the more they loved one another. It was hot and crowded in their hut, and there were children everywhere—on the floors, in the windows, on the stove. . . . In spite of her advanced years Stepanida was still bearing children, and now, looking at the crowd of children, it was hard to distinguish which were Rodion's and which were Volodka's. Volodka's wife, Lukerya, a plain young woman with prominent eyes and a nose like the beak of a bird, was kneading dough in a tub; Volodka was sitting on the stove with his legs hanging.

"Oh the road near Nikita's buckwheat . . . the engineer with his dog . . ." Rodion began, after a rest, scratching his ribs and his elbow. "'You must pay,' says he . . . 'coin,' says he. . . . Coin or no coin, we shall have to collect ten kopecks from every hut. We've offended the gentleman very much. I am sorry for him. . . ."

"We've lived without a bridge," said Volodka, not looking at anyone, "and we don't want one."

"What next; the bridge is a government business."

"We don't want it."

"Your opinion is not asked. What is it to you?"

"'Your opinion is not asked,'" Volodka mimicked him. "We don't want to drive anywhere; what do we want with a bridge? If we have to, we can cross by the boat."

Someone from the yard outside knocked at the window so violently that it seemed to shake the whole hut.

"Is Volodka at home?" he heard the voice of the younger Lychkov. "Volodka, come out, come along."

Volodka jumped down off the stove and began looking for his cap.

"Don't go, Volodka," said Rodion diffidently. "Don't go with them, Son. You are foolish, like a little child; they will teach you no good; don't go!"

"Don't go, Son," said Stepanida, and she blinked as though about to shed tears. "I bet they are calling you to the tavern."

"'To the tavern,'" Volodka mimicked.

"You'll come back drunk again, you currish Herod," said Lukerya, looking at him angrily. "Go along, go along, and may you burn up with vodka, you tailless Satan!"

"You hold your tongue," shouted Volodka.

"They've married me to a fool, they've ruined me, a luckless orphan, you redheaded drunkard . . ." wailed Lukerya, wiping her face with a hand covered with dough. "I wish I had never set eyes on you."

Volodka gave her a blow on the ear and went off.

## 3.

Elena Ivanovna and her little daughter visited the village on foot. They were out for a walk. It was a Sunday, and the peasant women and girls were walking up and down the street in their brightly colored dresses. Rodion and Stepanida, sitting side by side at their door, bowed and smiled to Elena Ivanovna and her little daughter as to acquaintances. From the windows more than a dozen children stared at them; their faces expressed amazement and curiosity, and they could be heard whispering:

"The Kucherov lady has come! The Kucherov lady!"

"Good morning," said Elena Ivanovna, and she stopped; she paused, and then asked: "Well, how are you getting on?"

"We get along all right, thank God," answered Rodion, speaking rapidly. "To be sure we get along."

"The life we lead!" smiled Stepanida. "You can see our poverty yourself, dear lady! The family is fourteen souls in all, and only two breadwinners. We are supposed to be blacksmiths, but when they bring us a horse to shoe we have no coal, nothing to buy it with. We are worried to death, lady," she went on, and laughed. "Oh, oh, we are worried to death."

Elena Ivanovna sat down at the entrance and, putting her arm round her little girl, pondered something, and, judging from the little girl's expression, melancholy thoughts were straying through her mind, too; as she brooded she played with the sumptuous lace on the parasol she had taken out of her mother's hands.

"Poverty," said Rodion, "a great deal of anxiety—you see no end to it. Here, God sends no rain . . . our life is not easy, there is no denying it."

"You have a hard time in this life," said Elena Ivanovna, "but in the other world you will be happy."

Rodion did not understand her and simply coughed into his clenched hand by way of reply. Stepanida said:

"Dear lady, the rich men will be all right in the next world, too. The rich put up candles, pay for services; the rich give to beggars, but what can the poor man do? He has no time to make the sign of the cross. He is the beggar of beggars himself; how can he think of his soul? And many sins come from poverty; from trouble we snarl at one another like dogs, we haven't a good word to say to one another, and all sorts of things happen, dear lady—God forbid! It seems we have no luck in this world nor the next. All the luck has fallen to the rich."

She spoke gaily; she was evidently used to talking of her

hard life. And Rodion smiled, too; he was pleased that his old woman was so clever, so ready of speech.

"It is only on the surface that the rich seem to be happy," said Elena Ivanovna. "Every man has his sorrow. Here my husband and I do not live poorly, we have means, but are we happy? I am young, but I have had four children; my children are always being ill. I am ill, too, and constantly being doctored."

"And what is your illness?" asked Rodion.

"A woman's complaint. I get no sleep; a continual headache gives me no peace. Here I am sitting and talking, but my head is bad, I am weak all over, and I should prefer the hardest labor to such a condition. My soul, too, is troubled; I am in continual fear for my children, my husband. Every family has its own trouble of some sort; we have ours. I am not of noble birth. My grandfather was a simple peasant, my father was a tradesman in Moscow; he was a plain, uneducated man, too, while my husband's parents were wealthy and distinguished. They did not want him to marry me, but he disobeyed them, quarreled with them, and they have not forgiven us to this day. That worries my husband; it troubles him and keeps him in constant agitation; he loves his mother, loves her dearly. So I am uneasy, too, my soul is in pain."

Peasants, men and women, were by now standing round Rodion's hut and listening. Kozov came up, too, and stood twitching his long, narrow beard. The Lychkovs, father and son, drew near.

"And say what you like, one cannot be happy and satisfied if one does not feel in one's proper place," Elena Ivanovna went on. "Each of you has his strip of land, each of you works and knows what he is working for; my husband builds bridges —in short, everyone has his place, while I, I simply walk about. I have not my bit to work. I don't work, and feel as though I were an outsider. I am saying all this that you may not judge from outward appearances; if a man is expensively dressed and has means it does not prove that he is satisfied with his life."

She got up to go away and took her daughter by the hand.

"I like your place here very much," she said, and smiled, and from that faint, diffident smile one could tell how unwell she really was, how young and how pretty; she had a pale, thinnish face with dark eyebrows and fair hair. And the little girl was just such another as her mother: thin, fair, and slender. There was a fragrance of scent about them.

"I like the river and the forest and the village," Elena Ivanovna went on; "I could live here all my life, and I feel as though here I should get strong and find my place. I want to help you—I want to dreadfully—to be of use, to be a real friend to you. I know your need, and what I don't know I feel, my heart guesses. I am sick, feeble, and for me perhaps it is not possible to change my life as I would. But I have children. I will try to bring them up that they may be of use to you, may love you. I shall impress upon them continually that their life does not belong to them, but to you. Only I beg you earnestly, I beseech you, trust us, live in friendship with us. My husband is a kind, good man. Don't worry him, don't irritate him. He is sensitive to every trifle, and yesterday, for instance, your cattle were in our vegetable garden, and one of your people broke down the fence to the beehives, and such an attitude to us drives my husband to despair. I beg you," she went on in an imploring voice, and she clasped her hands on her bosom, "I beg you to treat us as good neighbors; let us live in peace! There is a saying, you know, that even a bad peace is better than a good quarrel, and, 'Don't buy property, but buy neighbors.' I repeat my husband is a kind man and good; if all goes well we promise to do everything in our power for you; we will mend the roads, we will build a school for your children. I promise you."

"Of course we thank you humbly, lady," said Lychkov the father, looking at the ground; "you are educated people; it is for you to know best. Only, you see, Voronov, a rich peasant at Eresnevo, promised to build a school; he, too, said, 'I will do this for you,' 'I will do that for you,' and he only put up the framework and refused to go on. And then they made the peasants put the roof on and finish it; it cost them a thousand rubles. Voronov did not care; he only stroked his beard, but the peasants felt it a bit hard."

"That was a crow, but now there's a rook, too," said Kozov, and he winked.

There was the sound of laughter.

"We don't want a school," said Volodka sullenly. "Our children go to Petrovskoe, and they can go on going there; we don't want it."

Elena Ivanovna seemed suddenly intimidated; her face looked paler and thinner, she shrank into herself as though she had been touched with something coarse and walked away without uttering another word. And she walked more and more quickly, without looking round.

"Lady," said Rodion, walking after her, "lady, wait a bit; hear what I would say to you."

He followed her without his cap, and spoke softly as though begging.

"Lady, wait and hear what I will say to you."

They had walked out of the village, and Elena Ivanovna stopped beside a cart in the shade of an old mountain ash.

"Don't be offended, lady," said Rodion. "What does it mean? Have patience. Have patience for a couple of years. You will live here, you will have patience, and it will all come round. Our folks are good and peaceable; there's no harm in them; it's God's truth I'm telling you. Don't mind Kozov and the Lychkovs, and don't mind Volodka. He's a fool; he listens to the first that speaks. The others are quiet folks; they are silent.

Some would be glad, you know, to say a word from the heart and to stand up for themselves, but cannot. They have a heart and a conscience, but no tongue. Don't be offended . . . have patience. . . . What does it matter?"

Elena Ivanovna looked at the broad, tranquil river, pondering, and tears flowed down her cheeks. And Rodion was troubled by those tears; he almost cried himself!

"Never mind . . ." he muttered. "Have patience for a couple of years. You can have the school, you can have the roads, only not all at once. If you went, let us say, to sow corn on that mound, you would first have to weed it out, to pick out all the stones, and then to plow, and work and work . . . and with the people, you see, it is the same . . . you must work and work until you overcome them."

The crowd had moved away from Rodion's hut and was coming along the street towards the mountain ash. They began singing songs and playing the concertina, and they kept coming closer and closer. . . .

"Mamma, let us go away from here," said the little girl, huddling up to her mother, pale and shaking all over; "let us go away, Mamma!"

"Where?"

"To Moscow. . . . Let us go, Mamma."

The child began crying.

Rodion was utterly overcome; his face broke into profuse perspiration; he took out of his pocket a little crooked cucumber, like a half-moon, covered with crumbs of rye bread, and began thrusting it into the little girl's hands.

"Come, come," he muttered, scowling severely; "take the little cucumber, eat it up. . . . You mustn't cry. Mamma will whip you. . . . She'll tell your father of you when you get home. Come, come. . . ."

They walked on, and he still followed behind them, wanting to say something friendly and persuasive to them. And, seeing that they were both absorbed in their own thoughts and their own griefs, and not noticing him, he stopped and, shading his eyes from the sun, looked after them for a long time till they disappeared into their copse.

## 4.

The engineer seemed to grow irritable and petty, and in every trivial incident saw an act of robbery or outrage. His gate was kept bolted even by day, and at night two watchmen walked up and down the garden beating a board; and they gave up employing anyone from Obruchanovo as a laborer. As ill luck would have it someone (either a peasant or one of the workmen) took the new wheels off the cart and replaced them by old ones, then soon afterwards two bridles and a pair of pincers were carried off, and murmurs arose even in the village. People began to say that a search should be made at the Lychkovs' and at Volodka's, and then the bridles and the pincers were found under the hedge in the engineer's garden; someone had thrown them down there.

It happened that the peasants were coming in a crowd out of the forest, and again they met the engineer on the road. He stopped, and without wishing them good day he began, looking angrily first at one, then at another:

"I have begged you not to gather mushrooms in the park and near the yard, but to leave them for my wife and children, but your girls come before daybreak and there is not a mushroom left. . . . Whether one asks you or not it makes no difference. Entreaties, and friendliness, and persuasion I see are all useless."

He fixed his indignant eyes on Rodion and went on:

"My wife and I behaved to you as human beings, as to our equals, and you? But what's the use of talking! It will end by our looking down upon you. There is nothing left!"

And making an effort to restrain his anger, not to say too much, he turned and went on.

On getting home, Rodion said his prayer, took off his boots, and sat down beside his wife.

"Yes . . ." he began with a sigh. "We were walking along just now, and Monsieur Kucherov met us. . . . Yes. . . . He saw the girls at daybreak. . . . 'Why don't they bring mushrooms,' he said . . . 'to my wife and children?' he said. . . . And then he looked at me and he said: 'I and my wife will look after you,' he said. I wanted to fall down at his feet, but I hadn't the courage. . . . God give him health. . . . God bless him! . . ."

Stepanida crossed herself and sighed.

"They are kind, simplehearted people," Rodion went on. "'We shall look after you.' . . . He promised me that before everyone. In our old age . . . it wouldn't be a bad thing. . . . I should always pray for them. . . . Holy Mother, bless them. . . ."

The Feast of the Exaltation of the Cross, the fourteenth of September, was the festival of the village church. The Lychkovs, father and son, went across the river early in the morning and returned to dinner drunk; they spent a long time going about the village, alternately singing and swearing; then they had a fight and went to the New Villa to complain. First Lychkov the father went into the yard with a long ashen stick in his hands. He stopped irresolutely and took off his hat. Just at that moment the engineer and his family were sitting on the veranda, drinking tea.

"What do you want?" shouted the engineer.

"Your honor . . ." Lychkov began, and burst into tears. "Show the Divine mercy, protect me . . . my son makes my life a misery . . . your honor. . . ."

Lychkov the son walked up, too; he, too, was bareheaded and had a stick in his hand; he stopped and fixed his drunken senseless eyes on the veranda.

"It is not my business to settle your affairs," said the engineer. "Go to the rural captain or the police officer."

"I have been everywhere. . . . I have lodged a petition . . ." said Lychkov the father, and he sobbed. "Where can I go now? He can kill me now, it seems. He can do anything. Is that the way to treat a father? A father?"

He raised his stick and hit his son on the head; the son raised his stick and struck his father just on his bald patch such a blow that the stick bounced back. The father did not even flinch, but hit his son again and again on the head. And so they stood and kept hitting one another on the head, and it looked not so much like a fight as some sort of a game. And peasants, men and women, stood in a crowd at the gate and looked into the garden, and the faces of all were grave. They were the peasants who had come to greet them for the holiday, but seeing the Lychkovs, they were ashamed and did not go in.

The next morning Elena Ivanovna went with the children to Moscow. And there was a rumor that the engineer was selling his house. . . .

## 5.

The peasants had long ago grown used to the sight of the bridge, and it was difficult to imagine the river at that place without a bridge. The heap of rubble left from the building of it had long been overgrown with grass, the navvies were forgotten, and instead of the strains of the "Dubinushka" that they used to sing, the peasants heard almost every hour the sounds of a passing train.

The New Villa has long ago been sold; now it belongs to a government clerk who comes here from the town for the holidays with his family, drinks tea on the terrace, and then goes back to the town again. He wears a cockade on his cap; he talks and clears his throat as though he were a very important official, though he is only of the rank of a collegiate secretary, and when the peasants bow he makes no response.

In Obruchanovo everyone has grown older; Kozov is dead. In Rodion's hut there are even more children. Volodka has grown a long red beard. They are still as poor as ever.

In the early spring the Obruchanovo peasants were sawing wood near the station. And after work they were going home; they walked without haste one after the other. Broad saws curved over their shoulders; the sun was reflected in them. The nightingales were singing in the bushes on the bank, larks were trilling in the heavens. It was quiet at the New Villa; there was not a soul there, and only golden pigeons—golden because the sunlight was streaming upon them—were flying over the house. All of them—Rodion, the two Lychkovs, and Volodka—thought of the white horses, the little ponies, the fireworks, the boat with the lanterns; they remembered how the engineer's wife, so beautiful and so grandly dressed, had come into the village and talked to them in such a friendly way. And it seemed as though all that had never been; it was like a dream or a fairy tale.

They trudged along, tired out, and mused as they went. . . . In their village, they mused, the people were good, quiet, sensible, fearing God, and Elena Ivanovna, too, was quiet, kind, and gentle; it made one sad to look at her, but why had they not got on together? Why had they parted like enemies? How was it that some mist had shrouded from their eyes what mattered most and had let them see nothing but damage done by cattle, bridles, pincers, and all those trivial things which now, as they remembered them, seemed so nonsensical? How was it that with the new owner they lived in peace, and yet had been on bad terms with the engineer?

And, not knowing what answer to make to these questions, they were all silent except Volodka, who muttered something.

"What is it?" Rodion asked.

"We lived without a bridge . . ." said Volodka gloomily. "We lived without a bridge and did not ask for one . . . and we don't want it. . . ."

No one answered him and they walked on in silence with drooping heads.

# IN THE RAVINE

## 1.

THE VILLAGE OF Ukleyevo lay in a ravine, so that only the belfry and the chimneys of the printed-cottons factories could be seen from the highroad and the railway station. When visitors asked what village this was, they were told:

"That's the village where the deacon ate all the caviar at the funeral."

It had happened at the dinner at the funeral of Kostukov that the old deacon saw among the savories some large-grained caviar and began eating it greedily; people nudged him, tugged at his arm, but he seemed petrified with enjoyment: felt nothing, and only went on eating. He ate up all the caviar, and there were four pounds in the jar. And years had passed since then, the deacon had long been dead, but the caviar was still remembered. Whether life was so poor here or people had not been clever enough to notice anything but that unimportant incident, which had occurred ten years before, anyway the people had nothing else to tell about the village Ukleyevo.

The village was never free from fever, and there was boggy

mud there even in the summer, especially under the fences over which hung old willow trees that gave deep shade. Here there was always a smell from the factory refuse and the acetic acid which was used in the finishing of the cotton print.

The three cotton factories and the tanyard were not in the village itself, but a little way off. They were small factories, and not more than four hundred workmen were employed in all of them. The tanyard often made the water in the little river stink; the refuse contaminated the meadows, the peasants' cattle suffered from Siberian plague, and orders were given that the factory should be closed. It was considered to be closed, but went on working in secret with the connivance of the local police officer and the district doctor, who was paid ten rubles a month by the owner. In the whole village there were only two decent houses built of brick with iron roofs: one of them was the local court; in the other, a two-storied house just opposite the church, there lived a shopkeeper from Epifan called Grigory Petrovich Tsybukin.

Grigory kept a grocer's shop, but that was only for appearance's sake: in reality he sold vodka, cattle, hides, grain, and pigs; he traded in anything that came to hand, and when, for instance, magpies were wanted abroad for ladies' hats, he made some thirty kopecks on every pair of birds; he bought timber for felling, lent money at interest, and altogether was a sharp old man, full of resources.

He had two sons. The elder, Anisim, was in the police in the detective department and was rarely at home. The younger, Stepan, had gone in for trade and helped his father: but no great help was expected from him as he was weak in health and deaf; his wife Aksinya, a handsome woman with a good figure, who wore a hat and carried a parasol on holidays, got up early and went to bed late, and ran about all day long, picking up her skirts and jingling her keys, going from the granary to the cellar and from there to the shop, and old

Tsybukin looked at her good-humoredly while his eyes glowed, and at such moments he regretted she had not been married to his elder son instead of to the younger one, who was deaf, and who evidently knew very little about female beauty.

The old man had always an inclination for family life, and he loved his family more than anything on earth, especially his elder son, the detective, and his daughter-in-law. Aksinya had no sooner married the deaf son than she began to display an extraordinary gift for business, and knew who could be allowed to run up a bill and who could not: she kept the keys and would not trust them even to her husband; she kept the accounts by means of the reckoning beads, looked at the horses' teeth like a peasant, and was always laughing or shouting; and whatever she did or said the old man was simply delighted and muttered:

"Well done, daughter-in-law! You are a smart wench!"

He was a widower, but a year after his son's marriage he could not resist getting married himself. A girl was found for him, living twenty miles from Ukleyevo, called Varvara Nikolaevna, no longer quite young, but good-looking, comely, and belonging to a decent family. As soon as she was installed into the upper-story room everything in the house seemed to brighten up as though new glass had been put into all the windows. The lamps gleamed before the icons, the tables were covered with snow-white cloths, flowers with red buds made their appearance in the windows and in the front garden, and at dinner, instead of eating from a single bowl, each person had a separate plate set for him. Varvara Nikolaevna had a pleasant, friendly smile, and it seemed as though the whole house were smiling, too. Beggars and pilgrims, male and female, began to come into the yard, a thing which had never happened in the past; the plaintive singsong voices of the Ukleyevo peasant women and the apologetic coughs of weak, seedy-looking men, who had been dismissed from the factory for drunkenness, were heard under the windows. Varvara helped them with money, with bread, with old clothes, and afterwards, when she felt more at home, began taking things out of the shop. One day the deaf man saw her take four ounces of tea and that disturbed him.

"Here, Mother's taken four ounces of tea," he informed his father afterwards; "where is that to be entered?"

The old man made no reply but stood still and thought a moment, moving his eyebrows, and then went upstairs to his wife.

"Varvarushka, if you want anything out of the shop," he said affectionately, "take it, my dear. Take it and welcome; don't hesitate."

And the next day the deaf man, running across the yard, called to her:

"If there is anything you want, Mother, take it."

There was something new, something gay and lighthearted in her giving of alms, just as there was in the lamps before the icons and in the red flowers. When at Carnival or at the church festival, which lasted for three days, they sold the peasants tainted salt meat, smelling so strong it was hard to stand near the tub of it, and took scythes, caps, and their wives' kerchiefs in pledge from the drunken men; when the factory hands stupefied with bad vodka lay rolling in the mud, and sin seemed to hover thick like a fog in the air, then it was a relief to think that up there in the house there was a gentle, neatly dressed woman who had nothing to do with salt meat or vodka; her charity had in those burdensome, murky days the effect of a safety valve in a machine.

The days in Tsybukin's house were spent in business cares. Before the sun had risen in the morning Aksinya was panting and puffing as she washed in the outer room, and the samovar was boiling in the kitchen with a hum that boded no good. Old Grigory Petrovich, dressed in a long black coat, cotton breeches, and shiny top boots, looking a dapper little figure, walked about the rooms, tapping with his little heels like the father-in-law in a well-known song. The shop was opened. When it was daylight a racing droshky was brought up to the front door and the old man got jauntily on to it, pulling his big cap down to his ears; and, looking at him, no one would have said he was fifty-six. His wife and daughter-in-law saw him off, and at such times when he had on a good, clean coat, and had in the droshky a huge black horse that had cost three hundred rubles, the old man did not like the peasants to come up to him with their complaints and petitions; he hated the peasants and disdained them, and if he saw some peasants waiting at the gate, he would shout angrily:

"Why are you standing there? Go further off."

Or if it were a beggar, he would say:

"God will provide!"

He used to drive off on business; his wife, in a dark dress and a black apron, tidied the rooms or helped in the kitchen. Aksinya attended to the shop, and from the yard could be heard the clink of bottles and of money, her laughter and loud talk, and the anger of customers whom she had offended; and at the same time it could be seen that the secret sale of vodka was already going on in the shop. The deaf man sat in the shop, too, or walked about the street bareheaded, with his hands in his pockets, looking absent-mindedly now at the huts, now at the sky overhead. Six times a day they had tea; four times a day they sat down to meals; and in the evening they counted over their takings, put them down, went to bed, and slept soundly.

All the three cotton factories in Ukleyevo and the houses of the factory owners—Khrymin Seniors, Khrymin Juniors, and Kostukov—were on a telephone. The telephone was laid on in the local court, too, but it soon ceased to work as bugs and beetles bred there. The elder of the rural district had had little education and wrote every word in the official documents in capitals. But when the telephone was spoiled he said:

"Yes, now we shall be badly off without a telephone."

The Khrymin Seniors were continually at law with the Juniors, and sometimes the Juniors quarreled among themselves and began going to law, and their factory did not work for a month or two till they were reconciled again, and this was an entertainment for the people of Ukleyevo, as there was a great deal of talk and gossip on the occasion of each quarrel. On holidays Kostukov and the Juniors used to get up races, used to dash about Ukleyevo and run over calves. Aksinya, rustling her starched petticoats, used to promenade in a low-necked dress up and down the street near her shop; the Juniors used to snatch her up and carry her off as though by force. Then old Tsybukin would drive out to show his new horse and take Varvara with him.

In the evening, after the races, when people were going to bed, an expensive concertina was played in the Juniors' yard and, if it were a moonlight night, those sounds sent a thrill of delight to the heart, and Ukleyevo no longer seemed a wretched hole.

## 2.

The elder son Anisim came home very rarely, only on great holidays, but he often sent by a returning villager presents and letters written in very good writing by some other hand, always on a sheet of foolscap in the form of a petition. The letters were full of expressions that Anisim never made use of in conversation: "Dear Papa and Mamma, I send you a pound of flower tea for the satisfaction of your physical needs."

At the bottom of every letter was scratched, as though with a broken pen: "Anisim Tsybukin," and again in the same excellent hand: "Agent."

The letters were read aloud several times, and the old father, touched, red with emotion, would say:

"Here he did not care to stay at home, he has gone in for an intellectual line. Well, let him! Every man to his own job!"

It happened just before Carnival there was a heavy storm of rain mixed with hail; the old man and Varvara went to the window to look at it, and lo and behold! Anisim drove up in a sledge from the station. He was quite unexpected. He came indoors, looking anxious and troubled about something, and he remained the same all the time; but there was something free and easy in his manner. He was in no haste to go away, it seemed, as though he had been dismissed from the service. Varvara was pleased at his arrival; she looked at him with a sly expression, sighed, and shook her head.

"How is this, my friends?" she said. "Tut, tut, the lad's in his twenty-eighth year, and he is still leading a gay bachelor life; tut, tut, tut. . . ."

From the other room her soft, even speech sounded like tut, tut, tut. She began whispering with her husband and Aksinya, and their faces wore the same sly and mysterious expression, as though they were conspirators.

It was decided to marry Anisim.

"Oh, tut, tut . . . the younger brother has been married long ago," said Varvara, "and you are still without a helpmate like a cock at a fair. What is the meaning of it? Tut, tut, you will be married, please God, then as you choose—you will go into the service and your wife will remain here at home to help us. There is no order in your life, young man, and I see you have forgotten how to live properly. Tut, tut, it's the same trouble with all you townspeople."

When the Tsybukins married, the most handsome girls were chosen as brides for them as rich men. For Anisim, too, they found a handsome one. He was himself of an uninteresting and inconspicuous appearance; of a feeble, sickly build and short stature. He had full, puffy cheeks, which looked as though he were blowing them out; his eyes looked with a keen, unblinking stare; his beard was red and scanty, and when he was thinking he always put it into his mouth and bit it; moreover he often drank too much, and that was noticeable from his face and his walk. But when he was informed that they had found a very beautiful bride for him, he said:

"Oh well, I am not a fright myself. All of us Tsybukins are handsome, I may say."

The village of Torguevo was near the town. Half of it had lately been incorporated into the town, the other half remained a village. In the first—the town half—there was a widow living in her own little house; she had a sister living with her who was quite poor and went out to work by the day, and this sister had a daughter called Lipa, a girl who went out to work, too. People in Torguevo were already talking about Lipa's good looks, but her terrible poverty put everyone off; people opined that some widower or elderly man would marry her regardless of her poverty, or would perhaps take her to himself without marriage, and that her mother would get enough to eat living with her. Varvara heard about Lipa from the matchmakers, and she drove over to Torguevo.

Then a visit of inspection was arranged at the aunt's, with lunch and wine all in due order, and Lipa wore a new pink dress made on purpose for this occasion, and a crimson ribbon like a flame gleamed in her hair. She was pale-faced, thin, and frail, with soft, delicate features sunburnt from working in the open air; a shy, mournful smile always hovered about her face, and there was a childlike look in her eyes, trustful and curious.

She was young, quite a little girl, her bosom still scarcely perceptible, but she could be married because she had reached the legal age. She really was beautiful, and the only thing that might be thought unattractive was her big masculine hands, which hung idle now like two big claws.

"There is no dowry—and we don't think much of that," said Tsybukin to the aunt. "We took a wife from a poor family for our son Stepan, too, and now we can't say too much for her. In house and in business alike she has hands of gold."

Lipa stood in the doorway and looked as though she would say: "Do with me as you will, I trust you," while her mother Praskovya, the workwoman, hid herself in the kitchen numb with shyness. At one time in her youth a merchant whose floors she was scrubbing stamped at her in a rage; she went chill with terror and there always was a feeling of fear at the bottom of her heart. When she was frightened her arms and legs trembled and her cheeks twitched. Sitting in the kitchen, she tried to hear what the visitors were saying, and she kept crossing herself, pressing her fingers to her forehead, and gazing at the icons. Anisim, slightly drunk, opened the door into the kitchen and said in a free-and-easy way:

"Why are you sitting in here, precious Mamma? We are dull without you."

And Praskovya, overcome with timidity, pressing her hands to her lean, wasted bosom, said:

"Oh, not at all. . . . It's very kind of you."

After the visit of inspection the wedding day was fixed. Then Anisim walked about the rooms at home whistling, or, suddenly thinking of something, would fall to brooding and would look at the floor fixedly, silently, as though he would probe to the depths of the earth. He expressed neither pleasure that he was to be married, married so soon, on Low Sunday, nor a desire to see his bride, but simply went on whistling. And it was evident he was only getting married because his father and stepmother wished him to, and because it was the custom in the village to marry the son in order to have a woman to help in the house. When he went away he seemed in no haste, and behaved altogether not as he had done on previous visits—was particularly free and easy, and talked inappropriately.

## 3.

In the village Shikalovo lived two dressmakers, sisters, belonging to the Flagellant sect. The new clothes for the wedding were ordered from them, and they often came to try them on, and stayed a long while drinking tea. They were making Varvara a brown dress with black lace and bugles on it, and Aksinya a light green dress with a yellow front, with a train. When the dressmakers had finished their work Tsybukin paid them not in money but in goods from the shop, and they went away depressed, carrying parcels of tallow candles and tins of sardines which they did not in the least need, and when they got out of the village into the open country they sat down on a hillock and cried.

Anisim arrived three days before the wedding, rigged out in new clothes from top to toe. He had dazzling India-rubber galoshes, and instead of a cravat wore a red cord with little balls on it, and over his shoulder he had hung an overcoat, also new, without putting his arms into the sleeves.

After crossing himself sedately before the icon, he greeted his father and gave him ten silver rubles and ten half rubles; to Varvara he gave as much, and to Aksinya twenty quarter rubles. The chief charm of the present lay in the fact that all the coins, as though carefully matched, were new and glittered in the sun. Trying to seem grave and sedate, he pursed up his face and puffed out his cheeks, and he smelled of spirits. Probably he had visited the refreshment bar at every station. And again there was a free-and-easiness about the man—something superfluous and out of place. Then Anisim had lunch and drank tea with the old man, and Varvara turned the new coins over in her hand and inquired about villagers who had gone to live in the town.

"They are all right, thank God, they get on quite well," said Anisim. "Only something has happened to Ivan Yegorov: his old wife Sofya Nikiforovna is dead. From consumption. They ordered the memorial dinner for the peace of her soul at the confectioner's at two and a half rubles a head. And there was real wine. Those who were peasants from our village—they paid two and a half rubles for them, too. They ate nothing, as though a peasant would understand sauce!"

"Two and a half," said his father, shaking his head.

"Well, it's not like the country there; you go into a restaurant to have a snack of something, you ask for one thing and another, others join till there is a party of us, one has a drink—and before you know where you are it is daylight and you've three or four rubles each to pay. And when one is with Samorodov he likes to have coffee with brandy in it after everything, and brandy is sixty kopecks for a little glass."

"And he is making it all up," said the old man enthusiastically; "he is making it all up, lying!"

"I am always with Samorodov now. It is Samorodov who writes my letters to you. He writes splendidly. And if I were to tell you, Mamma," Anisim went on gaily, addressing Varvara, "the sort of fellow that Samorodov is, you would not believe me. We call him Muhtar, because he is black like an Armenian. I can see through him, I know all his affairs like the five fingers of my hand, and he feels that, and he always follows me about; we are regular inseparables. He seems not to like it in a way, but he can't get on without me. Where I go he goes. I have a correct, trustworthy eye, Mamma. One sees a peasant selling a shirt in the market place. 'Stay, that shirt's stolen.' And really it turns out it is so: the shirt was a stolen one."

"What do you tell from?" asked Varvara.

"Not from anything, I have just an eye for it. I know nothing about the shirt, only for some reason I seem drawn to it: it's stolen, and that's all I can say. Among us detectives it's come to their saying, 'Oh, Anisim has gone to shoot snipe!' That means looking for stolen goods. Yes. . . . Anybody can steal, but it is another thing to keep! The earth is wide, but there is nowhere to hide stolen goods."

"In our village a ram and two ewes were carried off last week," said Varvara, and she heaved a sigh, "and there is no one to try and find them. . . . Oh, tut, tut. . . ."

"Well, I might have a try. I don't mind."

The day of the wedding arrived. It was a cool but bright, cheerful April day. People were driving about Ukleyevo from early morning with pairs or teams of three horses decked with many-colored ribbons on their yokes and manes, with a jingle of bells. The rooks, disturbed by this activity, were cawing noisily in the willows, and the starlings sang their loudest unceasingly, as though rejoicing that there was a wedding at the Tsybukins'.

Indoors the tables were already covered with long fish, smoked hams, stuffed fowls, boxes of sprats, pickled savories of various sorts, and a number of bottles of vodka and wine; there was a smell of smoked sausage and of sour tinned lobster. Old Tsybukin walked about near the tables, tapping with his heels and sharpening the knives against each other. They kept calling Varvara and asking for things, and she was constantly, with a distracted face, running breathlessly into the kitchen, where the man cook from Kostukov's and the woman cook from Khrymin Juniors' had been at work since early morning. Aksinya, with her hair curled, in her stays without her dress on, in new creaky boots, flew about the yard like a whirlwind showing glimpses of her bare knees and bosom.

It was noisy, there was a sound of scolding and oaths; passers-by stopped at the wide-open gates, and in everything there was a feeling that something extraordinary was happening.

"They have gone for the bride!"

The bells began jingling and died away far beyond the village. . . . Between two and three o'clock people ran up: again there was a jingling of bells: they were bringing the bride! The church was full, the candelabra were lighted, the choir was singing from music books as old Tsybukin had wished it. The glare of the lights and the bright colored dresses dazzled Lipa; she felt as though the singers with their loud voices were hitting her on the head with a hammer. Her boots and the stays, which she had put on for the first time in her life, pinched her, and her face looked as though she had only just come to herself after fainting; she gazed about without understanding. Anisim, in his black coat with a red cord instead of a tie, stared at the same spot lost in thought, and when the singers shouted loudly he hurriedly crossed himself. He felt touched and disposed to weep. This church was familiar to him from earliest childhood; at one time his dead mother used to bring him here to take the sacrament; at one time he used to sing in the choir; every icon he remembered so well, every corner. Here he was being married; he had to take a wife for the sake of doing the proper thing, but he was not thinking of that now, he had forgotten his wedding completely. Tears dimmed his eyes so that he could not see the icons, he felt heavy at heart; he prayed and besought God that the misfortunes that threatened him, that were ready to burst upon him tomorrow, if not today, might somehow pass him by as storm clouds in time of drought pass over the village without yielding one drop of rain. And so many sins were heaped up in the past, so many sins, all getting away from them or setting them right was so beyond hope that it seemed incongruous even to ask forgiveness. But he did ask forgiveness, and even gave a loud sob, but no one took any notice of that, since they all supposed he had had a drop too much.

There was a sound of a fretful childish wail:

"Take me away, Mamma darling!"

"Quiet there!" cried the priest.

When they returned from the church people ran after them; there were crowds, too, round the shop, round the gates, and in the yard under the windows. The peasant women came in to sing songs of congratulation to them. The young couple had scarcely crossed the threshold when the singers, who were already standing in the outer room with their music books, broke into a loud chant at the top of their voices; a band ordered expressly from the town began playing. Foaming Don wine was brought in tall wineglasses, and Elizarov, a carpenter who did jobs by contract, a tall, gaunt old man with eyebrows so bushy that his eyes could scarcely be seen, said, addressing the happy pair:

"Anisim and you, my child, love one another, live in God's way, little children, and the Heavenly Mother will not abandon you."

He leaned his face on the old father's shoulder and gave a sob.

"Grigory Petrovich, let us weep, let us weep with joy!" he said in a thin voice, and then at once burst out laughing in a loud bass guffaw. "Ho-ho-ho! This is a fine daughter-in-law for you too! Everything is in its place in her; all runs smoothly, no creaking, the mechanism works well, lots of screws in it."

He was a native of the Yegoryevsky district but had worked in the factories in Ukleyevo and the neighborhood from his youth up and had made it his home. He had been a familiar figure for years as old and gaunt and lanky as now, and for years he had been nicknamed "Crutch." Perhaps because he had been for forty years occupied in repairing the factory machinery, he judged everybody and everything by its soundness or its need of repair. And before sitting down to the table, he tried several chairs to see whether they were solid, and he touched the smoked fish also.

After the Don wine, they all sat down to the table. The visitors talked, moving their chairs. The singers were singing in the outer room. The band was playing, and at the same time the peasant women in the yard were singing their songs all in chorus—and there was an awful, wild medley of sounds which made one giddy.

Crutch turned round in his chair and prodded his neighbors with his elbows, prevented people from talking, and laughed and cried alternately.

"Little children, little children, little children," he muttered rapidly. "Aksinya, my dear, Varvara darling, we will live all in peace and harmony, my dear little axes. . . ."

He drank little and was now drunk from only one glass of English bitters. The revolting bitters, made from nobody knows what, intoxicated everyone who drank it as though it had stunned them. Their tongues began to falter.

The local clergy, the clerks from the factories with their wives, the tradesmen and tavern-keepers from the other villages were present. The clerk and the elder of the rural district who had served together for fourteen years, and who had during all that time never signed a single document for anybody nor let a single person out of the local court without deceiving or insulting him, were sitting now side by side, both fat and well fed, and it seemed as though they were so saturated in injustice and falsehood that even the skin of their faces was somehow peculiar, fraudulent. The clerk's wife, a thin woman with a squint, had brought all her children with her, and like a bird of prey looked aslant at the plates and snatched anything she could get hold of to put in her own or her children's pockets.

Lipa sat as though turned to stone, still with the same expression as in church. Anisim had not said a single word to her since he had made her acquaintance, so that he did not yet know the sound of her voice; and now, sitting beside her, he remained mute and went on drinking bitters, and when he got drunk he began talking to the aunt who was sitting opposite:

"I have a friend called Samorodov. A peculiar man. He is by rank an honorary citizen, and he can talk. But I know him through and through, Auntie, and he feels it. Pray join me in drinking to the health of Samorodov, Auntie!"

Varvara, worn out and distracted, walked round the table pressing the guests to eat, and was evidently pleased that here were so many dishes and that everything was so lavish—no one could disparage them now. The sun set, but the dinner went on: the guests were beyond knowing what they were eating or drinking, it was impossible to distinguish what was said, and only from time to time when the band subsided some peasant woman could be heard shouting:

"They have sucked the blood out of us, the Herods; a pest on them!"

In the evening they danced to the band. The Khrymin Juniors came, bringing their wine, and one of them, when dancing a quadrille, held a bottle in each hand and a wineglass in his mouth, and that made everyone laugh. In the middle of the quadrille they suddenly crooked their knees and danced in a squatting position; Aksinya, in green, flew by like a flash, stirring up a wind with her train. Someone trod on her flounce and Crutch shouted:

"Aie, they have torn off the panel! Children!"

Aksinya had naive gray eyes, which rarely blinked, and a naive smile played continually on her face. And in those unblinking eyes, and in that little head on the long neck, and in her slenderness there was something snakelike; all in green but for the yellow on her bosom, she looked, with a smile on her face, as a viper looks out of the young rye in the spring at the passers-by, stretching itself and lifting its head. The Khrymins were free in their behavior to her, and it was very noticeable that she was on intimate terms with the eldest of them. But her deaf husband saw nothing, he did not look at her; he sat with his legs crossed and ate nuts, cracking them so loudly that it sounded like pistol shots.

But, behold, old Tsybukin himself walked into the middle of the room and waved his handkerchief as a sign that he, too, wanted to dance the Russian dance, and all over the house and from the crowd in the yard rose a roar of approbation:

"*He's* going to dance! *He* himself!"

Varvara danced, but the old man only waved his handkerchief and kicked up his heels, but the people in the yard, propped against one another, peeping in at the windows, were in raptures, and for the moment forgave him everything—his wealth and the wrongs he had done them.

"Well done, Grigory Petrovich!" was heard in the crowd. "That's right, do your best! You can still play your part! Ha-ha!"

It was kept up till late, till two o'clock in the morning. Anisim, staggering, went to take leave of the singers and bandsmen and gave each of them a new half ruble. His father, who was not staggering but still seemed to be standing on one leg, saw his guests off, and said to each of them:

"The wedding has cost two thousand."

As the party was breaking up, someone took the Shikalovo innkeeper's good coat instead of his own old one, and Anisim suddenly flew into a rage and began shouting:

"Stop, I'll find it at once; I know who stole it, stop."

He ran out into the street and pursued someone. He was caught, brought back home, and shoved, drunken, red with anger, and wet, into the room where the aunt was undressing Lipa, and was locked in.

## 4.

Five days had passed. Anisim, who was preparing to go, went upstairs to say good-bye to Varvara. All the lamps were burning before the icons, there was a smell of incense, while she sat at the window knitting a stocking of red wool.

"You have not stayed with us long," she said. "You've been dull, I dare say. Oh, tut, tut. . . . We live comfortably; we have plenty of everything. We celebrated your wedding properly, in good style; your father says it came to two thousand. In fact we live like merchants, only it's dreary. We treat the people very badly. My heart aches, my dear; how we treat them, my goodness! Whether we exchange a horse or buy something or hire a laborer—it's cheating in everything. Cheating and cheating. The Lenten oil in the shop is bitter, rancid; the people have pitch that is better. But surely, tell me pray, couldn't we sell good oil?"

"Every man to his own job, Mamma."

"But you know we all have to die? Oy, oy, really you ought to talk to your father . . . !"

"Why, you should talk to him yourself."

"Well, well, I did put in my word, but he said just what you do: 'Every man to his own job.' Do you suppose in the next world they'll consider what job you have been put to? God's judgment is just."

"Of course no one will consider," said Anisim, and he heaved a sigh. "There is no God, anyway, you know, Mamma, so what considering can there be?"

Varvara looked at him with surprise, burst out laughing, and clasped her hands. Perhaps because she was so genuinely surprised at his words and looked at him as though he were a queer person, he was confused.

"Perhaps there is a God, only there is no faith. When I was being married I was not myself. Just as you may take an egg from under a hen and there is a chicken chirping in it, so my conscience was beginning to chirp in me, and while I was being married I thought all the time there was a God! But when I left the church it was nothing. And indeed, how can I tell whether there is a God or not? We are not taught right from childhood, and while the babe is still at his mother's breast he is only taught 'every man to his own job.' Father does not believe in God, either. You were saying that Guntorev had some sheep stolen. . . . I have found them; it was a peasant at Shikalovo stole them; he stole them, but father's got the fleeces . . . so that's all his faith amounts to."

Anisim winked and wagged his head.

"The elder does not believe in God, either," he went on. "And the clerk and the deacon, too. And as for their going to church and keeping the fasts, that is simply to prevent people talking ill of them, and in case it really may be true that there will be a Day of Judgment. Nowadays people say that the end of the world has come because people have grown weaker, do not honor their parents, and so on. All that is nonsense. My idea, Mamma, is that all our trouble is because there is so little conscience in people. I see through things, Mamma, and I understand. If a man has a stolen shirt, I see it. A man sits in a tavern and you fancy he is drinking tea and no more, but to me the tea is neither here nor there; I see further, he has no conscience. You can go about the whole day and not meet one man with a conscience. And the whole reason is that they don't know whether there is a God or not. . . . Well, good-bye, Mamma, keep alive and well; don't remember evil against me."

Anisim bowed down at Varvara's feet.

"I thank you for everything, Mamma," he said. "You are a great gain to our family. You are a very ladylike woman, and I am very pleased with you."

Much moved, Anisim went out but returned again and said:

"Samorodov has got me mixed up in something: I shall either make my fortune or come to grief. If anything happens, then you must comfort my father, Mamma."

"Oh, nonsense, don't you worry, tut, tut, tut . . . God is merciful. And, Anisim, you should be affectionate to your wife, instead of giving each other sulky looks as you do; you might smile at least."

"Yes, she is rather a queer one," said Anisim, and he gave a sigh. "She does not understand anything, she never speaks. She is very young, let her grow up."

A tall, sleek white stallion was already standing at the front door, harnessed to the chaise.

Old Tsybukin jumped in jauntily with a run and took the reins. Anisim kissed Varvara, Aksinya, and his brother. On the steps Lipa, too, was standing; she was standing motionless, looking away, and it seemed as though she had not come to see him off but just by chance for some unknown reason. Anisim went up to her and just touched her cheek with his lips.

"Good-bye," he said.

And, without looking at him, she gave a strange smile; her face began to quiver, and everyone for some reason felt sorry for her. Anisim, too, leaped into the chaise with a bound and put his arms jauntily akimbo, for he considered himself a good-looking fellow.

When they drove up out of the ravine Anisim kept looking back towards the village. It was a warm, bright day. The cattle were being driven out for the first time, and the peasant girls and women were walking by the herd in their holiday dresses. The dun-colored bull bellowed, glad to be free, and pawed the ground with his forefeet. On all sides, above and below, the larks were singing. Anisim looked round at the elegant white church—it had only lately been whitewashed—and he thought how he had been praying in it five days before; he looked round at the school with its green roof, at the little river in which he used once to bathe and catch fish, and there was a stir of joy in his heart, and he wished that walls might rise up from the ground and prevent him from going further, and that he might be left with nothing but the past.

At the station they went to the refreshment room and drank a glass of sherry each. His father felt in his pocket for his purse to pay.

"I will stand treat," said Anisim. The old man, touched and delighted, slapped him on the shoulder, and winked to the waiter as much as to say, "See what a fine son I have got."

"You ought to stay at home in the business, Anisim," he said; "you would be worth any price to me! I would shower gold on you from head to foot, my son."

"It can't be done, Papa."

The sherry was sour and smelled of sealing wax, but they had another glass.

When old Tsybukin returned home from the station, for the first moment he did not recognize his younger daughter-in-law. As soon as her husband had driven out of the yard, Lipa was transformed and suddenly brightened up. Wearing a threadbare old petticoat, with her feet bare and her sleeves tucked up to the shoulders, she was scrubbing the stairs in the entry and singing in a silvery little voice, and when she brought out a big tub of dirty water and looked up at the sun with her childlike smile it seemed as though she, too, were a lark.

An old laborer who was passing by the door shook his head and cleared his throat.

"Yes, indeed, your daughters-in-law, Grigory Petrovich, are a blessing from God," he said. "Not women, but treasures!"

## 5.

On Friday the eighth of July, Elizarov, nicknamed Crutch, and Lipa were returning from the village of Kazanskoe, where they had been to a service on the occasion of a church holiday in the honor of the Holy Mother of Kazan. A good distance after them walked Lipa's mother Praskovya, who always fell behind, as she was ill and short of breath. It was drawing towards evening.

"A-a-a . . ." said Crutch, wondering as he listened to Lipa. "A-a! . . . We-ell!"

"I am very fond of jam, Ilya Makarich," said Lipa. "I sit down in my little corner and drink tea and eat jam. Or I drink it with Varvara Nikolaevna, and she tells some story full of feeling. We have a lot of jam—four jars. 'Have some, Lipa; eat as much as you like.'"

"A-a-a, four jars!"

"They live very well. We have white bread with our tea; and meat, too, as much as one wants. They live very well, only I am frightened with them, Ilya Makarich. Oh, oh, how frightened I am!"

"Why are you frightened, child?" asked Crutch, and he looked back to see how far Praskovya was behind.

"To begin with, when the wedding had been celebrated I was afraid of Anisim Grigorich. Anisim Grigorich did nothing, he didn't ill-treat me, only when he comes near me a cold shiver runs all over me, through all my bones. And I did not sleep one night, I trembled all over and kept praying to God. And now I am afraid of Aksinya, Ilya Makarich. It's not that she does anything, she is always laughing, but sometimes she glances at the window, and her eyes are so fierce and there is a gleam of green in them—like the eyes of the sheep in the shed. The Khrymin Juniors are leading her astray: 'Your old man,' they tell her, 'has a bit of land at Butyokino, a hundred and twenty acres,' they say, 'and there is sand and water there, so you, Aksinya,' they say, 'build a brickyard there and we will go shares in it.' Bricks now are twenty rubles the thousand, it's a profitable business. Yesterday at dinner Aksinya said to my father-in-law: 'I want to build a brickyard at Butyokino; I'm going into business on my own account.' She laughed as she said it. And Grigory Petrovich's face darkened, one could see he did not like it. 'As long as I live,' he said, 'the family must not break up, we must go on all together.' She gave a look and gritted her teeth. . . . Fritters were served, she would not eat them."

"A-a-a! . . ." Crutch was surprised.

"And tell me, if you please, when does she sleep?" said

Lipa. "She sleeps for half an hour, then jumps up and keeps walking and walking about to see whether the peasants have not set fire to something, have not stolen something. . . . I am frightened with her, Ilya Makarich. And the Khrymin Juniors did not go to bed after the wedding, but drove to the town to go to law with each other; and folks do say it is all on account of Aksinya. Two of the brothers have promised to build her a brickyard, but the third is offended, and the factory has been at a standstill for a month, and my uncle Prokhor is without work and goes about from house to house getting crusts. 'Hadn't you better go working on the land or sawing up wood, meanwhile, Uncle?' I tell him; 'why disgrace yourself?' 'I've got out of the way of it,' he says; 'I don't know how to do any sort of peasant's work now, Lipinka.'"

They stopped to rest and wait for Praskovya near a copse of young aspen trees. Elizarov had long been a contractor in a small way, but he kept no horses, going on foot all over the district with nothing but a little bag in which there was bread and onions, and stalking along with big strides, swinging his arms. And it was difficult to walk with him.

At the entrance to the copse stood a milestone. Elizarov touched it; read it. Praskovya reached them out of breath. Her wrinkled and always scared-looking face was beaming with happiness; she had been at church today like anyone else, then she had been to the fair and there had drunk pear cider. For her this was unusual, and it even seemed to her now that she had lived for her own pleasure that day for the first time in her life. After resting, they all three walked on side by side. The sun had already set, and its beams filtered through the copse, casting a light on the trunks of the trees. There was a faint sound of voices ahead. The Ukleyevo girls had long before pushed on ahead but had lingered in the copse, probably gathering mushrooms.

"Hey, wenches!" cried Elizarov. "Hey, my beauties!"

There was a sound of laughter in response.

"Crutch is coming! Crutch! The old horse-radish."

And the echo laughed, too. And then the copse was left behind. The tops of the factory chimneys came into view. The cross on the belfry glittered: this was the village: "the one at which the deacon ate all the caviar at the funeral." Now they were almost home; they only had to go down into the big ravine. Lipa and Praskovya, who had been walking barefooted, sat down on the grass to put on their boots; Elizarov sat down with them. If they looked down from above, Ukleyevo was beautiful and peaceful with its willow trees, its white church, and its little river, and the only blot on the picture was the roofs of the factories, painted for the sake of cheapness a gloomy ashen gray. On the slope on the further side they could see the rye—some in stacks and sheaves here and there as though strewn about by the storm, and some freshly cut lying in swathes; the oats, too, were ripe and glistened now in the sun like mother-of-pearl. It was harvesttime. Today was a holiday, tomorrow they would harvest the rye and carry the hay, and then Sunday a holiday again; every day there were mutterings of distant thunder. It was misty and looked like rain, and, gazing now at the fields, everyone thought, "God grant we get the harvest in in time"; and everyone felt gay and joyful and anxious at heart.

"Mowers ask a high price nowadays," said Praskovya. "One ruble and forty kopecks a day."

People kept coming and coming from the fair at Kazanskoe: peasant women, factory workers in new caps, beggars, children. . . . Here a cart would drive by stirring up the dust and behind it would run an unsold horse, and it seemed glad it had not been sold; then a cow was led along by the horns, resisting stubbornly; then a cart again, and in it drunken peasants swinging their legs. An old woman led a little boy in a big cap and big boots; the boy was tired out with the heat and the heavy boots which prevented his bending his legs at the knees, but yet blew unceasingly with all his might at a tin trumpet. They had gone down the slope and turned into the street, but the trumpet could still be heard.

"Our factory owners don't seem quite themselves . . ." said Elizarov. "There's trouble. Kostukov is angry with me. 'Too many boards have gone on the cornices.' 'Too many? As many have gone on it as were needed, Vassily Danilich; I don't eat them with my porridge.' 'How can you speak to me like that?' said he. 'You good-for-nothing blockhead! Don't forget yourself! It was I made you a contractor.' 'That's nothing so wonderful,' said I. 'Even before I was a contractor I used to have tea every day.' 'You are a rascal,' he said. I said nothing. 'We are rascals in this world,' thought I, 'and you will be a rascal in the next. . . .' Ha-ha-ha! The next day he was softer. 'Don't you bear malice against me for my words, Makarich,' he said. 'If I said too much,' says he, 'what of it? I am a merchant of the first guild, your superior—you ought to hold your tongue.' 'You,' said I, 'are a merchant of the first guild and I am a carpenter, that's correct. And St. Joseph was a carpenter, too. Ours is a righteous calling and pleasing to God, and if you are pleased to be my superior you are very welcome to it, Vassily Danilich.' And later on—after that conversation I mean—I thought: 'Which is the superior? A merchant of the first guild or a carpenter?' The carpenter must be, my child!"

Crutch thought a minute and added:

"Yes, that's how it is, child. He who works, he who is patient is the superior."

By now the sun had set and a thick mist as white as milk was rising over the river, in the church enclosure, and in the open spaces round the factories. Now when the darkness was coming on rapidly, when lights were twinkling below, and when it seemed as though the mists were hiding a fathomless abyss, Lipa and her mother, who were born in poverty and prepared to live so till the end, giving up to others everything except their frightened, gentle souls, may have fancied for a minute perhaps that in the vast, mysterious world, among the endless series of lives, they, too, counted for something, and they, too, were superior to someone; they liked sitting here at the top, they smiled happily and forgot that they must go down below again all the same.

At last they went home again. The mowers were sitting on the ground at the gates near the shop. As a rule the Ukleyevo peasants did not go to Tsybukin's to work, and they had to hire strangers, and now in the darkness it seemed as though there were men sitting there with long black beards. The shop was open, and through the doorway they could see the deaf man playing draughts with a boy. The mowers were singing softly, scarcely audibly, or loudly demanding their wages for the previous day, but they were not paid for fear they should go away before tomorrow. Old Tsybukin, with his coat off, was sitting in his waistcoat with Aksinya under the birch tree, drinking tea; a lamp was burning on the table.

"I say, grandfather," a mower called from outside the gates, as though taunting him, "pay us half anyway! Hey, grandfather."

And at once there was the sound of laughter, and then again they sang hardly audibly. . . . Crutch, too, sat down to have some tea.

"We have been at the fair, you know," he began telling them. "We have had a walk, a very nice walk, my children, praise the Lord. But an unfortunate thing happened: Sashka, the blacksmith, bought some tobacco and gave the shopman half a ruble to be sure. And the half ruble was a false one," Crutch went on, and he meant to speak in a whisper, but he spoke in a smothered husky voice which was audible to everyone. "The half ruble turned out to be a bad one. He was asked where he got it. 'Anisim Tsybukin gave it me,' he said. 'When I went to his wedding,' he said. They called the police inspector, took the man away. . . . Look out, Grigory Petrovich, that nothing comes of it, no talk. . . ."

"Gra-andfather!" the same voice called tauntingly outside the gates. "Gra-andfather!"

A silence followed.

"Ah, little children, little children, little children . . ." Crutch muttered rapidly, and he got up. He was overcome with drowsiness. "Well, thank you for the tea, for the sugar, little children. It is time to sleep. I am like a bit of rotten timber nowadays, my beams are crumbling under me. Ho-ho-ho! I suppose it's time I was dead." And he gave a gulp.

Old Tsybukin did not finish his tea but sat on a little, pondering; and his face looked as though he were listening to the footsteps of Crutch, who was far away down the street.

"Sashka, the blacksmith, told a lie, I expect," said Aksinya, guessing his thoughts.

He went into the house and came back a little later with a parcel; he opened it, and there was the gleam of rubles—perfectly new coins. He took one, tried it with his teeth, flung it on the tray; then flung down another.

"The rubles really are false . . ." he said, looking at Aksinya and seeming perplexed. "These are those Anisim brought, his present. Take them, Daughter," he whispered, and thrust the parcel into her hands. "Take them and throw them into the well . . . confound them! And mind there is no talk about it. Harm might come of it. . . . Take away the samovar, put out the light."

Lipa and her mother, sitting in the barn, saw the lights go out one after the other; only overhead in Varvara's room there were blue and red lamps gleaming, and a feeling of peace, content, and happy ignorance seemed to float down from there. Praskovya could never get used to her daughter's being married to a rich man, and when she came she huddled timidly in the outer room with a deprecating smile on her face, and tea and sugar were sent out to her. And Lipa, too, could not get used to it either, and after her husband had gone away she did not sleep in her bed but lay down anywhere to sleep, in the kitchen or the barn, and every day she scrubbed the floor or washed the clothes, and felt as though she were hired by the day. And now, on coming back from the service, they drank tea in the kitchen with the cook, then they went into the barn and lay down on the ground between the sledge and the wall. It was dark here and smelled of harness. The lights went out about the house, then they could hear the deaf man shutting up the shop, the mowers settling themselves about the yard to sleep. In the distance at the Khrymin Juniors' they were playing on the expensive concertina. . . . Praskovya and Lipa began to go to sleep.

And when they were awakened by somebody's steps it was bright moonlight; at the entrance of the barn stood Aksinya with her bedding in her arms.

"Maybe it's a bit cooler here," she said; then she came in and lay down almost in the doorway so that the moonlight fell full upon her.

She did not sleep, but breathed heavily, tossing from side to side with the heat, throwing off almost all the bedclothes. And in the magic moonlight what a beautiful, what a proud animal she was! A little time passed, and then steps were heard again: the old father, white all over, appeared in the doorway.

"Aksinya," he called, "are you here?"

"Well?" she responded angrily.

"I told you just now to throw the money into the well, have you done so?"

"What next, throwing property into the water! I gave them to the mowers. . . ."

"Oh my God!" cried the old man, dumbfounded and alarmed. "Oh my God! you wicked woman. . . ."

He flung up his hands and went out, and he kept saying something as he went away. And a little later Aksinya sat up and sighed heavily with annoyance, then got up and, gathering up her bedclothes in her arms, went out.

"Why did you marry me into this family, Mother?" said Lipa.

"One has to be married, Daughter. It was not us who ordained it."

And a feeling of inconsolable woe was ready to take possession of them. But it seemed to them that someone was looking down from the height of the heavens, out of the blue from where the stars were seeing everything that was going on in Ukleyevo, watching over them. And however great was wickedness, still the night was calm and beautiful, and still in God's world there is and will be truth and justice as calm and beautiful, and everything on earth is only waiting to be made one with truth and justice, even as the moonlight is blended with the night.

And both, huddling close to one another, fell asleep comforted.

## 6.

News had come long before that Anisim had been put in prison for coining and passing bad money. Months passed, more than half a year passed, the long winter was over, spring had begun, and everyone in the house and the village had grown used to the fact that Anisim was in prison. And when anyone passed by the house or the shop at night he would remember that Anisim was in prison; and when they rang at the churchyard for some reason, that, too, reminded them that he was in prison awaiting trial.

It seemed as though a shadow had fallen upon the house.

The house looked darker, the roof was rustier, the heavy, iron-bound door into the shop, which was painted green, was covered with cracks, or, as the deaf man expressed it, "blisters"; and old Tsybukin seemed to have grown dingy, too. He had given up cutting his hair and beard and looked shaggy. He no longer sprang jauntily into his chaise, nor shouted to beggars: "God will provide!" His strength was on the wane, and that was evident in everything. People were less afraid of him now, and the police officer drew up a formal charge against him in the shop though he received his regular bribe as before; and three times the old man was called up to the town to be tried for illicit dealing in spirits, and the case was continually adjourned owing to the non-appearance of witnesses, and old Tsybukin was worn out with worry.

He often went to see his son, hired somebody, handed in a petition to somebody else, presented a holy banner to some church. He presented the governor of the prison in which Anisim was confined with a silver glass stand with a long spoon and the inscription: "The soul knows its right measure."

"There is no one to look after things for us," said Varvara. "Tut, tut. . . . You ought to ask some of the gentlefolks; they would write to the head officials. . . . At least they might let him out on bail! Why wear the poor fellow out?"

She, too, was grieved, but had grown stouter and whiter; she lighted the lamps before the icons as before, and saw that everything in the house was clean, and regaled the guests with jam and apple cheese. The deaf man and Aksinya looked after the shop. A new project was in progress—a brickyard in Butyokino—and Aksinya went there almost every day in the chaise. She drove herself, and when she met acquaintances she stretched out her neck like a snake out of the young rye, and smiled naively and enigmatically. Lipa spent her time playing with the baby which had been born to her before Lent. It was a tiny, thin, pitiful little baby, and it was strange that it should cry and gaze about and be considered a human being, and even be called Nikifor. He lay in his swinging cradle, and Lipa would walk away towards the door and say, bowing to him:

"Good day, Nikifor Anisimich!"

And she would rush at him and kiss him. Then she would walk away to the door, bow again, and say:

"Good day, Nikifor Anisimich!"

And he kicked up his little red legs, and his crying was mixed with laughter like the carpenter Elizarov's.

At last the day of the trial was fixed. Tsybukin went away five days before. Then they heard that the peasants called as witnesses had been fetched; their old workman who had received a notice to appear went too.

The trial was on a Thursday. But Sunday had passed, and Tsybukin was still not back, and there was no news. Towards the evening on Tuesday Varvara was sitting at the open window, listening for her husband to come. In the next room Lipa was playing with her baby. She was tossing him up in her arms and saying enthusiastically:

"You will grow up ever so big, ever so big. You will be a peasant, we shall go out to work together! We shall go out to work together!"

"Come, come," said Varvara, offended. "Go out to work, what an idea, you silly girl! He will be a merchant . . . !"

Lipa sang softly, but a minute later she forgot and again:

"You will grow ever so big, ever so big. You will be a peasant, we'll go out to work together."

"There she is at it again!"

Lipa, with Nikifor in her arms, stood still in the doorway and asked:

"Why do I love him so much, Mamma? Why do I feel so sorry for him?" she went on in a quivering voice, and her eyes glistened with tears. "Who is he? What is he like? As light as a little feather, as a little crumb, but I love him; I love him like a real person. Here he can do nothing, he can't talk, and yet I know what he wants with his little eyes."

Varvara was listening; the sound of the evening train coming in to the station reached her. Had her husband come? She did not hear and she did not heed what Lipa was saying, she had no idea how the time passed, but only trembled all over—not from dread, but intense curiosity. She saw a cart full of peasants roll quickly by with a rattle. It was the witnesses coming back from the station. When the cart passed the shop the old workman jumped out and walked into the yard. She could hear him being greeted in the yard and being asked some questions. . . .

"Deprivation of rights and all his property," he said loudly, "and six years' penal servitude in Siberia."

She could see Aksinya come out of the shop by the back way; she had just been selling kerosene, and in one hand held a bottle and in the other a can, and in her mouth she had some silver coins.

"Where is Father?" she asked, lisping.

"At the station," answered the laborer. "'When it gets a little darker,' he said, 'then I shall come.'"

And when it became known all through the household that Anisim was sentenced to penal servitude, the cook in the kitchen suddenly broke into a wail as though at a funeral, imagining that this was demanded by the proprieties:

"There is no one to care for us now you have gone, Anisim Grigorich, our bright falcon. . . ."

The dogs began barking in alarm. Varvara ran to the window, and, rushing about in distress, shouted to the cook with all her might, straining her voice:

"Sto-op, Stepanida, sto-op! Don't harrow us, for Christ's sake!"

They forgot to set the samovar, they could think of nothing. Only Lipa could not make out what it was all about and went on playing with her baby.

When the old father arrived from the station they asked

him no questions. He greeted them and walked through all the rooms in silence; he had no supper.

"There was no one to see about things . . ." Varvara began when they were alone. "I said you should have asked some of the gentry, you would not heed me at the time. . . . A petition would—"

"I saw to things," said her husband with a wave of his hand. "When Anisim was condemned I went to the gentleman who was defending him. 'It's no use now,' he said, 'it's too late'; and Anisim said the same: 'It's too late.' But all the same as I came out of the court I made an agreement with a lawyer, I paid him something in advance. I'll wait a week and then I will go again. It is as God wills."

Again the old man walked through all the rooms, and when he went back to Varvara he said:

"I must be ill. My head's in a sort of . . . fog. My thoughts are in a maze."

He closed the door that Lipa might not hear and went on softly:

"I am unhappy about my money. Do you remember how before his wedding Anisim brought me some new rubles and half rubles? One parcel I put away at the time, but the others I mixed with my own money. When my uncle Dmitri Filatich—the Kingdom of Heaven be his—was alive, he used constantly to go journeys to Moscow and to the Crimea to buy goods. He had a wife, and this same wife, when he was away buying goods, used to take up with other men. She had half a dozen children. And when uncle was in his cups he would laugh and say: 'I never can make out,' he used to say, 'which are my children and which are other people's.' An easygoing disposition, to be sure; and so I now can't distinguish which are genuine rubles and which are false ones. And it seems to me that they are all false."

"Nonsense, God bless you."

"I take a ticket at the station, I give the man three rubles, and I keep fancying they are false. And I am frightened. I must be ill."

"There's no denying it, we are all in God's hands.... Oh dear, dear..." said Varvara, and she shook her head. "You ought to think about this, Grigory Petrovich: you never know, anything may happen, you are not a young man. See they don't wrong your grandchild when you are dead and gone. Oy, I am afraid they will be unfair to Nikifor! He has as good as no father, his mother's young and foolish... you ought to secure something for him, poor little boy, at least the land, Butyokino, Grigory Petrovich, really! Think it over!" Varvara went on persuading him. "The pretty boy, one is sorry for him! You go tomorrow and make out a deed; why put it off?"

"I'd forgotten about my grandson," said Tsybukin. "I must go and have a look at him. So you say the boy is all right? Well, let him grow up, please God."

He opened the door and, crooking his finger, beckoned to Lipa. She went up to him with the baby in her arms.

"If there is anything you want, Lipinka, you ask for it," he said. "And eat anything you like, we don't grudge it, so long as it does you good...." He made the sign of the cross over the baby. "And take care of my grandchild. My son is gone, but my grandson is left."

Tears rolled down his cheeks; he gave a sob and went away. Soon afterwards he went to bed and slept soundly after seven sleepless nights.

## 7.

Old Tsybukin went to the town for a short time. Someone told Aksinya that he had gone to the notary to make his will and that he was leaving Butyokino, the very place where she had set up a brickyard, to Nikifor, his grandson. She was informed of this in the morning when old Tsybukin and Varvara were sitting near the steps under the birch tree, drinking their tea. She closed the shop in the front and at the back, gathered together all the keys she had, and flung them at her father-in-law's feet.

"I am not going on working for you," she began in a loud voice, and suddenly broke into sobs. "It seems I am not your daughter-in-law, but a servant! Everybody's jeering and saying, 'See what a servant the Tsybukins have got hold of!' I did not come to you for wages! I am not a beggar, I am not a slave, I have a father and mother."

She did not wipe away her tears; she fixed upon her father-in-law eyes full of tears, vindictive, squinting with wrath; her face and neck were red and tense, and she was shouting at the top of her voice.

"I don't mean to go on being a slave!" she went on. "I am worn out. When it is work, when it is sitting in the shop day in and day out, scurrying out at night for vodka—then it is my share, but when it is giving away the land then it is for that convict's wife and her imp. She is mistress here, and I am her servant. Give her everything, the convict's wife, and may it choke her! I am going home! Find yourselves some other fool, you damned Herods!"

Tsybukin had never in his life scolded or punished his children and never dreamed that one of his family could speak to him rudely or behave disrespectfully; and now he was very much frightened; he ran into the house and there hid behind the cupboard. And Varvara was so much flustered that she could not get up from her seat and only waved her hands before her as though she were warding off a bee.

"Oh, holy saints! what's the meaning of it?" she muttered in horror. "What is she shouting? Oh dear, dear! . . . People will hear! Hush. Oh, hush!"

"He has given Butyokino to the convict's wife," Aksinya

went on, bawling. "Give her everything now, I don't want anything from you! Let me alone! You are all a gang of thieves here! I have seen my fill of it, I have had enough! You have robbed folks coming in and going out; you have robbed old and young alike, you brigands! And who has been selling vodka without a license? And false money? You've filled boxes full of false coins, and now I am no more use!"

A crowd had by now collected at the open gate and was staring into the yard.

"Let the people look," bawled Aksinya. "I will shame you all! You shall burn with shame! You shall grovel at my feet. Hey! Stepan," she called to the deaf man, "let us go home this minute! Let us go to my father and mother; I don't want to live with convicts. Get ready!"

Clothes were hanging on lines stretched across the yard; she snatched off her petticoats and blouses still wet and flung them into the deaf man's arms. Then in her fury she dashed about the yard by the linen, tore down all of it, and what was not hers she threw on the ground and trampled upon.

"Holy saints, take her away," moaned Varvara. "What a woman! Give her Butyokino! Give it her, for the Lord's sake!"

"Well! Wha-at a woman!" people were saying at the gate. "She's a wo-oman! She's going it—something like!"

Aksinya ran into the kitchen where washing was going on. Lipa was washing alone, the cook had gone to the river to rinse the clothes. Steam was rising from the trough and from the caldron on the side of the stove, and the kitchen was thick and stifling from the steam. On the floor was a heap of unwashed clothes, and Nikifor, kicking up his little red legs, had been put down on a bench near them, so that if he fell he should not hurt himself. Just as Aksinya went in Lipa took the former's chemise out of the heap and put it in the trough, and was just stretching out her hand to a big ladle of boiling water which was standing on the table.

"Give it here," said Aksinya, looking at her with hatred, and snatching the chemise out of the trough; "it is not your business to touch my linen! You are a convict's wife, and ought to know your place and who you are."

Lipa gazed at her, taken aback, and did not understand, but suddenly she caught the look Aksinya turned upon the child, and at once she understood and went numb all over.

"You've taken my land, so here you are!" Saying this, Aksinya snatched up the ladle with the boiling water and flung it over Nikifor.

After this there was heard a scream such as had never been heard before in Ukleyevo, and no one would have believed that a little weak creature like Lipa could scream like that. And it was suddenly silent in the yard.

Aksinya walked into the house with her old naive smile.... The deaf man kept moving about the yard with his arms full of linen, then he began hanging it up again, in silence, without haste. And until the cook came back from the river no one ventured to go into the kitchen and see what was there.

## 8.

Nikifor was taken to the district hospital, and towards evening he died there. Lipa did not wait for them to come for her but wrapped the dead baby in its little quilt and carried it home.

The hospital, a new one recently built, with big windows, stood high up on a hill; it was glittering from the setting sun and looked as though it were on fire from inside. There was a little village below. Lipa went down along the road, and, before reaching the village, sat down by a pond. A woman brought a horse down to drink and the horse did not drink.

"What more do you want?" said the woman to it softly. "What do you want?"

A boy in a red shirt, sitting at the water's edge, was washing his father's boots. And not another soul was in sight either in the village or on the hill.

"It's not drinking," said Lipa, looking at the horse.

Then the woman with the horse and the boy with the boots walked away, and there was no one left at all. The sun went to bed wrapped in cloth of gold and purple, and long clouds, red and lilac, stretched across the sky, guarded its slumbers. Somewhere far away a bittern cried, a hollow, melancholy sound like a cow shut up in a barn. The cry of that mysterious bird was heard every spring, but no one knew what it was like or where it lived. At the top of the hill by the hospital, in the bushes close to the pond, and in the fields the nightingales were trilling. The cuckoo kept reckoning someone's years and losing count and beginning again. In the pond the frogs called angrily to one another, straining themselves to bursting, and one could even make out the words: "That's what you are! That's what you are!" What a noise there was! It seemed as though all these creatures were singing and shouting so that no one might sleep on that spring night, so that all, even the angry frogs, might appreciate and enjoy every minute: life is given only once.

A silver half-moon was shining in the sky; there were many stars. Lipa had no idea how long she sat by the pond, but when she got up and walked on everybody was asleep in the little village, and there was not a single light. It was probably about nine miles' walk home, but she had not the strength, she had not the power to think how to go: the moon gleamed now in front, now on the right, and the same cuckoo kept calling in a voice grown husky, with a chuckle as though gibing at her: "Oy, look out, you'll lose your way!" Lipa walked rapidly; she lost the kerchief from her head . . . she looked at the sky and wondered where her baby's soul was now: was it following her, or floating aloft yonder among the stars and thinking nothing now of his mother? Oh, how lonely it was in the open country at night, in the midst of that singing when one cannot sing oneself; in the midst of the incessant cries of joy when one cannot oneself be joyful, when the moon, which cares not whether it is spring or winter, whether men are alive or dead, looks down as lonely, too. . . . When there is grief in the heart it is hard to be without people. If only her mother Praskovya had been with her, or Crutch, or the cook, or some peasant!

"Boo-oo!" cried the bittern. "Boo-oo!"

And suddenly she heard clearly the sound of human speech:

"Put the horses in, Vavila!"

By the wayside a campfire was burning ahead of her: the flames had died down, there were only red embers. She could hear the horses munching. In the darkness she could see the outlines of two carts, one with a barrel, the other, a lower one with sacks in it, and the figures of two men; one was leading a horse to put it into the shafts, the other was standing motionless by the fire with his hands behind his back. A dog growled by the carts. The one who was leading the horse stopped and said:

"It seems as though someone were coming along the road."

"Sharik, be quiet!" the other called to the dog.

And from the voice one could tell that the second was an old man. Lipa stopped and said:

"God help you."

The old man went up to her and answered not immediately:

"Good evening!"

"Your dog does not bite, grandfather?"

"No, come along, he won't touch you."

"I have been at the hospital," said Lipa after a pause. "My little son died there. Here I am carrying him home."

It must have been unpleasant for the old man to hear this, for he moved away and said hurriedly:

"Never mind, my dear. It's God's will. You are very slow, lad," he added, addressing his companion; "look alive!"

"Your yoke's nowhere," said the young man; "it is not to be seen."

"You are a regular, Vavila."

The old man picked up an ember, blew on it—only his eyes and nose were lighted up—then, when they had found the yoke, he went with the light to Lipa and looked at her, and his look expressed compassion and tenderness.

"You are a mother," he said; "every mother grieves for her child."

And he sighed and shook his head as he said it. Vavila threw something on the fire, stamped on it—and at once it was very dark; the vision vanished, and as before there were only the fields, the sky with the stars, and the noise of the birds hindering each other from sleep. And the land rail called, it seemed, in the very place where the fire had been.

But a minute passed, and again she could see the two carts and the old man and lanky Vavila. The carts creaked as they went out on the road.

"Are you holy men?" Lipa asked the old man.

"No. We are from Firsanovo."

"You looked at me just now and my heart was softened. And the young man is so gentle. I thought you must be holy men."

"Are you going far?"

"To Ukleyevo."

"Get in, we will give you a lift as far as Kuzmenki, then you go straight on and we turn off to the left."

Vavila got into the cart with the barrel and the old man and Lipa got into the other. They moved at a walking pace, Vavila in front.

"My baby was in torment all day," said Lipa. "He looked at me with his little eyes and said nothing; he wanted to speak and could not. Holy Father, Queen of Heaven! In my grief I kept falling down on the floor. I stood up and fell down by the bedside. And tell me, grandfather, why a little thing should be tormented before his death? When a grown-up person, a man or woman, is in torment his sins are forgiven, but why a little thing, when he has no sins? Why?"

"Who can tell?" answered the old man.

They drove on for half an hour in silence.

"We can't know everything, how and wherefore," said the old man. "It is ordained for the bird to have not four wings but two because it is able to fly with two; and so it is ordained for man not to know everything but only a half or a quarter. As much as he needs to know so as to live, so much he knows."

"It is better for me to go on foot, grandfather. Now my heart is all of a tremble."

"Never mind, sit still."

The old man yawned and made the sign of the cross over his mouth.

"Never mind," he repeated. "Yours is not the worst of sorrows. Life is long, there will be good and bad to come, there will be everything. Great is Mother Russia," he said, and looked round on each side of him. "I have been all over Russia, and I have seen everything in her, and you may believe my words, my dear. There will be good and there will be bad. I went as a delegate from my village to Siberia, and I have been to the Amur River and the Altai Mountains and I settled in Siberia; I worked the land there, then I was homesick for Mother Russia and I came back to my native village. We came back to Russia on foot; and I remember we went on a steamer, and I was thin as thin, all in rags, barefoot, freezing with cold, and gnawing a crust, and a gentleman who was on the steamer—the Kingdom of Heaven be his if he is dead—looked at me pitifully, and the tears came into his eyes. 'Ah,' he said, 'your bread is black, your days are black. . . .' And when I got home, as the saying is, there was neither stick nor stall; I had a wife, but I left her behind in Siberia, she was buried there. So I am living as a day laborer. And yet I tell you: since then I have had good as well as bad. Here I do not want to die, my dear, I would be glad to live another twenty years; so there has been more of the good. And great is our Mother Russia!" and again he gazed to each side and looked round.

"Grandfather," Lipa asked, "when anyone dies, how many days does his soul walk the earth?"

"Who can tell! Ask Vavila here, he has been to school. Now they teach them everything. Vavila!" the old man called to him.

"Yes!"

"Vavila, when anyone dies how long does his soul walk the earth?"

Vavila stopped the horse and only then answered:

"Nine days. My uncle Kirilla died and his soul lived in our hut thirteen days after."

"How do you know?"

"For thirteen days there was a knocking in the stove."

"Well, that's all right. Go on," said the old man, and it could be seen that he did not believe a word of all that.

Near Kuzmenki the cart turned into the highroad while Lipa went straight on. It was by now getting light. As she went down into the ravine the Ukleyevo huts and the church were hidden in fog. It was cold, and it seemed to her that the same cuckoo was calling still.

When Lipa reached home the cattle had not yet been driven out; everyone was asleep. She sat down on the steps and waited. The old man was the first to come out; he understood all that had happened from the first glance at her, and for a long time he could not articulate a word, but only moved his lips without a sound.

"Ech, Lipa," he said, "you did not take care of my grandchild. . . ."

Varvara was awakened. She clasped her hands and broke into sobs, and immediately began laying out the baby.

"And he was a pretty child..." she said. "Oh dear, dear.... You only had the one child, and you did not take care enough of him, you silly girl...."

There was a requiem service in the morning and the evening. The funeral took place the next day, and after it the guests and the priests ate a great deal, and with such greed that one might have thought that they had not tasted food for a long time. Lipa waited at table, and the priest, lifting his fork on which there was a salted mushroom, said to her:

"Don't grieve for the babe. For of such is the Kingdom of Heaven."

And only when they had all separated, Lipa realized fully that there was no Nikifor and never would be, she realized it and broke into sobs. And she did not know what room to go into to sob, for she felt that now that her child was dead there was no place for her in the house, that she had no reason to be here, that she was in the way; and the others felt it, too.

"Now what are you bellowing for?" Aksinya shouted, suddenly appearing in the doorway; in honor of the funeral she was dressed all in new clothes and had powdered her face. "Shut up!"

Lipa tried to stop but could not and sobbed louder than ever.

"Do you hear?" shouted Aksinya, and she stamped her foot in violent anger. "Who is it I am speaking to? Go out of the yard and don't set foot here again, you convict's wife. Get away."

"There, there, there," the old man put in fussily. "Aksinya, don't make such an outcry, my girl.... She is crying, it is only natural... her child is dead...."

"'It is only natural,'" Aksinya mimicked him. "Let her stay the night here, and don't let me see a trace of her here tomorrow! 'It is only natural'!" she mimicked him again, and, laughing, she went into the shop.

Early the next morning Lipa went off to her mother at Torguevo.

## 9.

At the present time the steps and the front door of the shop have been repainted and are as bright as though they were new, there are gay geraniums in the windows as of old, and what happened in Tsybukin's house and yard three years ago is almost forgotten.

Grigory Petrovich is looked upon as the master as he was in old days, but in reality everything has passed into Aksinya's hands; she buys and sells, and nothing can be done without her consent. The brickyard is working well; and as bricks are wanted for the railway the price has gone up to twenty-four rubles a thousand; peasant women and girls cart the bricks to the station and load them up in the trucks and earn a quarter ruble a day for the work.

Aksinya has gone into partnership with the Khrymin Juniors, and their factory is now called Khrymin Juniors and Co. They have opened a tavern near the station, and now the expensive concertina is played not at the factory but at the tavern, and the head of the post office often goes there, and he, too, is engaged in some sort of traffic, and the stationmaster, too. Khrymin Juniors have presented the deaf man Stepan with a gold watch, and he is constantly taking it out of his pocket and putting it to his ear.

People say of Aksinya that she has become a person of power; and it is true that when she drives in the morning to her brickyard, handsome and happy, with the naive smile on her face, and afterwards when she is giving orders there, one is aware of great power in her. Everyone is afraid of her in the house and in the village and in the brickyard. When she goes to the post the head of the postal department jumps up and says to her:

"I humbly beg you to be seated, Aksinya Abramovna!"

A certain landowner, middle-aged but foppish, in a tunic of

fine cloth and patent leather high boots, sold her a horse, and was so carried away by talking to her that he knocked down the price to meet her wishes. He held her hand a long time and, looking into her merry, sly, naive eyes, said:

"For a woman like you, Aksinya Abramovna, I should be ready to do anything you please. Only say when we can meet where no one will interfere with us?"

"Why, when you please."

And since then the elderly fop drives up to the shop almost every day to drink beer. And the beer is horrid, bitter as wormwood. The landowner shakes his head, but he drinks it.

Old Tsybukin does not have anything to do with the business now at all. He does not keep any money because he cannot distinguish between the good and the false, but he is silent, he says nothing of this weakness. He has become forgetful, and if they don't give him food he does not ask for it. They have grown used to having dinner without him, and Varvara often says:

"He went to bed again yesterday without any supper."

And she says it unconcernedly because she is used to it. For some reason, summer and winter alike, he wears a fur coat, and only in very hot weather he does not go out but sits at home. As a rule, putting on his fur coat, wrapping it round him and turning up his collar, he walks about the village, along the road to the station, or sits from morning till night on the seat near the church gates. He sits there without stirring. Passers-by bow to him, but he does not respond, for as of old he dislikes the peasants. If he is asked a question he answers quite rationally and politely, but briefly.

There is a rumor going about in the village that his daughter-in-law turns him out of the house and gives him nothing to eat, and that he is fed by charity; some are glad, others are sorry for him.

Varvara has grown even fatter and whiter, and as before she is active in good works, and Aksinya does not interfere with her.

There is so much jam now that they have not time to eat it before the fresh fruit comes in; it goes sugary, and Varvara almost sheds tears, not knowing what to do with it.

They have begun to forget about Anisim. A letter has come from him written in verse on a big sheet of paper as though it were a petition, all in the same splendid handwriting. Evidently his friend Samorodov is sharing his punishment. Under the verses in an ugly, scarcely legible handwriting there was a single line: "I am ill here all the time; I am wretched, for Christ's sake help me!"

Towards evening—it was a fine autumn day—old Tsybukin was sitting near the church gates, with the collar of his fur coat turned up and nothing of him could be seen but his nose and the peak of his cap. At the other end of the long seat was sitting Elizarov, the contractor, and beside him Yakov, the school watchman, a toothless old man of seventy. Crutch and the watchman were talking.

"Children ought to give food and drink to the old. . . . Honor thy father and mother . . ." Yakov was saying with irritation, "while she, this daughter-in-law, has turned her father-in-law out of his own house; the old man has neither food nor drink; where is he to go? He has not had a morsel for these three days."

"Three days!" said Crutch, amazed.

"Here he sits and does not say a word. He has grown feeble. And why be silent? He ought to prosecute her, they wouldn't flatter her in the police court."

"Wouldn't flatter whom?" asked Crutch, not hearing.

"What?"

"The woman's all right, she does her best. In their line of business they can't get on without that . . . without sin, I mean. . . ."

"From his own house," Yakov went on with irritation. "Save up and buy your own house, then turn people out of it! She is a nice one, to be sure! A pla-ague!"

Tsybukin listened and did not stir.

"Whether it is your own house or others' it makes no difference so long as it is warm and the women don't scold . . ." said Crutch, and he laughed. "When I was young I was very fond of my Nastasya. She was a quiet woman. And she used to be always at it: 'Buy a house, Makarich! Buy a house, Makarich! Buy a house, Makarich!' She was dying and yet she kept on saying, 'Buy yourself a racing droshky, Makarich, that you may not have to walk.' And I bought her nothing but gingerbread."

"Her husband's deaf and stupid," Yakov went on, not hearing Crutch; "a regular fool, just like a goose. He can't understand anything. Hit a goose on the head with a stick and even then it does not understand."

Crutch got up to go home to the factory. Yakov also got up, and both of them went off together, still talking. When they had gone fifty paces old Tsybukin got up, too, and walked after them, stepping uncertainly as though on slippery ice.

The village was already plunged in the dusk of evening and the sun only gleamed on the upper part of the road which ran wriggling like a snake up the slope. Old women were coming back from the woods and children with them; they were bringing baskets of mushrooms. Peasant women and girls came in a crowd from the station where they had been loading the trucks with bricks, and their noses and their cheeks under their eyes were covered with red brick dust. They were singing. Ahead of them all was Lipa, singing in a high voice, with her eyes turned upwards to the sky, breaking into trills as though triumphant and ecstatic that at last the day was over and she could rest. In the crowd was her mother Praskovya, who was walking with a bundle in her arms and breathless as usual.

"Good evening, Makarich!" cried Lipa, seeing Crutch. "Good evening, darling!"

"Good evening, Lipinka," cried Crutch delighted. "Dear girls and women, love the rich carpenter! Ho-ho! My little children, my little children." (Crutch gave a gulp.) "My dear little axes!"

Crutch and Yakov went on further and could still be heard talking. Then after them the crowd was met by old Tsybukin and there was a sudden hush. Lipa and Praskovya had dropped a little behind, and when the old man was on a level with them Lipa bowed down low and said:

"Good evening, Grigory Petrovich."

Her mother, too, bowed down. The old man stopped and, saying nothing, looked at the two in silence; his lips were quivering and his eyes full of tears. Lipa took out of her mother's bundle a piece of savory turnover and gave it him. He took it and began eating.

The sun had by now set: its glow died away on the road above. It grew dark and cool. Lipa and Praskovya walked on and for some time they kept crossing themselves.

# THE BISHOP

## 1.

THE EVENING SERVICE was being celebrated on the eve of Palm Sunday in the Old Petrovsky Convent. When they began distributing the palm it was close upon ten o'clock, the candles were burning dimly, the wicks wanted snuffing; it was all in a sort of mist. In the twilight of the church the crowd seemed heaving like the sea, and to Bishop Pyotr, who had been unwell for the last three days, it seemed that all the faces—old and young, men's and women's—were alike, that everyone who came up for the palm had the same expression in his eyes. In the mist he could not see the doors; the crowd kept moving and looked as though there were no end to it. The female choir was singing, a nun was reading the prayers for the day.

How stifling, how hot it was! How long the service went on! Bishop Pyotr was tired. His breathing was labored and rapid, his throat was parched, his shoulders ached with weariness, his legs were trembling. And it disturbed him unpleasantly when a religious maniac uttered occasional shrieks in the gallery. And then all of a sudden, as though in a dream or delirium, it seemed to the bishop as though his own mother Marya Timofyevna, whom he had not seen for nine years, or some old woman just like his mother, came up to him out of the crowd, and, after taking a palm branch from him, walked away, looking at him all the while good-humoredly with a kind, joyful smile until she was lost in the crowd. And for some reason tears flowed down his face. There was peace in his heart, everything was well, yet he kept gazing fixedly towards the left choir, where the prayers were being read, where in the dusk of evening you could not recognize anyone, and—wept. Tears glistened on his face and on his beard. Here someone close at hand was weeping, then someone else farther away, then others and still others, and little by little the church was filled with soft weeping. And a little later, within five minutes, the nuns' choir was singing; no one was weeping and everything was as before.

Soon the service was over. When the bishop got into his carriage to drive home, the gay, melodious chime of the heavy, costly bells was filling the whole garden in the moonlight. The white walls, the white crosses on the tombs, the white birch trees and black shadows, and the faraway moon in the sky exactly over the convent seemed now living their own lives, apart and incomprehensible, yet very near to man. It was the beginning of April, and after the warm spring day it turned cool; there was a faint touch of frost, and the breath of spring could be felt in the soft, chilly air. The road from the convent to the town was sandy, the horses had to go at a walking pace, and on both sides of the carriage in the brilliant, peaceful moonlight there were people trudging along home from church through the sand. And all was silent, sunk in thought; everything around seemed kindly, youthful, akin, everything—trees and sky and even the moon, and one longed to think that so it would be always.

At last the carriage drove into the town and rumbled along the principal street. The shops were already shut, but at Erakin's, the millionaire shopkeeper's, they were trying the new electric lights, which flickered brightly, and a crowd of people were gathered round. Then came wide, dark, deserted streets, one after another; then the highroad, the open country, the fragrance of pines. And suddenly there rose up before the bishop's eyes a white turreted wall, and behind it a tall belfry in the full moonlight, and beside it five shining, golden cupolas: this was the Pankratievsky Monastery, in which Bishop Pyotr lived. And here, too, high above the monastery, was the silent, dreamy moon. The carriage drove in at the gate, crunching over the sand; here and there in the moonlight there were glimpses of dark monastic figures, and there was the sound of footsteps on the flagstones. . . .

"You know, Your Holiness, your mamma arrived while you were away," the lay brother informed the bishop as he went into his cell.

"My mother? When did she come?"

"Before the evening service. She asked first where you were and then she went to the convent."

"Then it was her I saw in the church, just now! Oh Lord!"

And the bishop laughed with joy.

"She bade me tell Your Holiness," the lay brother went on, "that she would come tomorrow. She had a little girl with her—her grandchild, I suppose. They are staying at Ovsyannikov's inn."

"What time is it now?"

"A little after eleven."

"Oh, how vexing!"

The bishop sat for a little while in the parlor, hesitating, and, as it were, refusing to believe it was so late. His arms and legs were stiff, his head ached. He was hot and uncomfortable. After resting a little he went into his bedroom, and there, too, he sat a little, still thinking of his mother; he could hear the lay brother going away, and Father Sisoi coughing the other side of the wall. The monastery clock struck a quarter.

The bishop changed his clothes and began reading the prayers before sleep. He read attentively those old, long familiar prayers, and at the same time thought about his mother. She had nine children and about forty grandchildren. At one time she had lived with her husband, the deacon, in a poor village; she had lived there a very long time from the age of seventeen to sixty. The bishop remembered her from early childhood, almost from the age of three, and—how he had loved her! Sweet, precious childhood, always fondly remembered! Why did it, that long-past time that could never return, why did it seem brighter, fuller, and more festive than it had really been? When in his childhood or youth he had been ill, how tender and sympathetic his mother had been! And now his prayers mingled with the memories, which gleamed more and more brightly like a flame, and the prayers did not hinder his thinking of his mother.

When he had finished his prayers he undressed and lay down, and at once, as soon as it was dark, there rose before his mind his dead father, his mother, his native village Lesopolye . . . the creak of wheels, the bleat of sheep, the church bells on bright summer mornings, the gypsies under the window—oh, how sweet to think of it! He remembered the priest of Lesopolye, Father Simeon—mild, gentle, kindly; he was a lean little man, while his son, a divinity student, was a huge fellow and talked in a roaring bass voice. The priest's son had flown into a rage with the cook and abused her: "Ah, you Jehud's ass!" and Father Simeon overhearing it, said not a word, and was only ashamed because he could not remember where such an ass was mentioned in the Bible. After him the priest at Lesopolye had been Father Demyan, who used to drink heavily, and at times drank till he saw green snakes, and was even nicknamed Demyan Snakeseer. The schoolmaster at Lesopolye was Matvei Nikolaich, who had been a divinity student, a kind and intelligent man, but he, too, was a drunkard; he never beat the school children, but for some reason he always had hanging on his wall a bunch of birch twigs, and below it an utterly meaningless inscription in Latin: "Betula kinderbalsamica secuta." He had a shaggy black dog whom he called Syntax.

And His Holiness laughed. Six miles from Lesopolye was the village Obnino with a wonder-working icon. In the summer they used to carry the icon in procession about the neighboring villages and ring the bells the whole day long; first in one village and then in another, and it used to seem to the bishop then that joy was quivering in the air, and he (in those days his name was Pavlusha) used to follow the icon, bareheaded and barefoot, with naive faith, with a naive smile, infinitely happy. In Obnino, he remembered now, there were always a lot of people, and the priest there, Father Alexei, to save time during mass, used to make his deaf nephew Ilarion read the names of those for whose health or whose souls' peace prayers were asked. Ilarion used to read them, now and then getting a five or ten kopeck piece for the service, and only when he was gray and bald, when life was nearly over, he suddenly saw written on one of the pieces of paper: "What a fool you are, Ilarion." Up to fifteen at least Pavlusha was undeveloped and idle at his lessons, so much so that they thought of taking him away from the clerical school and putting him into a shop; one day, going to the post at Obnino for letters, he had stared a long time at the post-office clerks and asked: "Allow me to ask, how do you get your salary, every month or every day?"

His Holiness crossed himself and turned over on the other side, trying to stop thinking and go to sleep.

"My mother has come," he remembered and laughed.

The moon peeped in at the window, the floor was lighted up, and there were shadows on it. A cricket was chirping. Through the wall Father Sisoi was snoring in the next room, and his aged snore had a sound that suggested loneliness, forlornness, even vagrancy. Sisoi had once been housekeeper to the bishop of the diocese, and was called now "the former Father Housekeeper"; he was seventy years old, he lived in a monastery twelve miles from the town and stayed sometimes in the town, too. He had come to the Pankratievsky Monastery three days before, and the bishop had kept him that he might talk to him at his leisure about matters of business, about the arrangements here. . . .

At half-past one they began ringing for matins. Father Sisoi could be heard coughing, muttering something in a discontented voice, then he got up and walked barefoot about the rooms.

"Father Sisoi," the bishop called.

Sisoi went back to his room and a little later made his appearance in his boots, with a candle; he had on his cassock over his underclothes and on his head was an old faded skullcap.

"I can't sleep," said the bishop, sitting up. "I must be unwell. And what it is I don't know. Fever!"

"You must have caught cold, Your Holiness. You must be rubbed with tallow." Sisoi stood a little and yawned. "O Lord, forgive me, a sinner."

"They had the electric lights on at Erakin's today," he said; "I don't like it!"

Father Sisoi was old, lean, bent, always dissatisfied with something, and his eyes were angry-looking and prominent as a crab's.

"I don't like it," he said, going away. "I don't like it. Bother it!"

## 2.

Next day, Palm Sunday, the bishop took the service in the cathedral in the town, then he visited the bishop of the diocese, then visited a very sick old lady, the widow of a general, and at last drove home. Between one and two o'clock he had welcome visitors dining with him—his mother and his niece Katya, a child of eight years old. All dinnertime the spring sunshine was streaming in at the windows, throwing bright light on the white tablecloth and on Katya's red hair. Through the double windows they could hear the noise of the rooks and the notes of the starlings in the garden.

"It is nine years since we have met," said the old lady. "And when I looked at you in the monastery yesterday, good Lord! you've not changed a bit, except maybe you are thinner and your beard is a little longer. Holy Mother, Queen of Heaven! Yesterday at the evening service no one could help crying. I, too, as I looked at you, suddenly began crying though I couldn't say why. His Holy Will!"

And in spite of the affectionate tone in which she said this, he could see she was constrained as though she were uncertain whether to address him formally or familiarly, to laugh or not, and that she felt herself more a deacon's widow than his mother. And Katya gazed without blinking at her uncle, His Holiness, as though trying to discover what sort of a person he was. Her hair sprang up from under the comb and the velvet ribbon and stood out like a halo; she had a turned-up nose and sly eyes. The child had broken a glass before sitting down to dinner, and now her grandmother, as she talked, moved away from Katya first a wineglass and then a tumbler. The bishop listened to his mother and remembered how many, many years ago she used to take him and his brothers and sisters to relations whom she considered rich; in those days she was taken up with the care of her children, now with her grandchildren, and she had brought Katya. . . .

"Your sister Varenka has four children," she told him; "Katya, here, is the eldest. And your brother-in-law, Father Ivan, fell sick, God knows of what, and died three days before the Assumption; and my poor Varenka is left a beggar."

"And how is Nikanor getting on?" the bishop asked about his eldest brother.

"He is all right, thank God. Though he has nothing much, yet he can live. Only there is one thing: his son, my grandson Nikolasha, did not want to go into the Church; he has gone to the university to be a doctor. He thinks it is better; but who knows! His Holy Will!"

"Nikolasha cuts up dead people," said Katya, spilling water over her knees.

"Sit still, child," her grandmother observed calmly, and took the glass out of her hand. "Say a prayer, and go on eating."

"How long it is since we have seen each other!" said the bishop, and he tenderly stroked his mother's hand and shoulder; "and I missed you abroad, Mother, I missed you dreadfully."

"Thank you."

"I used to sit in the evenings at the open window, lonely and alone; often there was music playing, and all at once I used to be overcome with homesickness and felt as though I would give everything only to be at home and see you."

His mother smiled, beamed, but at once she made a grave face and said:

"Thank you."

His mood suddenly changed. He looked at his mother and could not understand how she had come by that respectfulness, that timid expression of face: what was it for? And he did not recognize her. He felt sad and vexed. And then his head ached just as it had the day before; his legs felt fearfully tired, and the fish seemed to him stale and tasteless; he felt thirsty all the time. . . .

After dinner two rich ladies, landowners, arrived and sat for an hour and a half in silence with rigid countenances; the archimandrite, a silent, rather deaf man, came to see him about business. Then they began ringing for vespers; the sun was setting behind the wood and the day was over. When he returned from church, he hurriedly said his prayers, got into bed, and wrapped himself up as warm as possible.

It was disagreeable to remember the fish he had eaten at dinner. The moonlight worried him, and then he heard talking. In an adjoining room, probably in the parlor, Father Sisoi was talking politics:

"There's war among the Japanese now. They are fighting. The Japanese, my good soul, are the same as the Montenegrins; they are the same race. They were under the Turkish yoke together."

And then he heard the voice of Marya Timofyevna:

"So, having said our prayers and drunk tea, we went, you know, to Father Yegor at Novokatnoye, so . . ."

And she kept on saying, "having had tea," or "having drunk tea," and it seemed as though the only thing she had done in her life was to drink tea.

The bishop slowly, languidly, recalled the seminary, the academy. For three years he had been Greek teacher in the seminary: by that time he could not read without spectacles. Then he had become a monk; he had been made a school inspector. Then he had defended his thesis for his degree. When he was thirty-two he had been made rector of the seminary, and consecrated archimandrite: and then his life had been so easy, so pleasant; it seemed so long, so long, no end was in sight. Then he had begun to be ill, had grown very thin and almost blind, and by the advice of the doctors had to give up everything and go abroad.

"And what then?" asked Sisoi in the next room.

"Then we drank tea . . ." answered Marya Timofyevna.

"Good gracious, you've got a green beard," said Katya suddenly in surprise, and she laughed.

The bishop remembered that the gray-headed Father Sisoi's beard really had a shade of green in it, and he laughed.

"God have mercy upon us, what we have to put up with with this girl!" said Sisoi, aloud, getting angry. "Spoiled child! Sit quiet!"

The bishop remembered the perfectly new white church in which he had conducted the services while living abroad, the remembered the sound of the warm sea. In his flat he had five lofty light rooms; in his study he had a new writing table, lots of books. He had read a great deal and often written. And he remembered how he had pined for his native land, how a blind beggar woman had played the guitar under his window every day and sung of love, and how, as he listened, he had always for some reason thought of the past. But eight years had passed and he had been called back to Russia, and now he was a suffragan bishop, and all the past had retreated far away into the mist as though it were a dream. . . .

Father Sisoi came into the bedroom with a candle.

"I say!" he said, wondering, "are you asleep already, Your Holiness?"

"What is it?"

"Why, it's still early, ten o'clock or less. I bought a candle today; I wanted to rub you with tallow."

"I am in a fever . . ." said the bishop, and he sat up. "I really ought to have something. My head is bad. . . ."

Sisoi took off the bishop's shirt and began rubbing his chest and back with tallow.

"That's the way . . . that's the way . . ." he said. "Lord Jesus Christ . . . that's the way. I walked to the town today; I was at what's-his-name's—the chief priest Sidonsky's. . . . I had tea with him. I don't like him. Lord Jesus Christ . . . that's the way. I don't like him."

## 3.

The bishop of the diocese, a very fat old man, was ill with rheumatism or gout and had been in bed for over a month. Bishop Pyotr went to see him almost every day, and saw all who came to ask his help. And now that he was unwell he was struck by the emptiness, the triviality of everything which they asked and for which they wept; he was vexed at their ignorance, their timidity; and all this useless, petty business oppressed him by the mass of it, and it seemed to him that now he understood the diocesan bishop who had once in his young days written on "The Doctrines of the Freedom of the Will," and now seemed to be all lost in trivialities, to have forgotten everything, and to have no thoughts of religion. The bishop must have lost touch with Russian life while he was abroad; he did not find it easy; the peasants seemed to him coarse, the women who sought his help dull and stupid, the seminarists and their teachers uncultivated and at times savage. And the documents coming in and going out were reckoned by tens of thousands; and what documents they were! The higher clergy in the whole diocese gave the priests, young and old, and even their wives and children, marks for their behavior—a five, a four, and sometimes even a three; and about this he had to talk and to read and write serious reports. And there was positively not one minute to spare; his soul was troubled all day long, and the bishop was only at peace when he was in church.

He could not get used, either, to the awe which, through no wish of his own, he inspired in people in spite of his quiet, modest disposition. All the people in the province seemed to him little, scared, and guilty when he looked at them. Everyone was timid in his presence, even the old chief priests; everyone "flopped" at his feet, and not long previously an old lady, a village priest's wife who had come to consult him, was so overcome by awe that she could not utter a single word, and went away empty. And he, who could never in his sermons bring himself to speak ill of people, never reproached anyone because he was so sorry for them, was moved to fury with the people who came to consult him, lost his temper, and flung their petitions on the floor. The whole time he had been here, not one person had spoken to him genuinely, simply, as to a human being; even his old mother seemed now not the same! And why, he wondered, did she chatter away to Sisoi and laugh so much; while with him, her son, she was grave and usually silent and constrained, which did not suit her at all. The only person who behaved freely with him and said what he meant was old Sisoi, who had spent his whole life in the presence of bishops and had outlived eleven of them. And so the bishop was at ease with him, although, of course, he was a tedious and nonsensical man.

After the service on Tuesday, His Holiness Pyotr was in the diocesan bishop's house, receiving petitions there; he got excited and angry, and then drove home. He was as unwell as before; he longed to be in bed, but he had hardly reached home when he was informed that a young merchant called Erakin, who subscribed liberally to charities, had come to see him about a very important matter. The bishop had to see him. Erakin stayed about an hour, talked very loud, almost shouted, and it was difficult to understand what he said.

"God grant it may," he said as he went away. "Most essential! According to circumstances, Your Holiness! I trust it may!"

After him came the Mother Superior from a distant convent. And when she had gone they began ringing for vespers. He had to go to church.

In the evening the monks sang harmoniously, with inspiration. A young priest with a black beard conducted the service; and the bishop, hearing of the Bridegroom who comes at midnight and of the Heavenly Mansion adorned for the festival, felt no repentance for his sins, no tribulation, but peace at heart and tranquility. And he was carried back in thought to the distant past, to his childhood and youth, when, too, they used to sing of the Bridegroom and of the Heavenly Mansion; and now that past rose up before him—living, fair, and joyful as in all likelihood it never had been. And perhaps in the other world, in the life to come, we shall think of the distant past, of our life here, with the same feeling. Who knows? The bishop was sitting near the altar. It was dark; tears flowed down his face. He thought that here he had attained everything a man in his position could attain; he had faith and yet everything was not clear, something was lacking still. He did not want to die; and he still felt that he had missed what was most important, something of which he had dimly dreamed in the past; and he was troubled by the same hopes for the future as he had felt in childhood, at the academy and abroad.

"How well they sing today!" he thought, listening to the singing. "How nice it is!"

## 4.

On Tuesday he celebrated mass in the cathedral; it was the Washing of Feet. When the service was over and the people were going home, it was sunny, warm; the water gurgled in the gutters, and the unceasing trilling of the larks, tender, telling of peace, rose from the fields outside the town. The trees were already awakening and smiling a welcome, while above them the infinite, fathomless blue sky stretched into the distance, God knows whither.

On reaching home His Holiness drank some tea, then changed his clothes, lay down on his bed, and told the lay brother to close the shutters on the windows. The bedroom was darkened. But what weariness, what pain in his legs and his back, a chill heavy pain, what a noise in his ears! He had not slept for a long time—for a very long time, as it seemed to him now—and some trifling detail which haunted his brain as soon as his eyes were closed prevented him from sleeping. As on the day before, sounds reached him form the adjoining rooms through the walls, voices, the jingle of glasses and teaspoons. . . . Marya Timofyevna was gaily telling Father Sisoi some story with quaint turns of speech, while the latter answered in a grumpy, ill-humored voice: "Bother them! Not likely! What next!" And the bishop again felt vexed and then hurt that with other people his old mother behaved in a simple, ordinary way, while with him, her son, she was shy, spoke little, and did not say what she meant, and even, as he fancied, had during all these few days kept trying in his presence to find an excuse for standing up, because she was embarrassed at sitting before him. And his father? He, too, probably, if he had been living, would not have been able to utter a word in the bishop's presence. . . .

Something fell down on the floor in the adjoining room and was broken; Katya must have dropped a cup or a saucer, for Father Sisoi suddenly spat and said angrily:

"What a regular nuisance the child is! Lord forgive my transgressions! One can't provide enough for her."

Then all was quiet, the only sounds came from outside. And when the bishop opened his eyes he saw Katya in his room, standing motionless, staring at him. Her red hair, as usual, stood up from under the comb like a halo.

"Is that you, Katya?" he asked. "Who is it downstairs who keeps opening and shutting a door?"

"I don't hear it," answered Katya; and she listened.

"There, someone has just passed by."

"But that was a noise in your stomach, Uncle."

He laughed and stroked her on the head.

"So you say Cousin Nikolasha cuts up dead people?" he asked after a pause.

"Yes, he is studying."

"And is he kind?"

"Oh, yes he's kind. But he drinks vodka awfully."

"And what was it your father died of?"

"Papa was weak and very, very thin, and all at once his throat was bad. I was ill then, too, and Brother Fedya; we all had bad throats. Papa died, Uncle, and we got well."

Her chin began quivering, and tears gleamed in her eyes and trickled down her cheeks.

"Your Holiness," she said in a shrill voice, by now weeping bitterly, "Uncle, Mother and all of us are left very wretched.... Give us a little money... do be kind... Uncle darling...."

He, too, was moved to tears, and for a long time was too much touched to speak. Then he stroked her on the head, patted her on the shoulder, and said:

"Very good, very good, my child. When the holy Easter comes, we will talk it over.... I will help you.... I will help you...."

His mother came in quietly, timidly, and prayed before the icon. Noticing that he was not sleeping, she said:

"Won't you have a drop of soup?"

"No, thank you," he answered, "I am not hungry."

"You seem to be unwell, now I look at you. I should think so; you may well be ill! The whole day on your legs, the whole day.... And, my goodness, it makes one's heart ache even to look at you! Well, Easter is not far off; you will rest then, please God. Then we will have a talk, too, but now I'm not going to disturb you with my chatter. Come along, Katya; let His Holiness sleep a little."

And he remembered how once very long ago, when he was a boy, she had spoken exactly like that, in the same jestingly respectful tone, with a church dignitary.... Only from her extraordinarily kind eyes and the timid, anxious glance she stole at him as she went out of the room could one have guessed that this was his mother. He shut his eyes and seemed to sleep, but twice heard the clock strike and Father Sisoi coughing the other side of the wall. And once more his mother came in and looked timidly at him for a minute. Someone drove up to the steps, as he could hear, in a coach or in a chaise. Suddenly a knock, the door slammed, the lay brother came into the bedroom.

"Your Holiness," he called.

"Well?"

"The horses are here; it's time for the evening service."

"What o'clock is it?"

"A quarter-past seven."

He dressed and drove to the cathedral. During all the "Twelve Gospels" he had to stand in the middle of the church without moving, and the first gospel, the longest and the most beautiful, he read himself. A mood of confidence and courage came over him. That first gospel, "Now is the Son of Man glorified," he knew by heart; and as he read he raised his eyes from time to time, and saw on both sides a perfect sea of lights and heard the splutter of candles, but, as in past years, he could not see the people, and it seemed as though these were all the same people as had been round him in those days, in his childhood and his youth; that they would always be the same every year and till such time as God only knew.

His father had been a deacon, his grandfather a priest, his great-grandfather a deacon, and his whole family, perhaps from the days when Christianity had been accepted in Russia, had belonged to the priesthood; and his love for the church services, for the priesthood, for the peal of the bells, was deep in him, ineradicable, innate. In church, particularly when he took part in the service, he felt vigorous, of good cheer, happy. So it was now. Only when the eighth gospel had been read, he felt that his voice had grown weak, even his cough was inaudible.

His head had begun to ache intensely, and he was troubled by a fear that he might fall down. And his legs were indeed quite numb, so that by degrees he ceased to feel them and could not understand how or on what he was standing, and why he did not fall. . . .

It was a quarter to twelve when the service was over. When he reached home, the bishop undressed and went to bed at once without even saying his prayers. He could not speak and felt that he could not have stood up. When he had covered his head with the quilt he felt a sudden longing to be abroad, an insufferable longing! He felt that he would give his life not to see those pitiful cheap shutters, those low ceilings, not to smell that heavy monastery smell. If only there were one person to whom he could have talked, have opened his heart!

For a long while he heard footsteps in the next room and could not tell whose they were. At last the door opened and Sisoi came in with a candle and a teacup in his hand.

"You are in bed already, Your Holiness?" he asked. "Here I have come to rub you with spirit and vinegar. A thorough rubbing does a great deal of good. Lord Jesus Christ! . . . that's the way . . . that's the way. . . . I've just been in our monastery. . . . I don't like it. I'm going away from here tomorrow, Your Holiness; I don't want to stay longer. Lord Jesus Christ . . . that's the way. . . ."

Sisoi could never stay long in the same place, and he felt as though he had been a whole year in the Pankratievsky Monastery. Above all, listening to him, it was difficult to understand where his home was, whether he cared for anyone or anything, whether he believed in God. . . . He did not know himself why he was a monk, and, indeed, he did not think about it, and the time when he had become a monk had long passed out of his memory; it seemed as though he had been born a monk.

"I'm going away tomorrow; God be with them all."

"I should like to talk to you. . . . I can't find the time," said the bishop softly with an effort. "I don't know anything or anybody here. . . ."

"I'll stay till Sunday if you like; so be it, but I don't want to stay longer. I am sick of them!"

"I ought not to be a bishop," said the bishop softly. "I ought to have been a village priest, a deacon . . . or simply a monk. . . . All this oppresses me . . . oppresses me."

"What? Lord Jesus Christ . . . that's the way. Come, sleep well, Your Holiness! . . . What's the good of talking? It's no use. Good night!"

The bishop did not sleep all night. And at eight o'clock in the morning he began to have hemorrhage from the bowels. The lay brother was alarmed, and ran first to the archimandrite, then for the monastery doctor, Ivan Andreyich, who lived in the town. The doctor, a stout old man with a long gray beard, made a prolonged examination of the bishop, and kept shaking his head and frowning, then said:

"Do you know, Your Holiness, you have got typhoid?"

After an hour or so of hemorrhage the bishop looked much thinner, paler, and wasted; his face looked wrinkled, his eyes looked bigger, and he seemed older, shorter, and it seemed to him that he was thinner, weaker, more insignificant than anyone, that everything that had been had retreated far, far away and would never go on again or be repeated.

"How good," he thought, "how good!"

His old mother came. Seeing his wrinkled face and his big eyes, she was frightened; she fell on her knees by the bed and began kissing his face, his shoulders, his hands. And to her, too, it seemed that he was thinner, weaker, and more insignificant than anyone, and now she forgot that he was a bishop and kissed him as though he were a child very near and very dear to her.

"Pavlusha darling," she said; "my own, my darling son! . . . Why are you like this? Pavlusha, answer me!"

Katya, pale and severe, stood beside her, unable to understand what was the matter with her uncle, why there was such a look of suffering on her grandmother's face, why she was saying such sad and touching things. By now he could not utter a word, he could understand nothing, and he imagined he was a simple ordinary man, that he was walking quickly, cheerfully, through the fields, tapping with his stick, while above him was the open sky bathed in sunshine, and that he was free now as a bird and could go where he liked!

"Pavlusha, my darling son, answer me," the old woman was saying. "What is it? My own!"

"Don't disturb His Holiness," Sisoi said angrily, walking about the room. "Let him sleep . . . what's the use . . . it's no good. . . ."

Three doctors arrived, consulted together, and went away again. The day was long, incredibly long, then the night came on and passed slowly, slowly, and towards morning on Saturday the lay brother went in to the old mother who was lying on the sofa in the parlor, and asked her to go into the bedroom: the bishop had just breathed his last.

Next day was Easter Sunday. There were forty-two churches and six monasteries in the town; the sonorous, joyful clang of the bells hung over the town from morning till night unceasingly, setting the spring air aquiver; the birds were singing, the sun was shining brightly. The big market square was noisy, swings were going, barrel organs were playing, accordions were squeaking, drunken voices were shouting. After midday people began driving up and down the principal street.

In short, all was merriment, everything was satisfactory, just as it had been the year before, and as it will be in all likelihood next year.

A month later a new suffragan bishop was appointed, and

no one thought anything more of Bishop Pyotr, and afterwards he was completely forgotten. And only the dead man's old mother, who is living today with her son-in-law the deacon in a remote little district town, when she goes out at night to bring her cow in and meets other women at the pasture, begins talking of her children and her grandchildren, and says that she had a son a bishop, and this she says timidly, afraid that she may not be believed. . . .

And, indeed, there are some who do not believe her.

# BETROTHED

## 1.

IT WAS TEN o'clock in the evening and the full moon was shining over the garden. In the Shumins' house an evening service celebrated at the request of the grandmother, Marfa Mihalovna, was just over, and now Nadya—she had gone into the garden for a minute—could see the table being laid for supper in the dining-room, and her grandmother bustling about in her gorgeous silk dress; Father Andrei, a chief priest of the cathedral, was talking to Nadya's mother, Nina Ivanovna, and now in the evening light through the window her mother for some reason looked very young; Andrei Andreyich, Father Andrei's son, was standing by listening attentively.

It was still and cool in the garden, and dark peaceful shadows lay on the ground. There was a sound of frogs croaking, far, far away beyond the town. There was a feeling of May, sweet May! One drew deep breaths and longed to fancy that not here but far away under the sky, above the trees, far away in the open country, in the fields and the woods, the life of spring was unfolding now, mysterious, lovely, rich, and holy, beyond the understanding of weak, sinful man. And for some reason one wanted to cry.

She, Nadya, was already twenty-three. Ever since she was sixteen she had been passionately dreaming of marriage and at last she was engaged to Andrei Andreyich, the young man who was standing on the other side of the window; she liked him, the wedding was already fixed for July 7, and yet there was no joy in her heart; she was sleeping badly, her spirits drooped. . . . She could hear from the open windows of the basement, where the kitchen was, the hurrying servants, the clatter of knives, the banging of the swing door; there was a smell of roast turkey and pickled cherries, and for some reason it seemed to her that it would be like that all her life, with no change, no end to it.

Someone came out of the house and stood on the steps; it was Alexandr Timofeich, or, as he was always called, Sasha, who had come from Moscow ten days before and was staying with them. Years ago a distant relation of the grandmother, a gentleman's widow called Marya Petrovna, a thin, sickly little woman who had sunk into poverty, used to come to the house to ask for assistance. She had a son Sasha. It used for some reason to be said that he had talent as an artist, and when his mother died Nadya's grandmother had, for the salvation of her soul, sent him to the Komissarovsky school in Moscow; two years later he went into the school of painting, spent nearly fifteen years there, and only just managed to scrape through the leaving examination in the section of architecture. He did not set up as an architect, however, but took a job at a lithographer's. He used to come almost every year, usually very ill, to stay with Nadya's grandmother to rest and recover.

He was wearing now a frock coat buttoned up, and shabby canvas trousers, crumpled into creases at the bottom. And his shirt had not been ironed and he had somehow all over a look of not being fresh. He was very thin, with big eyes, long thin fingers, and a swarthy bearded face, and all the same he was handsome. With the Shumins he was like one of the family, and in their house felt he was at home. And the room in which he lived when he was there had for years been called Sasha's room. Standing on the steps, he saw Nadya and went up to her.

"It's nice here," he said.

"Of course it's nice, you ought to stay here till the autumn."

"Yes, I expect it will come to that. I dare say I shall stay with you till September."

He laughed for no reason and sat down beside her.

"I'm sitting gazing at Mother," said Nadya. "She looks so young from here! My mother has her weaknesses, of course," she added, after a pause, "but still she is an exceptional woman."

"Yes, she is very nice . . ." Sasha agreed. "Your mother, in her own way of course, is a very good and sweet woman, but . . . how shall say? I went early this morning into your kitchen and there I found four servants sleeping on the floor, no bedsteads, and rags for bedding, stench, bugs, beetles . . . it is just as it was twenty years ago, no change at all. Well, Granny, God bless her, what else can you expect of Granny? But your mother speaks French, you know, and acts in private theatricals. One would think she might understand."

As Sasha talked, he used to stretch out two long wasted fingers before the listener's face.

"It all seems somehow strange to me here, now I am out of the habit of it," he went on. "There is no making it out. Nobody ever does anything. Your mother spends the whole day walking about like a duchess, Granny does nothing either, nor you either. And your Andrei Andreyich never does anything either."

Nadya had heard this the year before and, she fancied, the year before that too, and she knew that Sasha could not make any other criticism, and in old days this had amused her, but now for some reason she felt annoyed.

"That's all stale, and I have been sick of it for ages," she said, and got up. "You should think of something a little newer."

He laughed and got up too, and they went together toward the house. She, tall, handsome, and well made, beside him looked very healthy and smartly dressed; she was conscious of this and felt sorry for him and for some reason awkward.

"And you say a great deal you should not," she said. "You've just been talking about my Andrei, but you see you don't know him."

"My Andrei. . . . Bother him, your Andrei. I am sorry for your youth."

They were already sitting down to supper as the young people went into the dining-room. The grandmother, or Granny as she was called in the household, a very stout, plain old lady with bushy eyebrows and a little mustache, was talking loudly, and from her voice and manner of speaking it could be seen that she was the person of most importance in the house. She owned rows of shops in the market, and the old-fashioned house with columns and the garden, yet she prayed every morning that God might save her from ruin and shed tears as she did so. Her daughter-in-law, Nadya's mother, Nina Ivanovna, a fair-haired woman tightly laced in, with a pince-nez, and diamonds on every finger, Father Andrei, a lean, toothless old man whose face always looked as though he were just going to say something amusing, and his son, Andrei Andreyich, a stout and handsome young man with curly hair, looking like an artist or an actor, were all talking of hypnotism.

"You will get well in a week here," said Granny, addressing Sasha. "Only you must eat more. What do you look like!" she sighed. "You are really dreadful! You are a regular prodigal son, that is what you are."

"After wasting his father's substance in riotous living," said

Father Andrei slowly, with laughing eyes. "He fed with senseless beasts."

"I like my dad," said Andrei Andreyich, touching his father on the shoulder. "He is a splendid old fellow, a dear old fellow."

Everyone was silent for a space. Sasha suddenly burst out laughing and put his dinner napkin to his mouth.

"So you believe in hypnotism?" said Father Andrei to Nina Ivanovna.

"I cannot, of course, assert that I believe," answered Nina Ivanovna, assuming a very serious, even severe, expression; "but I must own that there is much that is mysterious and incomprehensible in nature."

"I quite agree with you, though I must add that religion distinctly curtails for us the domain of the mysterious."

A big and very fat turkey was served. Father Andrei and Nina Ivanovna went on with their conversation. Nina Ivanovna's diamonds glittered on her fingers, then tears began to glitter in her eyes, she grew excited.

"Though I cannot venture to argue with you," she said, "you must admit there are so many insoluble riddles in life!"

"Not one, I assure you."

After supper Andrei Andreyich played the fiddle and Nina Ivanovna accompanied him on the piano. Ten years before he had taken his degree at the university in the Faculty of Arts but had never held any post, had no definite work, and only from time to time took part in concerts for charitable objects; and in the town he was regarded as a musician.

Andrei Andreyich played; they all listened in silence. The samovar was boiling quietly on the table and no one but Sasha was drinking tea. Then when it struck twelve a violin string suddenly broke; everyone laughed, bustled about, and began saying good-bye.

After seeing her fiancé out, Nadya went upstairs where she and her mother had their rooms (the lower story was occupied by the grandmother). They began putting the lights out below in the dining-room, while Sasha still sat on drinking tea. He always spent a long time over tea in the Moscow style, drinking as much as seven glasses at a time. For a long time after Nadya had undressed and gone to bed she could hear the servants clearing away downstairs and Granny talking angrily. At last everything was hushed, and nothing could be heard but Sasha from time to time coughing on a bass note in his room below.

## 2.

When Nadya woke up it must have been five o'clock, it was beginning to get light. A watchman was tapping somewhere far away. She was not sleepy, and her bed felt very soft and uncomfortable. Nadya sat up in her bed and fell to thinking as she had done every night in May. Her thoughts were the same as they had been the night before, useless, persistent thoughts, always alike, of how Andrei Andreyich had begun courting her and had made her an offer, how she had accepted him and then little by little had come to appreciate the kindly, intelligent man. But for some reason now, when there was little more than a month left before the wedding, she began to feel dread and uneasiness as though something vague and oppressive were before her.

"Ticktock, ticktock..." the watchman tapped lazily. "... Ticktock."

Through the big old-fashioned window she could see the garden and at a little distance bushes of lilac in full flower, drowsy and lifeless from the cold; and the thick white mist was floating softly up to the lilac, trying to cover it. Drowsy rooks were cawing in the faraway trees.

"My God, why is my heart so heavy?"

Perhaps every girl felt the same before her wedding. There was no knowing! Or was it Sasha's influence? But for several years past Sasha had been repeating the same thing, like a copybook, and when he talked he seemed naive and queer. But why was it she could not get Sasha out of her head? Why was it?

The watchman left off tapping for a long while. The birds were twittering under the windows and the mist had disappeared from the garden. Everything was lighted up by the spring sunshine as by a smile. Soon the whole garden, warm and caressed by the sun, returned to life, and dewdrops like diamonds glittered on the leaves and the old neglected garden on that morning looked young and gaily decked.

Granny was already awake. Sasha's husky cough began. Nadya could hear them below, setting the samovar and moving the chairs. The hours passed slowly; Nadya had been up and walking about the garden for a long while and still the morning dragged on.

At last Nina Ivanovna appeared with a tear-stained face, carrying a glass of mineral water. She was interested in spiritualism and homeopathy, read a great deal, was fond of talking of the doubts to which she was subject, and to Nadya it seemed as though there were a deep mysterious significance in all that.

Now Nadya kissed her mother and walked beside her.

"What have you been crying about, Mother?" she asked.

"Last night I was reading a story in which there is an old man and his daughter. The old man is in some office and his chief falls in love with his daughter. I have not finished it, but there was a passage which made it hard to keep from tears," said Nina Ivanovna, and she sipped at her glass. "I thought of it this morning and shed tears again."

"I have been so depressed all these days," said Nadya after a pause. "Why is it I don't sleep at night!"

"I don't know, dear. When I can't sleep I shut my eyes very

tightly, like this, and picture to myself Anna Karenina moving about and talking, or something historical from the ancient world. . . ."

Nadya felt that her mother did not understand her and was incapable of understanding. She felt this for the first time in her life, and it positively frightened her and made her want to hide herself; and she went away to her own room.

At two o'clock they sat down to dinner. It was Wednesday, a fast day, and so vegetable soup and bream with boiled grain were set before Granny.

To tease Granny, Sasha ate his meat soup as well as the vegetable soup. He was making jokes all through dinnertime, but his jests were labored and invariably with a moral bearing, and the effect was not at all amusing when, before making some witty remark, he raised his very long, thin, deathly-looking fingers; and when one remembered that he was very ill and would probably not be much longer in this world, one felt sorry for him and ready to weep.

After dinner Granny went off to her own room to lie down. Nina Ivanovna played on the piano for a little, and then she too went away.

"Oh, dear Nadya!" Sasha began his usual afternoon conversation. "If only you would listen to me! If only you would!"

She was sitting far back in an old-fashioned armchair, with her eyes shut, while he paced slowly about the room from corner to corner.

"If only you would go to the university," he said. "Only enlightened and holy people are interesting, it's only they who are wanted. The more of such people there are, the sooner the Kingdom of God will come on earth. Of your town then not one stone will be left, everything will be blown up from the foundations, everything will be changed as though by magic. And then there will be immense, magnificent houses here, wonderful gardens, marvelous fountains, remarkable people. . . . But that's not what matters most. What matters most is that the crowd, in our sense of the word, in the sense in which it exists now—that evil will not exist then, because every man will believe and every man will know what he is living for and no one will seek moral support in the crowd. Dear Nadya, darling girl, go away! Show them all that you are sick of this stagnant, gray, sinful life. Prove it to yourself at least!"

"I can't, Sasha, I'm going to be married."

"Oh, nonsense! What's it for!"

They went out into the garden and walked up and down a little.

"And however that may be, my dear girl, you must think, you must realize how unclean, how immoral this idle life of yours is," Sasha went on. "Do understand that if, for instance, you and your mother and your grandmother do nothing, it means that someone else is working for you, you are eating up someone else's life, and is that clean, isn't it filthy?"

Nadya wanted to say "Yes, that is true"; she wanted to say that she understood, but tears came into her eyes, her spirits drooped, and shrinking into herself she went off to her room.

Towards evening Andrei Andreyich arrived and as usual played the fiddle for a long time. He was not given to much talk as a rule and was fond of the fiddle, perhaps because one could be silent while playing. At eleven o'clock when he was about to go home and had put on his greatcoat, he embraced Nadya and began greedily kissing her face, her shoulders, and her hands.

"My dear, my sweet, my charmer," he muttered. "Oh, how happy I am! I am beside myself with rapture!"

And it seemed to her as though she had heard that long, long ago, or had read it somewhere . . . in some old tattered novel thrown away long ago.

In the dining-room Sasha was sitting at the table drinking tea with the saucer poised on his five long fingers; Granny was laying out patience; Nina Ivanovna was reading. The flame crackled in the icon lamp and everything, it seemed, was quiet and going well. Nadya said good night, went upstairs to her room, got into bed, and fell asleep at once. But just as on the night before, almost before it was light, she woke up. She was not sleepy, there was an uneasy, oppressive feeling in her heart. She sat up with her head on her knees and thought of her fiancé and her marriage. . . . She for some reason remembered that her mother had not loved her father and now had nothing and lived in complete dependence on her mother-in-law, Granny. And however much Nadya pondered she could not imagine why she had hitherto seen in her mother something special and exceptional, how it was she had not noticed that she was a simple, ordinary, unhappy woman.

And Sasha downstairs was not asleep, she could hear him coughing. "He is a queer, naive man," thought Nadya. And in all his dreams, in all those marvelous gardens and wonderful fountains, one felt there was something absurd. But for some reason, in his naiveté, in this very absurdity there was something so beautiful that as soon as she thought of the possibility of going to the university, it sent a cold thrill through her heart and her bosom and flooded them with joy and rapture.

"But better not think, better not think . . ." she whispered. "I must not think of it."

"Ticktock," tapped the watchman somewhere far away. "Ticktock . . . ticktock. . . ."

## 3.

In the middle of June Sasha suddenly felt bored and made up his mind to return to Moscow.

"I can't exist in this town," he said gloomily. "No water supply, no drains! It disgusts me to eat at dinner; the filth in the kitchen is incredible. . . ."

"Wait a little, prodigal son!" Granny tried to persuade him, speaking for some reason in a whisper, "the wedding is to be on the seventh."

"I don't want to."

"You meant to stay with us until September!"

"But now, you see, I don't want to. I must get to work."

The summer was gray and cold, the trees were wet, everything in the garden looked dejected and uninviting, it certainly did make one long to get to work. The sound of unfamiliar women's voices was heard downstairs and upstairs, there was the rattle of a sewing machine in Granny's room, they were working hard at the trousseau. Of fur coats alone, six were provided for Nadya, and the cheapest of them, in Granny's words, had cost three hundred rubles! The fuss irritated Sasha; he stayed in his own room and was cross, but everyone persuaded him to remain, and he promised not to go before the first of July.

Time passed quickly. On St. Peter's day Andrei Andreyich went with Nadya after dinner to Moscow Street to look once more at the house which had been taken and made ready for the young couple some time before. It was a house of two stories, but so far only the upper floor had been furnished. There was in the hall a shining floor, painted and parqueted, there were Viennese chairs, a piano, a violin stand; there was a smell of paint. On the wall hung a big oil painting in a gold frame—a naked lady and beside her a purple vase with a broken handle.

"An exquisite picture," said Andrei Andreyich, and he gave a respectful sigh. "It's the work of the artist Shismachevsky."

Then there was the drawing-room with the round table, and a sofa and easy chairs upholstered in bright blue. Above the sofa was a big photograph of Father Andrei wearing a priest's velvet cap and decorations. Then they went into the dining-room in which there was a sideboard; then into the bedroom; here in the half dusk stood two bedsteads side by side, and it looked as though the bedroom had been decorated with the idea that it would always be very agreeable there and could not possibly be anything else. Andrei Andreyich led Nadya about the rooms, all the while keeping his arm round her waist; and she felt weak and conscience-stricken. She hated all the rooms, the beds, the easy chairs; she was nauseated by the naked lady. It was clear to her now that she had ceased to love Andrei Andreyich or perhaps had never loved him at all; but how to say this and to whom to say it and with what object she did not understand, and could not understand, though she was thinking about it all day and all night. . . . He held her round the waist, talked so affectionately, so modestly, was so happy, walking about this house of his; while she saw nothing in it all but vulgarity, stupid, naive, unbearable vulgarity, and his arm round her waist felt as hard and cold as an iron hoop. And every minute she was on the point of running away, bursting into sobs, throwing herself out of a window. Andrei Andreyich led her into the bathroom and here he touched a tap fixed in the wall and at once water flowed.

"What do you say to that?" he said, and laughed. "I had a tank holding two hundred gallons put in the loft, and so now we shall have water."

They walked across the yard and went out into the street and took a cab. Thick clouds of dust were blowing, and it seemed as though it were just going to rain.

"You are not cold?" said Andrei Andreyich, screwing up his eyes at the dust.

She did not answer.

"Yesterday, you remember, Sasha blamed me for doing nothing," he said, after a brief silence. "Well, he is right, absolutely right! I do nothing and can do nothing. My precious, why is it? Why is it that the very thought that I may some day fix a cockade on my cap and go into the government service is so hateful to me? Why do I feel so uncomfortable when I see a lawyer or a

Latin master or a member of the Zemstvo? O Mother Russia! O Mother Russia! What a burden of idle and useless people you still carry! How many like me are upon you, long-suffering Mother!"

And from the fact that he did nothing he drew generalizations, seeing in it a sign of the times.

"When we are married let us go together into the country, my precious; there we will work! We will buy ourselves a little piece of land with a garden and a river, we will labor and watch life. Oh, how splendid that will be!"

He took off his hat, and his hair floated in the wind, while she listened to him and thought: "Good God, I wish I were home!"

When they were quite near the house they overtook Father Andrei.

"Ah, here's Father coming," cried Andrei Andreyich, delighted, and he waved his hat. "I love my dad really," he said as he paid the cabman. "He's a splendid old fellow, a dear old fellow."

Nadya went into the house, feeling cross and unwell, thinking that there would be visitors all the evening, that she would have to entertain them, to smile, to listen to the fiddle, to listen to all sorts of nonsense, and to talk of nothing but the wedding.

Granny, dignified, gorgeous in her silk dress, and haughty as she always seemed before visitors, was sitting before the samovar. Father Andrei came in with his sly smile.

"I have the pleasure and blessed consolation of seeing you in health," he said to Granny, and it was hard to tell whether he was joking or speaking seriously.

## 4.

The wind was beating on the window and on the roof; there was a whistling sound, and in the stove the house spirit was plaintively and sullenly droning his song. It was past midnight; everyone in the house had gone to bed, but no one was asleep, and it seemed all the while to Nadya as though they were playing the fiddle below. There was a sharp bang; a shutter must have been torn off. A minute later Nina Ivanovna came in in her nightgown, with a candle.

"What was the bang, Nadya?" she asked.

Her mother, with her hair in a single plait and a timid smile on her face, looked older, plainer, smaller on that stormy night. Nadya remembered that quite a little time ago she had thought her mother an exceptional woman and had listened with pride to the things she said; and now she could not remember those things, everything that came into her mind was so feeble and useless.

In the stove was the sound of several bass voices in chorus, and she even heard "O-o-o my G-o-od!" Nadya sat on her bed, and suddenly she clutched at her hair and burst into sobs.

"Mother, Mother, my own," she said. "If only you knew what is happening to me! I beg you, I beseech you, let me go away! I beseech you!"

"Where?" asked Nina Ivanovna, not understanding, and she sat down on the bedstead. "Go where?"

For a long while Nadya cried and could not utter a word.

"Let me go away from the town," she said at last. "There must not and will not be a wedding, understand that! I don't love that man . . . I can't even speak about him."

"No, my own, no!" Nina Ivanovna said quickly, terribly alarmed. "Calm yourself—it's just because you are in low spirits. It will pass, it often happens. Most likely you have had a tiff with Andrei; but lovers' quarrels always end in kisses!"

"Oh, go away, Mother, oh, go away," sobbed Nadya.

"Yes," said Nina Ivanovna after a pause, "it's not long since you were a baby, a little girl, and now you are engaged to be married. In nature there is a continual transmutation of substances. Before you know where you are you will be a mother yourself and an old woman, and will have as rebellious a daughter as I have."

"My darling, my sweet, you are clever you know, you are unhappy," said Nadya. "You are very unhappy; why do you say such very dull, commonplace things? For God's sake, why?"

Nina Ivanovna tried to say something but could not utter a word; she gave a sob and went away to her own room. The bass voices began droning in the stove again, and Nadya felt suddenly frightened. She jumped out of bed and went quickly to her mother. Nina Ivanovna, with tear-stained face, was lying in bed wrapped in a pale blue quilt and holding a book in her hands.

"Mother, listen to me!" said Nadya. "I implore you, do understand! If you would only understand how petty and degrading our life is. My eyes have been opened, and I see it all now. And what is your Andrei Andreyich? Why, he is not intelligent, Mother! Merciful heavens, do understand, Mother, he is stupid!"

Nina Ivanovna abruptly sat up.

"You and your grandmother torment me," she said with a sob. "I want to live! to live," she repeated, and twice she beat her little fist upon her bosom. "Let me be free! I am still young, I want to live, and you have made me an old woman between you!"

She broke into bitter tears, lay down and curled up under the quilt, and looked so small, so pitiful, so foolish. Nayda went to her room, dressed, and, sitting at the window, fell to waiting for the morning. She sat all night thinking, while someone seemed to be tapping on the shutters and whistling in the yard.

In the morning Granny complained that the wind had blown down all the apples in the garden and broken down an old plum tree. It was gray, murky, cheerless, dark enough for candles; everyone complained of the cold, and the rain lashed on the windows. After tea Nadya went into Sasha's room and, without saying a word, knelt down before an armchair in the corner and hid her face in her hands.

"What is it?" asked Sasha.

"I can't . . ." she said. "How I could go on living here before, I can't understand, I can't conceive! I despise the man I am engaged to, I despise myself, I despise all this idle, senseless existence."

"Well, well," said Sasha, not yet grasping what was meant. "That's all right . . . that's good."

"I am sick of this life," Nadya went on. "I can't endure another day here. Tomorrow I am going away. Take me with you for God's sake!"

For a minute Sasha looked at her in astonishment; at last he understood and was delighted as a child. He waved his arms and began pattering with his slippers as though he were dancing with delight.

"Splendid," he said, rubbing his hands. "My goodness, how fine that is!"

And she stared at him without blinking, with adoring eyes, as though spellbound, expecting every minute that he would say something important, something infinitely significant; he had told her nothing yet, but already it seemed to her that something new and great was opening before her which she had not known till then, and already she gazed at him full of expectation, ready to face anything, even death.

"I am going tomorrow," he said after a moment's thought. "You come to the station to see me off. . . . I'll take your things in my portmanteau, and I'll get your ticket, and when the third bell rings you get into the carriage, and we'll go off. You'll see me as far as Moscow and then go on to Petersburg alone. Have you a passport?"

"Yes."

"I can promise you, you won't regret it," said Sasha, with

conviction. "You will go, you will study, and then go where fate takes you. When you turn your life upside down everything will be changed. The great thing is to turn your life upside down, and all the rest is unimportant. And so we will set off tomorrow?"

"Oh yes, for God's sake!"

It seemed to Nadya that she was very much excited, that her heart was heavier than ever before, that she would spend all the time till she went away in misery and agonizing thought; but she had hardly gone upstairs and lain down on her bed when she fell asleep at once, with traces of tears and a smile on her face, and slept soundly till evening.

## 5.

A cab had been sent for. Nadya in her hat and overcoat went upstairs to take one more look at her mother, at all her belongings. She stood in her own room beside her still warm bed, looked about her, then went slowly in to her mother. Nina Ivanovna was asleep; it was quite still in her room. Nadya kissed her mother, smoothed her hair, stood still for a couple of minutes . . . then walked slowly downstairs.

It was raining heavily. The cabman with the hood pulled down was standing at the entrance, drenched with rain.

"There is not room for you, Nadya," said Granny, as the servants began putting in the luggage. "What an idea to see him off in such weather! You had better stop at home. Goodness, how it rains!"

Nadya tried to say something but could not. Then Sasha helped Nadya in and covered her feet with a rug. Then he sat down beside her.

"Good luck to you! God bless you!" Granny cried from the steps. "Mind you write to us from Moscow, Sasha!"

"Right. Good-bye, Granny."

"The Queen of Heaven keep you!"

"Oh, what weather!" said Sasha.

It was only now that Nadya began to cry. Now it was clear to her that she certainly was going, which she had not really believed when she was saying good-bye to Granny, and when she was looking at her mother. Good-bye, town! And she suddenly thought of it all: Andrei, and his father, and the new house and the naked lady with the vase; and it all no longer frightened her, nor weighed upon her, but was naive and trivial and continually retreated further away. And when they got into the railway carriage and the train began to move, all that past which had been so big and serious shrank up into something tiny, and a vast wide future which till then had scarcely been noticed began unfolding before her. The rain pattered on the carriage windows, nothing could be seen but the green fields, telegraph posts with birds sitting on the wires flitted by, and joy made her hold her breath; she thought that she was going to freedom, going to study, and this was just like what used, ages ago, to be called going off to be a free Cossack.

She laughed and cried and prayed all at once.

"It's a-all right," said Sasha, smiling. "It's a-all right."

## 6.

Autumn had passed and winter, too, had gone. Nadya had begun to be very homesick and thought every day of her mother and her grandmother; she thought of Sasha too. The letters that came from home were kind and gentle, and it seemed as though everything by now were forgiven and forgotten. In May after the examinations she set off for home in good health and high spirits and stopped on the way at Moscow to see Sasha. He was just the same as the year before, with the same beard and unkempt hair, with the same large beautiful eyes, and he still wore the same coat and canvas trousers; but he looked unwell and worried, he seemed both older and thinner, and kept coughing, and for some reason he struck Nadya as gray and provincial.

"My God, Nadya has come!" he said, and laughed gaily. "My darling girl!"

They sat in the printing room, which was full of tobacco smoke, and smelled strongly, stiflingly, of India ink and paint; then they went to his room, which also smelled of tobacco and was full of the traces of spitting; near a cold samovar stood a broken plate with dark paper on it, and there were masses of dead flies on the table and on the floor. And everything showed that Sasha ordered his personal life in a slovenly way and lived anyhow, with utter contempt for comfort, and if anyone began talking to him of his personal happiness, of his personal life, of affection for him, he would not have understood and would have only laughed.

"It is all right, everything has gone well," said Nadya hurriedly. "Mother came to see me in Petersburg in the autumn; she said that Granny is not angry and only keeps going into my room and making the sign of the cross over the walls."

Sasha looked cheerful, but he kept coughing, and talked in a cracked voice, and Nadya kept looking at him, unable to decide whether he really were seriously ill or whether it were only her fancy.

"Dear Sasha," she said, "you are ill."

"No, it's nothing, I am ill, but not very . . ."

"Oh, dear!" cried Nadya, in agitation. "Why don't you go to a doctor? Why don't you take care of your health? My dear, darling Sasha," she said, and tears gushed from her eyes and for some reason there rose before her imagination Andrei Andreyich and the naked lady with the vase, and all her past which seemed now as far away as her childhood; and she began crying because Sasha no longer seemed to her so novel, so cultured, and so interesting as the year before. "Dear Sasha, you are very, very ill. I would do anything to make you not so pale and thin. I am so indebted to you! You can't imagine how much you have done for me, my good Sasha! In reality you are now the person nearest and dearest to me."

They sat on and talked, and now, after Nadya had spent a winter in Petersburg, Sasha, his works, his smile, his whole figure had for her a suggestion of something out of date, old-fashioned, done with long ago and perhaps already dead and buried.

"I am going down the Volga the day after tomorrow," said Sasha, "and then to drink koumiss. I mean to drink koumiss. A friend and his wife are going with me. His wife is a wonderful woman; I am always at her, trying to persuade her to go to the university. I want her to turn her life upside down."

After having talked, they drove to the station. Sasha got her tea and apples; and when the train began moving and he waved his handkerchief at her, smiling, it could be seen even from his legs that he was very ill and would not live long.

Nadya reached her native town at midday. As she drove home from the station the streets struck her as very wide and the houses very small and squat; there were no people about, she met no one but the German piano tuner in a rusty greatcoat. And all the houses looked as though they were covered with dust. Granny, who seemed to have grown quite old, but was as fat and plain as ever, flung her arms round Nadya and cried for a long time with her face on Nadya's shoulder, unable to tear herself away. Nina Ivanovna looked much older and plainer and seemed shriveled up, but was still tightly laced, and still had diamonds flashing on her fingers.

"My darling," she said, trembling all over, "my darling!"

Then they sat down and cried without speaking. It was evident that both mother and grandmother realized that the past was lost and gone, never to return; they had now no position in society, no prestige as before, no right to invite visitors; so it is when in the midst of an easy careless life the police suddenly burst in at night and make a search, and it turns out that the head of the family has embezzled money or committed forgery—and good-bye then to the easy careless life for ever!

Nadya went upstairs and saw the same bed, the same windows with naive white curtains, and outside the windows the same garden, gay and noisy, bathed in sunshine. She touched the table, sat down, and sank into thought. And she had a good dinner and drank tea with delicious rich cream; but something was missing, there was a sense of emptiness in the rooms and the ceilings were so low. In the evening she went to bed, covered herself up and for some reason it seemed to her to be funny lying in this snug, very soft bed.

Nina Ivanovna came in for a minute; she sat down as people who feel guilty sit down, timidly, and looking about her.

"Well, tell me, Nadya," she inquired after a brief pause, "are you contented? Quite contented?"

"Yes, Mother."

Nina Ivanovna got up, made the sign of the cross over Nadya and the windows.

"I have become religious, as you see," she said. "You know I am studying philosophy now, and I am always thinking and thinking. . . . And many things have become as clear as daylight to me. It seems to me that what is above all necessary is that life should pass as it were through a prism."

"Tell me, Mother, how is Granny in health?"

"She seems all right. When you went away that time with Sasha and the telegram came from you, Granny fell on the floor as she read it; for three days she lay without moving. After that she was always praying and crying. But now she is all right again."

She got up and walked about the room.

"Ticktock," tapped the watchman. "Ticktock, ticktock. . . ."

"What is above all necessary is that life should pass as it were through a prism," she said; "in other words, that life in consciousness should be analyzed into its simplest elements as into the seven primary colors, and each element must be studied separately."

What Nina Ivanovna said further and when she went away, Nadya did not hear, as she quickly fell asleep.

May passed; June came. Nadya had grown used to being at home. Granny busied herself about the samovar, heaving deep sighs. Nina Ivanovna talked in the evenings about her philosophy; she still lived in the house like a poor relation and had to go to Granny for every farthing. There were lots of flies in the house, and the ceilings seemed to become lower and lower. Granny and Nina Ivanovna did not go out in the streets for fear of meeting Father Andrei and Andrei Andreyich. Nadya walked about the garden and the streets, looked at the gray fences, and it seemed to her that everything in the town had grown old, was out of date, and was only waiting either for the end, or for the beginning of something young and fresh. Oh, if only that new, bright life would come more quickly—that life in which one will be able to face one's fate boldly and directly, to know that one is right, to be lighthearted and free! And sooner or later such a life will come. The time will come when of Granny's house, where things are so arranged that the four servants can only live in one room in filth in the basement—the time will come when of that house not a trace will remain, and it will be forgotten, no one will remember it. And Nadya's only entertainment was from the boys next door; when she walked about the garden they knocked on the fence and shouted in mockery: "Betrothed! Betrothed!"

A letter from Sasha arrived from Saratov. In his gay dancing handwriting he told them that his journey on the Volga had been a complete success, but that he had been taken rather ill in Saratov, had lost his voice, and had been for the last fortnight in the hospital. She knew what that meant, and she was overwhelmed with a foreboding that was like a conviction. And it vexed her that this foreboding and the thought of Sasha did not distress her so much as before. She had a passionate desire for life, longed to be in Petersburg, and her friendship with Sasha seemed now sweet but something far, far away! She did not sleep all night, and in the morning sat at the window, listening. And she did in fact hear voices below; Granny, greatly agitated, was asking questions rapidly. Then someone began crying. . . . When Nadya went downstairs Granny was standing in the corner, praying before the icon and her face was tearful. A telegram lay on the table.

For some time Nadya walked up and down the room, listening to Granny's weeping; then she picked up the telegram and read it.

It announced that the previous morning Alexandr Timofeich, or more simply, Sasha, had died at Saratov of consumption.

Granny and Nina Ivanovna went to the church to order a memorial service, while Nadya went on walking about the rooms and thinking. She recognized clearly that her life had been turned upside down as Sasha wished; that here she was, alien, isolated, useless, and that everything here was useless to her; that all the past had been torn away from her and vanished as though it had been burnt up and the ashes scattered to the winds. She went into Sasha's room and stood there for a while.

"Good-bye, dear Sasha," she thought, and before her mind rose the vista of a new, wide, spacious life, and that life, still obscure and full of mysteries, beckoned her and attracted her.

She went upstairs to her own room to pack, and next morning said good-bye to her family, and full of life and high spirits left the town—as she supposed for ever.

## ABOUT THE TYPE

The text of this book has been set in Trump Mediaeval. Designed by Georg Trump for the Weber foundry in the late 1950s, this typeface is a modern rethinking of the Garalde Oldstyle types (often associated with Claude Garamond) that have long been popular with printers and book designers.

Trump Mediaeval is a trademark of
Linotype-Hell AG and/or its subsidiaries

Printed and bound by R. R. Donnelley & Sons,
Harrisonburg, Virginia

Book design by Red Canoe, Deer Lodge, Tennessee
Caroline Kavanagh
Deb Koch

## TITLES IN SERIES

HINDOO HOLIDAY
MY DOG TULIP
MY FATHER AND MYSELF
WE THINK THE WORLD OF YOU
J. R. Ackerley

THE LIVING THOUGHTS OF KIERKEGAARD
W. H. Auden, editor

PRISON MEMOIRS OF AN ANARCHIST
Alexander Berkman

HERSELF SURPRISED (First Trilogy, Volume 1)
TO BE A PILGRIM (First Trilogy, Volume 2)
THE HORSE'S MOUTH (First Trilogy, Volume 3)
Joyce Cary

PEASANTS AND OTHER STORIES
Anton Chekhov

THE WINNERS
Julio Cortázar

MEMOIRS
Lorenzo Da Ponte

A HIGH WIND IN JAMAICA
THE FOX IN THE ATTIC
THE WOODEN SHEPHERDESS
Richard Hughes

THE OTHER HOUSE
Henry James

BOREDOM
CONTEMPT
Alberto Moravia

MORTE D'URBAN
THE STORIES OF J. F. POWERS
WHEAT THAT SPRINGETH GREEN
J. F. Powers

THE FIERCE AND BEAUTIFUL WORLD
Andrei Platonov

MEMOIRS OF MY NERVOUS ILLNESS
Daniel Paul Schreber

RECORDS OF SHELLEY, BYRON, AND THE AUTHOR
Edward John Trelawny

JAKOB VON GUNTEN
Robert Walser

LOLLY WILLOWES
Sylvia Townsend Warner